The Whipple Wash Chronicles

BOOK ONE

Enjoy the Journey

S. D. Ferrell

The Whipple Wash Chronicles

THE VALLEY TIME FORGOT

S.D. FERRELL

ELSBRIER INK

First published in Canada in 2012 by
Elsbrier Ink, Brantford, ON
elsbrier.ink@gmail.com
www.whipplewashchronicles.com

SECOND EDITION

ISBN-10: 1489528962
ISBN-13: 978-1489528964

For my daughters, the Whipple Wash Fairies

ACKNOWLEDGMENTS

I would like to thank my family and friends for their encouragement and support throughout the creation of this book; it has been in itself an amazing journey. To show my gratitude I have given them characters in the story. By no means however are they a true representation of them, or events that have taken place. A special thank you to my daughters; Natasha, Kay'la, Whitnee, Elisha and Gabrielle- my muses, who have sat through what seemed like a million changes to the plot. I would also like to thank my daughter Kay'la for helping me edit the many versions of the manuscript. Lastly, I would like to thank you, my valued readers, for joining me on this grand and epic adventure; I hope you will enjoy reading it as much as I have enjoyed creating it!

PROLOGUE

A long time ago, in a far off land, when the earth was young and mankind still believed in magic and miracles; an evil worse than anything you could imagine was haunting and ravishing the northern kingdoms.

The evil; Lord Canvil from the Moors of Erebos, had one purpose and only one purpose. He was determined to conquer this world one nation at a time and greedily take for himself the spiritual artifacts -- Artifacts that would wield him ultimate power -- A power that would be mightier than the force of nature herself. He would manipulate this power and use it against his nemesis the Light of Goodness.

Many of the people, like the warrior dwarfs from Mount Albyawn, the horse riders from the Albertian Grasslands and the elves from the Waterfalls of Glenevie perished in the wake of his fiery hell and their lands were left in charred ruin. Those who didn't perish were forced into servitude in Canvil's army or transported to his fortress on the moors where they would live out the rest of their days in slavery.

Canvil had amassed a huge army and ruled them with an iron fist and a heartless soul. The new recruits, under his command, soon succumbed to the tyranny of his ways and lost all resemblance of who they once were. Quickly they became as callous and as black-hearted as Canvil; they carried out with deadly accuracy his every bidding with no question, conscience or regret. They were known as the Venom Horde and just the whisper of their name left grown, seasoned men shaking and cowering in their boots.

On Canvil's order, a scouting party left to search for and steal The Gilded Hand of the Hawthorn Springs. Canvil had heard that the hand gave the bearer of it eternal life. Upon reaching Runbo's Garden, where the gilded hand was located, they came upon a lone unarmed woman; Queen Faywyn of the Whipple Wash Valley. She had been on her annual sabbatical to the springs. With no guard to protect her she was left at the mercy and whim of the scouting party. Instead of killing her, Jaja, the leader and Canvil's oldest son, stole the gilded hand and kidnapped Faywyn -- He had a more sinister purpose in mind for her.

On their way back to Canvil, who was plundering a humble nation at the foothills of Mount Aspentonia the last stronghold before the southern kingdoms, an unwilling member of the scouting party defected. He had befriended Faywyn and with her encouragement, that he would be safe, he made his way back to the Hawthorn Springs. From there he traveled west towards the Whipple Wash Valley and the village of Elsbrier where Faywyn ruled with her daughters, the Seven Elders.

Upon hearing the strangers tale the Elders not sure whether to believe him or not deployed a troupe of Hummingmoth Messengers- Their mission; to find Faywyn and discover if the stranger's tale of Canvil was true.

That fateful day the smallest and youngest of the Hummingmoth Messengers, Jasper the unlikeliest of heroes, left with his brothers; setting in motion a chain of events that would change the course of time. But would it be enough to stop Canvil and his army of Venom Horde from taking over the southern kingdoms?

CHAPTER 1
That Odd Little Fellow

Bitter cold winds howled through a small village, causing the doors and shutters on the hut-like buildings to rattle on their hinges. The wind churned up the decaying leaves and the light coating of snow that covered the ground, making visibility nearly impossible.

It was in the wee hours of the morning, on the last day of winter. The storm had been raging for weeks. The sky overhead was thick with dark clouds that were eerily tinted with hues of bright purple and green. It looked as though at any moment that the small village would be buried under a mountain of snow. Instead, explosive bouts of ear piercing thunder rumbled unnervingly throughout the night and barely any snow had fallen.

A small creature, no bigger than a man's hand, flew through the village looking for a safe and sheltered place to land. However, the winds were strong and he could barely see what was right in front of him. It took all of his flying skills not to be blown into one of the huts or a large tree. That would have been the end of him or at least the end of his flying days.

Suddenly the winds became fiercer and nearly blew the poor little fellow into a hut, but he swerved just in time, narrowly missing the thick wall. Two seconds later, however he came to an abrupt stop and fell to the ground.

One of the villagers had stepped out of her hut and did not see the creature until he bumped into her. Bending down she gently picked him up. Shivering uncontrollably with cold and fright he stared nervously up at her until she smiled warmly at him. He sighed in relief and instantly felt safe -- a feeling he hadn't experienced in a very long time.

"Jasper...my name...is Jasper," he said weakly before falling unconscious in her hands. The villager looked curiously for several moments at Jasper. As she did, her brow furled with concern. He was an odd-looking creature. She had never seen anything quite like him before.

Jasper looked like a black and brown striped moth. The forest, where the village was located, was full of them. However, that is where the similarity ended. His wings were large, almost transparent and had iridescent stripes of green and dark brown running through them. They reminded her of the hummingbirds' that nested in the bushes beside her hut each spring.

His body was almost five times the size of a regular moth and was covered in fine hairs. His head was round, his cheeks chubby and he had two large dark brown eyes. As she looked at him, his long and thin snout curled up into a small ball and lay against his face. His mouth located just under his snout was full of tiny white teeth. If all that was not strange enough for a moth he also had human-like legs and arms. They too were covered in fine hairs. Jasper was a sight to see and looked like he hadn't bathed in weeks. His hands and feet were filthy and the small hairs on his body were matted with knots.

The villager peered into the darkness to see if anyone else had seen what just happened. Being so early in the morning everyone else was sound asleep in their huts and no doubt snuggled beneath a thick layer of covers. She should have been as well, but an unexpected event that happened earlier that night had kept her from sleeping. The villager carefully carried Jasper into her hut, closing the door tightly behind her. The wind blew aggressively at the thick wooden door, as if it too wanted to come in.

"Oh do shut up will you! You can't come in," the villager said as she struggled to take off her scarf and overcoat.

"Lizbeth who are you talking to?" a voice called from across the room.

"Just the wind Marla," Lizbeth said than chuckled lightly. Marla had made her way to Lizbeth's hut several hours earlier. A loud cracking noise had woken Marla from her sleep. She looked out of her door and noticed that a large tree branch was hanging precariously from the tree right beside her hut. She gathered what she could as quickly as she could and ran out just before the branch crashed through the roof. With a sleigh full of her belongings, she made her way across the village to Lizbeth's hut.

Lizbeth had been sitting at her table writing on parchment when she heard a loud knock at her door and Marla frantically calling out her name. After Marla explained what happened, they were both too anxious to sleep. Lizbeth brought over a chair from the dining table and sat it beside the rocking chair in front of the fireplace. Throughout the night, they talked about the storm, sipped on herbal tea and hooked sweaters for one of the villager's underlings.

"The wind…you are talking to the wind?" Marla asked as she turned to look at Lizbeth. Lizbeth was hanging her overcoat and scarf on a large wooden hook by the door while carefully cradling Jasper in her left arm. Marla seeing this quickly jumped up from the rocking chair nearly tipping over her cup of tea that sat on the small table between the two chairs. The pink ball of bimble yarn that she was using rolled off her lap and onto the floor. The blanket she had covered her legs with also fell.

"Lizbeth what do you have there? It doesn't look like firewood to me?" Marla asked as she made her way over to Lizbeth. Lizbeth was supposed to be fetching wood for the fireplace; while they talked, the fire had burned low and the hut had cooled.

"No it is not wood Marla," Lizbeth said. Marla peeked over Lizbeth's shoulder then screwed up her face.

"Oh my…what in the name of Zenrah do you have there?" Marla asked. "Not what, but who," Lizbeth said. She walked over to the rocking chair; Marla tagged behind her. Lizbeth picked the blanket up off the floor and placed it on the seat of the rocker. She laid Jasper on the blanket; took a corner of it and covered him with it. She looked at him nervously for a moment than sighed in relief as Jasper's chest steadily rose and fell with each breath.

"Where do you think he came from?" Marla asked. She had never seen anything quite like him before either.

"I don't know." Lizbeth said shaking her head. "Not from around here that is for sure." Marla nodded her head in agreement.

"Odd looking fellow isn't he," Marla said.

"Yes, he certainly is," Lizbeth said, as the frown on her face grew deeper. "And he speaks elfish…clearly."

"Elfish?" Marla questioned then looked curiously down at Jasper as Lizbeth nodded her head.

"He said his name was Jasper, and then he passed out." Lizbeth said.

"What do you think the elders will say?" Marla asked. Lizbeth shook her head. The council of elders would have to be told that Jasper was among them. Nothing happened in the small village without their approval first.

"I guess we will have to wait and see." Lizbeth said. "For now I think we should both try and get some sleep. I think we are in for a very interesting day." Marla looked at Lizbeth with a puzzled expression but did not comment on her words. They both went to their beds but thoughts of Jasper, and where he came from, kept them from sleeping soundly.

The next morning, Jasper woke to find himself snuggled beneath a soft cover in the rocking chair. He felt very small in the chair; however, he was thankful that he no longer had to fight for survival against the wind that still howled outside. Curious to know where he was Jasper looked around. The rocking chair was standing in front of a stone fireplace located on the back wall of a large room. The room, rectangular in shape, had rounded corners and walls that were made from several large posts set evenly apart; thick branches were stacked between them. The holes between the branches were packed solidly with a thick grayish brown mud. Above, spanning the width of the room, were large rugged beams. Above the beams was a peaked roof made of thick, tightly weaved branches. On the left side of the room was a cot piled high with thick covers and plump pillows. Between the cot and fireplace was a door that Jasper presumed lead into another room. At the front of the room was a large wooden door. Along that wall was also a window with solid wood shutters that were latched tightly shut. Jasper could hear the wind banging against them. In front of the window was a round wooden table with four wooden chairs.

Hearing a noise, Jasper turned around. Along the last wall of the hut was a stone counter with wooden cupboards above and below it. Standing in front of the counter were two creatures. They were talking quietly while they prepared food. Jasper's stomach rumbled with hunger as the delicious smell reached his snout. He tried to remember when he had eaten last. His mind grew foggy with the attempt. Jasper began to worry about his lack of recollection, until his stomach rumbled again. He looked over at the two creatures and hoped they wouldn't mind sharing their meal with him. Mustering up his courage Jasper squeaked out a greeting.

"H...h...hello," he said shakily. The creatures turned and greeted him warmly with large toothy smiles. Jasper's nerves immediately eased.

"Well hello little one," The shorter of the two said. "It is good to see you awake." She smiled warmly at him. Jasper smiled back.

"My name is Lizbeth. I am the one you bumped into last night, and this is Marla," she said. Jasper looked at them as curiously as they had looked at him the previous night. Lizbeth was only about two and half feet tall. Her face showed the weathered lines of age but she had a bright twinkle in her eyes. Marla was younger by several years and was about two feet taller than Lizbeth. Their facial features were similar, a long thin nose, small pointed ears and large eyes. They were also similarly dressed. They wore long tunics with pants underneath and thick socks that covered their feet.

"Are you hungry?" Lizbeth asked. Jasper eagerly nodded his head and unconsciously licked his lips.

As Marla set the table, Lizbeth slowly walked over to Jasper and held out her hands. He looked up at her cautiously; she smiled warmly back at him. Seeing the kindness in her eyes Jasper knew no harm would come to him so he stood slowly and stretched. His little body hurt but he was able to step onto her hands unassisted. His wings unfolded, fluttered lightly behind him then settled snuggly against his back. He sighed in relief that everything was in working order.

Lizbeth carried Jasper to the table and placed him on top of it, as he was too small to sit in one of the chairs. She placed in front of him a mug of warm herbal tea, a plate of hot biscuits and a bowl of warm vegetable soup. Lizbeth and Marla smiled as Jasper immediately pulled off a chunk of the biscuit, dipped it into the soup and ate it with a ravenous hunger.

They had eaten earlier; the soup was to be for their midday and evening meals. As they sipped on tea, they watched in amusement as Jasper eagerly ate all of his food. Just as Jasper unfurled his snout and dipped it into the teacup Marla leaned towards him. "Jasper, where did you come from?" she asked. Jasper looked up at her as she sat back in her chair. He had been thinking about that while he ate. Unfortunately, he couldn't remember where he came from or how he got to their village. It was as if all but his name had been erased from his memory.

"I don't know," Jasper said. His bottom lip started to tremble as tears formed in his eyes. He sniffled, ran his finger under his snout and tried not to cry.

"Now, now little one," Lizbeth said soothingly. "Don't fret. I am sure your memory will return after you have rested. How you got here and who you are can wait for another day." Jasper nodded as a tear dripped onto his cheek. "For the time being would you like to hear about where you are?
Do you think that will make you feel better?" Lizbeth asked. Jasper nodded eagerly then took another sip of his tea.

Lizbeth and Marla took turns telling Jasper about themselves and their home. Lizbeth was the Keeper of the Woods and was at least three hundred years old. Marla was the apprentice to Aldwin the village healer and was only fifty years old. Jasper found it interesting to learn they were members of an ancient tribe called Elfkins. According to folklore, they were the only beings left from a catastrophic event that vanquished everyone else in the world thousands of years ago.

They went on to talk about the village. It was located in a large forest called the Greenwood Forest. The forest was in a valley that was surrounded by mountain ranges. They talked about the villagers, some in length like Aldwin and Old Barty who literally whittled his days away making flutes, toys and rocking chairs. He learned about the forest creatures, how they lived in harmony with the Elfkins and worked beside them. They spoke fondly of a badger named Bauthal who was an elder of the forest creatures. Lizbeth said Bauthal would be very interested to learn about Jasper once he awoke from hibernation. They then talked in length about the winter storm that brought Jasper to them. He could tell by the expressions on their faces that the storm had worried them. However, none of what they spoke of seemed familiar to him. A couple of hours had gone by and Jasper could not stop himself from yawning--Lizbeth smiled.

"Well that is enough." She said just as Marla had started to talk with pride about two of the village fishermen; Rangous and Septer. "Why don't you rest," Lizbeth said. "It sounds like the winds have died down. Maybe we can get some work done before the sun sets." While Marla cleared the table, Lizbeth carried Jasper back to the rocking chair and started to cover him with the blanket. Jasper reached out his hand and held onto her finger squeezing lightly. Lizbeth's breath caught in her throat; her face softened with a loving smile.

"Thank you Lizbeth," Jasper said. Yawning loudly he released Lizbeth's hand, pulled the blanket up to his chin and yawned again.

"You are most welcome little one," Lizbeth said than smiled; Jasper was already asleep.

That evening Jasper once again found himself on top of Lizbeth's table; only this time he was being poked and prodded by Aldwin.

Aldwin stood about five feet tall and had a lean build. His facial features were similar to Lizbeth's and Marla's. He had dark brown hair and a neatly trimmed beard. Aldwin was older then Marla by twenty-five summers. He was dressed in dark pants and a thick brown sweater. After examining Jasper thoroughly, Aldwin stood back from the table, folded his arms across his chest and scowled.

"What is it Aldwin?" Lizbeth asked with worry. She had invited Aldwin over to examine Jasper, hoping to discover how Jasper lost his memory. She needed as much information about him as she could before she met with the elders.

"Nothing," Aldwin said. "He has no bump on the head; none of his bones are broken. Other than a few cuts, scraps and needing a good bath I can't find anything wrong with him."

"Why can't he remember then?" Lizbeth asked.

"I don't know Lizbeth." Aldwin said shaking his head as he picked up his medicine bag. "Perhaps he is suppressing it." Lizbeth walked with Aldwin to the door. He put on his overcoat, slung the medicine bag over his shoulder then looked worriedly at Lizbeth. He leaned down and spoke quietly so only Lizbeth could hear.

"Lizbeth are you sure you can trust this little fellow? I mean after all, we know nothing about him or where he came from." They both looked over at Jasper. A large bouquet of white flowers stood in a container in the middle of the table; Jasper had taken one of the blooms in his hand and inhaled its delightful scent. He sighed heavily then smiled goofily in satisfaction.

"Oh yes I am sure I can trust him," Lizbeth smiled. "Besides Marla is staying with me until the carpenters fix her hut. I suspect it will take several weeks." Aldwin looked around the room for his apprentice.

"She is visiting Mirabella. We hooked sweaters for the underlings last night." Lizbeth said.

"Ahh yes," Aldwin said. Mirabella and Marla were close friends and she often went over to help with the underlings. Mirabella and Pothos had their hands full with seven underlings -- all under the age of nine summers.

"And what of the elders," Aldwin continued. "There will be resistance."

Lizbeth had decided to keep the knowledge of Jasper to just the three of them until Aldwin had a chance to examine him. Lizbeth looked up at Aldwin then over at Jasper who was now running his fingers through the fine hairs on his legs trying to comb out the knots. An overwhelming sensation made Lizbeth's heart swell with love. She couldn't explain her feelings for Jasper to Aldwin so instead she said. "If it comes to it I will protect Jasper with my life."

"Well now," Aldwin chuckled, as he stood upright "I know you don't get on well with the elders but I don't think it will come down to that." He opened the door, but before leaving, he said, "I will stop by before the meeting with the elders and see if there has been a change with Jasper."

"Alright," Lizbeth said. "Would you like to come with us?" she asked. Aldwin could hear a slight hesitation in her voice. Aldwin nodded and Lizbeth smiled. She feared the elders would banish Jasper without a second thought. The elders could be obstinate when they chose to be. Lizbeth was not one of their favorite Elfkins. With Aldwin there supporting them they might have a fighting chance.

"Get some rest Lizbeth. You look tired," Aldwin said as he looked at the expression of concern on her face. Lizbeth smiled at his words and nodded. He scowled down at her.

"Go on now," she said. "I will be fine." Aldwin knew better than to argue with her. He sighed heavily before bidding her goodnight. Lizbeth closed the door tightly behind him and made her way across the room to the cupboards. She was not worried about her safety as she readied a bowl so that Jasper could bathe.

She sat the bowl in front of Jasper and laid a towel and a bar of soap beside it. Jasper looked up at her questioningly. They had already eaten he wasn't sure what the bowl of water was for. He looked at the soap as if he had never seen one before. Taking his finger he scrapped the bar and was about to put his finger in his mouth when Lizbeth stopped him.

"It's not for eating, it's for cleaning you silly creature," Lizbeth said. Jasper screwed up his face. "Surely you have taken a bath before." Jasper shrugged his shoulders and looked sheepishly at her. "Alright I will show you how it's done. Then after this you can wash yourself... at least once a week," she added.

Lizbeth introduced Jasper to bathing and after it was done they sat in the rocking chair together. She spoke to him about the elders, the medallions they wore and how they were chosen to be a member of the council. Lizbeth talked until Jasper fell asleep in her arms. As she rocked in the chair waiting for Marla to come home she wondered with apprehension about what the elders would say.

Gradually Lizbeth's thoughts turned to the one they called Zusie. She lived deep in the side of the mountain in a crystal cave. Like Jasper, she was different and most of the villagers had never met her. Lizbeth however had a long standing friendship with her. Lizbeth was certain that Zusie would want to meet Jasper and decided that a trek up the mountain was in order.

The winds outside howled loudly and blew with great force against the door and shutters to the window. They rattled violently on their hinges but the latches were strong and the shutters stayed shut. Lizbeth looked over her shoulder and whispered crossly, "As it was before and is now, you can't come in. Do shut up and go away." The wind banged loudly again at the door. Jasper squirmed and whimpered restlessly in his sleep. Lizbeth calmed him with a soothing song that she hummed and he quickly settled back down.

"Poor little fellow," she whispered. "Don't you worry. I will keep you from harm." Jasper smiled in his sleep and curled closer to her. Lizbeth's heart melted. Was it by a mere coincidence that Jasper landed on her doorstep, she thought as she smiled at him. Or was there a greater purpose to their meeting? Lizbeth instinctively knew that the latter was the reasoning. As she continued to rock in the chair and hum softly Lizbeth wondered once again what the elders would say in the morning.

CHAPTER 2

The Council of Elders

The next day the winds had died down completely -- the sky was clear, the sun shone brightly and the temperature was refreshingly cool. With the break in the weather, the Elfkin village erupted into a frenzy of controlled motion. Every villager was out of their hut; even the youngest of them who were warmly clothed in thick hooded overcoats and boots. The smallest of the underlings were snuggled against their ma's chest in sling-like wraps called swaddles.

Most of the Elfkin men had immediately gone into the forest to gather wood for their fires. They brought it back to the village by way of two-wheeled trolleys. The wood was stacked neatly in sheds located at the back of their huts. The men repeatedly went back and forth until every wood shed was full. The women and older underlings stayed to check their dwellings for damage and repairs if needed. Thrilled to be outside, the younger underlings played catch-me-up; a game of chase and tag.

Other than a couple of toppled benches, the only hut that had extensive damage was Marla's. Several of the village carpenters went to work on removing the rubble. It took all of them to move the heavy branch. Once it was gone, they found more damage than was previously estimated. The entire roof needed rebuilding along with the cabinets dining table, and two of the chairs lay in splinters on the floor. After speaking with Griffyn, the head carpenter with a no nonsense attitude, Marla realized that she would be staying with Lizbeth for some time. Marla was reassured before Lizbeth left with Aldwin and Jasper; who was hidden from view in the pocket of Aldwin's tunic, that she could stay as long as was needed.

Marla was thankful for Lizbeth's kindness. The storage room where she would be staying was larger than most and quite comfortable. Instead of feeling sorry for herself, she worked with the carpenters to remove the broken furniture and cupboards.

After speaking with Marla, Lizbeth and Aldwin quickly walked down a winding path that led out of the village to a large clearing. In the center of the clearing was a large building. Aldwin looked around the clearing. Seeing no one, he helped Jasper out of his pocket. As Jasper hovered between Lizbeth and Aldwin, he looked in awe at the building. It was three times taller than Lizbeth's hut, four times wider and five times the length. It was made out of rugged beams and the thick wooden doors were massive. The roof, like on Lizbeth's hut, was made from tightly weaved branches.

Aldwin opened one of the large doors. Jasper was surprised that it opened with little resistance. Curious to see more Jasper followed behind Lizbeth and Aldwin as they stepped inside. The outside of the building had impressed Jasper, but the interior left him speechless. It was extraordinary.

Large rugged beams spanned the length of it. Thick posts placed twelve feet apart held up the beams. A massive stone fireplace sat at the back of the room. Along the walls were multi-tiered benches. Above the benches were long shuttered windows. The floor, made from large flat stones, was clear of debris. Jasper could tell that the structure meant a lot to the Elfkins.

They walked to the center of the room; a low bench was placed in front of a long table that sat on a raised platform. Behind the table were five high-back chairs. Aldwin motioned for Jasper to sit on the bench; Aldwin and Lizbeth sat on either side of him. The three of them waited quietly for the elders to appear. Jasper was the only one that seemed nervous. His stomach churned with anxiety even though Lizbeth reassured him all would go well. She had gone to each of the elders huts earlier that day and told them that she had something very important to show them. Each of them had refused her an audience until she explained Jasper to them. Curious, they agreed.

Jasper jumped when a door, located at the back of the room beside the fireplace, opened and the elders appeared. They walked in single file with stern expressions on their weathered faces to the table. They each took a chair and sat down. They did not acknowledge Jasper until Lizbeth introduced him. As instructed, Jasper greeted them politely and tried not to fret as he waited for their response. None of them responded in kind. Instead they looked at him with the same expression of disdain. It was hard for Jasper to think that anything positive was going to come out of the meeting.

The Council of Elders was made up of five members: Markhum, Bertrum, Farringdum, Gradum and Tad. They all looked similar in build and facial features except Tad who was taller and thinner. Other than Tad, it was difficult for Jasper to tell the others apart. Each had a long white beard, long thin nose, bushy eyebrows and large pointed ears. They were robust in stature, had large, beefy hands, and each wore a long white robe. Around their necks a medallion hung. Lizbeth had told Jasper all about them. Instead of looking at the Elders' faces, Jasper concentrated on the medallions as Lizbeth began to state her request.

The medallions were circular and made from the inner ring of an old tree. In the center was a stylistic depiction of the fir tree they were carved out of. Surrounding it were the Elfkin symbols for the four basic elements of life; earth, water, air and fire. Carved into the trunk of the tree were the words; "Truth in honesty above all."

Time passed slowly as Jasper recalled what Lizbeth had told him about the medallions and the elders. 'The elders are given the position at high council because of their age, or longevity, which is one of the seven ancient symbolic meanings for the fir tree,' he remembered her saying. 'It has nothing to do with the other six meanings; honesty, progress, resilience, friendship, remembrance and perceptiveness. This lot is as close-minded and thickheaded as they come. Not a progressive or perceptive thinker in any of them. I think the other meanings have gotten lost in translation over the years as well. But it is what it is and we shall follow tradition and introduce you to them tomorrow,' Lizbeth said. Rather than comment, Jasper wondered whether or not the elders would see the truth in his fateful predicament and allow him to stay.

Jasper however did not know that the elders disliked Lizbeth greatly. She annoyed them with her 'forward thinking' as they called it. She openly challenged their decisions that vexed them to no end. He also did not know that behind closed doors Aldwin and Lizbeth often spoke of the validity of the council and whether or not it had run its course. However, there were other villagers, who like the elders, were set in their ways and preferred tradition over forward thinking. They too disliked Lizbeth but tolerated her because of her knowledge. Other villagers, those who respected Lizbeth, often said that she should be a member of the council. Her retort was always the same -- 'I am too open-minded to be a member.' That however was not the real reason why.

Even though Lizbeth was older than the council members were, she was female and for as long as anyone could remember only males sat at council. Lizbeth didn't really mind as she enjoyed her position as the Keeper of the Woods. It was a fascinating job. She not only had to keep records of weather patterns and how much precipitation fell each year, but she also had to know the beneficial properties of each plant.

Part of her responsibilities also included keeping track of each species of life in the Greenwood Forest, including the Elfkins. Lizbeth had just finished a detailed journal of all that she knew just before Marla had frantically knocked on her door. While Marla placed her belongings in the storeroom, Lizbeth wrapped the journal in a thick piece of cloth and placed it in the chest at the end of her cot. She was not quite ready to share it with anyone.

Now, just a day later, they sat in front of the elders. Lizbeth had instructed Jasper not to fidget as the elders might see it as a sign of hostility. However, Lizbeth had started to raise her voice and Jasper, a nervous creature by nature, started to fidget. The longer Lizbeth argued the more stern the elder's expressions became which worried Jasper. With no memory of how he got there, or how to get home, he had no idea what he would do if they banished him from the village.

"We know nothing of him!" Markhum stated, repeating an earlier comment. This time however he said it with an edge of contempt. The other elders nodded and Jasper's heart began to thump harder.

"We know not where he came from!" Farringdum said with the same edge of contempt. The others nodded again. Sweat began to bead on Jasper's forehead.

The tension in the room became thick and Jasper wrung his hands together. Lizbeth's composure changed from tolerance for the elder's lack of imagination to anger. It seethed just beneath the surface as she watched them nodding their heads in unison. Not one of them had the backbone to stand up against the others -- they thought singularly. If one said no, they all said no. If one said yes, they all said yes. And Zenrah forbid if anything out of the ordinary should happen because it was always seen as an omen of misfortune. Any new idea of how to do something was talked about for days sometimes months before a decision was made. Their conclusion was always the same 'That is not the way we do things,' and that would be the end of it.

Lizbeth knew that Jasper's arrival to their village was a sign of change. To voice that however would surely mean that the elders would banish him, as it looked like they were about to do. It was a desperate moment and Lizbeth needed to sway them to her side.

"Look at him!" Lizbeth yelled allowing her anger to boil over. "He is no bigger than your hand. How could one so small be of concern to any of us?"

"Know your place Lizbeth!" Bertrum sneered as he leaned forward and scowled at her. The others nodded and glared at her. Lizbeth sighed heavily and shook her head. Over the years, she and Bertrum had several run-ins. He had a foul temper and so did his father before him.

Bertrum was usually the one who spoke for the lot of them. They followed his lead out of fear more so than because they agreed with his arguments.

Lizbeth opened her mouth to speak again but stopped when Bertrum pounded his fist on the table and bellowed "Enough!" Jasper jumped in surprise and so did the other elders. His heart thumped loudly. Anxiety tweaked his imagination and as a vision of him being caught and thrown in a dark cave came to the forefront of his mind, his wings involuntarily unfolded behind him and his snout began to unfurl.

Aldwin, sensing Jasper's distress, whispered softly to him that all would be fine. To reassure him Aldwin picked Jasper up and placed him on his right shoulder. Jasper's nerves instantly eased. As he leaned his head against Aldwin's cheek and whispered a thank you, his snout re-curled up and his wings lay flat against his back. The Elders, seeing the exchange, gasped in shock. Lizbeth turned around sharply then smiled when she saw the exchange of kindness from Aldwin to Jasper. There was more to Jasper's story, she was sure of it and would not rest until she knew what it was.

She turned back to the elders and looked at each of them, but directed her next words to Bertrum. "If you banish Jasper from the village I will have no recourse but to go with him," Lizbeth said. The elders gasped again in shock. Aldwin looked at Lizbeth with surprise before masking his expression. They hadn't talked about the steps they would take if the elders banished Jasper from the village.

Jasper, still sitting on Aldwin's shoulder, looked fearfully at Lizbeth then frowned deeply. In the short time he had known her he had come to love her. He couldn't explain the feeling or why it was so intense. He did not want her to leave on his account and was about to say so. Before he could however Lizbeth turned and winked at them. Jasper confused as to what that meant stayed quiet. Aldwin knowing what it meant stood up.

The elders watched in astonishment as Aldwin walked over to Lizbeth and stood by her side. The elders were not as dense as Lizbeth thought. They knew implacably what the show of solidarity meant -- Aldwin would leave as well. To lose Lizbeth and all of her knowledge would be bad, but they would survive. However to lose their village healer would not bode well with the other villagers. Even though they had Marla, she was not yet fully trained.

"We need to discuss this," Bertrum said barely keeping his anger in check as he got up from the table. The other elders huffed in annoyance as well, but each of them stood and walked in single file to the back of the room. Bertrum opened the door and waited impatiently for the others to enter. He sneered at Lizbeth before he slammed the door shut. Lizbeth and Aldwin, with Jasper on his shoulder, stood still and listened. The muffled voices of the elders could be heard from behind the door -- They were arguing. Lizbeth smirked -- Arguing was a good sign.

Lizbeth's expression instantly changed however when the door suddenly opened and Bertrum glared at her with deep hatred. Solemnly the elders walked back to the table in a single file and sat on their chairs again. They looked at Lizbeth with contempt, but each of them nodded their heads; which meant Jasper could stay. Inwardly Lizbeth smiled with satisfaction, the elders were not as thickheaded as she thought. Outwardly, her expression however was as solemn as theirs was.

"Thank you," Lizbeth said. Aldwin nodded his head and Jasper, not able to look at the elders, whispered a thank you. Bertrum sneered at them as they walked to the big doors. He waited until they shut the door behind them before he reprimanded the other elders with coarse words.

With Jasper still on Aldwin's shoulder, the three of them started down the path that led to the village. Their faces were lit with bright smiles. Caught up in their victory they did not see a portly villager standing at the corner of the building. Nor did they feel his steely gaze burning into their backs before he opened one of the big doors and stepped inside. Bertrum's angry voice could be heard over the other elders as they tried to reason with him. The villager looked at them in disgust; they were weak-minded and he hated all of them. His anger boiled to the surface as he dramatically shut the heavy door. The loud bang startled the elders into silence. As they turned to see who had come in all of them but Bertrum moaned with displeasure. They sighed heavily as they slumped in their chairs – it was going to be a very long day.

CHAPTER 3

The Elfkin Village

"You know we haven't heard the last of this," Aldwin said as he looked out over the village.

"I know," Lizbeth replied. "But for now, Jasper is safe and that is all that matters."

"What now?" Aldwin asked looking down at Lizbeth.

"I am going to show Jasper his new home," Lizbeth said. Aldwin's sudden outburst of laughter startled Jasper. He flew off Aldwin's shoulder and hovered in mid-air in front of them.

"Sorry," Aldwin said to Jasper before addressing Lizbeth, "You are a force to be reckoned with. I am sure the elders are scratching their heads trying to figure out how you got another one passed them!"

Lizbeth smiled. Jasper looked curiously at them, wondering what Aldwin spoke of. "Enjoy the day," Aldwin said.

"You as well," Lizbeth said. Aldwin started to walk toward his hut then stopped and looked at Jasper.

"Welcome to your new home Jasper. I hope you will enjoy living here," Aldwin said.

"Thank you," Jasper said smiling brightly. Aldwin smiled in return, nodded his head to Lizbeth and as he started to walk away they could hear him whistling a merry tune.

"Well now," Lizbeth said as she clapped her hands together. "Let us get on with the showing shall we? There is a lot of ground to cover." Jasper nodded his head eagerly.

"That as you know was the Gathering Hall. It is where we have our village meetings and festive celebrations," Lizbeth said. She walked briskly away from the hall and the elders who she thought were no doubt still talking about Jasper. "That," she said pointing to a large flat stone that hung in a small hut in the middle of the village "is the summoning stone. We only use it for emergencies." Jasper intrigued by the stone wanted to take a closer look, but Lizbeth started walking down a path that led out of the village.

At the first bend in the path she pointed to a building on her right, stating it was the bathing huts. As she quickly walked on, Lizbeth said that she would take him there after the evening meal. He only nodded in agreement.

The first place they stopped at along the path was a grove of trees that were unlike the other trees in the forest. They were only about ten feet tall and had spirally branches. Lizbeth called them bimble trees.

"We harvest the pods from the bimble tree in mid-summer," Lizbeth said. "The pods are full of silky strands of fiber. We spin the strands of fibers together using spinning wheels. The strands are dyed using a colour solution made from crushed flower petals; the finished product, which we call bimble yarn, is rolled into balls. We use the yarn to make our sweaters, blankets and socks." Jasper nodded in response. He remembered seeing a basket of colourful yarn by the rocking chair.

Beside the grove was a long building. Lizbeth walked to the building, unlatched the thick wooden door and went inside. Jasper followed her in. "This is the wheel house. It is where we weave the fiber and dye the yarn," she said. After Jasper's eyes adjusted to the dim light, he looked around. In the middle of the room were several spinning wheels. A small three-legged stool sat beside each wheel. Along the back wall were several large bins. Along each of the sidewalls were low shelving units that were bare. Spanning the length of every wall were shuttered windows. Satisfied that Jasper had seen enough Lizbeth walked briskly out of the building and onto the next point of interest; a very large clearing that was devoid of bushes and trees.

"This is one of three vegetable patches," she said with pride. " It is too early to see anything, but soon, once the ground is thawed, we will sow seeds and grow a variety of vegetables that we will harvest from late spring to fall," Beside the vegetable patches was a grove of neatly trimmed bushes. "Those are berry bushes," she added. "We harvest the fruit in early fall. This grove is one of many." Again, Jasper nodded but did not say anything, so Lizbeth continued to show him around his new home.

She led him down a steep path to a winding river that she called the Bantor River. There were large chunks of ice in it but for the most part the river ran quick. They came to a massive tree that had a large hole in the trunk of it. Lizbeth walked around the tree but Jasper stopped in front of it and looked curiously at it. "What is it Jasper?" Lizbeth asked. Before Jasper could respond, they heard a gale of laughter coming from around the next bend in the river. Lizbeth walked quickly towards the sound. Rounding several large bushes, she came to an immediate stop and sighed heavily. Jasper nearly bumped into her but swerved just in time. He looked curiously at the scene before him then smiled.

"Rangous and Septer, isn't it too early to fish?" Lizbeth questioned them.

"Too early to fish," Rangous said before clicking his tongue loudly. Rangous was tall for an Elfkin at five feet three inches. He was ruggedly handsome with dark brown eyes, black hair and neatly trimmed beard. He was struggling with a rather large fish that was swinging wildly on the end of the fishing line. The fishing pole bowed from the weight of the fish.

"Too early," Septer said then smiled broadly, as he positioned a net under the fish. Rangous took the fish off the hook and dropped it into the net. Septer was almost as tall as Rangous, and was handsome with blue eyes and sandy coloured hair. He had a twinkle to his eyes and an infectious smile. Shivering violently he chuckled and said, "There's no such thing as too early."

Jasper thought the two of them looked quite comical dressed as they were with thick overcoats, their pants rolled up to their knees and no boots on their feet. Rangous turned and smiled broadly at Lizbeth. Noticing Jasper fluttering beside her he looked inquiringly for a moment but his smile did not falter.

"And who do you have with you today Lizbeth?" Rangous asked. Septer looked over- his smile did not falter either.

"This is Jasper," Lizbeth said than looked at them nonchalantly as if a stranger to the village was an everyday occurrence.

"Hello Jasper," Rangous and Septer said in unison- their smiles becoming broader. They both respected Lizbeth greatly. If she was not worried about Jasper than neither were they. Jasper smiled in return and instantly took a liking to both of them.

"Would you and Jasper like to join us?" Septer asked.

Lizbeth shook her head. "I am giving Jasper a tour of his new home," she said as she walked passed them.

"Perfect," they said in unison. Jasper followed Lizbeth and waved goodbye to them; Rangous and Septer waved in return. If Rangous and Septer were weary of Jasper, they did not show it. Instead, they welcomed him. That pleased Lizbeth. Perhaps, she thought, the other villagers would as well.

They left Septer and Rangous behind and walked in silence along the river for several paces until them came to a clearing that had eight small stone huts with peaked roofs sitting evenly apart in the middle of it. "These are drying huts," Lizbeth said as she opened up the door to one of the huts. Jasper again waited for his eyes to adjust to the darkness before looking around. Several long poles spanned the width of the building. Along one wall was a bench-like table that was neatly stacked with coils of rope. "This is where we dry the various tea leaves and spices that we harvest from the gardens. We wash them in large tubs then hang them in bunches from those poles." Jasper again just nodded his head but did not comment. Lizbeth looked at Jasper curiously before she carefully closed the door behind them.   They walked several paces away to a large rectangular building. Lizbeth unlatched the door and they both went in.

"This is the pottery hut and these are pottery wheels," Lizbeth said. Jasper looked on in surprise. Several pottery wheels sat in the middle of the room. A small stool sat beside each of them. Along the walls of the room were bench-like tables. Most of the tables had stacks of bowls, cups and plates on them. Hanging on the wall just above the table were small hook-like tools. Along the walls of this building were shuttered windows as well. Jasper looked at everything curiously but did not comment on any of it.

Lizbeth left the building and walked around to the back; Jasper followed. At the back of this building were several large stone fireplaces. Lizbeth explained that they were used to bake the pottery and every Elfkin over ten summers old knew how to make pottery. "If the weather permits, tomorrow I will show you the waterfall. It is not far from here and is quite lovely." Jasper only smiled in response. Lizbeth took a path leading out of the clearing. They walked several paces before she spoke again. "Jasper you have been quiet. Is something bothering you?" Lizbeth asked, stopping at a fork in the pathway. When Jasper did not respond right away, Lizbeth continued speaking. "This pathway will take you to the base of Mount Aspentonia," she said pointing to the right. "And this one will take us back to the village," Lizbeth pointed to the left.

"I am getting hungry. Are you?" she asked. Jasper nodded and they started on their way back to the village. All the while he flew with a perplexed expression on his face but remained quiet. Lizbeth was concerned. She had so hoped that by showing him around it would have jogged his memory of his own home. "Jasper does any of this seem familiar to you? Do you remember anything about where you came from?" Lizbeth asked.

"I can't remember Lizbeth," Jasper said sadly. Tears welled up in his eyes just as they had when Marla asked him that same question the day before.

"Do not fret little one," Lizbeth said soothingly. "We will get to how you got here and who you are another day. For now know that you are welcome to stay for as long as you like." Jasper smiled and tried not to worry.

CHAPTER 4

An Invitation to Tea

A full moon rotation and then some had passed since Jasper's arrival in the Elfkin village. Most of the villagers had accepted him as Lizbeth hoped they would. However, there were some who kept their distance, whispered about him behind his back and wondered in private where he came from.

Jasper didn't mind as he had Lizbeth. He also had Marla, Aldwin, Septer, Rangous and of course Bauthal. Who, as Lizbeth had predicted, was very interested in Jasper and where he came from. With Jasper's memory still absent, Bauthal and Lizbeth decided to put Jasper to work collecting sapple. Sapple was a gooey substance that pooled at the base of flower blooms and was collected by sapple gathers. They used their long thin snouts to collect the sapple then emptied it into clay pots. The Elfkins used the sapple to sweeten their various teas and baked goods.

There were three species of sapple gathers: bumbled beetles, frilly bees and pesty gnats. Until Jasper came along a bumbled beetle named Monto, was the largest of the sapple gatherers. He was big for a bumble beetle at four inches round and five inches long. Like the other bumble beetles, Monto had black and green spotted hard-shelled wings that covered his entire body when he was not in flight. He had an overly large head, tiny eyes and a moderately long snout that stuck out three inches from between his eyes. Monto was not very bright and had a rather sour disposition. He was also a bully and caused problems with the smaller creatures in the forest. Monto, for no reason at all, took an immediate disliking to Jasper. Once again, Jasper didn't mind as the other sapple gathers, like most of the villagers, had welcomed him warmly.

As it turned out, Jasper loved to collect sapple and was not just good at it but quick as well. It was his favorite thing to do, besides flying that is. With his swift wings, he covered more ground than anyone else and was finished his share of the chores well before the midday break. With the time remaining, Jasper explored the forest south of the village. He found the Greenwood Forest quite charming and often thought while exploring it that he would stay. That was until he heard about the Outer Bound Meadow.

Just the day before, after he finished his chores, Marla asked Jasper if he wouldn't mind taking a basket of food to Septer and Rangous. They were fishing in the pool at the base of the waterfall. They had been talking about the meadow when Jasper arrived. "Not even you, Rangous, the bravest and strongest of the Elfkins, would go to the Outer Bound Meadow," Septer said as he laid his fishing pole beside a bucket that was full of fish. He took the basket of food from Jasper, walked over to a large rock and sat on it --Then he motioned for Jasper to sit beside him. Septer took a large biscuit out of the basket and gave Jasper a piece of it. Jasper listened with interest to their conversation as he ate the biscuit.

"There would be no need Septer," Rangous retorted as he took a large brown and green speckled fish off the hook dangling from his fishing pole. He threw the fish into the bucket, smiled broadly and added, "All we need is right here in the Greenwood Forest."

Jasper did not question them about the meadow. Instead, he wondered for the rest of the day if that was where he came from. He went to sleep at his usual time but was awoken by a fretful dream. He couldn't remember the dream but he desperately felt that he needed to find his way home. Before he fell back to sleep he decided he would fly to the meadow. He awoke early and missed breakfast just so he could have enough time to get to the meadow before the forest became too dark to find his way through it. He had no idea how far away the meadow was. He was however the fastest flyer of all the winged creatures. Jasper was confident that he would make it there before the sunset.

Jasper was on his last flower -- A particularly large purple willynad that had unusual thick petals. His head was buried deep in the flower so that he could reach the sapple. The petals effectively muffled even the beating of his wings. So when a piercing sound disturbed the morning air every forest creature and Elfkin in hearing range stopped what they were doing except Jasper. The noise came again and this time everyone standing near Jasper looked curiously in his direction. Even the underlings playing a game of paddleball -- A game played with two paddles and a ball made from the gooey sap of the bimble trees, stopped playing and looked in his direction. The sound had come from the cave where Zusie lived.

Jasper finished sucking up the last of the sapple and was about to leave the flower when he was pushed deeper into it. By the time he wiggled his way out of it, he was fit to be tied.

"What is this all about?" he growled angrily. Expecting to see Monto, Jasper balled his little hands into fists. The previous day Monto had tried to knock Jasper out of the air while he carried a pot of sapple back to Lizbeth's hut. Jasper had held on tight however and did not drop the pot. Lizbeth seeing what had happened, loudly chastised Monto in front of the other sapple gathers and warned him that if he tried something like that again she would report him to the elders. Embarrassed, Monto had flown off in a huff and no one had seen him for the rest of the afternoon. However later that day when Lizbeth and Jasper returned home, after having dinner at Aldwin's, they right away noticed that something was wrong. The bench that sat beside the door to Lizbeth hut was toppled over. The clay pots that Jasper had filled earlier that day lay in pieces on the ground. Lizbeth never bothered to ask the other villagers if they had seen what had happened; she knew with certainty that Monto had done it.

Still angry at Monto for spoiling his hard work and breaking Lizbeth's possessions, Jasper was ready to give him a well-deserved bop on the snout. When he turned around however it was Lizbeth, not Monto, who stood before him. Jasper unclenched his fist, lowered them to his side and looked curiously at Lizbeth. Her hands were on her hips and her left foot tapped impatiently on the ground. The force of the tapping scattered a herd of red dapple spider ants that were making their way back to their nest with several large brown mushrooms. The ants yelled up at Lizbeth to watch what she was doing. Lizbeth ignored the ants. Instead, she looked at Jasper with a stern expression that made her right eye twitch. He looked wearily at her, wondering what he could have done to warrant such an awful expression.

Since his arrival Jasper noticed a subtle change in Lizbeth. She had become fatigued and weary. Most nights she fell asleep just after they finished their evening meal. Her demeanor gradually changed as well, she became irritable at the slightest noise. When he mentioned it to Marla, she said it was because Lizbeth took on more work than most of the other villagers half her age. Jasper didn't mention it again but in private he worried about her.

"Jasper," Lizbeth began to scold him loudly. "Did you not hear that?"

"Hear what, Lizbeth?" Jasper replied. Then he looked at her with concern. Her face had gone quite pale except for two red blotches on her cheeks.

"Your name, Jasper," she said. "You are being summoned to the cave." Lizbeth pointed to a spot on the side of the mountain.

"The cave...what cave? Are you jesting Lizbeth?" Jasper questioned, as he looked in the direction to where she pointed. He could see that there was indeed a cave at the back of a thick stone ledge just above a crop of Aspens.

"Don't you know about Zusie and the Crystal Cave of Aspentonia?" Lizbeth asked in astonishment.

"The what? I've never heard of a...a what did you call it? Crystal Cave...and what the heck is a Zusie?" Jasper stammered.

"Zusie is the Keeper of the Crystal Cave and to some of us she is the knower of all things," Lizbeth said calmly. The red blotches on her cheeks paled to a soft pink.

"When did she get here? How long has she been up there? And why is she calling my name?" Jasper asked quickly with a suspicious look on his face, still thinking that Lizbeth was jesting. Lizbeth shook her head and sighed heavily.

"Long before you Jasper; long before you. And I am not sure why she is calling your name." However, the look in Lizbeth's eyes, which she quickly masked, had Jasper wondering if she did know why Zusie was summoning him.

"You are always flying off into the forest by yourself," she began to scold him again, her cheeks getting redder as she did. "It's no wonder that you have never heard of her." Jasper looked at her with a sad expression. Lizbeth sighed heavily. "I am sorry Jasper. It is not your fault. I blame myself. I should have told you about Zusie long before now, but we were so busy getting ready for the spring planting," she said, more so to herself. Lizbeth shook her head in dismay and looked kindly at Jasper. "You best be getting up there to see what it is she wants before she calls your name again."

Just then, the noise came from the mouth of the cave again, only this time Jasper did hear it ringing loud and clear. The one they called Zusie was calling his name.

"What should I do Lizbeth?" Jasper asked nervously, tapping his little fingers together as his wings beat rapidly to keep him hovering in midair.

"Go," she urged gently. "Go and see what it is that she wants. Maybe she just wants to invite you for tea," Lizbeth said, more cheerily than she felt.

Jasper looked at Lizbeth strangely as if she had two heads and didn't move. Lizbeth, tired of waiting, pushed him forward. Not as hard as she had pushed him into the flower, but hard enough that he bumped into

Bauthal who was standing near by. Jasper apologized to him -- Bauthal gave a nod than looked up at the cave.

As Jasper flew towards stone steps that lead up the side of the mountain to the cave he passed several villagers. Some encouraged him; while others said nothing and turned back to their work. One in particular however named Camcor snarled as Jasper flew by. Jasper quickened his pace. Camcor was Bertrum's grandson and Jasper often saw them talking with Monto. Why the three of them took an immediate dislike to him Jasper didn't know. Perhaps Zusie the knower of all things would be able to tell him.

Flying low to the ground Jasper started to make his way up the steps. The steps were the only clear path up the side of the mountain that was thick with trees and bushes. As he flew around a large fir tree, odd visions of what Zusie looked like popped into his head. The vision was of a hairy bucktoothed Elfkin. As he flew on the vision changed to a more sinister one and by the time Jasper reached the stone ledge he was petrified of what he would see. Hovering just below the ledge he cautiously peered over the top. He looked to the left then to the right; no one was there to greet him. Sighing in relief he flew up and hovered several feet from the entrance to the cave. Turning around, he looked back to the village below.

The villagers who had encouraged him were waving at him. He smiled halfheartedly and waved back. Seeing that he was all right, they turned and went back to their chores. Jasper noticed that Lizbeth and Bauthal were the only two who stayed. His nerves began to waver and he wished that Lizbeth had come with him.

"What do you think this means, Lizbeth?" Bauthal asked without taking his eyes off Jasper, who started to fly nervously back and forth in front of the cave's opening.

"I'm not sure, Bauthal," Lizbeth openly lied, as she too watched Jasper and wished that she had gone with him.

"Well," Bauthal said gruffly as he turned back to his chores, "it can't be good, whatever it is."

CHAPTER 5

The Crystal Cave of Aspentonia

The Crystal Cave of Aspentonia, so named for the mountain it was located in, was as new and mysterious to Jasper as anything he had ever seen before. Well, anything he could remember seeing that is.

The arched entrance was twenty feet high and fifteen feet wide. Large yellow crystal blocks that shone golden in the sun lined the entrance. Jasper, immediately comforted by their glow, sighed heavily. The ugly visions he had while flying up the stairs receded to the back of his mind.

The archway opened into a long narrow passageway that curved out of sight. White crystal blocks lined these walls and lit it in a soft glow. Anyone walking down the passageway or in Jasper's case, flying down, needed no lantern. Large stone tiles uniformly cut in three-foot squares lay on the floor. The stones were light grey in colour, pitted and grooved. The surface of them looked rough.

No one had come to meet Jasper, so he nervously flew back and forth just outside the entrance, trying to muster up the courage to fly in. Perhaps, he thought to himself, this is a test.

"Yes, that's it," he said nervously. "They are testing me to see if I have enough courage to fly into the cave, passageway or whatever this thing is." He waved his little hand at the golden entrance. "How bad can it be?" he said, gaining courage. "Zusie, the knower of all things, must be very old if she knows everything. Besides, she couldn't even walk down the passageway to greet me." Puffing out his chest, he boasted, "I'm the fastest flyer in the whole forest. If she tries anything, I'll just fly away!" Jasper said then chuckled nervously.

Just as he was about to enter the cave, the horrible vision he had while flying up the stairs popped back into his mind. However, the vision had changed to a ghastly-disfigured Elfkin with a hunchback. It was playing a game of paddleball with Jasper as the ball and the crystal wall as the second paddle. The vision frightened Jasper so much he was about to turn around and go back to the village when a voice hollered at him.

"Oh for goodness sake, will you just get in here already!"

Shocked, Jasper abruptly stopped flying back and forth and hovered in midair. Wide-eyed and terrified, he frantically looked around. No one was there and yet the voice sounded like it was right next to him.

"Sometime today would be nice!" the voice impatiently rang out again. Jasper again looked frantically about.

"Wh...wh...who's there? Show yourself." Terrified, Jasper balled his little hands into fists just in case he would have to fight his way free. However, no one came forward. The air was still and Jasper, at that very moment, felt like he was the only one in the valley. Several minutes passed then the voice came again, only this time it sounded strained as it politely spoke to him.

"Please...Jasper...if you enter the cave you will see that no harm will come to you." Jasper furrowed his eyebrows as a peculiar thought came to him: the voice actually sounded like it was in his head. Jasper jumped when he heard a loud smack like someone clapping their hands sharply.

"You got it," the voice said. "Now come on down."

The voice, when not yelling at him, was quite lovely. Jasper, although scared, was intrigued to see what Zusie looked like. Cautiously, he started to make his way down the long winding passageway.

Back in the village, Lizbeth sighed as she watched Jasper enter the cave. Turning wearily, she noticed a large group of villagers standing nearby. They were whispering urgently among themselves with heated voices. "I believe there is still work to be done!" she said sternly. "There is no need to fret; things are as they should be." Seeing them disburse Lizbeth walked slowly towards her hut. She did not see however, that Camcor and a couple of the villagers stayed to finish their heated conversation.

As Lizbeth stepped inside her hut, she eyed her sleeping cot and wished she could take a nap. However, there was still work to do. Instead, she walked to the cupboards and started to prepare a meal for the midday break. She decided to make vegetable soup. It was Jasper's favorite meal. She slowly chopped vegetables into tiny pieces and threw them into a small pot. She added water and a handful of dried herbs and carried the pot to the fireplace.

Lizbeth placed the pot of soup on the hook in the fireplace. She stirred it quickly with a large wooden spoon that hung on a hook on the wall. She then walked to the window and opened the shutters. A soft breeze blew through the open window. She smiled then looked at the center of the table. Something was out of place. She normally had a pot of flowers on the table. Lizbeth enjoyed it when the breeze blew the scent of them around her hut. She decided that after Jasper got back they would pick a bouquet of flowers. Sitting on a chair Lizbeth thought of Jasper. He was such a wonder -- kindhearted, hardworking, intelligent and curious. Not even the elders could argue that Jasper was unworthy to stay in the village. He had proved his worth and then some.

As she waited for the soup to come to a boil Lizbeth's thoughts turned to that fateful day Jasper landed on her doorstep. The storm that brought him to them was the worst she had ever seen. How someone so small was able to fly through it without getting hurt was beyond her comprehension. A greater power must have been keeping an eye on Jasper that day. Lizbeth said a quick thank you to Zenrah. The winds had been fierce and bitter cold. She shivered as she remembered that the younger underlings were not allowed outside without their ma or da for fear that the winds would carry them away.

The soup started to boil and Lizbeth got up from the table and walked slowly over to the fireplace. Every muscle in her body ached and she moaned as she stirred the soup. Instead of walking back to the table, she sat in the rocking chair and waited for the soup to finish cooking.

As she rocked in the chair her thoughts again turned to the day she met Jasper. She remembered how the winds banged at her door after she carried him inside. It was if the winds were trying to get at him. She shuttered again at the odd thought and chuckled nervously.

The savory smell of soup filled the room and Lizbeth got up from the chair and ladled a spoonful into a bowl. Carrying it back to the table her brow furled as she thought of the wind trying to get at Jasper. "Come now Lizbeth," she scolded herself aloud. "You're starting to sound like the elders with all these foreboding, ominous thoughts." She chuckled nervously again then sat down at the table.

Banishing all thoughts of the storm and Jasper's arrival to their village, she thought of what she still had to accomplish before the sunset. When she was finished eating Lizbeth put the bowl and spoon in the washbasin and walked to the door. She eyed her cot again with longing but put on her coat and opened the door.

As she stood on the threshold to her hut, she looked out over the village. Old Barty sat in front of his hut as he did most days on his rocking chair. That day he was whittling what looked like a new walking stick. A group of underlings were playing a game of catch-me-up around the summoning hut. Another group of underlings were playing a game of paddle-ball. Accidentally one of the balls flew through the open window of Old Barty's hut. He growled at them but allowed them to go inside his hut and get it. Lizbeth chuckled. Old Barty was a cantankerous sort most days but she knew he was kind. Lizbeth looked and waved a hello to Mirabella as she and several other women entered the village from one of the pathways. They each carried a basket full of winterberries. Mirabella waved in return before going into her hut. Lizbeth smiled. Everyone would have a winterberry pie for dessert. She knew that Mirabella would make her one and looked forward to sharing it with Jasper.

The wind blew and Lizbeth inhaled the sweet smell of the air. She loved the spring season. It was her favorite time of the year. It was unusually warm however, especially so after the bitter cold winter they had. All the trees had budded early and were almost in full bloom. The sun was warm against her skin and she smiled. It was almost too warm to wear a jacket but she felt chilled and put it on anyway. Then quite unexpectedly, she leaned heavily against the door. Every ounce of energy was taken from her and she would have fallen to the ground if not for Aldwin.

Aldwin lived in a hut about twenty paces from Lizbeth's home. Marla had told him that Lizbeth had been acting strangely. Instead of staying up late, as was her custom, she was falling into a dead sleep every night just after they ate their evening meal. As each day passed, she noticed it took Lizbeth longer and longer to get started with her day. The carpenters were finished with her hut and Marla was worried about what would happen to Lizbeth when she was not there to help her. She had spoken to Aldwin about it just the day before. Worried, Aldwin had made his way to Lizbeth's hut to check in on her and caught her just before she fell to the ground.

"Lizbeth," he said calmly, trying to keep the concern out of his voice. "Are you alright dear? Would you like to sit down?"

Lizbeth did not budge and stared blankly at Aldwin as thoughts of the storm and where Jasper came from whirled around in her mind. Aldwin shook her lightly and spoke sternly to her. "Lizbeth, Lizbeth can you hear me?" Aldwin asked as he watched the colour in her cheeks drain to a pale white; she leaned heavily into his embrace and started mumbling incoherently. Aldwin held onto her tightly. "Shh now Lizbeth, all will be well," he said soothingly.

Septer and Rangous were walking by on their way to the fishing pool; seeing them, Aldwin called them over. Just as they reached the hut, Lizbeth started to moan and in a hoarse whisper, they heard her say, "Life beyond the mountains, Jasper is proof," then she fainted. Aldwin immediately started to bark out orders.

"Septer, go find Marla and bring her back here. I saw her take a group of underlings into the forest towards the grove of bimble trees. And Septer," Aldwin said with a serious tone to his voice, "Mention this to no one else." Septer nodded as he placed his fishing gear against Lizbeth's hut and went to find Marla.

"Rangous, help me bring Lizbeth to her sleeping cot." Rangous lifted Lizbeth's slight frame easily into his muscular arms and carried her into the hut. Laying her down gently, he tucked the cover around her.

"Aldwin, did Septer and I hear right?" Rangous asked as Aldwin removed the pot of soup from the fireplace and quickly filled another with water. He added something from his medicine bag into the water and placed the pot on the hook in the fireplace. When Aldwin did not acknowledge Rangous' question he asked another. "Did Lizbeth say there was life beyond the mountains?"

"Hush Rangous!" Aldwin looked nervously towards the open door and window, making sure no one had overheard what Rangous had said. "Lizbeth knows not what she speaks of," Aldwin said while he stirred the pot with a long wooden spoon.

Aldwin put the spoon to rest on the mantle of the fireplace and walked over to stand beside Rangous at Lizbeth's cot. Taking his arm, he walked Rangous to the door, saying, "She has worked herself ill and has become delirious with fatigue. Go back to your fishing and mention this to no one." Rangous hesitantly picked up his fishing gear and, just as he was about to step off the front landing, Aldwin grabbed his arm again. "Please, Rangous. Make sure you and Septer tell no one of this. Lizbeth is tired. Her words are ramblings brought on by fatigue and nothing more. There is no need to worry. All is well."

Rangous respected Aldwin so he did not argue or voice his thoughts that he and Septer had been wondering where Jasper had come from -- So had many of the villagers. Instead, he nodded in agreement that he and Septer would keep it between them. As Rangous walked to the fishing pool, he hoped Lizbeth was wrong, as her words contradicted their teachings. In his heart though, he knew they held substance and truth. He promised himself he would check in on her after he finished with the day's chores.

Back at Lizbeth's hut, Aldwin stood impatiently in the doorway waiting for Septer and Marla to return. Lizbeth stirred in her sleep.

Looking at her, Aldwin frowned as her words flooded his mind. He looked to the entrance of the Crystal Cave and back to Lizbeth again. His frown grew deeper.

Aldwin thought over what he had said to Rangous. While he had denied the words they had overheard, Lizbeth and he often spoke of the possibility that life flourished outside the seclusion of their valley. However, they dispelled the thoughts as quickly as they had thought them. But, the more Aldwin dwelled on it, the more worried he became. He wondered why Zusie wanted to meet Jasper. She had not mentioned it the last time he had visited her, which was just the other day. His brow furled deeper with concern as he shook his head. Surely if something had happened, he would have been called to the cave and not Jasper.

Lizbeth moaned and shivered violently under her covers. Aldwin closed the door and the shutters to the window then went directly to the cupboard and took out a medium sized bowl. He walked to the fireplace, ladled several scoops of what he called 'soothe ease potion' into the bowl and carried it to the small table beside Lizbeth's cot. He then walked into the storeroom and brought back a thick cloth. He quickly dipped the cloth in the warm solution, wrung out the excess water, and placed it on Lizbeth's forehead.

Her moaning instantly eased as the aroma from the warm cloth filled her senses. Aldwin laid a thicker blanket on her and checked her pulse. He was surprised to find that it was not racing, as he expected it to be -- It was beating quite slowly. Worried, he looked down at her. He once again took the cloth from her forehead and dipped into the warm water. "I hope whatever is ailing you, dear Lizbeth," he said as he wrung out the cloth and put it back on her forehead, "is not contagious."

Aldwin grabbed a chair from the table, placed it beside the cot and waited for Marla and Septer to return. Several minutes passed before he finally heard someone approaching. Expecting it to be Marla and Septer, he stood to open the door. However, halfway to the door he stopped and listened. Septer was exchanging heated words and it was not with Marla. Aldwin sighed heavily when he recognized the voice. It was Camcor. He had hoped that he could have kept Lizbeth's condition quiet until Jasper returned. Camcor started to pound on the door. Aldwin walked wearily towards the door. If Camcor knew, the elders would soon know, as would the whole village.

Just as Aldwin placed his hand on the handle of the door, a foreboding feeling consumed him; Jasper being called to the Crystal Cave and Lizbeth falling ill was just the beginning of a very bad turn of events. Aldwin sighed heavily again and opened the door.

While Lizbeth lay sick in her bed, Jasper had traveled far into the side of the mountain. The passageway to the Crystal Cave was long and curved wildly. As he flew, his nerves began to twitch again. The visions he had earlier tried to make their way to the front of his mind. He pushed them back and continued to fly forward. Finally he heard a noise coming from up ahead. He was delighted and displeased at the same time as the noise he heard were voices-- they were talking about him.

"You would think being the fastest flyer in the whole forest he would have been here by now," someone said rudely as he approached an entranceway to a large cave with crystal-lined walls.

"Now be patient. I am sure he is confused and scared. I mean after all, yelling for him through that horn Aldwin gave you was not very polite. You know you could have just as easily gone down to the village and invited him for tea," another said kindly.

"Yes, he certainly was scared. You should have seen the visions he had while flying up the stairs! I think he was thinking of you," the first being replied.

Jasper turned the last corner and stopped abruptly. Two creatures (that looked nothing like the visions he had) stood not two paces from the entrance to the room. The creatures turned when they heard Jasper's sharp intake of breath and looked at him -- One had a broad welcoming smile, the other had a frown. The one with the smile said sweetly, "Welcome Jasper."

Jasper looked at the one with the frown. She stared calculatingly back at him. As she sized him up the frown grew deeper and she pierced him with evil eyes. Jasper shivered despite the warmth coming from the crystals. Before he had a chance to say hello the one with the frown abruptly turned and walked down an arched hallway. The other one still looked at Jasper with a soft inviting smile and motioned for him to follow her into the room. As she spoke, she walked slowly backwards towards a large stone table.

"Hello. My name is Chrystalina and that was my sister Saphina. She left to fetch Zusie -- Sorry for her rudeness. She's a tad bit grumpy today." Jasper thought to himself: a tad bit grumpy – what would she look and act like if she was angry? Chrystalina stopped walking backwards but only because she had bumped into the table. She smiled warmly at Jasper and motioned with her hand for him to come forward. Jasper's nerves eased and he slowly flew towards the centre of the room.

"You look thirsty. Would you like some tea or something to eat perhaps?" Before he could respond, she too abruptly turned and left the room. Only she had gone through an archway that had a wooden door.

Jasper stopped flying forward and hovered. What should I do now? He thought to himself. Lizbeth never told me there was more than one. He wondered needlessly of how many more there were. Not knowing what else to do, he decided to explore the room, hoping it would help keep his mind off the one called Saphina. She seemed to have taken an immediate disliking to him. He wondered, as he looked around the room, if she was friends with Bertrum, Camcor and Monto.

The room, Jasper noticed, was a perfect circle. The same white crystals in the passageway leading to it lined the walls of this room as well. The flooring was the same too. However, the high ceiling had large clear crystals jutting down in varying lengths from one foot to three. Jasper made a mental note not to fly too near as their tips looked quite sharp. The soft glow radiating from the crystals comforted Jasper just as the crystals at the front entrance had.

Jasper relaxed and flew to the stone table. Upon reaching it, he looked at it with pure delight. The table, oblong in shape, had intricate etchings carved into it. The etchings depicted all manner of creatures living in the Greenwood Forest, the plant life and the changing of the seasons. Words, in a language that Jasper could not read, intertwined with the pictures, spiraling and flowing around them like a breeze. Eight wooden chairs made from different trees growing in the forest sat evenly around the table. Jasper looked at one closely and decided it looked very much like the ones Old Barty made, only much larger.

No one had reentered the chamber, so Jasper continued to fly around the room. His nerves calmed as his interest piqued with each new discovery. Nine archways, including the one he entered from, sat evenly apart around the room. Each archway was about eight feet high and three feet wide. The archway directly behind the table was the only one with a door.

Between each archway was an arched cubbyhole: two feet high, one foot wide and nine inches deep. In each cubbyhole was a statue made from the same golden crystals as the outer archway to the cave. Words were etched into the crystal wall above the cubbyholes. Jasper flew quickly to the first statue on the left hand side of the entranceway and hovered in front of it. The statue was of a female being, dressed in a long flowing gown. Jasper was surprised to find that it was not of an Elfkin. Neither was it of Saphina or Chrystalina. He stayed long enough to take in its sophisticated beauty before flying to the next one.

As he flew around the room, he noticed that each statue was holding a plant, an animal or a strange being in the open palms of its hands. He came to the second last cubbyhole and lightly ran his little finger along the animal that the statue was holding. Jasper expected the statue to be cold, but it was warm. So captivated by it, Jasper did not realize he was no longer alone in the room until he heard a gentle but strong voice say, "Curious little fellow, isn't he?"

Startled, Jasper turned quickly to see who had spoken. His snout caught the edge of the animal in the statue's hands. The statue wobbled precariously in the cubbyhole. Jasper heard a collective gasp and turned back just in time to steady the statue with his little hands. Curling up his snout, he looked apologetically towards the entrance to the hallway that Saphina had gone down.

Looking genuinely delighted to see him was another creature, which he could only assume was Zusie. Jasper looked at her in awe- she was beautiful. Her hair- silvery white fine strands- cascaded over her shoulders and down her back to her hips. She was quite tall. Jasper surmised that she was probably as tall as Lizbeth's hut. She was definitely not an Elfkin, as her features were more delicate. Her eyes were the colour of the sky on a clear summer's day, her nose was small and rounded at the end and her ears were small and rounded at the top. She was dressed in a pale blue flowing tunic and her stature was neither slim nor round, but sturdy.

She was standing next to Saphina who looked displeasingly at him. Now able to take a better look at her, Jasper saw that she too was not of Elfkin kind. She was shorter than Zusie but a little taller than Rangous. She was slim with the same kind of features as Zusie except her ears were slightly pointed. Her hair was cropped at the nape of her neck and dark brown in colour. She was dressed in a pale yellow floor-length tunic with a scooped neckline. A white beaded sash encircled her waist and its ends hung down past her knees.

Jasper was just about to say hello when Chrystalina came through the archway with a door, pushing a wooden cart that had four small wooden wheels. Jasper noticed that she too was not Elfkin. Like Saphina in height, stature and facial features, she had long flowing dark brown hair that cascaded over her shoulders to the middle of her back. Her tunic was also floor-length but was dark green in colour. The neckline however was v-shaped and trimmed with a white, delicately woven material that also trimmed the edge of the long flowing sleeves.

Jasper's stomach rumbled loudly. The cart Chrystalina had brought into the room was full of food and the delicious aroma made its way to him. Jasper looked at the cart longingly. It was laden with a teapot and mugs, and a woven basket overflowing with thick slices of bread. Three large wooden bowls and a smaller one were filled to the top with what looked and smelled like a savory vegetable soup. His stomach rumbled loudly again as he swallowed the saliva that had started to gather in his mouth.

Zusie smiled warmly as she motioned for him to come to the table. He looked cautiously at the three of them. They seemed rather nice, other than Saphina, who scowled at him. His stomach rumbled again as he looked at the cart of food; he was quite hungry.

"It's not good to skip meals, little one," Zusie said, still smiling as she waited for him to come forward. He looked curiously at her, wondering if she could read minds. Saphina huffed loudly and Jasper looked suspiciously at her. *I am still the fastest flyer in the village,* he thought confidently, and slowly flew towards the table.

CHAPTER 6
Zusie's Tale

"Welcome, little one. As you have surmised, my name is Zusie. We are the keepers of the Crystal Cave of Aspentonia. We are glad you were able to join us today."

Jasper looked at her, thinking he did not have much of a choice, but quickly stopped this train of thought after he heard a nasty humph from Saphina. She sat in a chair on the left side of the table; he could feel her looking at him as he flew by her. Afraid to look her way, he picked a spot on the table to sit on then looked intently at the etching before him, and tried not to think of anything. Chrystalina came around the table with the cart and placed the small bowl of soup and a small spoon in front of him.

"Would you like a spoonful of sapple for your tea, Jasper?" Chrystalina asked him kindly. He nodded his reply as he looked timidly at Saphina, unsure if he should speak or not. Chrystalina placed a small cup filled with herbal tea in front of his bowl. She patted his tiny hand with the tip of one of her fingers and smiled at him encouragingly.

"It's okay, Jasper. Don't let Saphina frighten you. She woke up on the wrong side of her sleeping cot and, like I said before, has been a tad bit grumpy all morning." Chrystalina placed one of the large bowls of soup, a piece of bread and a large cup of tea in front of Saphina. She moved along the table and placed the same in front of Zusie who sat on the left side of Saphina.

"It would have been difficult to wake up on the wrong side as I would have hit my head on the wall," Saphina retorted as she pulled off a piece of bread and aggressively dipped it into her soup.

"My point exactly," replied Chrystalina smartly as she sat down in the chair on the other side of Zusie. "You must have knocked your head or did you forget that it was you who thought it wise to summon him here today?" Chrystalina said as she put three heaping spoonful's of sapple into her tea. She stirred it vigorously; splashing a bit on the table, then took a quick sip. As she added another teaspoon she said, "You've done nothing but treat him rudely."

Saphina replied quickly and in a harsh tone, "He was thinking of flying to the Outer Bound Meadow before we had a chance to talk with him! What was I supposed to do? Allow him to go?"

Hearing this, Jasper dropped a large piece of bread into his soup. The thick liquid splashed over the side and onto the lovely tabletop. He quickly looked up at Saphina, expecting her to yell at him.

"It is alright Jasper," Zusie said kindly. "The table is made of stone. A little bit of broth will not harm it. Please continue to eat." As Jasper picked up the chunk of bread and took a tentative bite, Zusie spoke to Saphina. "Saphina, please go fetch a wet cloth to wipe up the spill and mind that when you come back you are in a better mood. I think you have indeed frightened our guest." Zusie's voice was kind but had a commanding edge to it that had Saphina leaving the table without a word of complaint.

Once Saphina finished cleaning the spill, the four of them ate the rest of their meal in silence. Zusie finished first, with Saphina and Chrystalina finishing next. While Jasper enthusiastically ate his soup, they sipped their tea and waited for him to finish before they spoke. He took the last chunk of his bread, ran it around the inside of his bowl, sopping up the last little bit of soup. Satisfied that he got everything, he popped it into his mouth and chewed on it thoughtfully. He took a long sip of his tea then looked up and smiled awkwardly. The three of them had been watching him. Zusie and Chrystalina looked at him with amusement while Saphina looked disinterested.

Jasper knit his brow together, wondering why she disliked him, then promptly covered his mouth with his little hand and burped much more loudly than he meant to. Saphina clicked her tongue at his ill manners. Embarrassed, Jasper looked away and smiled sheepishly at Zusie who smiled warmly back at him.

"Thank you very much. Vegetable soup is my favorite. It was quite delicious," Jasper said as he patted his full stomach and licked his lips.

"You're welcome, but your thanks should be directed to Saphina as she made the soup especially for you," Zusie said. Jasper looked sharply at Saphina, wondering how she knew. He was going to ask her, but seeing the scowl on her face he simply thanked her instead.

"You're welcome Jasper," she said kindly. Jasper looked at her strangely; she actually smiled at him. "I apologize for being so short with you earlier," Saphina said warmly. Jasper smiled at her cautiously, wondering why she was all of a sudden being nice to him.

"Now that we have that over with, why did you want to fly to the Outer Bound Meadow?" she asked curtly. Jasper noticed that Saphina's moods changed as quickly as a blink of an eye.

"Saphina, that can wait," Zusie interrupted. "I am sure Jasper is more curious about the Crystal Cave and the three of us than he is about the reason why we summoned him here today." All three of them looked at Jasper, expecting him to respond.

"Yes, I am curious about the cave and who you are," he said slowly. He deliberately avoided looking at Saphina, as he was sure she would be scowling at him again. He was curious as to why they summoned him. However, the cave, the table, the statues and the three of them intrigued him more.

"I know the story and have work to do," Saphina said than stood up quickly. "Please call me when you are finished." Without another word, she turned and briskly walked down one of the hallways and disappeared around a corner. Jasper wondered if she always left a room so abruptly. Chrystalina stood slowly, walked around the table and picked up the empty dishes.

"Since Saphina made lunch, I will tidy these up and start the preparations for the evening meal," she said. "I think fish would be lovely with tossed greens and maybe berry tarts for a treat." Chrystalina pushed the trolley through the archway with a door. Jasper just noticed that the door swung both ways.

"Well then," Zusie said when the room was quiet "since it is just the two of us, why don't you make yourself comfortable and I will tell you the tale of the Crystal Cave and how the three of us came to live here." Jasper settled himself down using his teacup as a backrest. He propped his elbows on his knees and placed his chin in his hands. Seeing that he was quite comfortable, Zusie started her tale.

"We are not sure how the Crystal Cave came to be," she said, surprising Jasper who immediately sat up straight. He looked at her curiously, as he wondered how that could be if she was the 'knower of all things.' "The cave was here long, long before we arrived. We have tried to find out its origin but to date we have not been able to." Jasper continued to look at her curiously. "All that you see, the table, the statues and the chairs, were already here. It was as if someone had just left the day before I arrived and never returned." Jasper wondered if she expected them to and missed completely that she had said 'I' and not 'we.' "I know that surprises you Jasper...I think you were hoping for more. But that is all we know." Jasper's features changed from curious to sad.

"Well, not quite all we know." His expression brightened. "We found in one of the antechambers," he looked as she pointed to the archway on the right side of the entrance to the cave, "several scrolls," she said with a smile. "Hundreds in fact, all neatly stacked on shelves.

Over the years, we have been deciphering them, or trying to that is. The words above the cubbyholes are written in the same language. It is a very old language. In fact, it could be thousands upon hundreds of thousands of years old, but there are no dates on any of the scrolls, so we can't be sure." Jasper did not understand what "dates" meant. Not wanting to sound silly by asking, he continued to look at her. His expression however had changed to one of confusion. "You look troubled. Is there something you want to ask me, Jasper?" Zusie said.

"If you were not already here, where did you come from?" Jasper asked hopefully.

"Ah, now that is a tale worth telling and it is almost as mysterious as the Crystal Cave," Zusie said smiling at him. However, her smile did not quite meet her eyes. "I was found much like you were -- wandering the forest in a mighty storm. One of Lizbeth's ancestors rescued me actually. Yes," she continued as she saw the calculating look on his face, "that would make me very old. I do not age like Elfkins do." She noticed that he still looked confused and continued, "Years to them would be like a day to me."

Jasper's confused expression did not change so Zusie carried on with her tale. "Once the storm subsided, Panmara, Lizbeth's great grandma, tried to introduce me to the Council of Elders just like Lizbeth did with you. Some of the elders, ancestors to the present elders, wanted to kill me right away. Even though I was just an underling, I was different and I came with a storm that almost destroyed the village. Back then the elders was a superstitious lot and they saw me as a bad omen." Jasper thought that not much had changed. "I was to be executed the next day," Zusie said. Jasper gasped.

Seeing the distressed look on Jasper's face she quickly added, "Panmara did not believe that I was a bad omen. Instead, she believed I was the forbearer of good news. In the middle of the night, while the rest of the villagers slept, she and her mate Omar brought me to this cave. They were the only villagers who knew of its existence. Panmara showed me the statues and I saw for myself that my features resembled theirs."

"Did the elders not question where you went?" Jasper asked as he looked at the nearest statue, plainly seeing the resemblance. Zusie smiled. Jasper was indeed curious and bright; it pleased her greatly.

"Oh yes they did, but with no proof of who set me free they in a very short time forgot about me. In return for Panmara's kindness, I learned to decipher the scrolls and taught her all that I learned. As you might have guessed, Panmara was the very first keeper of the woods. Panmara passed her knowledge of the cave, the scrolls and me to her daughter. I then taught her daughter, Lizbeth's grandma, her name was Rosie. She taught her daughter Mararose who in turn taught Lizbeth. They kept the knowledge of the Crystal Cave, the scrolls and me to themselves and their mates; for fear that the elders would exile me or worse, kill me." Zusie sighed. "It was necessary but it made for a very lonely existence." Zusie sighed again at the memory of those days.

Jasper looked at her, not quite understanding, then asked a very insightful question. "If you were here first, when did your sisters arrive?" He looked at her hopefully.

A sad expression passed over Zusie's face. She looked at Jasper as she said calmly, "Saphina and Chrystalina are not my sisters. They are my daughters. Their father was an Elfkin."

She looked at him sadly. The questions he was about to ask were going to be difficult ones for her to answer, but she was sure they would be more difficult for him to understand. Jasper saw the look on her face but could not stop himself from asking. "Who is your mate and where is he now?"'

"Willman left the village a long time ago," Zusie said sadly.

"If none of the villagers knew about you, how did you meet him?"

"He was best friends with Lizbeth's mate Horman and was kin to Rangous' da."

Jasper interrupted her. "Lizbeth has a mate?" Not able to stop himself, he asked, "I have yet to meet him. Where is he?"

Zusie looked at him with great sorrow. "Willman and Horman left the village many years ago in search of a pass through the mountains to the south and…they never returned. The night before he left, I conceived. He never knew I was with child and that he was to be a da." Jasper looked at her with sympathy. "I at least have my daughters," Zusie said. "Lizbeth, the poor dear, was left to live the rest of her life by herself." As if knowing his next question, Zusie continued, "It is in the nature of Elfkins to mate for life. Once one is gone, the other continues to live out their existence by themselves. Sad, I know," she said while looking at Jasper, knowing he was thinking of Lizbeth, "but it is the way that it is and has been so for thousands of years."

Reluctantly, he asked his next question, not sure he wanted to know the answer. "If Lizbeth does not have a daughter to pass the knowledge onto, who will be the next keeper of the woods?"

Zusie smiled. Jasper grasped new ideas quickly. She thought that perhaps he would indeed come in handy as Lizbeth assured her he would.

"Well now…that is a very interesting question," she said brightly. "Once Lizbeth and I came to terms with the fact that Willman and Horman would not be returning and long after the birth of my twin daughters, Lizbeth decided that it was time that the other villagers knew about us. One night, she gathered some of the villagers together -- The ones she thought she could trust and she told them our story. It was difficult at first to convince them. But she, as I am sure you know firsthand, has a very persuasive nature." Jasper nodded in agreement. "She brought a couple of villagers to meet us; they were Aldwin and Rangous' das. Rangous, as you now know, is kin to Willman. Therefore, my daughters are also his kin." Jasper nodded as he rapidly thought through all she was saying.

"They went back to the village…more enlightened you might say, and it was easy to convince the other villagers and elders that I, and now my daughters, were not evil omens. Eventually the Elfkins came to regard me as the 'knower of all things,' which isn't really the truth. I only know what I know because I am able to decipher the scrolls. It is the elders you see depicted in the statues who are the knowledgeable ones."

Jasper got up and paced back and forth in front of his cup, going over all that she had said. Finally, he stopped and looked at her disapprovingly. "Do you mean to tell me that you, the knower of all things, can't remember where you came from or how you got to the Evergreen Forest?"

Zusie looked at him thoughtfully, but decided not to correct his mistake of calling the Greenwood Forest the Evergreen Forest. If she had corrected him however, she might have been surprised at his response. Instead, she was not surprised that this would be the next question he would ask, especially since he had been so keen on trying to remember where he came from. Zusie did not need to be a mind reader to know where Jasper's thoughts were leading. She was sure he was wondering if she, the knower of all things, could not remember where she came from then how was he supposed to.

"I am sorry Jasper, but no, I don't remember. After Lizbeth and I realized that Willman and Horman were never coming home, I thought that knowledge was truly lost to us forever." Jasper hung his head and frowned as tears welled up in his eyes. "Until you came along that is,Zusie said, looking at him hopefully. He glanced at her with a surprised look on his face. "We summoned you here today because we are hoping you will be able to help me remember."

CHAPTER 7

The Memory Nut

"Yes, you see, we are going to knock you over the head in the hopes that it will bring back your memory," Saphina said cheekily as she entered the room carrying a large wooden mallet in her right hand. Tapping the thick, round head of the mallet gently on the side of her head, she looked at him mischievously.

Jasper took one look at the mallet and jumped into the air; knocking over his teacup. The remains of the tea splashed onto the table. The frantic beat of his wings made a humming noise that echoed off the crystal walls. Jasper quickly looked towards the entrance of the cave wondering if he could make it there before one of them caught him.

"Saphina!" Zusie gasped. Horrified by her daughter's words, Zusie looked at Saphina with great restraint. If she had said that a few years ago, Zusie would have sent her to her room as a punishment. However, her daughters were women now and past the age of punishment. Zusie knew the reason why Saphina was so hard on Jasper, but that was not an excuse for her to be so mean to him. "Why would you say that?" Zusie asked her.

"Yes, why would you say that?" Chrystalina asked haughtily as she entered the room. "He is jittery enough as it is without you threatening him like that!" She looked scathingly as at her sister. "It took great courage for him to meet with us."

"I was not threatening him. I was jesting!" Saphina said while plunking the mallet on the stone table, which made Jasper even more wary. The mallet sounded very heavy as it hit the table with a dull thud. The noise reverberated around the room and echoed down the hallways, drowning out the humming of Jasper's wings. Petrified, he looked at the mallet. A hit on the head would not bring his memory back it would kill him! Saphina looked at the petrified expression on Jasper's face and said lightly, "I was only jesting. Please sit back down. No one is going to hurt you."

Despite her assurance, Jasper continued to hover over his teacup. He looked at the big mallet and stumbled over his words as he asked nervously, "Wh...wh...what is the mallet for then?"

"The mallet is for this nut," Chrystalina said plainly, holding the nut up for Jasper to see. Jasper took a closer look at the nut as Chrystalina placed it on the table beside the mallet. It was rather big and oblong in shape. The shell, covered in fine, dark green hairs, wobbled back and forth on the table. Chrystalina steadied it with her hand.

"What is the nut for?" Jasper asked a little less nervously, looking from the nut to Chrystalina and back again.

"The nut is from a very rare plant called a reminiscence plant," Chrystalina said soothingly. She was obviously the kinder of the two sisters. "The plant that the nut comes from is quite interesting really," she said, sitting in the same chair she had earlier. "It only blooms," she continued to say in a soft voice, hoping to calm Jasper's jagged nerves, "every five hundred years; producing one nut. The nut takes a year to mature."

"I haven't been quite honest with you, Jasper," Zusie said while running her hand along the roughness of the nut's shell. Jasper looked at her suspiciously, as he continued to hover in the air. The girls looked at their mother compassionately, knowing she was thinking of their father. "You see Jasper, after all these years I haven't really given up hope of finding a way to remember where I came from." Jasper's expression eased as he looked at the sadness on Zusie's lovely face.

"I read about a rare plant that restores memory in the scrolls shortly after Lizbeth and I realized that Willman and Horman were not returning. I knew that it wouldn't bring Willman back to me. However, I thought if I could just get home, then I would be with my own kind and not feel so lonely. I searched the countryside for years looking for it to no avail. I finally gave up. My daughters needed me to be there for them, not traveling around the countryside for a miracle plant that might not even exist."

The room was quiet as she continued to tell her story. "Then, quite by accident just over a year ago, two fishermen, I think you know them, Rangous and Septer," Zusie said questioningly. Jasper nodded his head. "Well, they found a cave behind the waterfall and decided to explore it. Carrying a lantern to light their way, they wandered deep inside the cave. At the end of the long passageway was a smaller cave. Growing in the center was a strange plant about five feet tall with large, dark green, broad leaves. They had never seen anything like it before and, not wanting to disturb it, they left the cave. They sought out Lizbeth to ask if she knew anything about it. After describing the plant to her, she made her way to us. I remember the day like it was yesterday," Zusie said wistfully.

"I got very excited. We all ran to the cave and there it was! The plant I had looked for and thought I would never find! To think," Zusie said, chuckling lightly, "it was there all the time; a stone's throw away. I was searching all over the countryside for a plant that grew in the shade, when in reality it grows in darkness." As an afterthought, Zusie added, "We will have to re-transcribe that bit in the scrolls; 'sulshay' means darkness, not shade."

"I have already corrected it," Chrystalina said in matter of fact tone. Zusie smiled at her daughter. Out of the three of them, Chrystalina had the keenest interest in the scrolls and took it upon herself to make sure that they were properly sorted and catalogued. Zusie continued with her story.

"To my delight, the reminiscence plant was just coming into bloom. The flower was as large as a plate and bright pink in colour with a bright white center. It was lovely to behold." Zusie smiled warmly. Chrystalina smiled at the memory and Saphina's features softened. "I would just have one year to wait for the nut to mature and then I would have my memory back and be able to go home. Well, of course, you can imagine how excited I have been all year," she looked at Jasper with a girlish grin that brightened her pretty features.

He flinched as Saphina pulled out the chair she sat in earlier. Zusie motioned for Saphina to sit in the chair next to Chrystalina on the other side of the table. Saphina went grudgingly without a word of complaint and, as she sat in the chair, she looked sternly at Jasper. Her expression reminded him of the way the council of elders looked at him whenever he flew by them.

"Mother has kept an eye on the nut all year, watching it grow, making sure that no one disturbed it" Saphina said. "We have been waiting patiently for it to mature so that we can crack it open and mother can drink the nectar within."

"Well, some of us have been waiting patiently," Chrystalina said. She smiled and nudged Saphina's arm. Saphina ignored her.

"How can you be sure it is the plant you have been looking for?" Jasper asked.

"From the scrolls," Zusie replied patiently. "It was described in great detail right down to the size, shape and colour of the nut and the leaves on the plant. The person who kept the scrolls was very detailed in their description. They left nothing to the imagination."

"It also helped that there was a drawing of it," Saphina said rudely.

"Oh," was all Jasper could say as he looked at the nut. "Why do you need me?" he asked to no one in particular. Still looking curiously at the nut, his fear ebbed slightly and he drifted down to hover over it.

"Because," Chrystalina piped up to answer the question before the other two, "there is a glitch in our plan. Earlier this year, while I was sorting through the scrolls, I came across one that had to do with the reminiscence plant- A continuation of what mother had found you might say. The nut is as hard as rock and actually can't be split open with this mallet." Jasper looked at her strangely, wondering why they brought the mallet out and why they needed him. Surmising what Jasper was thinking, Chrystalina explained.

"See this little nub here?" She pointed at the top of the nut. Jasper peered intensely at the nut. There was indeed a small round nub no bigger than Jasper's hand sitting on top of the nut. The fine hair on the shell camouflaged it. Jasper would not have seen it if Chrystalina had not pointed it out. "When the nub is broken off, it will leave a tiny hole in the shell. Inside the center of the nut is a smaller nut about the length of my finger." She held up her index finger so Jasper could see. "That nut has a soft outer shell with a liquid center. Once the nub is off, the nectar can be sucked out and put into a cup so that mother can drink it."

"We gave up all hope of ever getting the nectar out until Lizbeth told us of your unique feature," Zusie said while pointing at her own nose.

Jasper looked down the length of his snout and a spark of realization shone in his eyes. Jasper realized what they needed him for and asked nervously, "How do you know the nut is mature?"

"Because it fell off the plant," Saphina said rudely, again. Seeing the stern look on her mother and sister's faces, she said in a gentler voice. "We read it in the scroll. That's how we knew it was mature and that we couldn't crack it open with the mallet."

"In fact," Zusie continued, "and this is very interesting indeed, it fell off the very night you arrived in the village. We had been taking turns watching over it. Chrystalina was in the chamber when it fell off. Once the weather cleared, we brought it here."

Jasper looked at the nut in astonishment then at Chrystalina who nodded. A thought quickly came to his mind as he looked at Saphina. "What if you deciphered the scrolls wrong and it is actually poisonous? I mean it could happen. You deciphered shade and darkness wrong." But, Jasper was not able to finish his sentence as Saphina jumped up from her chair and yelled at him.

"Oh for Zenrah's sake, Jasper," Saphina said as she pounded her fist on the table; no longer able to keep her temper in check. "The plant is not poisonous! If Lizbeth trusts us, why can't you?"

Jasper, still hovering over the nut, flew a little closer to the entrance of the cave, looking anxiously from the mallet to the nut then to Saphina.

"Saphina, sit down now!" Zusie said finally, having had enough of her daughter's rudeness towards Jasper. Saphina sat down in a huff, knocking Chrystalina's arm as she did. Chrystalina looked at her reproachfully as she rubbed her elbow. Saphina apologized to her under her breath.

"Jasper, I know you are scared and Saphina's rudeness is not helping any," Zusie looked crossly at her daughter and back at Jasper. "Why don't you take the night to think about it and come back tomorrow?" Jasper didn't say anything as he nodded his head in agreement.

As he was exiting the room, something sitting on the wall to right of the entrance caught his eye. Instead of flying out of the cave, he flew towards the last statue; the one he had yet to look at. Upon reaching it, he gasped in astonishment. He looked questionably at Zusie and then back again at the statue.

"Is that...is that what I think it is?" he said, hovering closer as he peered intently at the creature poised on the statue's outstretched hand.

"Yes, I think it is," Zusie nodded as she walked slowly towards him; not wanting to frighten him into a hasty departure.

Jasper's mouth dropped open. The statue was holding a creature that looked very much like him. "Who is she?" Jasper asked, not taking his eyes off the statue. Zusie looked at the words inscribed above the cubbyhole. "Jolise Neru – Keeper of the Hummingmoth Messengers." Shocked, Jasper gasped and stopped flapping his wings. He would have dropped to the floor if Zusie had not reached out her hand to catch him.

"It's alright, little one. Just relax. I have you," Zusie said kindly.

Jasper looked up at her. His little body shook as if he were a leaf caught in an updraft. A million thoughts flooded his mind but he was unable to articulate any of them aloud. Jasper was stunned into silence. Three questions immediately came to his mind: Was he a Hummingmoth messenger? Why could he not remember being one? And where were the elders depicted in the statues?

Seeing the perplexed expression on Jasper's face, Zusie said soothingly "It's okay dear. We know it is a lot to take in. Think about all you have learned and seen here today, and come back tomorrow with your answer."

Jasper looked at her and then over at the other two staring at him from the table. Chrystalina had a concerned look on her face while Saphina's expression was of great sadness, so much so that there were tears in her eyes. Jasper did not expect this response from thcm. Not knowing what to say, Jasper left the room. Zusie looked at her daughters and said quite confidently, "I am sure he will be back tomorrow with a favorable response."

"I hope you are right mother," Saphina said as she wiped the tears from her eyes and stood up. "I need to know why I have this connection to Jasper and why I can read his thoughts even when he is in the village and I am up here."

"But Saphina," Chrystalina said, "you have the gift of reading minds. I don't understand why this upsets you so."

"No...that's just it. You don't understand," Saphina interrupted angrily as she walked around the back of Chrystalina's chair. "You don't know what it's like. Yes, I can read his mind, but it's more. I can feel his every emotion and hear his every thought whether I try to or not. It's like he's...inside my head. The worst part is the dream! I don't think Jasper even realizes he is having it- But I do. It is as if I am in the dream with him. Every night I awake in the wee hours of the morning covered in sweat and trembling. I am unable to recall the dream, but I know it's the same one over and over again," she said miserably as she ran her hands through her hair.

"Saphina," Zusie said soothingly as she walked towards her daughter, arms outstretched to give her a hug.

"No, mother," Saphina said shaking her head aggressively. She put her hand up to stop her mother from coming forward. "A hug won't help this. I am not an underling anymore. This is not a scraped knee or banged elbow." Zusie stopped and looked apprehensively at her daughter. Why Zenrah gave Saphina the gift of mind reading and what purpose it had, she did not know. Most of the time, Saphina ignored it and was able to turn it off and on at will. Usually the intended participant had to be in the room facing Saphina for her to read his or her thoughts. However, Jasper was different and none of them knew why.

Consumed with anguish, Saphina continued. "I need to know why there is this connection with Jasper," she said, rubbing her temples as if to ease a pain. "I need to know before it drives me insane." She looked forlornly at them. Not knowing what to say, they looked helplessly back at her. Saphina sighed deeply. "I am going to rest. Please do not disturb me," she said. Without waiting for a reply, she walked slowly from the room.

Jasper made his way back down the long passageway, gaining speed as he flew towards the golden entrance. What he had learned disturbed him and he desperately needed to speak with Lizbeth about it. *Perhaps, he thought, Lizbeth will be able to make sense of it all*. He was sure Lizbeth would have the answers. She was the keeper of the woods after all and her knowledge surpassed all others. Well not Zusie and her daughters, but then Lizbeth saw things in a different way -- A matter of fact, no nonsense way. She would know the right thing to do and would help him through this. With renewed purpose, Jasper sped along, blissfully ignorant to the events that would soon transpire and his role in changing the course of time.

CHAPTER 8

Jasper's Flight

As Jasper reached the mouth of the cave, he noticed that dusk had fallen over the Greenwood Forest. He huffed in annoyance as he made his way quickly but carefully down the winding stairs.

"Now it is too late to fly to the Outer Bound Meadow," he mumbled with dismay. A thought popped into his head just as he reached the bottom stair. He looked back up through the trees to the mouth of the cave. "Perhaps that is what Zusie and her daughters meant to do; keep me in the cave until it was too dark for me to fly away," he said aloud. In his mind Jasper could see the scowl on Saphina's face and hear her abrupt humph.

Disappointed that he would not see the meadow that day Jasper started to make his way to Lizbeth's hut. It took him a minute to realize that something was out of place. The village was quiet; there was no one in sight. All he could hear as he flew through the village was the occasional slamming of a door. It must be time for the evening meal, he thought to himself. If Jasper only knew what took place while he was visiting with Zusie he would not have returned to the village. Instead, he would have flown to the Outer Bound Meadow straight away. Unaware of the plan for his demise that was being planned at that very moment Jasper eagerly flew on to Lizbeth's hut -- He had many questions to ask her and would not stop asking them until he was satisfied.

Upon reaching Lizbeth's hut Jasper noticed something else out of place. The shutters to the window were shut. He pushed on them but met resistance. Odd he thought -- Lizbeth normally kept them open until the sunset. He pounded as hard as he could on the thick wood and yelled out her name. Jasper was surprised when the shutters were thrown open and saw Aldwin not Lizbeth standing before him. Aldwin rudely hushed Jasper into silence and stepped aside so that he could enter. Jasper's stomach churned with anxiety as he flew through the opening and looked questioningly at Aldwin.

"Lizbeth has fallen ill and we have just now quieted her down," Aldwin said. Jasper could see that Aldwin was quite worried.

51

Jasper dropped to the table and looked passed Aldwin to Lizbeth's cot. She lay motionless under several layers of blankets. Her face, he noticed, was very pale except for bright red blotches on her cheeks. She looked like she had earlier that day when she was scolding him and tapping her foot impatiently. Only then, she looked formidable -- now she looked quite helpless.

"What is wrong with Lizbeth? Will she be alright?" Jasper asked in a low whisper.

"I am not sure what is wrong with her, Jasper," Aldwin replied in a whisper as well. "She came back to her hut for the midday meal just after you left to speak with Zusie. She ate and was about to go back to work when I saw her at the door. When I came to see if she was alright, she fainted and is now in a deep but restless sleep." Aldwin purposely left out the part that Lizbeth had been talking about life outside the valley and that Jasper was proof.

"Marla has been here helping out," Aldwin said. Jasper noticed Marla standing by the fireplace, ladling a light green liquid from a pot hanging over the fire into a bowl. Before Jasper could ask what the liquid was, Aldwin told him. "The potion is a mix of seven different herbs and water. When placed in warm water the herbs blend together and release an aroma that soothes the nerves. A cloth is dipped into the mixture and placed on the forehead." As Aldwin talked, Marla dipped a cloth in the mixture, wrung it out and placed it on Lizbeth's forehead. "The cloth needs to be kept warm so the changing of it happens quite frequently."

Jasper sniffed the air as the soothe ease potion reached the table. It was a pleasant smell and it instantly calmed his nerves. "Is there nothing else you can do for her?"

"No, Jasper. This is all I can do until I know what is wrong." Aldwin looked at Jasper thoughtfully, pulled out a chair and sat down wearily. Jasper slumped down and looked sadly at Lizbeth. He had so many questions to ask her but how was he going to get the answers when she lay unconscious in her bed? He immediately felt guilty for thinking of himself. Marla came to the table, sat down on the chair next to Aldwin and gently rubbed Jasper's arm.

"You look exhausted, Jasper. Why don't you have something to eat and then go off to bed?" Marla said. "I brought over fish and a mixed vegetable salad for the evening meal. Lizbeth had cooked a vegetable soup however we are not sure if that is what made her ill so we disposed of it." Jasper whimpered as emotion caught in his throat. Lizbeth had made him his favorite soup. Somehow, she knew he would need to be comforted.

"Aldwin and I have already eaten," Marla said. "I left a bowl for you." She pointed to a bowl on the counter by the washbasin. Jasper looked over at the washbasin and saw the empty pot that Lizbeth had used to cook the soup.

Emotion overwhelmed him. He shuddered heavily than placed his head in his hands and began to cry.

"Don't be upset Jasper. I am sure Lizbeth will be fine. She has just overworked herself," Marla said soothingly.

"I don't think that is the only reason why he is upset Marla," Aldwin said, looking sternly at Jasper. "What did Zusie say to you Jasper? What is it that they want from you?" Aldwin leaned towards Jasper and gently took his hands away from his face. Aldwin asked the question again, ignoring the tears that dripped from Jasper's eyes. "What is it that they want from you?" Jasper sniffled loudly and looked over at Lizbeth.

"I…I wanted to talk to Lizbeth about the meeting. I…I have so many questions and now…," Jasper stumbled over his words, sniffing loudly again as he tried to hold back the tears. "Now I don't know what to do." He shook his head, collapsed on the table, buried his head under his arms and wept uncontrollably.

"Hush now, Jasper. Calm yourself," Aldwin said. "I won't pressure you into telling us tonight. Have something to eat and then go off to bed. We will talk about this first thing in the morning."

Jasper stopped crying and sniffled loudly again than looked at them with a saddened expression. He flew up and hovered just inside the open window. He took one last pitiful look at Lizbeth then left without a word or backward glance at Aldwin and Marla.

"Jasper, wait! Don't you want something to eat?" Marla called after him.

"Leave him, Marla. I suspect he has much to think about."

"What do you think Zusie wants from him Aldwin?" Marla asked with concern.

"I don't know Marla, but I can't worry about it now. I have to find out what is wrong with Lizbeth. It is much graver than I let on in front of Jasper. If I can't find a cure, we may lose her."

"Do you really think her condition is that dire?" Marla asked as her eyes welled up with tears.

Aldwin did not answer her. Instead, he stood up and walked over to Lizbeth's bedside. He placed his hand on her wrist and felt her faint pulse. He took the cloth off her forehead, dipped it into the warm water and wrung it out before placing it back. He sat heavily on the chair and spoke without looking at her. His eyes were welling up with tears as well. Aldwin controlled his emotions before he spoke.

"Why don't you get some rest Marla?" Aldwin said. "You can sleep on the cot in the storage room and I will sit with Lizbeth for a while."

Marla got up from the table and walked over to stand behind Aldwin. Knowing better than to pester him for an answer, she placed her left hand on his shoulder, squeezing it gently. "All will be well, Aldwin. You will see. Lizbeth is a tough old bird. She will outlive most of us, I am sure." Squeezing his shoulder again, she added, "Wake me if there is any change."

Aldwin looked up at Marla, smiled grimly and patted her hand. "Go and rest now, Marla. I will wake you if there is a change."

As Marla walked out of the room, Aldwin picked up Lizbeth's hand and clasped it firmly between his. He whispered words of encouragement to her sleeping form. Neither Aldwin nor Marla noticed that someone was watching from the dark shadows and heard everything Aldwin had said.

Jasper's tiny wings beat faster with the racing of his heart. He could not believe what he just heard -- Lizbeth might die. Tears poured from his eyes, soaking the hairs on his chest. Not able to stand looking at Lizbeth anymore, he flew away from her hut. So caught up in his sorrow Jasper passed several huts before he noticed that a group of villagers stood just outside of Old Barty's hut. Worried that Old Barty had fallen ill as well he started to fly over but stopped as soon as he heard one of villagers yell, "There he is! Catch him before he disappears into the forest!"

The rest of the villagers turned in Jasper's direction. Jasper noticed that some of them were carrying long poles with nets at the end of them. Jasper recognized the poles; they were the kind that Septer and Rangous used to scoop up fish. Shocked at seeing him fluttering in midair, it took them a moment before they started to run towards him. They yelled at him angrily to stay where he was while they waved the nets above their heads. Their angry voices and waving nets scared Jasper into action. He turned around and sped into the forest. The mob of villagers chased after him.

Jasper was used to flying around in the forest. There was no wind so he was able to dash around the trees without fear that he would be blown into one. The leaves on the branches however whipped at his face and battered his wings. He kept going though, instinctively knowing that only bad things would happen if he stopped and confronted the mob.

Jasper took the chance to look behind him to see if he had lost them. He could not see anyone but he could hear them yelling as they crashed through the forest after him. He slowed down to duck under several fallen trees and heard a familiar voice yelling. "I've spotted him. There he goes! Come on follow me! He went in this direction," Monto yelled.

Jasper cleared the fallen trees and sped away again. He turned back to see if Monto had made it through. Jasper saw Monto slowing down to maneuver through them. His heart pounded with concern; Monto could be quick when he chose to be. Jasper turned back around and only had time to curl in his snout and raise his arms to shield his face before he slammed full-tilt into a massive maple tree. Bouncing off the tree, he fell in a heap to the forest floor. From nowhere a gust of wind blew and stirred up a pile of leaves lying near Jasper. The breeze blew the leaves until Jasper's body was completely covered. It stopped blowing just as quickly as it had started. The leaves effectively hid him from sight.

Monto was the first to arrive to the point where he thought he had seen Jasper last. He looked around curiously, as he tried to catch his breath. Shortly afterward, most of the villagers caught up to him.

"Did you catch him? Where is he?" some of them yelled angrily while trying to catch their breaths.

"No," Monto said with confusion. "I looked away for a minute while I maneuvered through those fallen trees back there and when I cleared them he was gone." The villagers imaginations took over and they looked frantically around. This was the farthest any of them had been. The thought that Jasper could just disappear had some of them cowering in fright.

"What do you mean he's gone?" Camcor huffed indignantly as he entered the clearing. He clutched his side and tried to catch his breath. Bertrum and Tad trotted in behind him wheezing from the exertion that it took to run through the forest. "He couldn't have just disappeared, you imbecile!" Camcor said as he looked angrily at Monto. He took a step forward and raised his arm as if to strike Monto down. Monto quickly flew behind someone standing in the shadows.

"Calm down Camcor," Bauthal said gruffly as he stepped into the clearing. Monto flew to the nearest branch and sat on it. Bauthal was as tall as Camcor, but in much better physical condition. He had followed the mob without them knowing it and made it to the clearing before they had. He too had ducked under a fallen tree and lost sight of Jasper.

The clearing was the last place he saw him. Bauthal was quite sure that they would not catch Jasper, as he was the fastest flyer that Bauthal had ever seen. However, on the off chance that they did, he would step in and protect Jasper with his life. As an elder of the forest creatures it was his duty to protect him.

"What are you doing here," Camcor said with distain. "I thought you were a friend of Jasper's."

"Oh is that what you are all doing this deep in the forest. Chasing after Jasper," Bauthal said incredulously. "Yes well good luck with that," he said than chuckled.

"You never answered his question, what are you doing in the forest?" Bertrum sneered.

"The forest is my home Bertrum. Why wouldn't I be here," Bauthal said sternly.

"Not even you live this far out Bauthal, what are you doing here?" Camcor said.

"Oh well if you must know I heard you all thrashing through the forest so I came to see what it was all about," Bauthal said.

"So then you saw Jasper," Camcor said.

"No," Bauthal said.

"No, you didn't see him or no, you wouldn't tell us if you did," Camcor said.

"You're not as thickheaded as you look Camcor," Bauthal said.

"Know your place Bauthal," Bertrum said with a sneer. Then Bertrum started to ramble on about Jasper and how strange he was and that he was a forbearer of grave tidings. Camcor and the rest of the villagers nodded in reply. Bauthal gave Bertrum time to have his say. He had something more important to do. He leaned against a tree at the edge of the clearing and pretended to listen to Bertrum.

He however, was actually listening for a sound that might reveal where Jasper was hiding. A slight rustling of leaves sounded at his feet and he looked down casually. There Jasper lay in a heap barely breathing. Keeping the surprise out of his expression Bauthal carefully pushed the leaves back over Jasper. He looked to be hurt quite badly and Bauthal feared for Jasper's life. He needed to find a way to get the Elfkins back to the village so that he could bring Aldwin back. Desperate times called for desperate measures.

"Yes, yes Bertrum we all know how you and your family feel about Jasper and forest creatures," Bauthal said interrupting Bertrum's rant. He could hear the collective gasp from the villagers. Camcor looked at Bauthal in surprise as he walked into the clearing.

"What Camcor? You don't think we can't hear you and your grandda mumbling under your breath as we walk by. You are always saying that manual labour is for forest creatures, not Elfkins." Camcor and Bertrum sputtered as they tried to think of a reply, but stopped abruptly. Bauthal came towards them baring his teeth and growling lowly. Camcor took a step back and Bertrum quickly moved behind him.

It was the first time a forest creature had ever shown hostility towards an Elfkin. The other villagers shuttered in fright. If a fight were to happen between Bauthal and Camcor there was no doubt that Bauthal would be the victor. Nervously they shuffled their feet. None of them had thought of the consequences. Now however seeing how angry Bauthal was they worried how the other forest creatures would feel once they heard what had happened. Slowly the villagers backed away from Bertrum and Camcor. Even Tad had the common sense to join them. Bauthal however passed by Camcor and his grandda with nothing more than a smug expression and walked casually to the other side of the clearing.

"I don't know about the rest of you," Bauthal said loudly as he turned, making sure all eyes were on him, "but I have had enough of this rubbish," he said pointing at Camcor and Bertrum. "I suggest for your own good that you return to your families." For good measure Bauthal snarled at them before he turned and started to make his way back through the forest. The Elfkins, without hesitation, started to follow Bauthal and ignored the steely gazes of Camcor and Bertrum as they walked by them. Finally, Camcor and Bertrum left the clearing as well with Monto tagging beside them. Bauthal could hear Monto asking Camcor if he really would have knocked him to the ground. He however did not hear Camcor's reply.

Once they reached the village, Bauthal waited to make sure that all the Elfkins made it back. He watched as they walked to their huts and went quietly inside. Bauthal stepped into the shadows of the trees and made his way to the back of Lizbeth's hut. He knew Aldwin would be there. Slowly he made his way down the side of the hut. He peeked around the corner, seeing no one he quickly went to the door and knocked lightly on it.

"Come in, Bauthal," Marla said with a sleepy reply as she opened the door.

"Is Aldwin a...," he began, but before he could finish asking if he was awake, Aldwin stood up from the chair next to Lizbeth's cot and hurriedly walked over to him.

"Bauthal, what happened?" Aldwin said in an urgent whisper. "I heard the commotion in the village square and saw a group of villagers chasing after Jasper. Then, I saw you running after the villagers. Did they catch Jasper? Is he hurt?"

"Come with me Aldwin, and I will explain on the way. It's best that we stay in the shadows until we are away from the village," Bauthal said. Aldwin and Bauthal left Marla to look after Lizbeth. They quickly and quietly made their way through the forest towards Jasper.

Bauthal explained on the way what had happened. Aldwin did not look surprised that Camcor had headed up the mob and that Bertrum and Tad had followed. They had been angrier than the other elders had when he had refused them entry into Lizbeth's hut. He was surprised, however, at how many villagers had joined in the chase. Camcor and Bertrum's sway over the villagers was much stronger than Aldwin expected. When unrest was left to fester, chaos would follow, Aldwin thought to himself. He had no idea however how to stop it from happening so he cursed instead.

"You can't blame them, Aldwin," Bauthal said breathlessly as they came to the edge of the clearing. "Camcor and Bertrum can be very intimidating. They have a way of swaying the opinions of Elfkins who are not as strong willed as you and Lizbeth are."

"That is no reasonable excuse to hunt another villager down who has done nothing but be helpful," Aldwin said tersely as he followed Bauthal to the place where Jasper lay hidden under the leaves at the base of the maple tree. He had come to care about Jasper just as Lizbeth had.

Aldwin bent down and cautiously cleared the leaves away. Jasper's motionless body lay curled up in a ball. Aldwin was afraid that they were too late. He gently ran his finger down Jasper's left arm and leg, along his spine and finally felt gingerly around his head. Jasper whimpered lightly when Aldwin touched a large bump just above his left eye. Aldwin and Bauthal sighed with relief.

"Easy now, little one," Aldwin said. Jasper opened his eyes, squinted from the pain, and moaned heavily. "It's okay, Jasper, you are with friends. Easy now, try not to move." Jasper looked up at him hopefully. "Bauthal brought me to you. Can you speak? Can you tell me what happened?"

"Th...th...they were chasing after me," Jasper whimpered sadly, confused as to why the villagers would do such a thing. "They were so angry, so I flew as fast as I could," he continued to say slowly as if he was picking his words carefully. "Until I ran head first into that...that tree." He looked up at the tree through slotted eyes. He had a disgusted look on his face, as if the tree purposely moved so that Jasper would fly into it. Aldwin and Bauthal exchanged a comforting smirk at Jasper's indignation towards the tree.

"Does it hurt anywhere else other than your head?" Aldwin asked. Jasper thought for a moment then gingerly moved his arms and legs then stretched his body out before replying.

"No. No, I don't think so." He winced when his hand touched the bump on his forehead. "Why were they chasing me, Aldwin?" Jasper asked. Aldwin looked away as anger boiled up to the surface. With great restraint, he turned back and sighed heavily. He did not know how to answer the question so he changed the subject.

"Do you think it would be alright if I picked you up?" he asked. Jasper nodded and winced again as Aldwin picked him up. "I am going to take you back to Lizbeth's," Aldwin said as Jasper lay helplessly in the palm of his hands. Jasper shook his head and started to protest but Aldwin reassured him that all would be fine. Jasper looked from Aldwin to Bauthal then nodded his head slowly in agreement. He knew they were his friends and that they would keep him safe.

Once they reached the outskirts of the village, Aldwin and Bauthal agreed that it would be wise to keep to the shadows. For good measure, Aldwin put Jasper into the pocket of his tunic just in case someone had seen them leave and waited for their return.

Finally safe inside Lizbeth's hut, they sighed heavily in relief. Bauthal quickly closed the shutters and latched them shut before Aldwin placed Jasper on top of the table. Marla had been pacing back and forth in front of the fireplace waiting for them. Seeing that the three of them were well, she readied a pot of tea.

"Bauthal, can you grab an extra lantern from the storage room and bring it here? Aldwin asked. "I want to take a closer look at Jasper." After a quick examination, Aldwin found nothing else wrong with him. Other than the bump on his head and a bit of dirt, Jasper was right as rain.

Jasper sat upright and leaned against a teacup that Marla has placed on the table along with a plate of bread and a bowl of plump winterberries. The Elfkins called them winterberries because they were the first berries of the spring season and were ready to pick even though the air was still quite cool at night. She had picked them earlier while she was out with the underlings. The berries grew on small bushes and were easy for the underlings to reach.

The warmth from the teacup permeated through Jasper's sore body and he shivered out the last chill. The others pulled out chairs and sat around the table, keenly watching Jasper as he pulled a rather large chunk of bread from the slice that Marla had placed beside him. He devoured it quickly and licked the crumbs off his lips.

"You are lucky, little one. It could have been much worse," Aldwin said as Jasper pulled off another chunk of bread and popped the whole thing in his mouth. Jasper nodded in agreement. Aldwin looked at him amusedly and wondered how Jasper could eat so ravenously after his ordeal? Then he remembered that Jasper left without eating supper. That had been several hours ago and it was only right that the little guy would be hungry.

While Jasper ate, the others sat in silence sipping their tea and nibbled the slices of bread. Jasper suddenly looked up at Aldwin and said in astonishment, "Oh, oh my I remember!" then he smiled broadly.

"You remember what, Jasper?" Marla and Bauthal asked in unison. They looked at each other and smiled. Jasper stared at a spot on the wall beside Lizbeth's cot trying to gather his thoughts, not sure if what he was thinking was true.

"I remember where I came from," he said quietly. "At least...I think I do." His companions stared at him in amazement.

"It must have been the knock on the head that jarred his memory back," Aldwin said, looking at the others. They in turn nodded in agreement.

Jasper looked up at Aldwin and took a bite of one of the red berries. He thought carefully over what Aldwin said about the bump jarring his memory. Berry juice dripped down his chin and onto his fuzzy belly. Taking no notice, he continued to eat his berry then stopped and quite plainly said, "No."

Lizbeth stirred on her cot and Aldwin made to get up but Marla stayed him with her hand and went to tend to her. Aldwin watched Jasper as he ate the rest of his berry and smiled slightly as more juice dripped down onto his belly. "What do you mean 'no,' Jasper?"

Jasper did not answer him right away. Instead, he looked at a point on the wall again. He stared intensely at it as his mind raced over the dream he had. He reached for another berry but, before he could get one, Bauthal, now impatient with waiting, moved the bowl away. Jasper looked up and before he had a chance to ask why, Bauthal spoke sternly. "Jasper, if not from bumping your head then how do you remember?"

"From my dream," Jasper said simply, and then added, "at least...I think it was a dream." Aldwin and Bauthal looked at him questioningly as Marla sat back down at the table. Jasper looked at the three of them as if it made perfect sense.

"What dream, Jasper?" Aldwin spoke their collective thought. "Do you mean when you were unconscious on the forest floor? And what do you mean you think it was a dream?"

While eating the last slice of his bread, several berries and two cups of tea, Jasper recited his dream in full detail. Stunned into silence, the others listened attentively to every single word that Jasper spoke.

CHAPTER 9

Jasper's Dream

"I am to go back there in the morning," Jasper said sleepily in response to Aldwin's suggestion that they see Zusie right away. Jasper yawned loudly as he stretched out his arms and legs. With his tummy now full, he was quite tired. Every muscle in his little body screamed for him to rest. The bump on his head was still throbbing and he touched it absentmindedly as he yawned again. He propped himself against his teacup and started to close his eyes.

"No," Aldwin said sternly. "I mean now." Jasper, startled by the angry tone in Aldwin's voice, flinched.

"It was just a dream, Aldwin," Jasper said sleepily. He could barely keep his eyes open.

"I don't think it was, Jasper," Aldwin said.

"But Aldwin," Jasper whined. "It's not morning yet and I am so tired. Can't it wait?" He stretched out his arms and yawned loudly, curling his body into a ball before closing his eyes.

"Jasper," Aldwin whispered harshly, "don't you understand how important this information is?" Jasper looked at Aldwin through half-closed eyes and shook his head lazily from side to side. Aldwin stood-- Backing away from the table, he shook his head. "For all our lives," Aldwin continued, "and our ancestors' lives, we thought we were the only ones. We have to tell Zusie right away. She will want to hear this information now. Not in the morning." He looked around at the others. Bauthal was nodding in agreement, but Marla sat with her head bowed, staring fixedly at her clenched hands.

"Marla?" Aldwin said as he walked quickly back to the table. When she didn't answer immediately, he laid his right hand over hers and squeezed lightly. Still she did not respond. He leaned down and placed his left hand under her chin, and raised it up so that he could see into her eyes. Her eyes normally dark brown and lively, were glazed with unshed tears; her brows knitted together, and her lips trembled. "Marla," he said calmly, but with an authority borne of having to take control in difficult situations. "Are you alright?" he asked each word clearly.

She looked at him. Her mouth opened but the words she wanted to speak would not come out. Instead, she blinked her eyes a couple of times and shook her head quickly back and forth as if to clear it of the thoughts she was having. Now composed but not sure she could speak, she nodded. Aldwin let go of her hands.

"Are you sure Marla? I need you to watch over Lizbeth while Bauthal and I take Jasper to see Zusie." Jasper moaned and squirmed by his teacup, but Aldwin paid him no mind. Marla breathed in deeply and slowly exhaled before replying.

"Yes, yes of course." She said than sat up straight. She wiped the tears from her eyes with the backs of her hand. "It's just been a bit of a shock, hasn't it?" She chuckled nervously as she looked at each of the others in turn. "I mean to think all this time, just beyond…." She shook her head quickly again and chuckled as she looked up at Aldwin. Seeing the concerned look on his face, she stood up, scraping the legs of the chair against the stone floor. "Aldwin, don't worry. Please do what you have to do. I will take care of Lizbeth while you are gone," she said reassuringly -- Aldwin, seeing that she was in control of her emotions, nodded.

He had chosen Marla as his apprentice, for several reasons – Controlling her emotions when faced with adversity was one of them. Aldwin remembered the day he chose her. The elders frowned upon his choice because the village healer had always been male. However out of the seven who came forward Marla, the only female, was the one who knew each of the plants set before her and what healing properties, if any, they had. As time went by Marla demonstrated that she was the right choice. She had a rare gift of making the villagers, young and old alike, feel at ease while administering the medicine he prescribed. He had a feeling that her knowledgeable, levelheaded demeanor would come in handy in the very near future.

Seeing that Marla was all right, Bauthal stood and walked to the door. He opened it slowly and peeked outside to see if anyone was wandering around.

"It looks to be clear," he said over his shoulder. "Nevertheless, I think we should keep to the woods just in case Camcor and his followers are still awake and see us walking through the village. Aldwin nodded and picked up Jasper who was pouting and looked to be near crying again. Aldwin ignored him.

Tough times wrought tough measures and Aldwin had a feeling that very soon everyone would have to find the means to cope with the changes that were about to take place; and those who didn't, well, they would deal with that when they came to it.

"Send Rangous to fetch us if Lizbeth's condition changes," Aldwin said to Marla as he slipped out the door after Bauthal.

It was quiet and still in the wee hours of the morning. Sunrise was hours away. The sky overhead was clear but pitch-black. If it were not for the moon's rays that filtered through the trees, they would not be able to see two feet in front of them. They walked quickly behind Lizbeth's hut, picking each of their steps cautiously, and disappeared into the dark shadows of the trees. Going through the village to the stone steps would have been quicker, but not necessarily wiser. As they made their way through the forest, they were unaware that someone did see them leave and was following them.

On Camcor's orders, Monto secretly waited and watched to see if Jasper returned to the village. He sat in the little house that Lizbeth had asked the carpenters to make for Jasper. Earlier that day they had attached it to the tree beside Lizbeth's hut. Monto grinned; Jasper hadn't even had a chance to use it. Sitting, as he was high up in the tree Monto had seen Aldwin and Bauthal leave the hut. He was pleased that they had come back without Jasper (or so he thought). He smirked to himself, thrilled that Jasper had not returned to the village. Until Jasper, he had been the fastest flyer who everyone relied on to collect sapple.

In reality, the villagers tolerated Monto as they did Camcor and his grandda. They all had the same disposition and often picked on those smaller than themselves. In Monto's case, he often pestered the red dapple spider ants to the point that they complained to the elders. It had stopped for a time, but then it started again. Only this time, Monto would fly past the ants as they carried food to their nest and knocked it off their backs. As they yelled up at him, he would apologize halfheartedly, saying that he did not see them.

Pleased that Jasper had not returned, he lay on the soft bed that Lizbeth had made, opting not to use the warm cover. His last thoughts just before falling asleep, was that he would make this little home his own and too bad for Lizbeth if she did not like it. He awoke when he heard the door of Lizbeth's hut opening. Curious to see what was going on, he poked his head out from behind the flap that was used as a door. He watched curiously, as Bauthal stuck his head out and scanned one end of the village to the other. Monto could not hear what Bauthal said but looked on the scene with great displeasure as Aldwin, who was carrying Jasper, joined Bauthal at the door.

He watched as the three of them quickly made their way around to the back of Lizbeth's hut. Furiously Monto kicked the flap as hard as his spindly little legs would allow. To his surprise, a gust of wind blew the flap back at him and knocked him flat to the floor. Angrier now, he decided before reporting to Camcor that he would see what they were up to.

Flying unnoticed high above their heads, he followed them as they walked briskly and silently through the forest until they reached the stone steps. He did not need to fly up the steps after them. He knew who they were going to see -- Zusie. Instead, he made his way to Camcor's hut to report that Jasper was back.

Flying low through the village, Monto, caught up in his thoughts, did not see the fishing net until it was too late. Someone had caught him in one of the nets the mob of villagers had tried to catch Jasper in earlier. Before he had a chance to fly out, someone threw a thick blanket over the net. He started to squirm and yell for his captor to let him go. However, the blanket effectively muffled his voice and foiled any attempt he might make to get free.

Just a few moments passed before he heard the opening of a door. Then someone rudely dropped him into something very hard and dark. He was slightly relieved, as not enough time had passed for him to be out of the village. Once his eyes adjusted to the dark, he could see that he was in a solid wooden box. He immediately panicked, afraid that he would run out of air. He looked up as light from a lantern peeked through holes in the top of the box. The holes were big enough to let air in and, he hoped food, but not big enough for him to fly out of. He started to yell again but no one came to his aid. He yelled and yelled until his voice went hoarse. Finally exhausted, he curled up into a ball. Just before he fell asleep, Monto wondered who had captured him, why they had and if they would release him.

Meanwhile, Aldwin, Bauthal and Jasper had reached the ledge at the top of the stairs. The golden archway shone warmly before them even though the sun was not reflecting off it. Jasper looked at it strangely, wondering how that could be. Bauthal, who had never seen the archway this close before, was at first stunned by the sheer mass of it. Transfixed he looked at its beauty in awe. Aldwin nudged him with his elbow but Bauthal did not move.

"Bauthal," Aldwin said while he nudged him again. Bauthal forced himself to look at him and smiled oddly. He could feel the warmth of the archway's glow on the side of his face. "Don't you think it's time we go inside?" Aldwin said, smirking at him. He knew that he must have had the same dumbfounded expression on his face the first time he had seen the golden archway.

"Yes, yes of course," Bauthal said. He looked from Aldwin to Jasper, who flew up nervously from Aldwin's hand and hovered beside his shoulder.

Aldwin looked sideways at him. "All will be fine, Jasper. Don't worry." *Easy for you to say*, Jasper thought, *Saphina probably likes you.* The three of them traveled down the long passageway -- Bauthal first, with Aldwin following and Jasper flying behind them. To ease his nerves, Jasper asked Aldwin why the crystals in the entrance shone brightly without the sun reflecting on them. He explained that the crystals only shone when a friend stood before them. If a foe stood before them and tried to walk under the archway, an invisible barrier would block their way and they would not have access to the Crystal Cave. Jasper wondered how they knew that, but then realized that they must have read it in one of the scrolls.

Bauthal nodded, understanding what Aldwin said, but Jasper looked puzzled -- How could crystals tell whether a person was friend or foe? Instead of asking, he kept his question for another time. The three of them continued to walk down the passageway, each caught up in their own thoughts. Jasper wondered why he agreed to come back, not that he had had much say in it. He shuddered to think of the reception that they would receive from Saphina. Jasper was sure that they would get an earful for waking her at this early hour.

Bauthal's thoughts were of complete and utter wonderment as he looked around him. Never had he seen anything so amazing, and he wished he had made his way to the cave long before now.

Aldwin thought curiously about Jasper's dream and wondered how much truth was in it. The clarity of his recollection did seem to stem more from actuality than fantasy. Moreover, in the pit of his stomach, he knew it to be true.

Finally, they came to the end of the passageway and stopped abruptly. Jasper stopped because Aldwin had. He bumped into the back of Aldwin's head. Luckily, his snout was curled or else he would have stabbed Aldwin with it. Aldwin stopped because Bauthal had. Like Jasper, Aldwin bumped into Bauthal. Bauthal stopped and gazed at the sight before him. His first look upon the crystal cave filled him with a quiet peace and his fur vibrated with a tingling sensation that spread up and down his spine.

Aldwin grunted and nudged Bauthal to the left side of him. He reached for a rope attached to a hollowed out crystal bell that hung on the right side of the entranceway and gently pulled on it. Beside the rope was a large horn that looked like it had come from a three-toed hog. They were shorthaired creatures the size of Bauthal and had two horns that stuck out at odd angles from their snouts. Jasper wondered if the horn was what Saphina had used to call him to the cave.

The bell's ring penetrated the air and echoed down the long hallways. Bauthal, too enthralled with the cave to wait for someone to invite them in, stepped in front of Aldwin and started to look at the statues. They did not have to wait long however, for just a couple of moments passed before they heard the shuffling of feet coming down a hallway.

Jasper shivered and climbed into one of the pockets in Aldwin's tunic. The shuffling of feet was coming from the same hallway that Saphina used to come in and out of the cave.

"Calm yourself, Jasper. All will be well," Aldwin said. He looked curiously down at Jasper in his pocket, wondering why he was shivering from fright. Jasper was thinking that Aldwin said that a lot and always just before something awful happened. Therefore, his words did not ease Jasper's nerves as he looked towards the passageway. Saphina entered the room with a miserable scowl on her face and Jasper quickly ducked back down into Aldwin's pocket.

Saphina was dressed in a plain white night gown, but looked like she had not slept well. Her complexion was quite pale; dark bags had formed under her eyes and her hair was tousled as if she had been roughly running her hands through it. She looked haggard. Upon seeing that it was Aldwin who rang the bell, her face immediately brightened.

"Aldwin," she said cheerily as she walked quickly to him. She opened her arms, gave him a hug, and kissed him tenderly on each cheek.

"Are you alright?" Aldwin asked as he looked into her eyes with worry.

"Yes, yes," she said, waving her hand as if to swat away a band of pesty gnats. "I had a fretful dream earlier, that's all, and I've been tossing and turning trying to get back to sleep; nothing to worry about." The dream had been about Jasper and his flight through the forest. She did not realize it had actually happened. "Really," she said as Aldwin's expression showed that he did not quite believe her.

Changing the subject, she pouted and admonished him playfully, "It has been too long since your last visit my friend. Please, come in and sit. We will have tea and catch up on things." Not waiting for Aldwin's reply, Saphina started to walk towards the door leading to the kitchen.

Jasper wondered at Saphina's reaction to Aldwin coming to the Crystal Cave at such a late hour. She acted as if visits in the middle of the night by him were commonplace. Encouraged by her cheerful demeanor, he poked his head out from the pocket.

"Saphina, wait." Aldwin reached out and grabbed her hand to stay her. Hearing the concern in his voice, she stopped.

"What is it, Aldwin?" she said and turned back to him. Jasper watched as her expression instantly changed from pleasant to disdainful as she saw him in Aldwin's pocket. Jasper poked his head back into the pocket so that only the top of his head and eyes showed.

"Aldwin," Bauthal said excitedly from across the room, "These are amazing!" Saphina, shocked to hear another voice turned abruptly in Bauthal's direction. Bauthal at the same time turned to see if Aldwin had heard him and saw Saphina looking strangely at him. He too had not realized that she was in the room.

"Hello," he said politely and, when she did not immediately respond in kind, he turned back to the statue. "These are wonderful," he said, pointing at the statue in front of him. "Is that an Elfkin with this one? It looks like an Elfkin," he said then looked at it more closely. "Maybe not," he said to no one in particular.

Saphina looked back at Aldwin with a puzzled expression. "Aldwin, why did you bring a badger…?" She started to say then stopped.

"Bauthal," Bauthal interrupted her and walked on to the next statue.

"Sorry," Saphina said respectfully "Bauthal and…him with you," she said, nodding at Jasper. "Is there a problem in the village?"

"Yes, but that is not the only reason we have come here tonight. There is a matter of great concern that we need to speak with the three of you about," Aldwin said pointedly.

Seeing his troubled expression Saphina did not question his request and quickly left the room in search of her mother and sister. Several moments passed before they heard quick footsteps coming towards them. Zusie and Saphina stepped quickly into the room and Jasper instantly noticed the differences between the two. While Saphina had looked haggard, Zusie looked quite the opposite. She looked calm and collected even after being rudely awaken from her slumber.

Her long hair was neatly braided into a thick plait that hung over her right shoulder. Her dressing gown of soft pale blue material flowed down the length of her body to the floor. Where Saphina only had eyes for Aldwin, Zusie took everything in the instant she entered the room. She noticed that Jasper, who had left Aldwin's pocket and was now flying back and forth behind him, looked as agitated as he had earlier that day. She also noticed he had attained a rather large bump over his left eye since she last saw him. She wondered if that was the reason for the visit. She looked at Aldwin and sensed that he, although he did not look it outwardly, was just as agitated as Jasper was.

When she looked at Bauthal, she smiled. He had an edge of giddiness about him that he barely kept in check as he looked at the statue next to the kitchen door. Her smile deepened when she heard his sigh. Usually when villagers came to visit for the first time, they were somewhat afraid of the cave, but not Bauthal; he was completely enthralled with it. This pleased Zusie.

"Please, come and sit," she said, looking at each of the guests in turn. Bauthal turned when he heard her voice. He looked at her curiously for a moment then smiled – his fur began to vibrate again.

"Hello," he said when he was able to gather himself. "Do you mind if I continue to look around the room? These statues are really quite interesting."

"No, of course not, please continue," Zusie said with a smile than she looked at her daughter.

"Saphina, please fetch your sister for us. I believe she is in the observatory. Then stop in the kitchen on the way back and bring some tea with you." Just as she finished the last word, Chrystalina came through the kitchen door walking backwards. She had a cup of tea in one hand, a large slice of bread in the other, and a bunch of berries, still on the vine, hung from her mouth. Startled at seeing a badger in the room, she cried out and the berries fell from her mouth.

The berries plopped noisily into her hot cup of tea, spilling the tea over the edge of the cup. The tea burnt her hand before it splashed to the floor, pooling around her feet. She let go of the cup as the pain from the hot tea registered in her brain. The cup would have fallen to the floor as well, if Bauthal had not acted as quickly as he did and caught it just as her hand let go of it. He placed the berry-filled cup on the table. Aldwin rushed over to her side.

"Oh my Chrissie, are you alright?" he asked, taking her burnt hand in his. Aldwin was the only one who called her Chrissie. He clicked his tongue loudly at her clumsiness and said crossly, "Here, let me put some salve on that before it blisters." He released her hand so that he could dig into his medicine bag for a salve that would stop the burn from blistering. He spread a generous helping on the burn and immediately wrapped it with a long piece of white cloth. Her hand instantly felt better as the stinging sensation subsided.

"Feels better already, thank you Aldwin," Chrystalina said as she flexed her bandaged hand.

"Good, good," Aldwin said, as he put the salve away. Chrystalina looked around at the others. Bauthal stood by the table looking intently at the carvings beside the teacup. Saphina, unconcerned by her sister's injury, pulled out one of the chairs on the other side of the table and sat down. Chrystalina was prone to accidents and Saphina, the tougher of the two, quite often took care of her.

Jasper, Chrystalina noticed, hovered in midair staring cautiously at Saphina. If he only knew that she was actually a sweetheart, he would not be so wary of her. She did not blame him, though; Saphina had been quite harsh with him earlier that day. Chrystalina then looked at her mother and smiled at her awkwardly. Zusie smiled reassuringly at her – she too was use to her daughter's little accidents.

"I thought you were in the observatory?" Zusie said.

"I was, but I got hungry," Chrystalina said sheepishly. "I wasn't expecting to see anyone, let alone company this late at night, or should I say, this early in the morning. By the way, what is Aldwin doing here? It's a bit late," she shook her head. "Early, even for him," she finished saying.

Aldwin looked at Bauthal when Chrystalina asked the question. He looked over at Jasper who began to wring his hands together. The beating of his wings became faster and the humming carried throughout the room as it had earlier that day.

"Jasper had a dream," Aldwin said to everyone, but looked at Zusie.

"You came here in the middle of the night because Jasper had a dream?" Saphina said crossly as she looked at Jasper.

"Saphina don't start," Zusie said sternly. "Aldwin would not have come here if he didn't think that it was important." Saphina slumped down in her chair, embarrassed that her mother would admonish her in front of their guests. She looked away, staring at the entrance to the cave, uninterested in Jasper's story.

"Please, everyone, let's sit so that we can hear about Jasper's dream in comfort." Zusie motioned for everyone to take a chair as she pulled out one for herself next to Saphina. Once everyone else was seated, Jasper sat on the table as far away from Saphina as he could without looking like he was trying to avoid her. Seeing that they were comfortable, Zusie looked kindly at Jasper and said, "Go on, little one. You are among friends. Please tell us your dream."

"Well," Jasper said nervously, "while I lay unconscious on the forest floor," he stopped abruptly as he heard the sharp intake of breath coming from Zusie and Chrystalina. Saphina sat up, leaned forward, and rested her arms on the table. She was now very interested in Jasper's story.

Aldwin held up his hand to stop them from asking any questions. "Please," he said calmly, "hold your questions until Jasper is done. He has had quite the eventful day and has yet to sleep." As if on cue, Jasper yawned loudly.

"Go on then, Jasper," Zusie said, wondering if the bump over his left eye had to do with him lying unconscious on the forest floor.

"Well, like I said," Jasper looked at Zusie, "I had a dream or at least I think it was a dream." He looked puzzled and scratched his head as if he was not quite sure. "A lady came to me while I lay on the forest floor. She told me that I would be fine and that help was on its way. She floated in the air as if she had wings, only I don't think she had any." He shook his head in confusion then went on with his tale. "I felt all warm inside as she hovered above me. She went on to say that they needed me back home to hear about my mission and news from the land beyond the mountains."

Jasper stopped for a moment to take a deep breath. The retelling of the dream to Zusie and her daughters seemed more real to him now rather than something he had imagined. The three of them looked at Jasper with concern, but Chrystalina spoke first.

"Jasper, do you mean the mountains to the south? Are you to bring information from the south?" Jasper thought for a moment.

"No," he said shaking his head, trying to remember. He scrunched up his eyes, "I think she meant the lands to the north, past Mount Aspentonia. Yes, yes," he said with confidence. "She meant the land to the north. I am sure of it."

"Jasper, do you mean to say that your home is north of us?" Zusie asked as she sat forward.

"No," Jasper corrected her. "I was sent on a mission to the distant lands in the north." They could see him struggling to remember something more but nothing else came to him and he slumped down exhausted. Aldwin and Zusie looked at him uneasily.

"Zusie, Jasper has had a dreadful day to say the least. I am not sure how much longer he can keep going. Why don't we let him rest for a while?" Aldwin suggested. Zusie nodded in agreement and stood, indicating that the conversation was over.

"Saphina, please grab a blanket and bring it for Jasper to sleep on. Chrystalina, take Bauthal into one of the antechambers so he can rest. I would like to speak with Aldwin alone." Saphina made a motion to speak but seeing the stern look on her mother's face, she left the room in a huff for the blanket. Chrystalina thanked Aldwin again for bandaging her hand before she showed Bauthal to an antechamber where he could rest.

Saphina came back into the room and spread a blanket at the end of the table. She doubled it so that it would be softer for Jasper to sleep on. Aldwin noticed her kindness as she folded the blanket. Saphina turned back when she reached the entrance to the hallway that led to her sleeping chamber. She again opened her mouth to speak, but seeing the expression on Zusie's face, she instead bade them goodnight.

Aldwin picked up Jasper and placed him on the blanket. Jasper curled up into a ball and promptly fell asleep. After the room was once again quiet, Zusie looked at Aldwin with concern.

"There is something else troubling you, isn't there Aldwin," Zusie asked.

Aldwin would have looked at her in surprise if he had not known Zusie so well. However, he did know her and the close relationship she had with Lizbeth. Lizbeth had helped Zusie with the birth of her daughters and, for several weeks afterwards, she visited them daily. No one had questioned Lizbeth about where she went every day. As keeper of the woods she spent most of her time in the forest, and on occasion was gone for several days at a time. When Zusie and Lizbeth came to terms with the fact that their mates would not be returning, they comforted each other. Those days were especially hard on Lizbeth. Zusie at least had the girls, but Lizbeth had no one. However, the girls gave new purpose to Lizbeth's life and over the years, she became more like a second mother to them than just a friend. Aldwin knew Saphina and Chrystalina would be greatly upset to hear that Lizbeth was not well.

Aldwin tried to gage what Zusie's reaction would be upon hearing the news that her friend had fallen gravely ill. He thought, as he looked into the depths of her eyes and saw the sadness there that somehow she already knew.

"Lizbeth has fallen ill. I'm not sure…how much longer…she has to live," Aldwin said. He watched as Zusie stumbled backwards and slumped down in her chair. She closed her eyes, laid her head against the back of the chair, and breathed in deeply several times before she looked at Aldwin.

"I had a feeling," she said slowly, "that it had something to do with her." She looked sadly at Aldwin. "What happened?" she asked.

"I don't know," Aldwin said, shaking his head. "She fainted just after the noonday break and has not awakened. I looked her over thoroughly. The only thing I could find was a small hard lump under the skin on her forearm. It was warm to the touch but there was no bruising around it. Other than that, she looks to be in perfect health."

"A lump on her arm," Zusie repeated. "Could that be what has made her ill?'

"I don't know. She never complained to me about it. I asked Marla about it but she never mentioned it to her either."

Zusie thought over the last words that Aldwin spoke. Her eyebrows knitted together and she bit her bottom lip as she thought deeply. She sat forward in her chair and looked from Aldwin to Jasper and back again to Aldwin.

"Is the lump on her left arm just about here?" she said, pointing to a spot on her own arm between her shoulder and elbow.

"Why yes," Aldwin said in surprise. "Do you know something about it?" Zusie stood up and faced him, convinced that she knew what had happened to Lizbeth.

"Just after the last winter storm, Lizbeth came to tell us that Jasper was in the village. She told me that he had bumped into her." Aldwin looked at her as a question formed in his mind, but before he could ask it, Zusie answered. "No, she never told me that it was hurting." Aldwin asked his next question instead.

"Is there anything in the scrolls about the sting of a…moth?" He looked perplexed, as he was not sure what else to call Jasper.

"Hummingmoth messenger," Zusie replied. "No. However, I have not read all of them. Chrystalina is the one to ask. Out of the three of us she is the one who has taken a keen interest in deciphering the scrolls." Aldwin looked at her hopefully. "I don't want you to get your hopes up, Aldwin," Zusie said, seeing the change in his expression. "Is her condition stable?"

"Yes," he said, nodding his head. "It's more like she is in a deep sleep. Periodically she becomes fretful, tosses and turns. We have been applying a soothe ease compress on her forehead. It takes but seconds for her to settle back down." Zusie looked at him curiously but before she could ask her question, Aldwin answered in return. "Marla is taking care of her while we are here with you. She will send Rangous if Lizbeth's condition changes."

"Ah," Zusie said, nodding her head in approval. "I have heard good things about Marla from Lizbeth. She is very fond of her."

"Yes," Aldwin nodded. "I think the feeling is mutual. We need not worry about Lizbeth while Marla is looking after her. She is becoming a very accomplished healer herself. I fear she may even surpass me in the next few years." Aldwin chuckled lightly as he looked at Zusie. "What will I do with myself when the villagers no longer need me as their healer?" Not waiting for Zusie to reply, he answered his own question. "I suppose I could become a fishermen like Rangous and Septer," he chuckled again, which had Zusie smiling, as she could not see Aldwin as anything other than a healer.

A vision popped into her mind of him standing knee-deep in the water with a net in one hand and a fishing pole in the other, miserably failing at catching fish. Zusie chuckled lightly and the seriousness of the moment seemed to ease slightly with their shared laughter.

Aldwin was the first to get back to the other reason he was there. He told Zusie about what had happened to Jasper after he left the cave. She shook her head in disgust.

"Camcor is a bully like his grandda Bertrum. Their family has held into the old beliefs that we have tried so hard to dispel. Lizbeth has told me things." Zusie said wearily. "And she has feared for Jasper's safety from the moment he entered the village."

Aldwin did not know that and sighed heavily. "She carries more burdens then she ought to." Aldwin said, shaking his head. "I need to wake Bauthal and get back to the village. Marla will need to be relieved so that she too might rest. It has been a long and trying day for all of us."

"I think it best," Zusie said looking over at Jasper, "that he stays here for his own safety." Aldwin nodded in agreement. "As soon as Chrystalina rises, I will ask her to look through the scrolls for the answer to your question about the sting of the hummingmoth messenger."

"Good, good. Please send for me if you should learn anything new." Aldwin walked over to Jasper and looked at him. The bump on his head had turned a deep purple and he looked to be resting peacefully. Aldwin was sure that when Jasper woke he would be in great pain. Reaching into his medicine bag, he walked back to Zusie and placed a few leaves onto her open palm. "Crush these and put them in a black tea. Let it steep for a few minutes and make sure that he drinks all of it. I am sure when he wakes he will be very sore."

Zusie nodded and placed the leaves on the table. They said their customary goodbye by hugging each other and kissing each other's cheeks. It had always been this way with Zusie and her daughters. They were a loving, kindhearted people, even Saphina with her rough exterior and bossy ways. They had welcomed many of the villagers into their home and treated them with kindness. They were patient with their teachings of the scrolls and did not mind answering questions that they had answered several times before. Contrary to the belief of some like Camcor and Bertrum, Zusie and her daughters bore no ill feelings towards the Elfkins. They treated them with great respect and as equals.

Aldwin smiled warmly at Zusie and she wondered where his thoughts had taken him. Before he left the room to wake Bauthal, he hugged Zusie warmly once again, telling her to get some sleep as he gently patted her back. Zusie waited until he came back into the room with Bauthal and bade them both goodbye. She did not go back to her sleeping chamber as Aldwin suggested however. The morning was soon to break and she was well past sleep. She would need the energy that good food and warm tea provided her in order to get through what was going to be a trying day for them all.

She picked up the leaves that Aldwin left and, as she went to push open the door to the kitchen, she heard a sigh coming from Jasper. She quickly walked over to him to see if he was awake, but he was sleeping peacefully. She smiled down at him. He must have been dreaming of someone or something that made him very happy, because he had a big grin on his face. Zusie took a corner of the blanket and covered him with it. As she walked back to the kitchen, she wondered if Jasper was dreaming of the woman in white and his home.

CHAPTER 10

The Trance

"Little one, it is time to wake." A soft and gentle voice stirred Jasper out of his sleep. As he gingerly opened his eyes, he saw a grayish fog before him with figures moving around in it. The fog gradually cleared and a lovely vision stood before him, dressed in a long flowing gown of soft white material. Her hair, silvery white, hung long over her shoulders. Her eyes, bright blue, twinkled as she looked at him. She smiled at him warmly and said, "Jasper, it's time to come home." She stepped to the side so that he could see past her.

Jasper looked up first. Above him was a clear blue, endless sky dotted with white fluffy clouds that moved slowly with the breeze. He breathed in deeply and smelled the sweet air warmed by the summer sun. He exhaled slowly and sighed again. He looked past the vision and smiled. Behind her was a very large tree. It was the tallest tree he had ever seen. It was so tall it looked like the upper branches were touching the clouds.

The tree had an abundance of thin leafy, pale green, vine-like limbs that hung down from thick branches. They hung low to the ground and swayed with the cool breeze. Jasper could almost hear the swishing sound they made as they brushed along the grass. He knew the tree: it was the Whipple Wash Tree, home to the Whipple Wash fairies and the seven elders of the Whipple Wash Valley. The tree stood majestically upon a small round-top hill. Jasper called out with glee as he watched the limbs of the tree part. Stepping out from behind the limbs were the fairies. All five of them turned as they heard his shouts and waved back at him. Zabethile, the youngest of the fairies and his best friend, cried out, 'You promised you would come back. Do you remember? You promised me you would come home. Come home, Jasper. Come home.' The other fairies comforted their sister as they walked down the hill and disappeared from sight. Jasper knew they were on their way to Elsbrier; the village that spread south of the hill.

Jasper blinked his eyes. Like magic, he was now on the outskirts of the village. Elsbrier was alive with movement and noise as the villagers happily went about their daily chores. A large river called the

Grandiflora wound through the village. Jasper could see the arched, covered stone bridges that were located every hundred paces or so down the length of the river. The bridges connected both sides of the marketplace.

Several stone huts lined the marketplace on either side of the river. Each of them had a large canopy sticking out towards the front. Under the canopies were large wooden tables laden with all manner of food, handmade clothing, woodcarvings, paintings, artwork and everything else imaginable. Jasper knew the stone buildings had several wooden shelves lining the interior walls. They would be filled with all manner of goods as well. Jasper's smile broadened as he watched the shop owners calling out to the villagers as they passed by, enticing them to look at their wares. Jasper knew that much bartering went on with the exchange of goods or services between the villagers.

Several of the villagers closer to Jasper stopped to wave a friendly hello before they continued on their way. He recognized all of them and enthusiastically waved back at them. He watched and smiled as small children played in the main square while their mothers sat on low benches talking with each other. Older children lined the bridges and laughed as they fished in the river. It must be a holiday Jasper thought; normally the children would be in school.

Jasper then laughed outright when he saw Zan and Arnack, the town jesters, sitting in the outdoor patio of the Baron's Den. They were whistling and making rude jesters at Enyce, one of the seven elders, as she walked by. Walking with her was a large winged horse named Farley. He was the elder of the Avidraughts; the flying horses of the Whipple Wash Valley. Jasper watched as Hammy Baronden, the keeper of the Baron's Den, brought out two mugs of mead for Zan and Arnack. He laughed with them until Enyce and Farley looked at him sternly. He quickly went back inside, but not before he winked at Zan and Arnack who chuckled merrily. Knowing that he should not, but not being able to help himself, Jasper giggled gleefully at their antics.

A warm fuzzy feeling came over Jasper and he sighed heavily. Taking a deep breath, he whispered, "Home...I'm home again." He breathed in the familiar smells and giggled with glee as he exhaled.

"Jasper," the voice called to him sweetly again and he looked over at the lovely vision before him, now fully realizing who she was – Jolise Neru, Keeper of the Hummingmoth messengers and youngest sister of the seven elders of the Whipple Wash Valley.

Standing with her were the other elders Enyce, Rayley, Andi, Sianna, Phiney, and Athia. They smiled warmly at Jasper; he smiled back.

"It is time to come home," Jolise said. "You were sent on a mission and you have important information. We need you to come home." The other elders nodded in agreement. The elders parted and the fairies stepped forward: Shanata, Mariela, Enna, Ashlina and Zabethile. Jasper smiled at each of them. Oh, how he missed them. Jasper looked at Zabethile. Tears were dripping from her eyes and her lips trembled as she said, "You promised you would come back. Do you remember? You promised me you would come home. Come home, Jasper. Please come home," Zabethile cried softly.

Jasper reached out his hand to brush the tears from her cheek. As he did, she moved backwards. He stretched out his arm to touch her. This time everyone but Zabethile disappeared. Every time he reached for her, she moved further and further away. The thick fog rose again and Zabethile disappeared into the greyish void. All Jasper could hear was her voice saying repeatedly, "It's time to come home, you promised. It's time to come home."

Jasper moaned in despair and rushed headlong into the thick fog. He searched for her, but she was not there. Everything had vanished: the tree, the elders, the villagers. He frantically flew back and forth, calling out their names, but no one answered.

Suddenly, a bright red light flashed in the fog. Jasper gasped and shivered uncontrollably from fright. The light came barreling down on him and, the closer it got, the hotter it became. The scent coming from the now blinding light smelled like burnt flesh. The light made a strange humming sound like a million wings beating to the same drum. It hurt his ears and he winced from the pain. Jasper tried to fly away but he was stuck. He tried to free himself. However the more he struggled, the more entangled he became. The humming noise grew louder, piercing his eardrums. The red light became brighter and the heat from it became hotter, burning his flesh. He yelled until his voice was hoarse as the light overtook him, and he thrashed wildly from side to side, moaning in pain from the agony. Then suddenly, he was free -- The light vanished and with it the heat. The drumming of the million wings turned into a soft sound and he careened to hear it. However, all he could hear was the rapid beating of his own heart. With dismay, he moaned pathetically. He did not want the heat to return so he willed himself to lay still. The sound came again. It was someone calling his name.

"Jasper, Jasper, wake up. You've been dreaming, little one. Jasper, come back to us. It's time to wake up." Jasper recognized the voice.

Like a soothing balm, it quieted him. His breathing slowed and he instantly felt at ease. He slowly opened his eyes. Standing over him was Chrystalina. She was smiling down at him as he lay on a blanket at the end of the stone table in the Crystal Cave of Aspentonia. He smiled at her and she returned the smile, but he could see concern in her eyes. She looked towards the other end of the table and nodded. He turned his head to see who was at the other end. Saphina, dressed in a pale yellow shift, was sitting down at the end of the table in her usual chair, dishing plump red berries onto a plate. He noticed that she did not look as haggard as she had earlier. The bags under her eyes were gone and she had brushed her hair. Perhaps she had gotten a restful sleep. He would be surprised to find out she hadn't slept at all.

Saphina paid Jasper no mind as she picked up a teacup, blew off the steam and took a sip before she put it back down on the table. She popped a berry in her mouth, unrolled a piece of parchment and started to read it. Jasper noticed that several scrolls sat in two piles on the other side of the teacup. Hearing a clink, he looked to the left of Saphina. Sitting a couple of chairs away from her was Zusie, dressed in a deep emerald green tunic. She was looking at him with her bright blue eyes and, although she smiled at him, he could tell that she too was concerned.

"Jasper," Chrystalina said softly and held out her hand. He got up slowly -- every muscle in his body hurt and he groaned in agony. He however stepped gingerly onto her hand than sat with a plump as she carried him carefully to the other end of table. She sat Jasper down in front of Zusie who placed a small cup of black tea and a plate of spiced nut bread and berries beside him.

"Are you alright?" Zusie looked at Jasper curiously. He nodded in reply. "You were having quite the dream, little one. You were giggling one moment then moaning the next and you tossed and turned for quite some time. Chrystalina," she turned to her daughter and smiled fondly at her, "jumped up just in time to stop you from falling off the edge of the table." Jasper turned to Chrystalina and smiled his thank you to her.

"I would have let him fall," Saphina said, not taking her eyes off the scroll she was reading. Her mother and sister looked at her crossly; Jasper could not bring himself to look at her. Saphina felt them staring at her so she looked up from the parchment. "What?" She chuckled. "It's one way to wake him up." Chrystalina kissed her teeth in disgust and Saphina went back to her reading, muttering under her breath that she was only jesting.

"Your wings got caught in the blanket, along with your arms and legs while you thrashed around. Are you sure you are alright?" Zusie asked him again. Jasper took a moment to move his arms and legs. He stood up and wiggled his body and wings. Although he was very sore, all seemed to be in working condition. He touched the bump on his head and winced from the pain.

"Drink your tea," Zusie said, pushing the cup closer to him. "Aldwin left some pain relief for you. It has been steeping in the tea." Jasper looked at the cup curiously. "It's okay, Jasper. It will make the pain go away," Zusie reassured him.

Jasper put his snout in the tea and sipped it. It was bitter but he drank it as Zusie instructed. While sipping the last of the tea, something caught his attention. He looked beyond Saphina to the other side of the room where the statue of Jolise Neru sat in its cubbyhole. The statue was glowing. Curious, Jasper started to fly slowly towards it. Zusie and Chrystalina stood up quickly and walked beside him, in case the medicine had made him dizzy or sick. It worked well enough on them and the Elfkins but no one was quite sure what effect it would have on someone so small. He seemed to be fine as he stopped and hovered in front of the statue.

Jasper could feel the warmth the statue emitted. He flew up and put his hand on its arm and was surprised to find it felt cool to the touch.

"She's been glowing like that for some time now, just before you started giggling in your dream in fact." Jasper turned his head and looked back at Zusie.

"She came to me in my dream," he said and turned back to the statue. "She told me it was time to come home. She said I was sent on a mission and I have important information for her." Saphina looked up from the scroll she was reading, interested in what he had to say.

"Do you remember what the information is?" Zusie asked. Jasper shook his head. "Do you remember why you were sent on a mission?" Jasper shook his head again. His wings began to flutter slowly and he dipped down. Jasper gave no complaint when Zusie held out her hand for him to rest on as they walked back to the table. He also nodded his head in agreement when she suggested he have something to eat.

Popping a chunk of bread in his mouth, he sat back against his now refilled teacup. He knit his brow as he tried to remember. Several minutes passed. The room was quiet; so quiet in fact; you could have heard a pair of red dapple spider ants talking. The others stared at Jasper expectantly. As time went by, the stillness in the room gradually slipped away. Zusie and Chrystalina seeing that Jasper wasn't coming to a revelation any time soon sipped their tea and ate their bread.

Saphina had tried to read Jasper's thoughts, but they were going by so quickly she couldn't keep up with them. She blocked him out as best she could and went back to reading the scrolls.

Occasionally, Jasper would move his leg or sigh as he munched on a piece of bread. Zusie and Chrystalina would look at him eagerly but then sigh in dismay; his face still showed that he was thinking intensely. Saphina would click her teeth in annoyance, huff loudly, and ruffle the scrolls before she went back to reading them. More time went by as Jasper tried to remember. The dream played over and over in his mind. The burning red light no longer scared him as he tried to recall the details.

Gradually the plates became bare, except for Saphina's plate. The tea left in the pot had become cold. Jasper had managed to eat all his bread and fruit but had only drunk a bit of his tea. Having drunk the medicated one earlier, he was now feeling like he had to relieve himself. Concentrating on remembering became more difficult. He was wondering where they relieved themselves when Saphina, who had picked up the change in his thinking pattern, disrupted his thoughts.

"Jasper!" she yelled as she jumped up from her chair, knocking it over.

Startled out of his wits, Jasper also jumped up. When he did he knocked over his teacup, spilling its contents all over the table. Saphina, seeing that the tea was making its way towards the scrolls, scooped them up quickly.

"You clumsy oaf," Saphina yelled. The tea ran to the edge, spilled over the side and splashed onto the floor. Jasper was fluttering quickly back and forth until he heard what she called him. Putting his hands on his hips, he leaned towards her and before he realized what he was doing, he scolded her.

"Well if you hadn't scared me half to death I wouldn't have knocked over the teacup." Jasper yelled. "You scared me so badly I almost peed right here on this lovely table!"

Saphina, shocked that Jasper would dare to yell at her in such a manner, looked over at her mother and sister. Zusie was suppressing a smirk behind her hand while Chrystalina was barely containing a giggle. Seeing that she was not going to receive any support from them, she looked back at Jasper. She expected to see a smug look on his face however; tears were in his eyes instead. He looked quite scared as he fluttered rapidly back and forth; keeping a wary eye on Saphina. Seeing the look on his face, Saphina's anger quickly deflated. She placed the scrolls on a dry spot on the table, righted her chair and slumped down in it. The edge of her yellow tunic lay in the puddle of tea on the floor. Not caring Saphina stared at her hands that lay clenched in her lap for a moment then she spoke quietly.

"I am sorry for scaring you like that Jasper," Saphina said. Not hearing a response, she looked up at him as he looked at her. "Sincerely Jasper, I am truly sorry." Jasper stopped fluttering from side to side and hovered in midair. Still looking at him, she shook her head slowly. "Do you not understand how important it is that you remember? Not just to you and the villagers in your homeland, but to us as well. Lizbeth lies ill in her bed and Aldwin has no means to cure her. There is great unrest in the village -- You experienced that for yourself last night,' she said pointedly. "Something terrible is about to happen that will bring death and destruction to this valley. We've been reading the signs for months now." Sadly, she looked at her mother and sister who were sitting quietly in their chairs, looking worriedly at Jasper as Saphina spoke.

What she said was true; they had been reading the signs -- Subtle as they were, but they did exist. It all started with the abnormal changes in weather patterns, the last winter storm being the oddest of them. On occasion, the crystals in the back caves glowed eerily and a sound rumbled behind them. From the observatory -- A room located high in the mountain that was accessed by a winding staircase just off the kitchen, they could see that even the stars shone abnormally and were out of alignment. From their perch, they could feel the unrest in the village. It was as if a cloud of doubt hovered over the forest and evil leered from the shadows. They did not know how to explain it to the Elfkins so they listened and kept watch from the cave.

Saphina stood up and paced the floor in front of her chair, the edge of her tunic getting wetter by the minute as she thought carefully about what she was going to say next. She stopped pacing and looked at Jasper again who seemed to be crying. Seeing his tears, Saphina sighed heavily and looked at him hopefully.

"Your unique capability is the door to life or death and we have the key to unlock it," she said, pointing at something behind Jasper. Jasper did not need to turn around to know what she pointed at; the memory nut still lay on the table beside the mallet. "Won't you please consider our request to suck up the nectar and empty it into a cup so that mother can drink it?"

"Perhaps," Zusie said, "Once I drink the nectar there will be enough left in the nut for you to drink and then you will remember where you came from and what your mission was."

Jasper sighed heavily, knowing that no matter how scared he was friends and family were counting on him. Jasper looked from Saphina to Zusie and Chrystalina. They all had the same expression of hope on their faces.

Jasper looked up at the crystal ceiling. His breathing came in quick bursts and his wings fluttered as fast as his heart. Between clenched teeth, he squeaked out a shaky "yes." Not sure that they had heard correctly they leaned forward. As he continued to look up at the crystal ceiling, not daring to look at the others, something caught his eye from across the room. Jasper looked over. The statue of Jolise Neru was shining brightly again. Even though Jasper was several feet away, he could feel the warmth of it penetrate his body. He felt an electric energy flow through his veins; it did not frighten him. Instead, his breathing eased and his heartbeat slowed. With renewed confidence, Jasper squared his shoulders and without hesitation clearly said, "Yes, I will do it."

Several things quickly happened in succession. Saphina whooped loudly and slipped on the puddle of tea as she ran towards the entranceway. She yelled back over her shoulder that she was going to fetch Aldwin and disappeared down the long hall to the golden archway before anyone could stop her.

Chrystalina clapped her hands, laughed outright, and said that she would be right back. She quickly left the room as well but went into the antechamber that housed the scrolls. Jasper watched her go and noticed that, as she passed the statue of Jolise Neru, it no longer emitted the warm glow. It was back to its normal state and he looked at it curiously until Zusie spoke.

"Thank you Jasper," Zusie said calmly as she smiled warmly at him. He nodded and landed on the table. He walked to his cup to right it and stopped short when Zusie said, "I will take care of that," and righted his cup before he could. "I believe you mentioned that you needed to…relieve yourself?"

Jasper's expression of embarrassment had Zusie smiling slightly. He had forgotten that he needed to go but, at the mention of it, he now had a hard time keeping it in. Normally he relieves himself behind a bush and the villagers use outhouses, but where does one go in a Crystal Cave? Zusie answered his unasked question.

"If you go down there," Zusie pointed to the hallway next to the kitchen door, "and take the first left, you will find the bathing and," she smiled, "relieving chamber." Jasper smiled awkwardly and left the room in a hurry.

Zusie cleared the table and mopped up the spilt tea while she waited for the others to return. When Jasper reentered the room, he noticed that only one of the scrolls that Saphina had been looking at still lay on the table. Zusie was sitting in her usual chair and Chrystalina sat next her. A stack of blank parchment, a writing stick and an inkwell sat on the table in front of her. Jasper looked curiously at the parchment as he flew into the room. Before he could question Chrystalina about it, Saphina called from the entrance to the cave.

"Look who I ran into as I was descending the stairs." Aldwin walked into the room with her. Both of them were chuckling heartily.

"What's so funny?" Chrystalina asked.

"I literally ran into him," Saphina chuckled again and looked fondly at Aldwin. Turning back to the others, she said excitedly, "You know halfway down the stairs where it curves sharply around that enormous fir tree? Well, I was running down the stairs, around the bend and slammed right into him. He grabbed me with one arm and a tree branch with the other. We both would have tumbled head over heels backwards if he hadn't grabbed that branch. My hero," she said playfully, and gave him a quick one-arm hug and a kiss on the cheek before she joyfully walked towards the table.

Jasper looked at the bright smile on her face as he flew to the table and sat on it. He thought Saphina was quite lovely when she wasn't scowling at him. Aldwin followed Saphina to the table but, instead of sitting in the chair next to her, he leaned over the table to examine Jasper.

"How are you feeling this morning?" Aldwin asked.

"I feel fine," Jasper said as Aldwin examined him from head to toe. He flinched slightly when Aldwin gently poked around the bump above his eye. Aldwin noticed that the swelling had gone down considerably however a dark purple and black bruise had spread out from the bottom of his eye and down his cheek.

"No pain?" Aldwin asked. When Jasper shook his head, Aldwin turned to Zusie.

"I put the purple lizben leaves in his tea as you suggested. He drank all of it."

"Ah, good, good," Aldwin said, nodding his head and looking back at Jasper. "I hear you have decided to sip the nectar from the memory nut. Are you sure that this is what you want to do?" Jasper looked around the table at Zusie and her daughters. Seeing their hopeful expressions, he nodded.

For good measure, to show that he was not afraid, he walked over to the nut and knocked on the outside of it three times. The others smirked at his cheekiness. Although the nut was larger than Jasper, he had no problems rolling it across the table. He stopped rolling the nut once he reached a spot in front of Saphina.

Surprised, she cocked her head to the right and stared at him. The others watched her reaction to his gesture. She smiled at him, leaned over the table and patted Jasper lightly on the back.

"It is a good thing you do here today. I am…proud of you." Her kind words had Jasper smiling brightly back at her and he decided at that moment that perhaps she wasn't as mean as she made out to be.

Saphina, hearing his thoughts, smiled as she got up from the chair. She walked around the table to where the mallet was, picked it up, carried it back and placed it beside the nut. While Jasper looked hesitantly at the mallet, a quick vision of Saphina knocking him over the head with it popped into his mind. She saw the image as he did and said softly, "Don't worry, Jasper. That would never happen."

Knowing this to be true Jasper smiled. He looked at the nut than folded his hands, as if in prayer, and closed his eyes. Time passed by slowly as he gathered his courage. When he opened his eyes, he looked at the nut and said clearly, "I am ready."

Saphina once again whooped loudly, startling the others. They looked at her and chuckled; even Jasper laughed. Saphina picked up the mallet, walked to her mother and held it out to her with great reverence.

"Would you like to do the honors?" Saphina asked.

"Thank you," Zusie said and took the mallet.

Jasper stood up. Eager to get it over with he started to roll the nut over to Zusie. Everyone was looking at Zusie and did not see the last little push that Jasper gave the nut. They turned just as the nut rolled off the table. Zusie scooped it up before it reached the floor. Jasper, horrified by what he did, started to stammer an apology.

"Don't worry, Jasper. If a swipe with this mallet can't crack it, I doubt dropping it on the floor could." Zusie said as she placed the nut back on the table. Relieved, Jasper sat down beside it.

Saphina unrolled the scroll in front of her and quickly read it over. "It says that you should strike the nub…from the top…and then it should pop right off." Saphina looked up at the others and said, "Easy enough."

Aldwin stood beside Zusie and turned the nut so the nub was facing forward and held it firmly in his hands. Zusie picked up the mallet and, to no one in particular, said, "Here's hoping." With one strike, she hit the top of the nub and, just as it said in the scroll, it popped right off, hit the table, bounced a couple of feet in the air and landed back down on to the table with a little thud. However, no one saw where the nub had landed; they were all watching the nut.

A whizzing sound came out first, followed by a white mist that spiraled in a thin stream towards the crystal ceiling. Everyone but Jasper suddenly plugged their nose and took a step back from the table.

"Oh my," Chrystalina said, waving her hand rapidly in front of her nose as she breathed through her mouth. Screwing up her face and smacking her lips together, she said, "It smells so bad I think I can taste it!"

"What?" Jasper said, looking strangely at Chrystalina.

"Doesn't the smell bother you?" she asked.

"What smell?" Jasper asked, giggling at the look of repulsion on her face.

"The smell Jasper, the smell coming from the nut, can't you smell it?" Chrystalina asked nasally.

"No," he said shaking his head, "I can't smell anything,"

"Interesting," Aldwin said as he took a couple more steps back from the table. The smell was really quite pungent. Jasper looked over at Saphina. She was breathing through her mouth as well. She smacked her lips together and screwed up her face just as her sister had. Jasper smiled broadly thinking how comical they all looked.

"It smells so bad I think I can taste it too," she said, waving the scroll in front of her face. Jasper giggled.

"I'll be right back," Chrystalina said as she ran from the room, still holding her nose. Jasper noticed that she had gone down the hallway that led to the bathing chamber.

"Is it supposed to smell like that?" asked Zusie fearfully.

Saphina stopped waving the scroll so that she could read it. She read carefully but quickly. She knew her mother was worried that perhaps the nut had gone bad.

"Yes," Saphina said brightly as she read aloud. "Be warned, after the nub is off, the gases trapped inside will escape. The smell is quite pungent." Zusie relaxed as did the others. Chrystalina came back into the room carrying a rather large candle. She lit the wick and the aroma from the candle filled the room, quickly dissipating the strong scent.

"Mmm that smells nice," Jasper said, breathing in deeply. Everyone looked at Jasper in astonishment.

"I thought you couldn't smell," Saphina said.

"Oh no, I can smell," Jasper said in a matter of fact way. "I just couldn't smell the nut." He looked over at the candle and then up at

Chrystalina curiously. "That smells like the winter moonlit flower tastes."

"Yes." Chrystalina looked at him, pleased that he recognized the smell. "During Lizbeth's last visit, she brought us some of the sapple you collected. I thought it smelled so good I mixed it in with some of the frilly beeswax that we have. It does smell delightful," she said, taking a long sniff of the air. "It has very soothing properties as well, don't you think?" Jasper took a long sniff and nodded. He did feel more relaxed.

"Strange, very strange," Aldwin said as he wondered why Jasper could smell the candle but not the nut. Zusie was also curious, but it would have to wait; there was something more important to take care of. If they had only thought it through, they would have realized that things would not go as planned, but time was of the essence. There was only a small window of opportunity before the soft nut inside shriveled up; the gases kept it moist. Once gone, the inner nut would dry out quickly.

Excited to have the chance to remember where she came from Zusie asked urgently, "So are we ready then?" Everyone nodded their head in agreement.

"It says here," Saphina started, "that you are to stick your snout into the hole quickly so that the tip of it pierces the inner nut. Then you suck up the nectar."

"Is that all?" Jasper asked, thinking it seemed simple enough.

"Yes, that's it," Saphina said rolling up the scroll. Chrystalina looked at her sister crossly.

"What my sister isn't telling you is that you might be affected by the nectar as well." Jasper looked at her curiously -- Chrystalina went on to explain. "Even though you will not be drinking it, you may feel some effects from the residue."

Saphina looked at her sister crossly. "Yes well there is that, but I left that part out because I didn't want you to be scared."

"Saphina," Zusie and Aldwin both said her name in the same manner that had Saphina defending herself.

"I,..I...thought it best to save him from any more fright," she looked back at them. "Honestly," she said as she looked at Jasper. "I didn't want to scare you more than you needed to be." Jasper looked at her and believed her words to be true.

Saphina opened the scroll and began to read again: "Upon the nectar touching the participant's taste buds, the participant will fall into a deep trance into which he or she will remember all that they have forgotten.

The trance could last several minutes to several hours depending on how the participant lost their memory and the severity of it.

Warning: depending on the event that took place and the reason why the participant lost their memory, the participant could become quite distraught and thrash around. It is advised that the participant be placed on a flat surface and given a wide berth in order to prevent them from hurting themselves or anyone else. During the trance, the participant will recall the events that took place before and after they lost their memory.' Saphina looked up from the scroll and said, "That's all there is. The scroll only talks of the one who drinks the nectar, not the one who sucks it out of the nut. Jasper should be fine as long as he does not drink the nectar in its entirety."

"Are there any side effects?" Aldwin asked the question that Jasper was about to ask.

"No," Saphina said sharply. They all looked at her, thinking that perhaps she was holding more back. She looked at them and said, "Oh for Zenrah's sake, there is nothing else. Honestly!" She held up the scroll so that they could see for themselves. Reading the last words that Saphina spoke at the bottom of the page, they all wondered if perhaps it continued on another scroll. However before any of them could voice their opinion, Saphina said tersely, "There are no other scrolls on this subject."

They looked from Saphina to Jasper and were surprised to see that he did not look afraid. In fact, he looked quite at ease as he stood up and walked over to the nut. Chrystalina placed a small cup beside him. Jasper looked at the cup; no one had to tell him what it was for. He placed his tiny hands on either side of the hole where the nub had been. The shell felt rough under his palms. He unfurled his snout and had to lean his head back a bit so that the tip lay just at the entrance. Without looking at anyone, he plunged his snout into the hole. It pierced the soft nut inside and Jasper sucked in deeply. The nectar from the inner nut had no taste either, at least not to Jasper. Before he could think any longer about why it had no taste a fuzzy feeling flooded his brain and washed away all thoughts.

He stepped back from the nut and his snout curled into a tight ball on its own accord. He opened his eyes and looked around the room. It seemed hazy, as if he stood in a thick fog. He could barely make out the others, who were leaning over the table anxiously yelling at him to unfurl his snout and empty the nectar into the cup. He tried to do their bidding but he could not -- Instinctively he swallowed. The nectar felt warm as it slowly went down his throat. With each passing moment, the room became foggier until it darkened to blackness. Jasper could no longer hear their voices yelling at him.

Suddenly, Jasper began to shake -- He crumpled to the hard tabletop. No one in the room expected this and they looked on in horror as Jasper entered the trance. There was no turning back now; he would have to endure whatever it brought him. They all said a silent prayer to Zenrah that Jasper would survive.

The shaking became fierce and both Zusie and Chrystalina reached out to touch him, but Aldwin stayed them with his hand and moved the nut, cup and mallet a safe distance away from Jasper. They were so worried for Jasper that no one noticed Saphina had slumped down in her chair and started to whimper. Aldwin rushed to her side, telling the other two to stay with Jasper but not to touch him. He looked into Saphina's eyes while Zusie and Chrystalina looked from Saphina to Jasper in helpless dismay. So concerned with Jasper and the memory nut, none of them thought that Saphina's gift of reading minds would put her in danger. However, it seemed that with her ability and her strange connection to Jasper, she had become an unwilling participant in the trance. It was not affecting her as intensely as it was Jasper. While he was shaking uncontrollably, she sat in her chair as if she was glued to it, staring into nothingness and whimpering.

Suddenly Jasper's shaking and whimpering stopped, and Aldwin came back to the table to look into Jasper's eyes. Although his eyes were open, they stared blankly back at Aldwin just as Saphina's had. Jasper could not see anyone or anything in the room, only the blackness that slowly cleared to a terrifying vision.

Flames leapt before his eyes and an awful heart-wrenching scream pierced the air, but only in his mind. All the others could hear was his heavy breathing and an occasional whimpering from Saphina. Jasper cried out as his memory came back to him in rapid flashes. Without realizing what he was doing Jasper immediately stood up and started to repeat everything that he saw. Chrystalina picked up the writing stick, shakily dipped it in the inkwell, and began to write on the parchment that she titled 'Jasper and the Memory Nut Trance'.

"I was running -- no flying -- away from something…dark-clothed warriors…there were several of them chasing after me. Up the side of the rocky foothills I flew, darting in and around a thick forest of pine trees. The landscape gave way to a rocky terrain that had several large boulders. I could hear the warriors catching up to me so I ducked behind the largest of the boulders. I looked around frantically for somewhere to hide. Several feet away, three large boulders grouped together lay at the base of a dead tree. One of the boulders had a large chunk out of it. The space between it and the boulder next to it was big enough for me to fit in to. I didn't want to take the chance of flying over to it so I crawled across the hard uneven ground, scraping my knees and the palms of my hands. My underbelly scraped against the boulder as I squeezed into the hole. Once inside, I found it to be bigger than I thought and was able to maneuver myself around. I peered out of the dark hole just as light from a torch flooded the area. I froze in fright as someone called out.

'Rishtoph, do you see him anywhere?' A warrior shouted as he walked by the rocks. A second later, another warrior joined him.

'No Jaja,' Rishtoph replied roughly. I could see them as they passed back and forth in front of the rocks. I was afraid that they had seen me, but they looked about half-heartedly. I relaxed; it was just a coincidence that they stopped right where I was hiding.

The one called Jaja stood in front of the rocks. With the light from the torches they carried, I could see him clearly. He was the one that had captured me and my brothers and was the king's eldest son. He tightly held onto the sword that he always carries; ready to strike with deadly force when necessary. A double-edged dagger with strange carvings on the hilt hung from a thick black belt around his waist. It was lethal looking and I shivered in fright.

The man named Rishtoph came to stand with Jaja. I believe he is the king's youngest son. He was dressed the same as his brother; the uniform of the Venom Horde. Rishtoph also wore a dagger at his waist, but not as big as his brother's. It was lethal looking all the same. I could tell they were Lord Canvil's sons; they had his nose. But where Jaja was tall and broad with dark features, Rishtoph was fair and gangly.

'Brother, call off the chase,' Rishtoph said gruffly. 'It is ridiculous for father to send us out after one measly winged beetle!' Jaja looked at Rishtoph with amusement.

'Watch what you say, little brother.' Jaja said as he looked around. 'Lord Canvil has ears, even out here.'

'Is that a threat, brother?' Rishtoph asked as he grabbed the hilt of his sword. With one fluid movement, the sword was out of its scabbard. Not intimidated by his younger brother Jaja continued to peer out into the dark night.

'Of course not, little brother,' he said in a smooth drawl, 'but we are not the only ones out looking…are we.' Just as the words left his lips, half a dozen men came up the side of the hill to where they stood. They bowed their heads to the two brothers and put their right arms across their chests in salute.

'There is no sign, my lord,' a tall heavyset man said to Jaja.

Jaja nodded and without looking at his brother, told the heavyset man to call off the chase. The man then held a large horn to his mouth and blew into it three times. I could hear men walking back down the mountainside, cursing loudly.

'Thank you brother,' Rishtoph said when the men were out of earshot.

Before Jaja answered him, he looked around in every direction. I'm not sure if he was looking for me or for someone who might be listening to their conversation. Finally, his eyes rested back on Rishtoph.

'You have much to learn little brother…if you want to take over the kingdom one day.' He was scolding his brother as if he were a young child. I could see by Rishtoph's expression that he did not appreciate the tone in his brother's voice.

Jaja looked around one more time than left his brother standing alone on the hillside. I watched Rishtoph tighten his hold on the hilt of his sword and with a mighty swing, he slammed it against the rocks where I lay hidden. The sound vibrated all around me and I cowered in fright. I thought for sure that he had heard the chattering of my teeth, but I could not stop myself from shaking. I watched as Rishtoph left in a huff, following his brother down the hill. I stayed where I was, shivering in fright, until I passed out.

I awoke sometime later, disoriented until I remembered what had happened. I knew I could not stay there; I had to leave and find my way back home. I listened to the sounds of the night; all I heard was the soft rustling of the leaves in the trees. Convinced that no one was around, I poked my head out from the crevice between the rocks. Seeing no one, I squeezed the rest of my body out. Without hesitation, I took flight up the foothills of Mount Aspentonia, all the while looking back several times to see if anyone had followed me. All I could see was an orange glow coming from the army's settlement in the valley far below. Although I was scared, I knew I had to go on. Joffro told me to."

Jasper hung his head. The others could see that this particular memory was difficult for him to recite. They looked curiously at each other, wondering who Joffro was. Chrystalina put the parchment that she was writing on to the side and picked up another one. In the top left hand corner, she wrote a symbol that indicated it was the second page - Jasper continued.

"Joffro, my leader, my brother in arms, ordered me to run away and find my way back home. I was trying to untie him from a wooden stake. 'Get away, Jasper. Fly over the mountains,' he urged me. 'It's the quickest way back home.' I tried desperately to free Joffro but the ropes would not give. Joffro, seeing that someone was coming to check on us, ordered me once again to fly away. 'You are our only hope, Jasper. I order you to fly away.' Seven Hummingmoth messengers were all that was left of the forty-five who flew out from our village that fateful day so many months ago. And now it was down to the last one -- Me, the smallest and youngest to get the message home.

I flew away, I had no choice, but not before they saw me. It was only by the grace of the Light of Goodness that I was able to get away. Trying not to think of my brothers and their fate in the hands of Canvil, I flew into the night; higher and higher up the foothills I sped. I sent a silent request to the Whipple Wash Tree that my brothers would survive the king's wrath when the news reached him that one of us got away."

The others looked at him strangely. How could he send a request to a tree and who or what was the Light of Goodness? Jasper continued.

"I flew all the next day and the day after that before I stopped to rest. I only rested for a few hours and then took off again, flying high over the rocky terrain. Time went by. I have no idea how many days passed, but the further up the hills I flew the fewer the trees were for me to hide in. I only stopped to eat and sleep a little every other day before I went on my way again. The valley, my valley I was sure, was just on other side of the mountain. If I could make my way there, I would be safe and could give my message to Jolise, keeper of the Hummingmoth messengers.

I flew for many more days and nights up the mountainside. The days had become colder and I had to find shelter for the nights, as they were colder still. If I had not, I would have frozen to death in mid-flight. One day, mid-afternoon, I finally reached the top of the mountain where I fluttered for a moment, looking down with glee onto the valley spreading out at the base of the mountain. However, that was not my valley, my home. It was nothing like the Whipple Wash Valley. It was too close to the mountainside, there was a meadow and a lake, and the other mountain range was too close. I cried out in agony.

How could Joffro have been so wrong? I surmised quickly that he could not have known. None of our maps showed the existence of this valley. Our folklore does not mention it. No one knows of this valley; the valley that time forgot. I realized it would take me several more weeks to pass through it, perhaps even months. I was not even sure that once I reached and crossed over the mountains on the other side of the valley that the Whipple Wash Valley would be there. I was disheartened and almost gave up, but I knew I had to get the message home, so I flew down the mountainside towards the valley below. I had to make it home no matter how long it took. I just hoped that there was still a home for me to come back to.

That first night, while I lay in a crevice on the mountainside, a mighty storm moved in and raged all through the night. Morning had risen and when I poked my head out from the crevice, the winds blew hard and chilled me to the bone but I started on my way.

The winds were proving to be too much for me and they blew me recklessly down the mountainside. I tried to find shelter but I could not. All I could do was keep my wings spread out and let the wind take me down into the valley. Several days had passed. I was exhausted beyond all measure when finally the wind blew me into the forest at the base of the mountain. It took all my skill and what energy

I had left not to fly into a tree. I found myself blowing around what looked to be a village. As I flew past huts, I was thinking to myself, 'I hope they are friendly,' when I bumped into someone coming out of a hut. I was knocked to the ground and all I could say before I passed out was my name."

Jasper stilled, blinked his eyes several times and shook his head. He had made it through the trance. The first person he saw once the fog cleared was Zusie. She was staring at him with tears in her eyes.

"I am sorry," was all he could manage to say. Zusie raised her hand as she was not able to speak and he knew, as he looked in her eyes, that she understood that he had no control over what had happened.

"Jasper, are you alright?" Aldwin asked. Jasper took a moment before he answered, then nodded as the last effects of the memory nut cleared from his mind.

Jasper heard the sigh of relief and looked around the room at the others. Chrystalina had tears spilling from her eyes and smiled at him while she wiped them away, leaving a dark smudge under her eyes from her fingertips that were black with ink.

Jasper's breath caught in his throat when he looked a Saphina. She had been crying and looked back at him with a mournful look that tore at his heart. She stood up and walked across the room, gathering her emotions before she spoke. Jasper looked at Aldwin, confused by the tortured expression he saw in Saphina's eyes.

"As you know, we did not realize that you would immediately go into the trance once the nectar entered your snout." Aldwin said. Jasper nodded, confirming that he understood. "What we also did not realize is that Saphina, with her unique ability to read minds and her strange connection to you that she would also go into the trance."

Realization dawned on Jasper. She had seen all that he had remembered and he felt badly for her. Before he could say he was sorry, she came back to the table and bent down so close that her face was mere inches from his. "I am so sorry, Jasper...I had no idea." Before he could register that she was apologizing to him, she scooped him up in her left hand and held him to her while she gently ran her right hand down his back. The warmth coming from her soothed him and he squirmed closer to her and sighed in great relief.

She held Jasper like that for a long time before she put him back down onto the table, smiling warmly at him as he sat there looking up at her. Although Saphina had not been on Jasper's journey to the valley, due to the clarity of his recollection and her unique connection to him, she might as well have been. Sharing that experience with him, as intimately as she had bonded them together for life.

The others around the table smiled as well, knowing that they had just witnessed the starting of a great friendship that would last a lifetime.

"Jasper," Zusie said, "I know you must be exhausted, but do you think you could tell us the message that you are to bring to Jolise?" Jasper sat for a moment. Looking up at Zusie, he smiled brightly.

"Yes, I do remember, and yes I will tell you. But might I have something to drink first?" he said, smacking his lips. His mouth felt quite dry as if he had not had anything to drink in days.

"Of course," Zusie said and was about to get up when Saphina jumped up from her chair, saying that she would get it. The others smiled as she quickly left the room. She came back with a cup of water and placed it in front of Jasper. He drank deeply from it. The water quenched his thirst instantly and washed away the residue left from the nectar.

Jasper sat back and looked at each of them in turn. All of them smiled back at him anxiously wanting to know what the message was. He was ready to tell them his message. However, it hurt him to think that, although they were smiling at him now, they would not be once he was finished. Nevertheless, he was a Hummingmoth messenger from the Whipple Wash Valley and he had a mission to complete. All else, even friendship, came second to finding his way home and delivering his message.

CHAPTER 11

The Hummingmoth's Message

"How long was I in the trance for?" Jasper asked to no one in particular.

"For several minutes," Zusie said.

"It felt like several hours," Jasper said with little emotion and looked over at Saphina who nodded. They smiled grimly at each other before Jasper looked back at Zusie. Chrystalina dipped the writing tool into the inkwell and held it above a fresh piece of parchment that she titled 'The Hummingmoth's Message.' Again, her hand was shaky, but not as shaky as it was when she was transcribing the trance.

"As you know I am a Hummingmoth messenger from the Whipple Wash Valley. My brothers and I were sent on a mission to find out if a rumor we heard of was true or not." The four of them looked curiously at Jasper but did not interrupt, so he continued. "A powerful, evil, spiritless man named Gregor Canvil or Lord Canvil as he likes to be called, has taken over all the lands to the north. He is hailed as the self-proclaimed king of the north." They all looked at Jasper, surprised to know that there were inhabited lands to the north. His words about Canvil however did not immediately register.

"Our queen, Queen Faywyn, went on her annual spiritual journey to the Gilded Hand of Hawthorn Springs. The water coming from the Gilded Hand is the purest water in the land and possesses rare spiritual healing powers. The spring feeds into the Grandiflora River. Once a year Queen Faywyn leaves the village on the morning of the spring equinox and returns with a crystal vessel of water on the morning of the summer solstice. However," Jasper stopped talking to swallow a lump of emotion that was forming in his throat "she did not return," he said sadly. The others looked at him with confused expressions. Wanting to hear more about the queen and the Gilded Hand, they started to ask their questions.

"Why does she take the trip to the Gilded Hand if the water coming from it flows into the Grandiflora River? Can you not just get the water from there?" Zusie asked. Jasper shook his head.

"No. By the time, the water reaches our village it is no longer pure.

We need it to be pure so that we can feed it to the Whipple Wash Tree." The others looked at him even more confused; was the Whipple Wash Tree not just a tree like any other? Seeing their confused expressions, he went on to recite the fable of his homeland.

"The Whipple Wash Tree is said to be older than the valley, the mountains, the sky, the water and the stars; older than time itself. It was there before life began; it was where life began. Queen Faywyn and her seven daughters, the elders of the Evergreen Forest and the Whipple Wash Valley, care for it. It is home to the Whipple Wash Fairies. The fairies were born from the tree itself. A prophecy reads that they will one day unite all the kingdoms and the people will, in harmony, live as one."

The others, except for Zusie, looked at him intrigued to hear more about the fairies who were born from a tree, as how could anyone be born from a tree? But, Zusie interrupted with a question that took Jasper by surprise.

"How did the elders get to your valley?"

"I...I don't know." Jasper said.

"What do you mean?" Zusie looked at him with a frown on her face.

"As far as I know, they have always been in the Whipple Wash Valley," Jasper said.

"But how can that be?" Zusie said, raising her voice in annoyance. "There are statues of them in this room. There must be a connection."

"I am sorry Zusie, but I do not know. Our folklore does not speak of this cave or the valley." Zusie looked confusedly at the others. Each of them shrugged their shoulders -- they did not understand either.

"Jasper, can you tell us what the message is," Zusie said as she calmed her emotions down.

Jasper nodded his head as he stood up. They would need to know, the message involved them as much as it did the people back home. He took a sip of his water and said grimly, trying to keep all emotion in check.

"Lord Canvil is ravenous for power and is planning on taking over all the lands until he has conquered this world. He is pure, unadulterated evil. To look into his eyes or hear him speak is like having ice run through your veins. No heart beats beneath his chest. No soul shines from the depth of his blacker than black eyes. He has no allegiance to anything or anyone except for himself and his insatiable thirst for power and riches."

Jasper could see their expressions growing grimmer with each word, but they had to know, as their lives depended on whether or not they believed him. He knew ugly truth was far better than sugarcoated half-truths, especially when lives were involved.

"He has amassed a huge army of soulless men who follow him without question, without regret or conscience. They are called the Venom Horde – men who are evil beyond all accounting and carry out with deadly accuracy the king's deplorable biddings."

Saphina winced as she could see the images of the Venom Horde in Jasper's mind.

"The countries that Lord Canvil conquers are given an ultimatum; forfeit all their holdings and people, or they will be killed, their fortunes taken away and his army of fireflies will destroy everything else that is left.

Chrystalina shivered in fright as she wrote the words, leaving splotches of ink on the paper. Zusie leaned sideways and steadied Chrystalina's hand.

"Would you like me to take over?" Chrystalina shook her head, as the others looked fearfully from her to each other, all of them hoping the same thing; that they never have the misfortune of meeting Canvil, his Venom Horde or the fireflies. They had no idea what fireflies were, but if they fought on the king's side, they must be just as evil as he is.

"What are those…fireflies you speak of?" Aldwin asked curiously. The others nodded, wanting to know as well. Jasper shivered but once again controlled his emotions just as the elder Jolise taught him to. The memories of them and their capabilities haunted his dreams.

"They are larger than I, perhaps five times my size. They have slim, elfish bodies, but their ears are large and pointed. They have red spiky hair that points out at odd angles. Their skin changes colour with their emotions, from pale yellow to orange to blood red. Once it is red…you want to make sure you are nowhere near them." Seeing their confused looks, he added, "When they turn red, they burst into flames and torch anything that is in their way, whether it be people, homes, livestock, trees, flowers -- Anything and everything burns to the ground."

The others looked at Jasper in shock as he continued. "Canvil keeps them locked up in cages that are fire resistant and only brings them out when he needs them." The others looked at him in disbelief. Saphina wondered what material other than rock was fire resistant.

"Why?" Zusie asked. She thought it an odd thing to do. If the fireflies fought willingly for Canvil, why did he need to lock them up? Jasper was confused by the question. "Why does he keep them locked up? Are they not his followers?" Zusie said.

"I don't know," Jasper said, shaking his head. "I never got close

enough to any of them to find out. We…we were trying to escape."
Jasper slumped down as the memory of his brothers tied helplessly to
stakes flooded his mind and he whimpered. The last memory he had of
his brothers was of the fireflies coming nearer as he sped away.

"Jasper, I am sure they are fine," Saphina said convincingly. Jasper
looked up at her and smiled at her kindness. He could not find the
words to explain to her that it did not feel like they were. The
Hummingmoths were connected much the same as she and he were.
Jasper could no longer sense them and wanted to believe that it was
because he had lost his memory. However, he resigned himself to the
alternative – Canvil, in his fury because Jasper escaped, ordered the
fireflies to dispose of Jasper's brothers. Tied to the stakes as they were,
they would have had no chance to escape.

For a minute, the room was quiet; all of them lost in their own
thoughts. The only sound was the scratching of the writing tool on the
parchment as Chrystalina finished writing what Jasper had said.

"Jasper," Zusie said, breaking the silence. "If Lord Canvil is taking
over all the lands, is he planning on coming to this valley?

"I don't believe the king knows about this valley," he said
cautiously. The others sighed and smiled. Jasper looked sadly at them.

"What is it, Jasper? This is good news," Aldwin said. Jasper shook
his head.

"I don't believe he knows about this valley," he repeated, "but he is
planning on coming over this mountain or perhaps through it. He thinks
that it will be the quickest way to the Whipple Wash Valley…and the
lands to the south," he said, trailing off quietly as he saw the look of
fear on all their faces. Saphina mulled something over for a moment
not quite believing all that she was hearing.

"If he kills all that resist him, who told you of the rumor?" Saphina
asked. Jasper sighed heavily.

"When Queen Faywyn did not return, a scouting party was sent out
to search for her. Obwyn, our village hunter, had a hunch about the
Firelog Forest and the flying rapcicors." The others looked confused.
Like the fireflies, they had never heard of flying rapcicors.

"They came across a band of rapcicors who had surrounded an old
man hiding in a thicket of prickly gooseberry bushes. Obwyn and the
band of villagers were able to chase away the rapcicors. The old man
was near death's door, but the Light of Goodness smiled upon him that
day. Obwyn and the others brought him to our village. Orliff, our
village healer, nursed him back to health. The man's name is Zander
and he is," Jasper corrected himself, "was the keeper of records." The

others looked even more confused.

"Do you mean he was the keeper of Canvil's scrolls?" Chrystalina asked.

"Yes," Jasper said. "He kept detailed records of all the lands and riches that Canvil plundered."

"How did he get away from Lord Canvil?" Zusie asked.

"He traveled with a band of scouts from the Venom Horde to the Gilded Hand. Canvil had heard of its mystical power and wanted it for himself." As they wondered what mystical powers it had, Jasper added, "He thought that the Gilded Hand gave the owner of it eternal life. He heard of the Whipple Wash Tree; that it was older than time itself and thought it was because of the water from the Gilded Hand."

The others looked curiously at him, wondering if it was true. Jasper went on to say, "He instructed Zander to keep a record of it in great detail; how it sat, what it looked like at night compared to day, what direction it faced and what happened to it every hour throughout the day. He also wanted detailed drawings of it at each hour."

Jasper's voice began to crack and falter, "They... came across...our queen and took her and, and...the Gilded Hand back to the king." Jasper's nerves faltered as sadness consumed him, but he went on with his tale. "Zander said he had befriended Faywyn. She told him of our village and the Whipple Wash Tree and the fairies. She told him that the Gilded Hand would be useless to the king. The hand and spring are connected, like clouds are connected with the sky, like trees are connected with the earth. The hand does not give its owner eternal life."

"What is the Gilded Hand?" Saphina asked.

"I've only seen drawings of it in the village library," Jasper said. "It is a five fingered open hand," Jasper raised his right hand, his palm faced upwards. "The hand is...was connected," Jasper corrected himself, "to the earth by way of a pedestal that looks like a wrist and part of an arm- carved from a rare stone. It stands about as tall as Aldwin and is four feet wide. The hand is located over the Hawthorn Springs. The water runs up through the arm and wrist and spills out of the open palm then it trickles down into the Grandiflora River."

"Where is it located?" Saphina inquired.

"In an enormous garden that covers the breadth of an island located in the middle of the Grandiflora River," Jasper said. "The only way to get to the island is by way of a covered bridge. Several statues of whimsical characters peek out at you from inside the trees, behind bushes and around every bend along the path that winds it way through the garden. The garden never ages nor is it affected by the changing of the seasons. In the garden, it is always a clear summer's day."

The others cooed in delight. "Does the garden have a name?" Saphina asked, intrigued to learn more. Jasper nodded.

"The plaque above the entrance to the covered bridge reads 'Runbo's Garden.'" Before the others could ask who Runbo was, Jasper answered pointedly, "No one knows who or what Runbo is."

Although the garden sounded intriguing, Aldwin thought that perhaps they were getting off topic; after all, an evil Lord was coming to conquer their valley.

"How did Zander get away from the Venom Horde?" Aldwin asked.

"In the still of the night, on their sixth day back to the king, Zander fled. He made his way back to the Grandiflora River and followed it for many days and nights. He did not know exactly where Elsbrier was. Queen Faywyn only told him that it was in the direction of where the sun kissed the land goodnight. He came to a fork in the river and took the way that continued to lead him west. For many more days and nights he continued on, living on roots and berries but not resting for long. He was afraid that Jaja, the commander of the Venom Horde, would send a party after him. Finally, he wandered into the Fire Log Forest where the flying rapcicors live."

It's all so strange," Zusie said nervously. The others nodded. They never imagined in their wildest dreams that there were such creatures in the world, or beings that would harm and destroy other beings and take over their lands. Jasper had been right – Surely, their valley was one that time had forgotten.

"Jasper," Zusie said, and asked the question they all feared the answer to, "how long before Lord Canvil comes to this valley?"

"I don't know," Jasper said, shaking his head. "He may already be on his way." The troubled looks on their faces spoke volumes and none of them needed to voice what they were thinking. Any time now, an evil Lord and his army of Venom Horde and fireflies could invade them. Peaceful in nature, the Elfkins would have no means to fight back. Being the only ones in the valley, there was no one they could call on to help.

"Well then," Zusie said, composing her thoughts as she spoke. "We will... have to gather the elders together."

"I will go," Aldwin said. "However, I think we should gather everyone in the village and tell them all together." Zusie thought for a moment.

"Yes...I think that would be wise as well. The elders may take days to decide the best course of action and I don't think we can spare the time for them to come to a decision."

"Jasper, might I have a word with you before I leave?" Aldwin asked. Jasper nodded. "I believe now that you have your memory back, you might be able to shed some light on Lizbeth's condition."

Jasper looked at him with a puzzled expression, and then he slumped down as if Aldwin's words knocked the air out of him.

"Oh Lizbeth," he moaned pathetically. "Dear Lizbeth," Jasper said, rocking from side to side.

"What is it?" Aldwin asked anxiously as he leaned over the table to look at Jasper. The others looked at him as well. He could see that they were worried; as they should be. He began to speak shakily as tears welled up in his eyes.

"Hummingmoth…messengers have…glands just inside the cheek that…are filled… with poison. If we are scared…or in great danger, the poison is secreted into our snouts." Jasper looked around the table apologetically. The others gasped. How many times did they carry Jasper in their hands with his snout unfurled when he was frightened? At any time they could have been stung and no one would have known what was wrong with them.

"We have no control over it. Self-preservation takes over…it is the only means we have of protecting ourselves…from predators," he said, snuffling loudly and wiping his hand under his curled up snout.

"Is there an antidote for the sting of a Hummingmoth?" Zusie asked, fearing the worse.

Jasper nodded his head. Zusie and the others smiled in relief.

"Do you know what it is?" Zusie asked anxiously. Afraid to look up at her, he shook his head sadly.

"The only one I know of that has the antidote is Orliff, our village healer. Orliff will know."

"But Orliff is so far away, Jasper. How he can possibly help Lizbeth?" Zusie slumped down in her chair; her smile from a moment ago vanished. Her lips trembled and her eyes filled with tears. Aldwin looked sadly at Zusie as her daughters comforted her; their own eyes holding unshed tears.

"What happens to the victims after they have been injected with the poison?" Aldwin asked, trying to keep his voice steady. Jasper did not want to tell them but they would need to know so he named off the stages.

"Gradual fatigue, drowsiness, disorientation…then they will fall into a deep sleep."

"How long will they stay in the sleep for, Jasper?" Aldwin asked.

"It could take days to several seasons, depending on how strong willed the victim is and how much they want to live."

"What will happen to the...victim?" Aldwin faltered. He was not sure he wanted to hear, as Zusie had not wanted to know what the conclusion would be without the antidote.

Jasper looked sadly at him and sniffed again, slowly saying what the others had feared to think. "Without the antidote... they will eventually... die." He sniffed loudly again, buried his head into his hands and rocked back and forth weeping. The moaning coming from him was heart wrenching. He had come to love Lizbeth and, because of him, she would die. The realization of it had his little body shaking violently as he sobbed.

Aldwin gathered himself as the others looked gloomily from each other to Jasper, trying to keep their emotions under control. He leaned into Jasper and gently took his tiny hands away from his face.

"I do not intend for that to happen, little one," Aldwin said with confidence, now fully in control of himself. Jasper sniffed loudly and saw the truth in his eyes.

"It is not your fault. You did not mean to cause Lizbeth harm. Spare your tears and gather your strength. Lizbeth needs you to be strong; we need you to be strong." Jasper steadied his emotions with great difficulty and stopped crying. Aldwin stood up. His emotions were now fully under control as he looked at Zusie.

"It seems as if we have less time than I thought. Lizbeth is the strongest willed of any of us and I know she would not want to leave this world this way." Aldwin said. He paused for a moment while he quickly thought. "We will tell the villagers of Jasper's message and those who choose to come with us can. We will leave in two days' time," he looked down at Jasper and smiled, "to Jasper's home."

Relieved that they believed him, Jasper stood up as well. He was going home and his newfound friends were coming with him. He smiled hopefully at them and gathered his courage as he wiped the tears from his eyes with the back of his hand. Zusie and her daughters gathered themselves as well and stood tall with straight backs, knowing that there was no other alternative.

"I think I should come with you," Zusie said. She had been to the village before but only at night when the others were asleep. Her presence still bothered some of them and she thought it best not to make them uncomfortable in their own village. In a brief moment however, everything had changed. Her presence, when Aldwin presented Jasper's message, would lend validity to the situation.

"Yes, I think that would be wise," Aldwin said. He bent down and opened his hand in front of Jasper. Jasper went willingly onto his hand even though the thought of seeing Camcor and Bertrum had him shaking a little. However, Aldwin was right; he needed to be strong. Lizbeth needed him to be strong.

"Pack only what you think we will need," Zusie said, turning to her daughters.

"And what of the scrolls and statues?" they both asked. Zusie mulled their question over for a moment before she answered.

"Pack the statues and only the scrolls you think might help us on our way."

"But we cannot leave the knowledge of the ancients for Canvil! He would surely find a way to use it against us," Chrystalina cried.

"Calm yourself, daughter," Zusie said, raising her hand. "We will pack the rest in wooden crates lined with thin pieces of crystal and put them in the cave behind the waterfall. I am sure they will be safe there." Aldwin nodded in agreement as did the others.

"Let's be on our way. The sun has risen and the villagers are sure to be up doing the day's chores," Aldwin said. Zusie, Jasper and Aldwin left the Crystal Cave. Chrystalina and Saphina left as well, each mentally making a list of things to pack for the journey.

Aldwin, Zusie and Jasper quickly made their way down the steps. Morning had indeed risen and the sky was a lovely shade of blue. Birds chirped merrily from tree branches as other winged creatures fluttered in and around the undergrowth that grew thickly along either side of the stone stairs. The morning seemed like any other; only the hurried steps and the tense expressions of the three coming from the Crystal Cave seemed out of place on such a lovely, warm spring day. Once they reached the bottom stair, Aldwin placed Jasper in the pocket of his tunic.

"I think it best if you stay hidden for now," he said. Jasper did not have to ask why as the night's events were still fresh in his mind. He was only too happy to shelter himself from view in Aldwin's pocket. However, before he went in, he made sure his snout was curled.

CHAPTER 12

The Ultimatum

Aldwin and Zusie quickly made their way through the village, only stopping once they reached the village square and the summoning hut. The hut was taller than Zusie but not by much. It had a peaked thatched roof made of twigs and mud. It was held up by four sturdy six-inch posts set four feet apart. Crossbeams at the bottom and halfway up the sides held it all together. In the middle of the hut was the large misshapen stone that Lizbeth had mentioned to Jasper. It was two and half feet in diameter and only two inches thick. It sparkled and shimmered with a multitude of colours. Jasper remembered the first day he saw it and how curious he was to learn more about it.

Aldwin reached into the hut and released the rope that held the stone in place. He then grabbed a large mallet off a hook hanging from one of the roof beams. The villagers used the summoning rock to warn each other when something terrible was taking place. The loud distinctive ping of the mallet hitting the rock would ring loudly throughout the village and into the forest. One strike of the rock meant fire; two strikes meant a flood. Upon hearing it, the Elfkins would fill either a bucketful of water or dirt and run to the summoning hut for further directions.

The stone had rarely been struck over the last hundred years. However, just the week before Mirabella's oldest son, Willbyn, had a go at it. He laughed heartily as everyone rushed towards the summoning hut-- the water in their buckets slushed over the sides. He did not laugh for long however. Mirabella pulled him by the ear towards their hut while she apologized profusely to everyone they passed. Unfortunately Willbyn had not learned his lesson because two days later he hit the stone again. That time, his da paddled his backside with a switch in front of everyone in the village. The villagers dropped their buckets full of sand and clapped their hands in approval.

Willbyn had always been a mischievous underling. He often played pranks that usually involved the elders. Nevertheless the pranks were never bad enough to warrant a strapping. Striking the summoning stone however was very, very serious business.

The stone, as far as Aldwin could recall, had never been struck three times. Three gongs meant mass destruction to all living things. Aldwin was going to strike the stone three times. A group of underlings playing nearby stopped and looked quizzically at Zusie and Aldwin as they stood beside the hut. Benly, the eldest of the underlings who were playing ran straight to his home. Upon reaching it he started to yell for his ma.

The other underlings stood looking in awe at Zusie – they had heard of her but had not met her yet. The youngest of the group, a girl named Isla, boldly walked over to Aldwin and Zusie. She looked questioningly at Aldwin.

"Aldwin can I use the mallet?" Isla asked as she swatted at a swarm of pesty gnats that had started to swarm around her head of curly red hair. Zusie smiled at the question as the mallet was almost as tall as Isla was. Aldwin scowled at the pesty gnats and they instantly flew away. He then turned his look on Isla.

"No, Isla," Aldwin said sternly. "Did you not see what happened to Willbyn last week when he used the mallet?" Aldwin asked. Isla nodded then covered her bottom with her hands. The other underlings also nodded, remembering quite visibly the terror on Willbyn's face as his da punished him in front of the whole village.

"Well then, go and fetch your ma and da. The rest of you too," he said, looking at the rest of the underlings. "We have important matters to discuss." The underlings scattered in all directions, yelling for their mas and das as they sped away.

"Aldwin, while we wait for the villagers to gather, I will go and look in on Lizbeth." Zusie said. Aldwin nodded. He gripped the mallet tightly and swung it towards the stone. As Zusie walked towards Lizbeth's hut, the noise from the summoning stone echoed throughout the village. Aldwin struck the stone twice more. The sound carried past the villager's huts and deep into the forest summoning all of the Elfkins and forest creatures to it.

Just as Zusie entered Lizbeth's hut, she heard Camcor's voice bellowing from somewhere in the forest. He was cursing then yelled loud enough for everyone to hear. "If this is Mirabella's brat of an underling Willbyn playing a prank on us again, I will tan his hide so bad he won't be able to sit down for a full moon rotation and then some!"

Zusie shuddered. She disliked Camcor. Not just for what he and Bertrum had done to Jasper but also because he forbade his mate Alma to meet with her. She could hear Bertrum urging Camcor on. She sighed heavily and shook her head. Bertrum and Camcor's rudeness was the least of their problems; there were more important things to worry about. The door clicked shut as Zusie leaned her back against it. She waited a moment while her eyes adjusted to the dim light in the room. Lizbeth's hut was tall and Zusie did not have to bend down to get through the door or to walk freely around the room. She was thankful for that as she looked around.

Nothing, she noticed, had changed since her last visit. Lizbeth liked her hut to be like her -- efficient. She had only what she needed to get through the day and nothing more. The only thing she did allow extra in the room was a bouquet of flowers. She usually had a bouquet of them sitting in pot on the table by the window. She liked when the breeze came through the open window and carried the scent of the flowers around her hut. Zusie looked over at the table – it was devoid of flowers. Frowning, Zusie looked over at Lizbeth.

Lizbeth was resting in a deep sleep, just as Aldwin had said. She looked comfortable; Marla was taking good care of her. As she was thinking of her, as if like magic, Marla walked out of the storage room carrying a rather large basket of brightly coloured bimble yarn. Shocked to see Zusie standing there, Marla dropped the basket onto the floor. The bimble yarn rolled out of it in every direction.

"Oh my," Marla said then added abruptly, "I wasn't expecting you." Zusie raised an eyebrow. Marla's face turned a crimson red from embarrassment. Not knowing what else to say she quickly bent down and started to pick up the balls of yarn.

Zusie walked over to the rocking chair, picked up the hook that had also fallen out of the basket and walked over to Marla. As she put the hook in the basket she smiled kindly at Marla. Before Marla could say thank you, Zusie bent down, picked up a ball of yarn, and put it in the basket as well.

"Y…y…you don't have to do that," Marla stammered as she watched Zusie bend over and pick up another ball of yarn.

"The work will go faster if we do it together," Zusie said as she put the ball in the basket. Getting on all fours, Zusie crawled after a ball of yarn that rolled under the table by Lizbeth's cot. Marla looked at her stunned into shock. She had heard great things about Zusie from Lizbeth, but she never thought she would be this kind or friendly.

Marla shook her head then smiled broadly as she heard Zusie gleefully say, "Gotcha." A ball of yarn had rolled under Lizbeth's cot. Together they picked up the rest of the yarn. When they were done Marla placed the basket on the floor on the other side of the rocking chair. She turned to say thank you but then stopped and looked sadly at Zusie. She was sitting in the chair beside Lizbeth's cot holding Lizbeth's left hand gently between hers.

"She's been sleeping soundly for several hours now," Marla said, as she walked over to the cot and sat on the edge of it. She looked fondly at Lizbeth, "Aldwin's soothe ease seems to be working." Zusie smiled and nodded. She did not want to frighten Marla by telling her that it was not going to be enough.

"Why don't you take a break?" Zusie said instead. "I am sure you must be weary from the night's vigil."

"Oh no…it is alright…Rangous had been here for several hours." Marla stopped talking and blushed. She looked up tentatively at Zusie who looked at her curiously and then smiled. "He, he was concerned about Lizbeth and came to see if there was anything he could do to help. Seeing that Aldwin was not here, he asked if he could stay. I, I thought that it was a good idea, considering what happened yesterday." Marla stammered apologetically, unsure of what Zusie's reaction would be upon hearing that she had been alone with Rangous unsupervised. Zusie leaned over and patted Marla's hand.

"It's alright Marla," she said.

As Zusie picked up Lizbeth's hand again, Marla calmed herself. She had always enjoyed Rangous' company, but the night before they seemed to have grown closer. She had stammered because she was embarrassed and did not want Zusie to think that anything had gone on between the two of them while Lizbeth slept. It was not in the Elfkin way for a male and female of the mating age to be alone together unless one or both had declared their intent. Rangous, Marla, Septer, Aldwin and several of the other villagers were in their mating years. In Elfkin terms, that was fifty summers or older. When Aldwin turned fifty, he had opted not to take a mate. Being alone with Aldwin, as Marla often was, was acceptable. She was his apprentice, so neither had to present their intentions for each other to the elders.

Marla had not thought of being alone with Rangous without an elder present when he asked her if he could stay. She was thankful for the company, as the night's events had shaken her. She did not feel guilty about it until Zusie unexpectedly showed up. Zusie had a way of making her feel at ease one moment and then on her guard the next.

"He left about an hour ago. We heard Camcor yelling up and down the village for him. Rangous left to see what he wanted and has not returned." Zusie stopped herself from saying something ill about Camcor.

"If you don't need to rest, could you do me a favor?" Zusie said.

"Of course, Zusie," Marla said.

"Lizbeth loves fresh flowers. Would you go and pick enough to fill a large pot?"

They both looked over to the open shelves where Lizbeth kept her pots. Zusie, seeing a large one on the second shelf, pointed. "See that one there? I think that will do nicely." It was quite a large pot; Marla recognized it as the one that Lizbeth sometimes used to dye the bimble yarn in when she didn't want to go to the wheel house. She turned to Zusie.

"They are still harvesting the nectar from the spring flowers. It will take many flowers to fill that pot."

Zusie stopped herself from saying 'in two days' time it will not matter.' Instead, she said, "Yes, yes you are quite right. Why don't you pick only the harvested flowers then and mix them with some greens like little ferns and bunroos? I want the hut to smell lovely when Lizbeth wakes." Marla smiled at the kind gesture. Before leaving the hut, she grabbed a basket out of the storeroom to carry the flowers in, as the stone pot would be too heavy.

"There's tea in the pot and I just finished making spicy scones if you are hungry," Marla said as she opened the door.

"Thank you, Marla. That is very kind of you. The scones smell wonderful," Zusie sad then smiled. Marla smiled brightly in return at the compliment and closed the door behind her.

The first thing Marla noticed as she stood on Lizbeth's doorstep was that the village was abuzz with commotion. Villagers were coming from all sides, talking agitatedly with each other. Marla looked over at a crowd standing around Aldwin who had the mallet in his hand. Forgetting the request from Zusie, Marla dropped the basket on the bench by the door and quickly walked towards the crowd, passing Camcor and the group of villagers who had been working with him as they slowly made their way towards the center of village. She noticed as she went by that their baskets were half-full of the early mushrooms that grew in patches near the river. She also noticed that Rangous was not with them.

She had been in the storeroom getting the yarn when she came out to see who had used the mallet. Seeing Zusie standing before her, she had completely forgotten about the summons.

An ominous feeling came over her as she walked closer to the crowd. Things were not right; things were not right at all. She had been working with Aldwin long enough to recognize the subtle signs when he was upset or worried. Although his outward composure was calm, she knew better; something terrible happened or was about to. She looked nervously around for Rangous and sighed when she saw him coming from the other side of the village with Bauthal and a large group of forest creatures.

Aldwin saw Marla walking towards the crowd that was quickly spreading out in a large half circle in front of him. The look he gave her was one of concern, but he quickly masked it because Camcor and Bertrum had made it to the outer edge of the circle and looked fit to be tied. Aldwin looked around the circle for the other elders. Markhum was standing next to Farringdum and Gradum. Their families stood next to them. Tad was standing in the entrance to his hut. He was the only elder who had not taken a mate and seemed to enjoy living his existence alone.

"What in the name of Zenrah is going on over here?" Camcor bellowed but stopped abruptly when he saw Aldwin standing on a side beam of the summoning hut. Aldwin wanted the villagers to see that it was he that summoned them and not one of the underlings.

Camcor and Bertrum looked scathingly at Aldwin. Camcor had been itching for a good fight ever since Jasper escaped and Monto never reported in. Oh well, he thought, the uppity Aldwin would do just as well. He started walking through the crowd leaving his grandda to follow or not. Bertrum chose not to follow and walked over to the other elders instead. The crowd in front of Aldwin had grown thick in numbers and Camcor recklessly pushed his way through. In his hurried steps to confront Aldwin he nearly knocked Old Barty off his cane.

The sack that Old Barty was holding over his right shoulder dropped to the ground with a dull thud as he tried to get his footing. The villagers standing nearby gasped as Old Barty stumbled backwards. He would have fallen to the ground if Rangous had not come through the crowd and steadied him. Old Barty thanked Rangous and asked him to pick up the sack and his cane. As Rangous handed the sack to Barty he noticed that something was wriggling around inside it. He was about to ask what was in the sack when Old Barty winked at him. Rangous handed Old Barty his cane and the sack but said nothing about its contents.

Without apologizing, Camcor continued to shove his way through the crowd. He only stopped when he was several feet from Aldwin. Camcor looked at him with hatred in his eyes. Why Camcor was so ornery no one really knew; he had been like that for as long as anyone could remember.

Camcor was short for a male Elfkin and when he was younger it bothered him to no end; especially when younger underlings like Rangous and Septer quickly grew taller than him. Camcor's anger boiled and churned inside of him and he started to bully Elfkins smaller than he. As he grew older, he became meaner and no longer bullied just the smaller ones. Most of the villagers kept clear of him and only spoke with him when necessary. They felt sorry for his mate and their three underlings, as he was just as unkind to them. However, as long as he didn't actually physically hurt anyone, there was nothing anyone could do.

Seeing the rage in Camcor's face, Rangous, Septer, Bauthal and Marla made their way out of the crowd to stand with Aldwin, just as some of Camcor's followers from the night before came forward to stand behind him. Aldwin jumped down from the summoning hut and stood with his friends. The two groups stood facing each other several feet apart. The rest of the villagers took several steps back, prodding their underlings behind them. It was very rare that a fight broke out in the village; in fact, no one could remember when it had happened last.

Aldwin had seen the subtle shift in attitudes with some of the younger villagers ever since the spring equinox celebration. He could not put his feeling into words, so he sat back and watched. He had an uneasy feeling that something was going to happen and when it did, lines would be drawn and sides would be taken, forever changing the humble, harmonious life in the village.

The crowd of villagers standing behind Camcor, about a hundred and fifty in all, started to buzz with heated conversations while the rest of the villagers who had not picked a side looked worriedly at the two groups. Aldwin was not surprised. The whole village by now had probably heard about the hunt for Jasper. He was sure that Camcor and Bertrum had tried to sway most of the villagers to their side. It looked to Aldwin that many of them had not picked one just yet.

Aldwin looked at Bauthal who stared at Camcor and the crowd. Aldwin had wondered where he had gone; Bauthal had quickly said goodbye when they had entered the village before disappearing into the woods. Aldwin realized that Bauthal must have spread word to the forest creatures that trouble was brewing. Aldwin himself had briefly gone to Lizbeth's hut but, seeing Rangous there, he went to his own hut instead. Marla had suggested that he get rest, but sleep eluded him as he pored over his own scrolls for an herbal concoction that would bring Lizbeth back to them.

The crowd around Camcor grew restless. Their grumblings became louder and angrier. Jasper shivered with fright in Aldwin's pocket.

"Courage, little one," Aldwin whispered. Jasper settled back down. "Calm down, everyone, calm down," Aldwin said, raising his voice. Gradually the crowd grew quiet. "We will wait a few more minutes before I tell you why I summoned you here today," he said, clearly and loud enough so that everyone could hear him.

"Wait for what?" Camcor asked rudely.

"For everyone else," Aldwin said as he stared at Camcor. His dislike for Camcor bubbled under the surface. "The words I am about to speak must be heard by everyone and, as you can see, there are still others coming out of the woods." Everyone turned to see that there indeed were still villagers hurriedly making their way to the center of the village.

Back in Lizbeth's hut, Zusie sat on the chair beside the sleeping cot, still holding Lizbeth's left hand in hers. She looked down at her friend and sighed heavily. No Elfkin was like Lizbeth. Her intelligence, kindness and fortitude set her apart from the others. She was one of a kind. If she were to leave them, still so young, it would be a solemn day. She leaned over, kissed Lizbeth on her forehead, and brushed the tendrils of curly hair from her face.

"Hold on, Lizbeth. You must hold on. Help is on the way," she said earnestly. Lizbeth did not move; Zusie wondered if she dreamed or if there was just an empty void.

Putting her hand back down to rest on the covers, Zusie picked up the bowl from the table and walked over to the fireplace. She filled it with soothe ease and walked back to the bed. Placing the bowl on the table, she picked up the cloth and dipped it into the warm water. She wrung it out, placed it on Lizbeth's forehead, and sat back down in the chair. The aroma was wonderful. Zusie could detect most of the herbs that Aldwin had used to make it and she breathed in deeply. She smiled as the aroma calmed her nerves. Aldwin was a talented healer, she thought to herself. It must have been driving him mad that he did not have a cure for Lizbeth.

"If you can hear me, my dear friend, all will be well. Just hold on," Zusie said lovingly as she picked up Lizbeth's hand again and pressed it gently between hers. Zusie reluctantly stood. She did not want to leave Lizbeth's side but knew that it was time to talk with the villagers. She was not looking forward to it. There would be resistance; that she was sure of. However there was no choice. They would have to leave. To survive and be free, they would have to leave the all they knew behind.

Zusie looked at the crowd that gathered around Aldwin. Most of them stood several paces away from Camcor and a group of villagers who stood directly behind him. They were looking angrily at Aldwin and his much smaller band of supporters. Zusie noticed that a large group of forest creatures stood off to the side. She shook her head in dismay; life was never going to be the same again, she thought to herself.

"Zusie, knower of all things," she sighed loudly and shook her head. "What a bunch of crock. If I had been the knower of all things, surely I would have seen this coming." She stepped onto the front stoop and saw the basket that Marla had left on the bench. She picked it up placing the handle of it over her arm. Quietly, she closed the door behind her and made her way to the circle.

The crowd parted as Zusie slowly walked towards Aldwin. Standing taller than all of them, she looked quite regal with her solid stature and confident stride. She exuded authority that garnered respect. As she passed, some of the villagers bowed their heads in greeting and Zusie returned the gesture with a slight smile. Others watched in awe as she went by, talking in whispers behind their hands about how lovely she was with her long flowing hair and emerald green dress.

Camcor faltered as he heard whispering behind him and turned to see Zusie walking purposely towards him. He caught his breath. She was taller than he imagined. As she neared, he had no choice but to look up. He thought she was lovely, lovelier in fact than anything or anyone he had ever seen before. His breath caught in his throat as she walked by and sternly looked down at him. His cheeks reddened with embarrassment, realizing that she had found out about his attempt to capture Jasper. When she got to Aldwin, she stopped and looked at him.

"Is he safe?" she asked as she quickly looked down at Aldwin's pocket. Aldwin nodded. She then smiled fondly at Bauthal, Rangous, Septer and Marla. They were very brave to stand with Aldwin when they were so outnumbered. She was thankful for it and bowed to them in greeting. They bowed to her in return.

They moved aside to allow her to stand by Aldwin. Seeing the position she took, the crowd standing behind Camcor dispersed, leaving only a handful standing with him. Camcor, noticing, glared after them with an evil eye, mentally remembering who they were; he would confront them about it later. He turned back to and noticed that Aldwin and his followers had amused looks on their faces. His face reddened again, only it was not from embarrassment but with hatred for them all. However, his apparent ill feeling towards them did not seem to bother them one bit.

Zusie, still holding the basket over her arm, handed it to Marla. Without comment, Marla took it, knowing that Zusie expected her to follow through with her request. Before Marla could take a step to leave, Rangous grabbed her hand and squeezed it gently.

"I will come for you," he whispered. Marla smiled at him warmly before she left. He turned back to see that his friends were looking at him with amused smiles on their faces.

"What?" Rangous said.

"Oh nothing," Septer said, barely keeping his smile in check.

"Oh do shut up," Rangous said.

"Again I said nothing here," Septer said his smile broadened. As Rangous stood beside Septer he cautiously looked at Aldwin. Aldwin nodded his head in approval. Rangous smiled boyishly and sighed in relief than looked out over the crowd.

The villagers were still whispering about having Zusie among them. Aldwin raised his hands again to quiet them. Zusie took a step forward.

"My fellow villagers," she said clearly. Instantly all eyes were on her as she bowed her head in respect. She then turned to the forest creatures standing on the other side of the main crowd. "And to you the noble creatures of the Greenwood Forest, thank you for joining us." She bowed to them as well, squelching any question as to whether or not Zusie had respect for the forest creatures. Camcor huffed indignantly. His supporters shuffled their feet nervously. One stern look from him, however, had them standing still again. Ignoring Camcor, Zusie spoke again.

"I have come to the village today to speak with you about a serious matter, but first I would like to set something straight." The crowd began to murmur. Camcor looked at Zusie suspiciously as she held her hand in front of Aldwin's pocket. "Come, little one," she said soothingly. Jasper popped his head out of the pocket. The murmuring in the crowd grew louder. Upon seeing Jasper, Camcor took a menacing step forward but stopped suddenly as Rangous and Septer took a step forward as well. The look on their faces showed that, if he were to try anything, they would not be above plummeting him with the summoning mallet. Camcor took a step back.

"What is he doing back here? We ran him out of the village last night," Camcor shouted angrily and pointed his finger at Jasper who was now sitting in Zusie's hand. She faced the crowd again. "He's nothing but a bad omen!" Camcor shouted. "Send him back where he came from." He then turned to the crowd. "He's the reason Lizbeth is sick." The crowd started to murmur with worry. "Before you know it," Camcor said, pointing at all the mas who held their underlings and stopped at Mirabella, who held the youngest of them, "we will all be sick and knocking at death's door, just like Lizbeth!" The crowd started yelling. The men stepped in front of their mates and underlings and started to raise their fists in anger.

"Nonsense," Zusie bellowed. The crowd instantly quieted as her voice rang throughout the village and into the forest. Looking past Camcor, she said, in a more dignified voice, "Jasper is a kind, wonderful soul." She held Jasper up so that the crowd could see him. "Jasper is of the noble Hummingmoth messengers and has brought a message to us from his homeland." The crowd stirred restlessly with her words.

"His homeland, his homeland!" Camcor yelled. "What is this you speak of? Everyone knows there is no life beyond this valley. We are all that there is."

"No," Zusie said, cutting Camcor off. "We are not all that there is. There is life." She took a step forward, beseeching the crowd to listen to her words. "There is life beyond the mountains to the south." Without looking down at Jasper, she said in dismay, "and... to the north as well."

The villagers, no longer looking to Camcor for direction, started yelling at Zusie, not in anger but in disbelief. Jasper shook in fright as he sat in her hand. His snout instinctively unfurled. He made ready to fly away but Zusie stopped him with a stern look. Camcor's voice rose above all.

"Do you believe this rubbish, these lies...these, these tellers of the untruth?" He looked triumphantly at Aldwin and the others as the crowd started to come forward, yelling angrily and waving their fists.

Before Aldwin and the others could think about what to do the forest creatures that had been quietly standing on the outskirts of the crowd moved quickly. They put themselves between the angry mob and Jasper. The villagers stopped and stared in disbelief -- They had always lived in harmony with the forest creatures. Now however, the creatures faced them growling lowly and baring their teeth.

Camcor, remembering how he felt when Bauthal had growled at him the night before, took a step back then turned abruptly when he heard a collective gasp behind him. Old Barty was making his way through the crowd. The villagers cried for him to stop. Coming up to Camcor, Old Barty dropped the sack he was holding at Camcor's feet.

"Your spy," was all he said. Barty raised his walking stick as if he were going to strike Camcor with it. Camcor raised his arms to cover his head but Old Barty just chuckled and walked away.

Camcor bent over and opened the sack. To his surprise, Monto flew out and almost hit him square in the face. Camcor straightened and looked incredulously at Old Barty's back as he walked towards the forest creatures. They parted, nodding to him in greeting. Old Barty walked past Zusie and winked at Jasper.

"Sorry men, but I don't walk as quickly as I use to," Old Barty said. Aldwin and the others smiled at him and stepped aside so that Old Barty could stand between them.

Jasper, seeing Old Barty's bravado, stood up straight on Zusie's hand. He looked at the villagers with courage. If Old Barty was not afraid, then neither would he be. Monto flew around Camcor's head until Camcor swatted at him and told him to find a place to land. Monto looked crossly at Camcor as he settled himself on Camcor's shoulder.

Aldwin made his way to the line of forest creatures, stood in front of them, and looked out over the crowd of villagers.

"Now that we have that settled, for those of you who do not want to listen to the message that Jasper has brought to us with great peril to himself…you can go back to your huts." The crowd murmured again. "But you must know this before you go." The crowd quickly became quiet again. "The truth as we know it does not exist. There is life beyond the Greenwood Forest. Jasper and Zusie are proof of this. If you choose not to believe, then so be it. However," he stopped to make sure he had everyone's attention, "there is an evil lord who lives in the lands past Mount Aspentonia to the north. He is making his way here and will destroy all that he touches. Our valley will be no more." Many of the villagers gasped and cried out, but Aldwin continued.

"This valley is no longer safe for us. We," Aldwin said, sweeping his hand towards those standing behind him, "are leaving this valley in two days' time." The villagers gasped again and started to murmur. Aldwin held up his hand, they quieted. "We will be traveling to the land beyond the Great Alps to the south and those of you that would like to join us are welcome to." A murmur started in the crowd again. "But know this," Aldwin said, raising his voice and looking straight at Camcor, "if you harbor any doubt as to the truth of this message or give us any trouble, we will leave you behind…and you can deal with the evil Lord and his army of Venom Horde and demon fireflies on your own."

"I don't believe this!" Camcor yelled, as the others grew restless around him. "You are all a bunch of fools," he said angrily as he looked straight at Jasper. "And he is a plague upon this village," Camcor said as he raised his voice and pointed at Jasper. "He should have been squashed like the useless pathetic bug that he is!"

Hearing Camcor's disdain for Jasper, Monto looked forlornly at Camcor, wondering if he felt that way about all bugs. Monto did not have long to wait for proof; Camcor swatted him off his shoulder. Monto fell to the ground with a heavy thud. "But Camcor," Monto whimpered as he looked up at him, "I thought…" Camcor interrupted him.

"There are no buts. If you had done your job last night, he would have been dead and none of this would be happening. You are as useless as he is." Camcor grabbed Alma's arm and pulled her towards their hut. She has stood quietly beside him the whole time, but everyone could see the worry on her face. She went unwillingly with him to her hut where Bertrum stood looking with satisfaction at Zusie and Aldwin. Monto, not able to look at the others, whimpered as he flew dejectedly off towards the forest.

Several villagers called after Camcor as he passed them, beseeching him to listen to reason, but he refused. All but the oldest of his underlings followed him; Benly looked pointedly at Jasper and saw the truth in his eyes. "Benly," Camcor bellowed as he ushered the rest of his family into the hut. Benly hesitated until Camcor bellowed for him again, then he ran to join his family.

Several of the other villagers left as well. Zusie looked at them anxiously as they dragged their underlings with them. By refusing to join them they were sealing their fate: death by the hand of Lord Canvil.

For those who remained, Aldwin motioned for them to come closer. Before they could leave the village there was work to do. Zusie looked towards Lizbeth's hut and saw that Marla had opened the window and placed a large pot of flowers on the table. She half listened as Aldwin started to tell the villagers of Jasper's message and all that he had endured before he came to their village. She looked from Lizbeth's hut to the villagers in front of her. It was going to be a daunting undertaking and not without peril, but it was the only choice they had.

She watched the villagers as they listened intently to Aldwin's words. She noticed as the expressions on their faces changed from fear, to belief, to resolve. This was a brave lot of Elfkins. They were to leave all they knew behind and embrace an unknown future to avoid slavery or death. She wondered if they would still be this brave once they reached the edge of the forest.

After listening to Aldwin's evacuation plans and agreeing to the specific tasks they were given, they walked over to Zusie and Jasper. Each of them shook Jasper's hand and the ma and underlings bowed to him in thanks for bringing them the message. Humbled by the reverence of their response to him, Jasper shyly said you're welcome. After the last family left, Jasper sighed heavily. Zusie looked down at him and smiled; he looked up at her and returned her smile. At the same time they both looked over at Lizbeth's hut and wondered the same thing. Did Lizbeth have enough resolve to survive the journey through the Greenwood Forest, the Outer Bound Meadow and beyond to the unknown? They both desperately hoped that she did.

CHAPTER 13

The Outer Bound Meadow

Rangous and Marla stood hand in hand at the very edge of the Greenwood Forest, the farthest either of them had ever been from the village. The farthest any of them had ever been, other than Willham and Horman. However, no one was sure if either of them had actually made it out of the forest, let alone the valley.

The caravan of Elfkins and forest creatures had arrived just before the sun set. They made camp in the protection of the forest a hundred feet back from where Rangous and Marla stood, keeping balance on an outcropping of rocks.

Before Rangous had bade Marla goodnight he had asked her if she wanted to join him in the morning to watch the sun rise over the meadow. She had agreed eagerly and they rose before everyone else had and quietly made their way to edge of the forest. As the sun bathed the meadow with light, Marla cooed breathlessly.

"Oh, it's lovely," she exclaimed as life in the meadow awoke to greet the new day. Rangous, thinking the same thing squeezed her hand softly.

As far as they could see, the meadow in varying shades of green and yellow stretched out before them. It rippled like water with the morning breeze. In some places, they could see patches of multicoloured flowers and were surprised that they could put a name to many of them. The grass in the meadow had been taller than they expected. If there were standing on the ground and not on the rocks, they would not have been able to see over it.

Marla looked up at Rangous, her face bright with a smile. The beauty of her smile and the shine of delight in her eyes had him catching his breath. He took her into his arms and embraced her warmly. She wrapped her arms around him in turn and laid her head on his chest. He had made known his intentions for Marla to the elders the day they heard Jasper's message. The elders rarely refused a union; it was more tradition than asking for permission. The only one of them who had voiced his concerns was Bertrum. However since he was not traveling with them his permission did not matter Marla and Rangous had agreed to postpone the three-day celebration of their union until they were safe.

They now looked out onto the meadow, both of them lost in their own thoughts. Rangous' thoughts were of the journey. Time had moved quickly over the last three weeks. They left in the two days that Aldwin had allotted. It was hard to leave the others behind who chose not to believe, especially the underlings who were too young to decide for themselves. The villagers who believed in Jasper's message quickly packed up their huts, only bringing with them what they could carry in sacks that had thick shoulder straps and belts they tied around their waists. Those who could took turns carrying them.

Six trolleys held food stores, blankets, candles and most of Aldwin's medicine. The Elfkins constructed several two-wheeled wooden trolleys that carried wood after it was gathered from the forest floor into six larger trolleys. They added more planks to increase the length and added two extra wheels so that they now sat on four wheels. They added two long poles to the front with three handles along each side so that six villagers could help pull them. They also added three pole-like handles along the sides so that other villagers could step in and help push the trolleys over tree roots and through mud. They made the sides larger as well to stop their goods from tumbling out.

They used thick blankets as tarps to keep the provisions dry. They tied the tarps to the sides of the trolleys with straps made from bimble yarn. The carpenters made a smaller trolley for Lizbeth. The extra blankets Lizbeth had made over the winter months came in handy. The Elfkins used them on the bottom of her trolley as a sleeping mat. The sides on this trolley were much larger than the others. It had five-foot poles strapped in place along the sides and front. Blankets were sewn together to make a canopy that, once in place, could either be rolled up to let fresh air in or tied down to keep the rain out. The trolley was big enough for two to travel in comfortably with room to spare for the scrolls, the statues and a book that they had found in Lizbeth's hut when they packed up her belongings.

The book intrigued everyone, especially Zusie, Aldwin and Chrystalina. It was a thorough account of life in the Greenwood Forest that included the Elfkins, Zusie and her daughters and the forest creatures. Lizbeth had also accounted for all of the plant life. There were detailed descriptions of what they looked like and what benefit, if any, they provided to the everyday survival. Zusie asked Chrystalina and Marla to continue with the book, gathering as much information as they could along their journey to Whipple Wash Valley; they agreed wholeheartedly.

As in the village, everyone had to help if they were to make it through the forest; even Old Barty. Aldwin had given him a special task. He was to look after Lizbeth. The warm soothe ease compresses were of no use on the trail, so each night Aldwin made up a soothe ease tea with extra nutrients from strained vegetables that could be fed to Lizbeth one spoonful at a time. If Lizbeth were to survive the trip, she would need nourishment. Every night, Zusie or Marla tended to Lizbeth; changing her undergarments, washing and feeding her. Old Barty used this time to stretch his legs and talk with the others.

The journey had started to take its toll on the elders and younger underlings. Their day's routine had not faltered from one day to the next. At first light, everyone rose, packed up their sleeping gear, ate quickly and was on their way. They ate at the midday break while they walked and did not stop walking until the sun was ready to set. They quickly made camp while there was still light, ate their evening meal and went to sleep. They had no idea if Lord Canvil was already on his way, so the greater the distance they put between themselves and Mount Aspentonia, the better their chance of escaping.

It was hard for the villagers to learn that someone would want to harm them. They had always lived in harmony. They quickly realized however that, once they traveled outside of the forest this may not necessarily be the case. After all, none of them really knew for sure what lay beyond the forest or of the creatures, if any, that lived in the meadow.

Two days into the journey, Rangous and Septer spoke with Zusie and Aldwin about arming themselves. They felt that fishing poles and knives were not going to be enough protection. Together they asked Chrystalina if she had read about anything in the scrolls that might help to protect them.

Chrystalina had packed several scrolls that showed how to make bows and arrows, spears and swords. They did not have the means to make the swords, but they could make the other weapons. Now, every Elfkin over the age of fifteen summers who was not carrying a sack carried a quiver of arrows and a bow on their back. Each had a knife strapped into the belt at their waist. They also made several long spears; anyone carrying a sack carried one, which they also used as a walking stick.

Each day, Septer and Rangous took a group of the Elfkins ahead of the caravan. They practiced shooting arrows at old tree stumps until the caravan caught up to them. Many of the villagers picked up the knack of shooting the arrows quickly, but everyone was surprised to see that Saphina had an innate ability for it and she no longer practiced with the rest of them.

The villagers, Rangous mused as he continued to hold Marla, had gradually become use to seeing Zusie and her daughters not only walking among them but doing their share of the work as well. They had opted to wear the same garb as the rest of the women – long tunics and thin-legged pants. They too carried knives in their belts. Saphina was the only one out of the three that carried a bow and quiver of arrows.

The departure, Rangous thought, had been especially hard on them. Zusie, who felt responsible for the villagers, was deeply saddened at how many did not believe and chose to stay behind. She resigned to the fact, after visiting each of their homes pleading with them to change their minds, that there was nothing else she could do for them.

Chrystalina was quite upset at having to leave most of the scrolls behind. The remaining scrolls were hid behind the waterfall in crystal-lined wooden boxes as Zusie had suggested. Rangous did not worry about them; it was Saphina who he wondered about. Most days she kept to herself and only joined the caravan during the evening meals. The rest of the time, she was off with Jasper, scouting the way ahead. Rangous smiled at the thought that Jasper rarely left her side and was often seen perched on her right shoulder, talking quietly in her ear. Rangous and Marla speculated at the things Jasper was saying to her. One night they asked Jasper what he was telling Saphina. Jasper however did not answer them; instead, he shrugged his shoulders and flew away.

Saphina suggested that he keep quiet about the things he told her of his homeland and what they could expect from Canvil and his Venom Horde. She worried that the information would confuse the Elfkins. The things he told her seemed so fantastical. If she did not know better Saphina would have thought Jasper had made it all up.

As they continued to stand on the outcropping of rocks, Marla's thoughts had been of the journey as well. As Aldwin had predicted, she stepped into a leadership role naturally. She taught the Elfkin women how to properly dress wounds, search for medicinal plants and how to make several different kinds of healing teas and salves from those plants. Her thoughts had gradually turned to her blooming love for Rangous.

Odd, she thought, how they had skirted around their attraction to each other for years. Odder still was that it took a tragedy like Lizbeth's illness and Jasper's message to finally bring them together. Marla sighed as she thought of Rangous being her mate. He was a strong, hard worker and readily jumped in when Zusie and Aldwin asked him to teach the others how to arm themselves and fend off attackers.

The other villagers began to rely on his knowledge of the forest with each passing day. Rangous and Septer had become capable leaders in the face of adversity. Marla blushed at her next thought -- that one day he would make a good, kind and capable da to their underlings as well. She sighed and tightened her arms around him. He in turn tightened his arms around her and kissed the top of her head.

Unnoticed behind them, Septer stood looking at the serene scene before him. For years, Septer had witnessed how Rangous looked at Marla when he thought no one was watching. Septer had teased Rangous; just two days before Lizbeth fell ill, that if he did not declare his intentions for Marla, he would do so and steal her away from him. Rangous laughed, as he had not taken Septer's words seriously. They often talked while fishing about whom they would choose when the time came to mate. For Rangous, it had always been Marla and no other.

For Septer, he always said that there were too many to choose from and that he was too much Elfkin for just one woman. Deep inside, however, he knew that he would never pick a woman from the village. For as long as he could remember, something nagged at him that if he wanted a mate, he would have to travel outside the Greenwood Forest. No one ever traveled outside of the village though, so Septer had resigned himself to live out his days without a mate. Now, as he too looked out at the meadow, he began to hope that perhaps his mate was out there waiting for him.

Cheered by the thought, he walked up to Rangous and Marla, climbed up on the next rock and smiled broadly.

"It's a glorious morning," he said and clapped Rangous heartily on the shoulder. The force of it almost knocked the three of them off the rocks, but they steadied themselves quickly. "With all that has happened, I have not taken the time to say that it's good to see that you two are finally together," Rangous and Marla smiled at him as they held hands. "You will be good for him, you know," he said to Marla. Playfully, he added as he looked out over the meadow, "You know… he has been mooning over you since we were underlings."

"Septer," Rangous said, feigning indignation, "you weren't supposed to tell her that!"

"I've known for some time," Marla said then smiled broadly." I've just been waiting for him to get up the nerve to ask." Rangous looked at her aghast which made Septer and Marla laugh.

"Come, it is time to wake the others," Septer said enthusiastically as he jumped off the rock. Marla and Rangous did not hesitate and jumped off the rocks after Septer. They were as excited as Septer was to get on with the next leg of their journey.

None of them saw the creature hiding in the tall grass, watching them with keen interest as they entered the woods.

An hour later Zusie stood with her daughters, Aldwin, Rangous, Septer, Bauthal and Jasper at the edge of the meadow. Everyone but Zusie and Jasper needed to stand on a rock to see over the meadow.

"Has there been any movement or show of life?" Zusie asked, turning to Septer. Saphina however answered the question.

"Jasper, Septer and I sat up in the trees all night watching and saw nothing moving or flying overhead other than the occasional bug."

"It doesn't mean that nothing more menacing is out there," Aldwin said.

"I flew out over the grass with a couple of the black winged parapeets, Knos and Alf, and saw no movement," Jasper said as he sat on Saphina's shoulder. "The grass is very tall and thick, however..." Jasper stopped talking, as he was not sure what else to say.

``Hmmm," Zusie said as she continued to look out over the meadow, "and there are no pathways into the meadow?"

"No" Aldwin said. Seeing Zusie's expectant look, he continued, "While the other villagers packed camp, Septer, Rangous, Bauthal and Saphina went in pairs...."

"Ah hum," Jasper interrupted.

"And Jasper," Aldwin corrected himself. "They went in either direction looking for signs of something or someone coming out of the meadow. There
were no signs."

"Would we not have seen some sign of creatures living in the meadow after all these years?" Chrystalina asked no one in particular as she half slipped, half jumped off the rock she was standing on.

"Not necessarily," Saphina said more sharply than she meant to as she looked down at her sister. "Perhaps," she said more calmly, "they have been under the same assumption as we have."

Seeing Chrystalina's puzzled look, Saphina sighed heavily. "We thought we were all that there was. The forest provided all that we needed, so there was no need to venture out of it. Perhaps it is the same for anything or anyone living in the meadow. It provides all that they need, so there was no need to venture into the forest." The others nodded in agreement.

"Well, I suppose we should just enter it and hope for the best," Chrystalina said cheerily.

"I think we can do a little better than that, Chrystalina," Saphina said sharply again, but meaning it this time. Turning to her mother and Aldwin, she said, "Mother, Septer and I talked at length last night about what the best course of action would be. We think it is best to send armed scouts ahead with several winged creatures. If the scouts find trouble, the winged creatures can fly back to warn the others."

"There'll be no need for that," the creature who had been hiding in the grass said with a thick accent.

All stood stunned as they looked in the direction where the thickly accented voice came from. Not eight feet from them, an enormous black snake reared its head just above the grass. However, it was not the snake that spoke; it was a small being no more than twelve inches tall. He sat in a wooden box strapped to the back of the snake just behind its head. The being was dressed in dark, leathery looking pants and a vest. His bright red hair was short and lay flat against his head. His face was round and tanned, his nose small, and he had a neatly trimmed beard. He did not look much different from an Elfkin. However, he did have the most unusual green eyes. His left hand held onto reins that went loosely around the snake's mouth and his right hand unconsciously held onto the hilt of a knife.

"I be Zeander," he said. He then whispered to the snake that immediately reared up into the air, bringing Zeander to the same height as Zusie. He held out his hand in greeting as the snake made its way slowly towards her.

Several things happened in rapid succession. Septer and Rangous quickly jumped off the rocks and stood in front of Zusie, their bows cocked with arrows, shielding her from the snake and its little rider. Septer pointed his arrow at the snake, Rangous at Zeander. Chrystalina cried out in fright and hid behind the rock her sister was standing on. Saphina held an arrow in her bow as well, but she was not looking at the snake or the rider. She was slowly looking around for more of them. Jasper unfurled his snout and flew up in the air, hovering above Saphina's head his little hands balled into fists. Aldwin, carrying no weapon, stood in front of the rock that Saphina was standing on.

Zeander dropped his hand and whispered to the snake again. The snake backed away slowly from Zusie.

"I mean ya no harm," Zeander said. Slowly he raised both his hands in the air; palms facing forward.

Zusie looked into his green eyes for a moment. "Saphina, anything," Zusie called over her shoulder. Saphina stopped looking around and stared at Zeander; quickly reading his thoughts.

Zeander looked back at her curiously, as she simply replied, "No." Zusie motioned for Septer and Rangous to lower their weapons but Saphina still held hers facing out towards the meadow while Jasper continued to hover over her head.

"We are sorry...Zeander," Zusie said. "However, up until three weeks ago we thought that we were the only life in this valley." She said then held out her hand as Zeander had. He whispered to the snake again and it reared its head to bring Zeander to the same height as Zusie, and then slithered closer. Zeander stuck out his hand for Zusie to shake, and spoke slowly so that they could understand him.

"Up till yesterday we didn't realize that there be anyone living in the forest," Zeander said. However, an odd light shone in his eyes than quickly disappeared -- Zusie saw it though and had the distinct feeling she had just been lied to. Zusie shook his small hand anyway and smiled at him. Chrystalina had to be encouraged to come out from behind the rock just as Saphina had to be encouraged to lower her weapon, however she did not come down from the rock. Jasper relaxed as well and fluttered down to Saphina's shoulder curling his snout as he did. The others slowly relaxed and in turn shook his hand and introduced themselves. Saphina nodded to them both when it was her turn. Jasper did the same.

"This be Paraphin," Zeander said, gesturing to the snake. "The last of the giant Abo snakes," he said sadly.

"How did you train him to carry you like that?" Saphina asked curiously. Paraphin looked crossly at her and hissed loudly. Her hand went automatically to the hilt of her knife.

"He did not train me misssssy," Paraphin addressed Saphina but looked at the others, "I chossse to allow Zeander to ride with me like thisss." Everyone noticed that he slurred his S's together but other than that, he was easier to understand than Zeander. "I got quite tired of having to ssstop all the time for him to catch up to me with hisss little legsss."

"Tis quite true," Zeander said, nodding his head and chuckling. "In fact, it be Paraphin who came up with the idea for the wooden holster. My missus and I made it according to Paraphin's instructions. It really has come in handy during our perimeter checks." The Elfkins looked at Paraphin with respect.

"Why do you have to do perimeter checks?" Rangous asked. "Are there others like you in the meadow?"

"Well, not like Paraphin. As I say, he be the last of his kind but ya, there be others." Everyone looked at him curiously waiting to hear more about the others. Zeander however said no more.

"Are there others like you?" Chrystalina asked, taking a step forward and looking at Zeander.

"Well, of course there are. I didn't say that I was the last of my kind, did I?" Zeander said.

"No, you didn't," Chrystalina said as she took a step back. Her cheeks reddened with embarrassment.

"How far is it to your village?" Zusie asked. Zeander looked at them and asked the question he already knew the answer to.

"Tis it just the five of ya then?"

"No," Aldwin said. "There are about four hundred and fifty of us, not counting the forest creatures that travel with us. And we have seven trolleys." Zeander, if surprised at the numbers, did not say so.

Zeander looked at him, knit his brows and said, "Are there elders and wee babes with ya as well?" Aldwin nodded his head. "Will you be leaving them behind with the trolleys?"

"No!" everyone shouted adamantly in unison.

"We will not be leaving anyone behind," Zusie said. A sad expression came over her face and Zeander was sure there was something more behind the look but did not question it.

"Will you need to rest?" Zeander said, looking at Aldwin.

"Only at night," Aldwin said.

Zeander scrunched up his eyebrows as he thought deeply then looked up at the sky. He ran his hand over the tall grass. The others looked at him curiously, as he grabbed some and pulled on it until it popped out of the ground. He sniffed the grass, bit a chunk off and chewed on it thoughtfully for a moment then spat it out. He looked at the group standing in front of him, still looking at him. Their curious looks changed to ones of skepticism – Zeander smiled.

"Well then, taking everything into consideration, it will take about three weeks to travel through the meadow to my village," Zeander said nonchalantly.

The others looked at him incredulously; the journey through the forest had taken that long.

"It's going to take three weeks to get through the meadow?" Saphina said rudely.

Zeander looked at her appraisingly. She was spunky and he could tell by her stance and the way she held her weapons that she could hold her own. He decided he liked her right off the bat. She was hiding something however, perhaps a special gift and he had an idea of what it was.

"Well, it won't take us that long," he said pointing to himself and Paraphin. "Nor the five of you," he added. But four hundred and fifty," he started to say then clicked his tongue in disgust as Chrystalina slipped on the dew-wet grass beneath her feet. "Wee ones, elders and seven trolleys", he finished saying as he watched Septer who quickly reached out and grab Chrystalina's arm steadying her. Zeander looked back up at the sky, counted a couple of times on his fingers and said, "Ya, I reckon it will take that long, give or take a week or two."

They looked at each other with wearied expressions. The journey through the valley was going to take longer than they thought and they had not even come to the difficult parts yet; crossing the lake and the mountain. Zusie looked out over the meadow, then back at the forest where some of the villagers had gathered. She saw their worried expressions and sighed. She then looked at Aldwin.

"How is Lizbeth doing?" Zusie asked.

"She is doing better than I expected her to," he said.

Zeander looked at them curiously, as they spoke. "Lizbeth, Lizbeth," he rolled the name quietly over his tongue before he decided that the name sounded familiar but could not remember where he had heard it. Dismissing it, he looked at Zusie and Aldwin as they talked more about a fellow named Old Barty and a couple of elders who he didn't catch their names. She was asking Aldwin how they were faring and Aldwin had retorted quietly that they were faring well under the circumstances.

"I don't mean to interrupt your chatter, but we best be going while we

still have daylight on our side." Zusie looked around at the others; they all nodded yes, without her even having to ask the question.

"Well then," she said turning back to Zeander, "we will tell the others. They should be finished with the packing by now."

"Great," Zeander said less-than enthusiastically. Then he looked around at the others and started pointing. "You, you, you and you two in the back there," He said. He had pointed to Rangous, Septer, Saphina and two of the villagers, Martan and Porthos. They who were among the group of villagers who had been watching with worried expressions from the protection of the trees. "Do ya actually know how to use those things on your backs or are they just for show?"

"We know how to use them well enough, little man," Saphina spoke for the group of them.

"Fine then," Zeander looked at Saphina and smiled at her cheekiness and courage. "You five will come with Paraphin and me. I suggest," he looked at Aldwin, "that you have the men walk along the outside. Make sure," he said, staring intently at Aldwin, "that the wee ones stay close to their mas and not wander off."

"Is all this precaution for our safety necessary?" Zusie questioned him. "Is there something you're not telling us?" She spoke to Zeander then quickly looked over to Saphina. Saphina looked at Zeander piercingly for a moment. She caught two rapid visions of animals that Zeander could not mask in time.

"It's probably best you tell them," she said.

Zeander looked at Saphina with an appreciative smile. Her gift, he knew from experience could come in handy, especially in times of trouble. However most of the time it was just annoying.

"We probably won't run into any trouble for several days. I've never seen giant salamites or longtooth grosshairs out this far, but one never knows. They get a sniff of ya and they might come after ya."

"Are they that vicious?" Chrystalina asked.

"Nah," said Zeander and she visibly relaxed until he looked incredulously at her and yelled. "Of course they're that mean! Why do ya think I suggested we have scouts n...n the men be on guard? Tis not the big ones they go after... 'tis the wee ones... and then you'll never see them again."

Chrystalina moved up behind Septer when Zeander starting yelling at her. Septer could feel her body shake as she clutched his arm.

"Now there's no need to yell at anyone or frighten us," he said as he looked sternly at Zeander.

"Why do you think I'm the lassst of my kind?" Paraphin said. He could hear the sharp intake of breaths from the tree line.

"Our saving grace," Zeander said so that all could hear, even the ones standing in the forest, "is that there are so many of you. They probably will not attack such a large group. Make sure ya keep to the path, keep the wee ones at arm's length, do as ya told and we should make it to my village safely."

"Alright then," Zusie said, raising her voice so that everyone could hear her clearly. "We will follow Zeander's lead and do as he suggests." The villagers at the forest's edge hesitated. "Go on now," she said sternly, "let's get moving. You know what awaits us if we don't at least try."

The others left in a hurry, going back into the woods to finish packing. Zusie her daughters and Jasper stayed. Zusie looked curiously at Zeander and Paraphin.

"You haven't asked us yet why we are leaving the forest…are you not even curious as to why?" Zeander looked back at them as they waited for him to answer.

"You're not the only ones who can read minds," he looked at Saphina. "Or read the stars," he said, looking at Chrystalina. "We knew you were coming months ago. Did you think it was just by happy coincidence that we happen to be here at the same time?" Zusie's breath caught in her throat, as did her daughters. Zeander looked at them smugly but did not offer up any more information.

"We are going to go ahead for a bit to check things over. We be back right soon. Make sure the others are ready to leave by the time we return. And I suggest" he said pointing at Jasper "that ya keep him close. No more flying ahead."

All they could do was nod and look curiously at the little man and the snake as they slithered silently into the tall grass where they quickly disappeared from view. Zusie and her daughters wanted to learn more about them. How did he know they were coming and why did Zeander make that comment about Jasper staying close? They knew however, that he would not offer the information until he was ready to.

CHAPTER 14

The Rains

A week into the journey across the Outer Bound Meadow and the villagers had not come across or even seen a single sign of a longtooth grosshair or a giant salamite. They did see many insects and birds that inhabited the forest. Most of the villagers found this quite comforting and strange at the same time. Strange because the animal life did not speak with them like the forest creatures did. When some of the villagers questioned Zeander about it he curtly replied that some of the creatures in the meadow could speak while others could not.

The villagers did not worry about it instead; they focused on the new species they discovered daily; like the midnight blue moths. They were lovely with large, deep blue wings that spanned the width of a large hand. They only came out at night when the moon was high in the sky. There were small red and white beetles that climbed to the top of a piece of grass in a single line then jumped into the air so that the wind could carry them to the next patch of grass. There were also dark brown ground snorkels: little hairless rodents with long whiskered snouts and large dark eyes. They lived in burrows in the ground and the underlings thrilled at seeing them. The ground snorkels were quite friendly and would come right up to the underlings and sniff their feet as they walked by, which made the underlings giggle with delight.

All and all, the first days in the meadow had been pleasant. Everyone was delighted at the new life and the wonder of it all. They forgot, for the time being, why they were in the meadow.

Night had fallen on the sixth day and as usual, the Elfkins put the trolleys into a large circle. The Elfkins and forest creatures then stomped down the grass in the circle and set up camp inside of it. A number of the villagers stood guard in the spaces between the trolleys. Zeander had suggested it the first night they made camp. It became a nightly ritual- three shifts, four hours long, four men per post each shift. Facing outward, the first watch of the night stood armed: watching and listening for any movement in the meadow.

The villagers huddled together in small groups, chatting among themselves while they ate their evening meal. There had been no rain since the week before they had reached the edge of the forest. The grass was getting drier as each day went by. They did not dare start a fire in the circle. So nightly, a group of villagers trekked to the river to cook the evening meal and refill the water pots while the rest of the villagers made camp. Most nights their meals consisted of simple fare of pan-fried fish and boiled vegetables. Occasionally, hard-dough dumplings accompanied the meal.

The first day out, Zeander had shown them how to look for early vegetables that grew in the ground among the grass. There was a tuber plant called sweet baroot that was thick at the top and tapered to a dull point, just like a carrot does. It was white in colour and crunchy, but its taste was bland. Zeander said they could eat it raw, boil it, or put it into a stew. There was another tuber plant called a borion that was round in shape, brown and grew in clusters. Its taste was sharp like a turnip. Zeander said that it was good for cooking and making one feel better if they had an upset stomach.

The underlings got good at spotting the mature plants and, while they walked along, they would stoop down, pick the vegetables out of the ground, and throw them into baskets in the trolleys.

Three days in, during one of the nightly treks to the river, they found a vine that wound its way up around the thickest grasses. Hanging from it were clusters of tiny purple berries that were sweet and juicy. Zeander said they were good to eat and helped to quench thirst. He also said not to eat the green ones as they were very bitter and would make one's stomach upset. The baroot, borion and purple berries were the only early vegetables and fruit available for picking. All the other vegetables, and there were plenty of them Zeander assured them, would not be ready to harvest until the fall.

The Elfkins understood this as it was the same way in the forest. There was an early spring harvest of nectar, mushrooms and winterberries. Most things they grew were not ready to harvest until the fall with the exception of a couple of vegetables that were ready mid-summer.

Most of the villagers, though they followed Zeander's orders, were cautious towards him and Paraphin and kept their distance. They also made sure that their 'wee ones' as Zeander called them did as well. Despite Zusie's attempt to encourage the others to get to know them, they stubbornly chose not to. Their standoffishness towards them reminded her of how Camcor's kin had treated her. Nothing good would come of it she was sure.

A small group consisting of Zusie, her daughters, Marla, Rangous,

Septer, Aldwin, Jasper and Bauthal quickly came to respect Zeander and Paraphin and enjoyed the time they spent with them. They were as knowledgeable of the meadow as the Elfkins were of the forest and many nights they swapped stories of their homelands and learned of each other's folklore. Saphina was especially keen to learn all she could and got quite good at deciphering Zeander's thick accent; often translating to the others what he said. Gradually, they too came to understand him, especially since he slowed his speech while he talked with them.

"They be out there," Zeander said while sitting with them. Saphina looked at him; she had been peering into the tall grasses. Zeander was nibbling on one of the baroots, crunching it loudly as he chomped away. If it were just he and Paraphin, he would not have taken the chance of eating a baroot, as they were so noisy. However, traveling with so many people it did not really matter, so he chomped away quite contently.

"I think you are right, Zeander," Saphina said as she popped a purple berry into her mouth. "I have not been able to shake the feeling that someone or something has been watching us all day."

"Humph," Zeander grunted. "'Tis better ya think ya being watched, than actually see them watching ya" Saphina looked at him strangely. Zeander sighed and shook his head; the Elfkins had so much to learn. "If ya can see them, Miss. Saphina, then ya be too close to them and it would not bode well for ya, that you can be sure." Saphina understood what he said and nodded.

"I had no idea it would take so long to get through the meadow," she sighed heavily. "It is much bigger than I thought." She paused and looked around the circle. "Than any of us thought it was." The others in the circle nodded.

"Ya indeed," Zeander said as he handed Paraphin a purple berry. Paraphin sniffed it loudly then turned his head.

"I think I will go in sssearch of a cricket or two," he said and slithered out of sight into the tall grass. The villagers had become used to Paraphin leaving the safety of the camp at night and not coming back until dawn. Some of the villagers often wondered where he went, Saphina included.

"Where does he go at night?" she asked Zeander as she popped another berry into her mouth. He looked up at her.

"He looks for something to eat and does a perimeter check," Zeander answered, biting into another baroot.

"Is he not afraid to go out on his own?" Marla asked, curious.

"Paraphin; afraid," Zeander chuckled. "No, Miss Marla, the creatures of the night be afraid of him. He be wicked fast and his bite is deadly. They won't take the chance. Besides, grosshairs and salamites like flesh and bone, not scales and forked tongues. They would only attack Paraphin if they had no other choice and only if there were several of them to do it. There's only one or two that follow us now."

Marla, sitting next to Rangous, shivered. He put his arm around her and pulled her closer. She looked over at Zeander. "Do you know which ones are out there?"

He sniffed the air. "There be too many different scents with the lot of ya to pick it up. But, they be out there, that ya can be sure of. Paraphin will probably dispatch of them." Marla shivered again.

"You have yet to tell us the story of your family," Marla said, changing the subject. Zeander looked at her intently for a moment. Sadness darkened his eyes and before he spoke he shook it away.

"I think I will go and find Paraphin and do the perimeter check with him. I can't let him have all the fun." Marla started to stammer that she did not mean to offend him, but Zeander had already walked into the tall grass and disappeared from sight. She looked around the small circle, bewildered at his reaction.

"It's alright, Marla," Saphina said. "I have my suspicions that it probably isn't a happy one to tell." Marla snuggled closer to Rangous as the others continued to eat their meal in silence.

Another week and a half had passed and the end of the meadow was still not in sight. Some of the villagers began to question Aldwin and Zusie daily. The question asked most was whether or not they could trust Zeander. On this particular day, a group of women came in search of Zusie. She could tell by the look on their faces that they were angry. She had come to know each of the villagers well over the passing weeks. This particular group complained the most and did the least work. Paramo, Martan's mate, was the leader of the group. She was a heavyset Elfkin who always seemed to be nagging either Martan or one of their underlings. Zusie jumped down from Lizbeth's trolley, landed softly on the ground, and walked a few paces away from the trolley. She had been talking with Lizbeth as she fed her the soothe ease broth. Lizbeth was still in a deep sleep but Zusie kept up hope that Lizbeth could hear and understand what she was saying to her.

Zusie ran her hands down the front of her tunic, straightening it and then she stood erect with her shoulders squared. She towered over the group of women. They had to bend their heads back to look up at her.

"Zusie," Paramo said angrily, "it has been over two weeks since we left the forest and entered the meadow. The underlings are getting tired of traveling. And frankly, we are all getting tired of traveling," she said then looked for support from the other women. They all nodded in agreement.

Hearing the anger in Paramo's voice, Chrystalina and Saphina, who were standing at the next trolley, walked over to stand on either side of their mother. Saphina's hand was on the hilt of her knife; her bow and quiver of arrows hung over her back. Paramo did not miss the slight gesture and instantly lowered her voice.

"Are you sure we can trust Zeander?" Paramo said.

Zusie looked sternly at Paramo and then at each of the women. It did not go unnoticed that they had taken a step back when Saphina had come to stand by her.

"As Aldwin told you yesterday, and I the day before that, and Saphina two days before that, I don't see that we have a choice, Paramo. Unless you know of a quicker way through the meadow," Zusie asked. Paramo looked at her with a blank stare. "Well then, we will have to trust Zeander." Paramo huffed indignantly. "Besides," Zusie said sternly, "he has given us no reason not to."

Not wanting to give in, Paramo raised her voice again. "But we will soon run out of food."

"What is this you speak of?" Saphina said harshly. Paramo and the other women took another step backwards. Some of the village women disliked Saphina because every time she overheard them whining about having to walk, she would quickly put them in their place. She would tell them that they had a choice -- they could continue to walk or stay where they were. This group of women had come to despise her a great deal, but secretly they were jealous of her skills and fortitude.

"Chrystalina and I have just finished taking count of the food stores and there is still a week's worth in the trolleys. And with Zeander's help," she emphasized her words so that the women had no doubt as to whose side she was on, "We have been able to replenish our stock. I don't think," she looked at Paramo with a sneer, "that you know what you speak of; as usual Paramo."

The women took another step back as Saphina raised her voice so that the other villagers, who were now looking at them with interest, could hear.

"How long did you think it was going to take? Aldwin was honest with us right from the start when he said it would be a long journey -

months in fact. Not a jolly little two-day trek through the woods. If you don't like how long it's been taking, you can go back to the village and wait with Camcor, Bertrum and the others who were foolish enough to stay."

"No, no," Paramo stammered and looked wildly about her for support from the other women. They, however, had already turned and were walking quickly back to their families.

"Sorry," Paramo said weakly as she looked down at the ground. "I won't bring it up again."

"Right you won't," Saphina said angrily as she took a menacing step towards Paramo. Paramo quickly turned and walked away as briskly as her little legs could carry her. Saphina turned and smiled broadly at her mother and sister.

"That was fun, wasn't it?" Saphina whispered as she barely contained a giggle. Her smile quickly faded however upon seeing the frowns on their faces. Saphina's shoulders slumped and she bowed her head. Her mother did not approve of her brashness, especially when she unleashed it on the villagers.

Saphina was surprised to feel her mother's finger under her chin. Zusie tilted Saphina's head up and winked at her.

"That was fun," Zusie said. Saphina looked from her mother to her sister who was also smiling. "Perhaps though," Zusie said, "the next time you could find a more…civil conclusion to a problem." Saphina wiped the smile off her face then looked at her mother.

"I will try to be more…," she started to say then looked up into the air trying to remember the word her mother had used, "Civil in the future." Zusie said. She knew that there would be no trying. When Saphina had a choice of walking away from a situation or arguing, nine times out of ten she chose to argue. Zusie put her hand on her daughter's shoulder and squeezed lightly, reassuring her that she was not upset.

"Go and tell the others that it's time to get started for the day's march. I think I will go in search of Zeander and ask again how much longer he thinks it will take."

Zusie motioned for Rangous to come and watch over Lizbeth until Old Barty returned from his morning meal. As she walked away, she did not see that the expression on Lizbeth's face had changed; she was now smiling slightly.

A loud clap of thunder rolled across the night sky, startling Zusie awake. A week had passed since the confrontation with Paramo and, for three days, they traveled without mishap until the fourth day when the rains came while they slept. They were not prepared that first night. Every Elfkin and forest creature was soaked to the bone while they waited for makeshift shelters to be built.

One of the trolleys had stakes in it and the men quickly unloaded them, hammering them into the ground. They put blankets over top and tied them to the stakes. The rain came in a torrential downpour and the blankets were soon soaked and dripped endlessly on whoever lay underneath. The following day, the rain continued and Zeander told them that it was not wise to travel through the meadow, as the trolleys would become stuck in the mud. The villagers complained about being soaked to the bone so Zeander showed them where a tar-like substance lay in puddles by the river. He told them to spread it on their blankets. It smelled awful but it would make the blankets waterproof.

He also showed them how to weave grass together to make thick mats to put under the shelters. It brought them up off the ground, keeping them dry while they slept. However, by the third day, two inches of water blanketed the ground. The water almost reached the top of the woven mats.

Lightning lit the sky and thunder rolled again; bringing with it a gale of wind that pelted the rain against the walls of the makeshift shelters. The blankets strained against the ropes holding them in place. Zusie tried to settle back down again but a terrible scream erupted. It was almost as loud as the thunder. Frightened that they were under attack, Zusie grabbed her knife before sticking her head out of the shelter. She looked around frantically. Several shelters away, Paramo was screaming at Martan. The wind and rain had caved-in their shelter and she was yelling at him to fix it. Their three underlings sat huddled together, looking on in fright, but dared not cry as Paramo would scold them for it.

Zusie started to crawl out of the shelter. Even though she disliked Paramo, she did like Martan and the underlings and would offer her assistance. Rangous ran by her however shouting for her to stay put. She watched as he reached Martan and offered to help. Two other villagers came to help as well and they quickly erected the shelter and secured it with extra ropes to the stacks.

Before ducking her head back into the safety of her shelter, Zusie looked at Paramo who was staring at her with open hatred. Zusie closed the flap of the shelter, shaking her head. Paramo had not approached Zusie again about Zeander nor did any of the other women who had come with her that day. However, occasionally Zusie could feel their eyes watching her, looking at her with disdain. Zusie shook her head again. It was as if Paramo and the others blamed her for their predicament. It did not bother Zusie for the most part. She had no control over the weather or the evil lord and his thirst for power. However just now, seeing the fury in Paramo's eyes, Zusie wondered how much longer it would be before there was a clash between the villagers and the small group that supported Zeander.

Zusie sighed heavily. Either they understood the severity of the situation or they did not. There was no going back to the forest. The only route open to them was through the meadow if they wanted to get to the mountain on the other side of the valley. What would happen once they made it through the meadow to the lake and then to the Mighty Alps she did not know? However, she was sure that the further away they were from Mount Aspentonia, the better the chance for their survival. She knew for sure that if the king had not already made his way over the mountain, he soon would and then Zenrah help them all.

She took a towel out of her pack and dried her hair. She understood the villagers' unrest and did not blame them, for the journey had been harder than any of them expected. The forest and their huts had always protected and sheltered them from severe weather storms. Being out in the open like this, with the elements pounding down on them, was as foreign to them as the threat of an attack from grosshairs, salamites and Canvil was. The thought that at any moment they could be attacked was grating on everyone's nerves. Thankfully, the grosshairs and salamites had kept their distance. It would seem that Zeander had been right; their caravan was too large.

As the lightning and thunder moved closer, Zusie looked up and said a quick prayer of thanks to Zenrah that they did not have to leave the protection of the forest in the middle of winter.

Lightning lit up the sky again, only this time it was right over their heads and the thunder clapped so loudly Zusie jumped in fright. Her heart raced as she looked over at Chrystalina who slept through it all. Zusie's thoughts then turned to Saphina who was out with Septer and a few of the other villagers for their turn at the night watch.

Where the village women kept their distance from Saphina and shot her dirty looks every chance they could, the men of the village had quite the opposite opinion of her. They respected her for her skills and strength. They also appreciated that she took advice well and shared her knowledge without being too bossy. They also noticed that she never complained about the work or the amount of walking they did, like some of the other women did.

Another strike of lightning lit up the sky and the clap of thunder that followed made Zusie jump again. Chrystalina stirred in her sleep this time but still did not wake. Zusie's thoughts turned to her daughter as she looked down at her. She had gained the respect of the villagers as well. However, where the women stayed clear of Saphina, many of them took Chrystalina into their fray. She was knowledgeable in healing and cooking and the women took naturally to her gentle, caring ways.

Zusie sighed heavily as the sky lit up again and another clap of thunder rolled across the valley, but this one was further away. The storm was moving quickly on. Zusie said another quick prayer to Zenrah. She asked him to look kindly on them by bringing clear skies in the morning.

Zusie knew as she settled down on her mat that they would not be able to pack up and move on for a couple of days or more. The sun's heat had to dry the meadow enough so they could move the trolleys safely over it. At least they could dry out their mats and assess the damage to the food stores while they waited for the ground to dry. Zusie sighed heavily again as she thought about what some of the villagers, like Paramo, would say once the rain stopped and they couldn't move until the ground dried. The trolleys would surely sink into the soft ground if they moved them too soon. The trolleys were hard enough to push on dry ground, let alone trying to pull them out of mud. She was not about to forfeit the trolleys and all their provisions just so they could move along before the ground had a chance to dry.

Who knew what lay ahead of them and what dangers they would encounter? They needed the trolleys and their contents if they were going to survive, Zusie was sure of it. She sighed as another clap of thunder rumbled still further yet. She smiled and thanked Zenrah, hoping he had answered her prayer for clear and sunny weather.

CHAPTER 15
Zeander's Homecoming

The rains stopped the night that Zusie had prayed to Zenrah. To everyone's delight, the morning greeted them with clear sunny skies. The wind blew warm and the air smelled fresh. The day continued with no sign that the rain would return; everyone sighed in relief.

The resentment the villagers harbored for Zusie, Aldwin and especially Zeander subsided as the day wore on. Some, however, like Paramo and her followers, continued to stare at Zusie and Zeander with disdain. Zeander had noticed it as they ate their midday meal and told Zusie not to worry. He had a feeling that one day Paramo would get what was coming to her. No one went through life with as much loathing in their soul without karma bouncing back and slapping them in the face.

Zusie asked what he meant by "karma" as she had never heard of it before. Over their meal, he explained to her what it meant. "Karma is the result of cause and effect, action and reaction,' Zeander said thoughtfully. 'I don't quite understand it myself,' he added. 'It is a term used by Desamiha the truth sayer,' he finished saying and left it at that.

Zusie wondered as she finished her meal if karma was bringing Canvil and his army to their valley. She could not think of one person or forest creature that had done something so terrible that they deserved the king's wrath. Not even Paramo, Camcor or Bertrum, regardless of how mean they were, deserved what Canvil and his army of Venom Horde and demon fireflies would do to them. She pondered over that thought for the rest of the day.

As suspected, it took days for the ground to dry. Before the caravan could get restless, Aldwin divided them into four groups. The first group gathered all the ground vegetables and berries they could find. The food stores had been damaged from the rain. Another group set about making clotheslines by using tall stakes with bimble yarn strung between them. The wind, blowing warmly, quickly dried the clothes and blankets hanging over the lines. The third group was in charge of weaving the grasses together into thick mats. The Elfkins placed the mats in the trolley that held the stakes or rolled them up and tied them to backpacks. The last group collected stones from the riverbed and brought them back to camp. They put them in small circles. Each night the Elfkins made small fires and cooked their meals over them. With all the rain they had, there was no fear of setting the meadow on fire.

The second day in, Mirabella had an idea for shelters in case the rain returned. Aldwin, Zusie and Zeander thought that the idea was a stroke of genius, and for several days, a large group of women was given the task of making the shelters. They soaked blankets with tar and dried them in the sun. They then sewed the blankets together, making large four-sided canopies that had a roof and floor. Large thick stakes on each outside corner held the shelter up. Bimble yarn tied to the tip of the stake and a smaller stake pounded into the ground about three feet from the shelter stopped it from caving in. A long center stake placed inside the middle of the shelter raised the roof so it peaked. This way, when it rained, the water would run off the slanted roof and not pool in the middle like it had with the first shelters. A split in the front side of the shelter made a doorway. The two flaps of the doorway could be tied open or left shut. To help secure the bottom of the shelter to the ground, braided bimble yarn was looped and the ends sewn on the bottom corners of the shelters and halfway along the bottom edge. Mirabella explained that curve-headed stakes, about twelve inches long pounded into the ground through the loops would hold the canopy in place. Old Barty and several of the older underlings whittled the hooked stakes.

Mirabella called her invention "clouts," short for cloth huts, and each family received one. The Elfkins practiced erecting them with the poles and stakes and found they went up quickly and, with a little practice, effortlessly. The clouts, when folded properly, rolled up like the woven mats and were placed in the trolley alongside the stakes and mats. Mirabella, quite happy with her invention, secretly wished it would rain again so she could see if it invention worked. However, the rain held off and, a week later, the meadow was dry enough to move the trolleys.

Aldwin jumped down from Lizbeth's trolley and held out his hand to help Saphina down. They had been tending Lizbeth while Old Barty helped with the packing of the supplies. After Aldwin examined Lizbeth and while Saphina fed her he rolled up the canopy to let in the warm breeze. Lizbeth surprisingly was the only who had stayed dry. The tightly woven blankets they used for her canopy had kept the water from dripping in on her. Touched by Aldwin's quaint gesture, Saphina took his hand. Immediately, a warm feeling shot up her arm and her cheeks warmed to a bright pink. Her breath caught in her throat.

Instantly she snatched her hand from his and jumped down from the trolley on her own. However, in her hurry, her pant leg caught on the side of the trolley and she tumbled out of it. She would have fallen to the ground if Aldwin had not caught her in his arms. As he steadied her, he could not help but notice that she seemed agitated and was becoming more so the longer he held her.

"Are you alright?" he asked with concern as he noticed how rosy her cheeks had become. He felt her forehead with the back of his left hand. With his right hand, he felt the pulse at her wrist. "You're not coming down with a fever are you?" he questioned as he stepped closer and peered into her eyes.

"No," she said rudely and pulled away from his touch. Aldwin looked at her with a bewildered expression. Saphina quickly walked away from him, mumbling that she had work to do. She passed Bauthal who had been in the next trolley counting provisions and re-packing the supplies. He had heard their exchange and watched as she stomped off.

"Are you alright?" Bauthal asked, but did not hear her mumbled reply as she walked briskly by him. He noticed that she rubbed her left wrist gently with her right thumb.

He looked curiously from Saphina to Aldwin's bewildered expression. Bauthal smirked and jumped down from the trolley and walked over to Aldwin.

"Morning, Aldwin," Bauthal said with a cheeky smile.

"Morning…Bauthal," Aldwin said absentmindedly as he continued to look at Saphina until she disappeared behind one of the trolleys. He shook his head slowly. He could not understand why she was so upset. They had been taking care of Lizbeth, feeding her the sooth-ease broth and readying her trolley for the journey. They had talked about how anxious and excited they were to finally be on their way again. Overall, it had been a pleasant conversation and he had enjoyed spending a few moments alone with her.

He shook his head, bent down and picked up his medicine bag that he had dropped to catch Saphina. "I hope she is not coming down with a fever." That was the only explanation he could think of for her instant change of attitude. "She has been out most nights with the rest of you as you keep watch over the camp. She hasn't had a good night's rest since we left the safety of the forest." He looked at Bauthal accusingly; Bauthal looked back at him with an amused expression. "Up until the rain, she walked all day with only a few hours of rest. Being out in the rain night after night could not have been good for her. After all this, I hope she is not coming down with something." Aldwin looked at

Bauthal who was still listening to him with an amused look on his face.

"Why are you looking at me like that?" Aldwin asked.

"I don't think it's a fever or any other aliment that she has," Bauthal said confidently. Aldwin's expression changed to a bemused one and Bauthal could barely contain chuckle. Ever since the night they saved Jasper from Camcor and took him to Zusie, they had become fast friends. Of course, they had known each other in the village, but it was rare that the forest creatures called on Aldwin to tend to them. Having in depth conversations with any of them or sharing an evening meal with them was even rarer.

Aldwin, respected and hardworking, was pleased to find Bauthal to be quite intelligent and ecstatic to learn that he could read the stars. The only others in the village that could understand their true meaning were Lizbeth and Chrystalina.

Aldwin was also delighted to find that the forest creatures respected Bauthal. On several occasions, he witnessed Bauthal talking to different groups of them, enquiring how they were faring, answering questions or directing them. He was not just a leader among the forest creatures, he was a great leader who did more than his own share of work and gained the respect of the village elders. Over the journey, he and Aldwin had become confidants and respected each other's opinions. Therefore, Bauthal had no problem voicing his opinion on the situation between Saphina and Aldwin.

"You know, my friend," Bauthal said, reaching up and clapping Aldwin on the shoulder as he did. "Even an old badger like me with bad eyes can see what the problem is with Saphina."

"You don't have bad eyes," Aldwin said. "You see better than most of us do. If your eyes are bad, then so are mine."

"You're right…you're right, my friend, neither of us has bad eyes," Bauthal said then chuckled. Aldwin was baffled as to why Bauthal was being so vague and why Saphina, if not sick, was acting so strangely.

"Never mind Aldwin, one day it will hit you over the head," Bauthal chuckled again and said over his shoulder as he walked away, "or she might."

Aldwin had no time to think about Bauthal's words because a group of underlings ran up to him. Each of them anxiously started to ask when they were leaving. None of them saw Old Barty amble up behind them or the scowl on his face.

"Give an Elfkin some room to breathe," Old Barty said before Aldwin had a chance to answer their question. The children parted as Barty walkedby them. "We will be going soon enough," he said gruffly. "Go and help your ma and da with the packing."

The underlings moaned but knew better than to argue with Old Barty. He often threatened that he would beat them with his walking stick. However, it was an empty threat. In all the years he had threatened to beat an underling, he never had. Aldwin chuckled as the underlings ran back to their ma and da frightened because Old Barty had raised his stick in the air.

"One of these days, underlings are going to clue in that you wouldn't really hit them with that thing." Aldwin looked down at Barty who was several inches shorter than he was. "Then what will you do?"

"I don't think we need to worry about that," Old Barty chuckled. "I often hear their mas threatening that if they do not behave they will come and fetch me to beat them."

Aldwin laughed as memories of his own ma threatening him with that very thing when he was an underling flashed before his eyes. Old Barty laughed with him, remembering the time that Aldwin's ma brought him to Barty's door for a beating. They looked at each other knowing they had been thinking of the same thing and laughed harder as neither of them could remember what had happened next. Barty walked past Aldwin still chuckling. Aldwin could see that Barty was leaning heavily on his walking stick.

"Are you alright, Barty?" Aldwin asked.

"Well as can be expected," Barty answered. He looked at Aldwin. "I am glad the rain is gone," he said as he leaned against the tailgate of Lizbeth's trolley. He ran his hand down the length of his right thigh as it helped with easing the pain. He accidentally knocked his cane to the ground but did not bend to pick it up.

Aldwin knew that Old Barty's hips and legs hurt more during the rainy times than any other time of the year. He opened his medicine bag and took out a little pouch.

"I won't...," Barty started to say, but seeing the stern look on Aldwin's face conceded with a loud humph. He did not usually take the medicine Aldwin offered to ease the pain, but the journey had been long and was taking its toll on him. Aldwin dipped his fingers into the pouch and brought out a small berry the size of a pea. Barty recognized it as the kind that grew on the stalks of the purple lizben and scowled.

``I want you to put this under your tongue," Aldwin said in his 'I am the healer and you are the patient and there will be no argument' voice. He handed Barty the berry. "Keep it there. It will only take a few moments before it dissolves and only a few moments more before the pain will ease."

Barty nodded and grudgingly put the berry under his tongue. It was tart, just as the nectar was, but ten times worse. Old Barty screwed up his face and was about to spit the berry out when Aldwin pointed at him.

"Keep it in there." Old Barty agreed, but screwed his face up even more as the saliva in his mouth started to dissolve the berry. Aldwin looked at the expression on Barty's face and smirked. "You're worse than the underlings. It's not that bad, just keep it in there." As Aldwin spoke, Barty could taste the bitterness easing as the berry dissolved under his tongue. Satisfied that Barty would not spit it out, Aldwin called Rangous. He was placing a freshly picked basket of baroots into the next trolley.

Together, they helped Old Barty into Lizbeth's trolley. Barty looked up at Aldwin with concern. His legs and arms felt heavy and his vision started to blur. It was all he could do to keep his eyes open.

"Am I...supposed to feel this way? I...can hardly move my legs and...arms," he said slowly then yawned loudly. Aldwin nodded as he and Rangous laid Barty down beside Lizbeth.

"Yes, besides easing the pain it will also help you sleep." Aldwin said. He could tell by the dark circles under Barty's eyes that he had not been sleeping well. A good days rest would also help ease the pain.

"B...b...but what of Lizbeth? Who will watch her?" Barty started to argue.

"Don't worry about that. I will send Jasper over to keep an eye on her for you." Old Barty tried to nod in agreement. However, he was so relaxed that his head fell back onto the mat. He sighed heavily and instantly fell asleep.

"Is he going to be alright?" Rangous asked while folding a blanket.

"Oh yes," Aldwin said, picking up the small pouch that held the purple lizben berries and tucked it back into his medicine bag. Rangous put the folded blanket under Barty's head. "He will sleep for several hours and, when he wakes up, the pain in his hip should have subsided enough for him to at least sit in comfort," Aldwin said. Then he added with a smile, "It won't do anything for his disposition though. He will still be as cantankerous as ever."

Rangous chuckled as he unfolded another blanket and put it over Barty.

"Probably even more so at me; I didn't tell him that it would make him sleep," Aldwin chuckled at the shocked look on Rangous' face. Rangous jumped down from the trolley. Seeing Barty's walking stick on the ground, he picked it up.

"I don't wish to be you when Old Barty wakes up," he said, "or anywhere near you when he starts swinging this walking stick at your head." Aldwin looked at the walking stick in Rangous' hand and thought for a moment before he took it from him and put it on Lizbeth's side of the trolley. Rangous looked at Aldwin and smiled. "I will go and see if the others are ready to go," he said.

Aldwin nodded and thanked Rangous before he left. He looked down at Barty sleeping beside Lizbeth and mused that even in his sleep he looked grumpy. His smiled faltered however, as he thought of what Rangous said. He immediately covered up the walking stick with a couple of blankets. Aldwin chuckled to himself as he went in search for Jasper -- not much had changed he was still afraid of being beat with Old Barty's walking stick.

The skies stayed clear for several more days as the caravan of Elfkins and forest creatures made their way across the meadow. Halfway through the fourth day, an excited murmur began to travel down the length of the caravan. The end of the meadow was now in sight and, if luck were on their side, they would be there before nightfall that day.

The underlings' laughter pealed happily over the breeze and it could be heard down the length of the caravan. Even the adults and the forest creatures were giddy with joy and relieved that this leg of the journey would soon end. They picked up the pace, talking excitedly with each other. An hour later however, everyone stopped talking as a loud booming noise echoed across the meadow. Mas, frightened by the sound, anxiously grabbed their underlings as the men cocked their bows and faced the meadow, ready to shoot at anything that moved.

Zeander, leading the caravan on the back of Paraphin, held up his hand for them to stop. The caravan slowly came to a standstill as the order passed down the line. They all listened intently for the sound again and jumped as it boomed across the meadow for a second and then a third time. Before anyone could question Zeander, he and Paraphin took off. All they heard before they disappeared into the grass was Zeander yelling that his village was under attack.

Rangous and Septer, who had been walking with Zeander, looked strangely at each other. Saphina ran up to them and asked what was going on.

"Zeander and Paraphin took off saying that their village was under attack," Septer said. Without thinking or asking for permission, Saphina took off after Zeander. Zusie and Aldwin had also come to see what was going on. Seeing only the top of Saphina's head as she ran into the grass, Zusie yelled for her to come back, but Saphina kept running after Zeander.

Without having to ask, Zusie sighed as Septer and Rangous ran after Saphina. Aldwin took command and ordered the villagers to make camp quickly. In no time at all, the Elfkins put the trolleys in a circle. The women, underlings and forest creatures sat huddled together in the middle. Every man and underling big enough to carry a bow and arrow stood guard at the edge of the circle. Seeing Aldwin at the weapons trolley, Jasper, who had been sitting with Lizbeth and Old Barty, flew over to him.

"What is going on? Jasper asked as he looked frantically around for Saphina. Aldwin did not answer him. "Where is Saphina?!" Jasper shouted at Aldwin.

Startled, Aldwin looked up from the trolley. "Jasper, go back to Lizbeth."

"But I want to see Saphina. She may need my help," Jasper whined.

"Jasper, I don't have time to argue with you! Go back to Lizbeth." Aldwin said sternly. Seeing the tears well up in Jasper's eyes, he calmed his tone. "Saphina will be alright. Rangous and Septer have gone after her and I am going as well." With that, he picked up a club. Its weight felt awkward in his hands. Aldwin abhorred violence, but if any harm should befall Saphina at the hands of a grosshair or salamite, well... may Zenrah have mercy on their souls. Jasper watched Aldwin run into the meadow, yelling for Saphina at the top of his lungs. Half a dozen armed villagers followed him. Jasper was just about to fly after him when Zusie stepped in his way. She looked sternly at him and pointed towards Lizbeth's trolley. Jasper looked at her painfully, but did as he was told and slowly flew back to Lizbeth.

Zusie looked sadly at him. She understood how he felt for she too feared for Saphina's life, but it was best that they stay in the protection of the circle until they heard news of what was happening. She walked slowly towards Chrystalina who was sitting on the ground near one of the trolleys. She was comforting some of the underlings. Zusie smiled at her tenderly as Chrystalina looked up at her. Zusie hoped that it would not be long before Saphina was back with them.

Two hours later, Saphina rushed out of the meadow with bow and arrow in hand. She had taken off without knowing the exact location of Zeander's village. She figured she would have caught up to them. However, that was not the case. Instead, Saphina put her faith in Zenrah that he would show her the way.

As Saphina gasped for air and her legs strained to keep her upright she looked around. The scene was as unfamiliar to her as the thought of carrying a bow and arrow for protection was. Yes, she had read about such things in the scrolls but never in her wildest imagination could she picture the destruction that lay before her. Holding an arrow cocked in the bow she looked for what might be a salamite or grosshair -- Thankfully the only thing she saw was the aftermath of the attack.

Zeander's village lay in ruin -- Many of the thatched roofs on the small, hut-like structures hung partially off or were laying in pieces beside the huts. The worship temple that was located in the middle of village was destroyed. The small benches, which the villagers sat on, lay broken and scattered in every direction. Great claw marks were everywhere on the ground. It looked like something very large had tried to dig into the ground to get at whatever lay beneath the soil.

Saphina's heart pounded in her chest. There was something else wrong -- something very wrong. She frantically looked around for Zeander's kinfolk; the Meadow Imps? There was no one there and she thought the worst – that they had been carried off or eaten alive. Sickened with the thought, raw emotion caught in her throat but she held it at bay she desperately needed to find Zeander. She cautiously walked forward. As she looked in all directions, she felt foolish for not bringing at least Rangous and Septer with her. As she moved forward, Saphina sensed that help was on its way.

Encouraged by the thought she walked through the village. When she came upon the worship temple, she stopped. Zeander had told them how important it was to his people. She squelched the need to right the benches and walked on to the other side of the village. She stopped at the entrance to a pathway that wound through the tall grasses. She knew the pathway would eventually lead her to the lake side of the village where she hoped to find Zeander and Paraphin.

Zeander had explained that a winding pathway through the meadow joined the two halves of his village. She stood in what they called the meadow side; the other half they called the lake side. She looked behind her, wondering if she should wait for the others, but she decided to go on. She needed to find Zeander and Paraphin; she needed to know that they were all right.

Saphina could not see over the tall grasses so she kept an arrow cocked in her bow as she cautiously turned one bend after another. She periodically looked behind her to make sure she was not being followed. Several paces later her heart skipped a beat; there were voices coming from around the next bend. Saphina quickly dropped to the ground. Lying on her belly, she shimmied her way along the dirt path and stopped just before the bend. Her heart pounded as she peered around the tall grass. That side of the village lay in ruin as well. However, she sighed when she caught a glimpse of Zeander. He was standing in the center of the village, talking earnestly with the most unusual creatures Saphina had ever seen.

One of the creatures, a female, was on bended knee listening intently to what Zeander was saying. The others, about a dozen in all, stood guard a couple of paces behind her. Saphina knew them the Tara Aquians. Zeander had described them to her and at the time, she had been eager to meet them. They sounded very interesting. However at first glance, standing guard as they were, they looked frightfully barbaric.

They were taller than Zusie and had lean, muscular bodies. Their smooth dark green skin shimmered iridescent in the daylight. Their shoulder length hair was black as the night sky and lay flat against their heads. They looked unapproachable and Saphina was not sure she wanted to meet them after all. She looked at the one talking with Zeander and noticed that her hair was different from the others. It was long and plaited in small braids that hung down her back. Like the others, her eyes were large and her eyebrows were dark and thin. She had no ears that Saphina could see and her nose sat almost flat against her face. Her mouth looked like an Elfkins,' however her lips were fuller.

All of them, except for the one talking with Zeander, were dressed the same. Their dark vests had shiny looking objects were layered one on top of the other. It reminded Saphina of fish scales. Their legs were clad in dark pants that clung to their bodies like a second skin; their slightly webbed feet and hands were bare. Each of them carried a long stick with a jagged white coloured object at the end. Saphina recognized the weapons. She had seen similar ones in the scrolls; the ancient ones called them warrior spears. They were made from thick wooden rods about six feet long and were topped with the jagged object that looked very sharp. Saphina noticed that some of the spearheads had bloodstains on them.

Each of them also carried a thick, round shield that had small jagged spikes sticking out along the edge of them. A larger spike protruded from the middle of them. Around their wrists, they wore thick bands that had the same type of spikes sticking out from them. In the belts around their waists, they had daggers made of the same material as the top of the spears; she noticed some of them carried two knives.

Saphina quickly assessed the situation. Zeander did not look to be in trouble. Saphina could not see Paraphin anywhere and hoped that he was unharmed. She tried to read the mind of the Tara Aquian speaking with Zeander. She knit her brows in concentration but all she could hear was a buzzing that sounded lyrical, like someone playing on one of Old Barty's flutes.

Saphina decided it was time to make her presence known. She quietly stood. Before she had a chance to move, the group of Tara Aquians standing guard quickly raised their weapons and pointed them menacingly at her. Zeander quickly turned; the hilt of his blade was instantly in his hand. Seeing that it was Saphina, he hurriedly spoke to her.

"Lower your weapons now." Saphina immediately stopped walking and dropped her bow and arrow to the ground. She slowly pulled the two knives out of her belt and dropped them as well. Saphina then put her hands in the air and turned around once so that they could see that she was not carrying any other weapons. Zeander said something to the Tara Aquians over his shoulder. They lowered their weapons and looked at Saphina with bland expressions.

"Saphina," Zeander said admonishingly as she slowly made her way to the group. Although the Tara Aquians' muscular arms were lax, she had no doubt that if she made one wrong move they would attack her in an instant. She looked down at Zeander, realizing that he was still scolding her. "You should not have come," he said as Saphina knelt down on one knee in front of him just as the Tara Aquian had done.

"We are friends, you and I. Is that not so?" Saphina asked. Although she was frightened, she masked it with a smile as she looked cheekily at Zeander. Zeander looked at her crossly but nodded.

"If I was in need of help, would you have come for me?" she asked more bravely.

"Yes, of course," Zeander said. He knew instantly that he was not going to win the argument. He had seen it too many times during the journey across the meadow. When Saphina set her mind to something, there was no stopping her. Not even Zusie, her own mother, could persuade her otherwise. She nodded at him, knowing by the look on his face that he would not argue with her.

"Now, introduce me to the Tara Aquians," she said boldly, her fear of them subsiding.

Zeander smiled and shook his head. Just as he was about to make the introduction, Rangous, Septer, Aldwin and six other villagers came running into the clearing with their bows cocked and ready to shoot anything that moved. All except Aldwin that is, who brought only a club. Zeander watched him swing it over his head and smirked as Aldwin yelled a battle cry—the others ducked out of his way. They skidded to halt however when Saphina raised her hand in greeting. The Tara Aquians again raised their weapons and pointed them at Aldwin and the others. Zeander spoke to them once again and they lowered them.

Seeing that Saphina and Zeander were all right Aldwin lowered the club to his side and motioned for the others to do the same. Bauthal, who had seen Aldwin take off after the others, followed with two dozen forest creatures. They made it through the meadow and the first clearing before the others even got to the first clearing. Instead of rushing as Aldwin and his group had done, they lay in wait, as Saphina had and assessed the situation. The Elfkins, he thought shaking his head, had much to learn about battle strategy. Seeing them lower their weapons, Bauthal and the other creatures came out of the meadow. To everyone's surprise, the Tara Aquians did not raise their weapons as the forest creatures made their way to the group of villagers.

"Having fun, are we?" Bauthal said as he stood beside Aldwin, looking amusedly at the club in his hand. Aldwin chose not to react to his friend's good-natured ribbing and instead looked over to Saphina and sighed heavily. He was relieved beyond measure that she was safe and smiled at her -- she warmly smiled back at him. Hmm, Bauthal thought to himself. Perhaps his friend was not as thick as he made out to be when matters concerned Saphina. Bauthal smiled; perhaps she would not have to knock him over the head after all.

They all started to walk slowly over to Saphina. Seeing her weapons on the ground, Aldwin bent down, picked them up, and handed them to her once he reached her. "Thank you," she said and took the weapons from him. Their hands brushed and electric energy shot up her arm again. Aldwin nodded at her then looked down at Zeander, who found the exchange between the two of them very interesting.

"So, is the battle over then?" Aldwin asked him.

"There was no battle," Zeander said, huffing in disgust. "It was a raid by the longtooths. They are so dim-witted that we don't battle them, we simply outwit them." Zeander motioned for them to sit. Six of the Tara Aquians sat, including the one that had been talking with Zeander. The remaining six took up post around the group. Aldwin and Saphina sat on the ground as well. The other villagers and forest creatures followed the Tara Aquians, and stood guard facing the meadow. They could not stop themselves from taking sidelong glances at the Tara Aquians as they stood nervously by them. The Tara Aquians however ignored them.

Saphina looked at Zeander and nodded in the direction of the female Tara Aquian. Zeander cleared his throat. "Oh right, sorry. Saphina this be Lindrella. She be the daughter of the high priest and priestess of the Tara Aquians. They, if you remember me telling you, dwell in the underwater caves of Lake Kellowash."

He turned to Lindrella and spoke to her in a language that Aldwin and Saphina could not understand. They looked at each other with confused expression. Once Zeander finished, he turned to them and told them what he had said.

"I told Lindrella that you were Saphina, daughter of Zusie, the knower of all things from the Crystal Cave of Aspentonia. And that Aldwin and the others were of the noble Elfkin tribe, and that Bauthal and the others were the mighty creatures of the Greenwood Forest." Bauthal turned at hearing this and nodded a thank you to Zeander. He was pleased that Zeander felt that the forest creatures were worthy enough to introduce. Zeander nodded back at Bauthal in kind.

Saphina put out her hand as Zeander had when they met him that first day at the edge of the forest. Instead of taking Saphina's hand, Lindrella put her hands together in front of her chest and bowed her head. Saphina looked at Aldwin who shrugged his shoulders and clasped his hands together as Lindrella had and bowed his head; Saphina followed suit.

Lindrella began to speak to them. Her voice was soft and lyrical like the low rhythmic sounds made from one of Old Barty's flutes. However, they still could not understand what she was saying. Saphina and Aldwin looked to Zeander for translation.

"Oh yes," he said, seeing their confused expressions. "Lindrella is welcoming you to the village." Lindrella began to speak again and Zeander continued to translate. "She would like to know why you have traveled so far from home," Zeander said.

"Wow, not one for small talk, is she?" Saphina said under her breath to Aldwin.

"Right to the point," Aldwin said. "Just like you."

Saphina smiled and looked at Lindrella. While she spoke, she never took her eyes off her; Zeander translated.

"Tell her that a Hummingmoth messenger brought us news of an evil Lord who lives in the land north of Mount Aspentonia. He is raging war and is on his way to this valley. He is pure evil and will destroy everything, everyone in this valley if they do not bow down to him and serve in his army."

Lindrella did not look surprised at her words or even worried as Zeander translated. She turned to one of her followers who quickly stood, picked up his spear and looked at two of the others. They also stood, picked up their weapons, and ran from the village in the direction of the lake.

They didn't say anything to each other," Saphina said as she looked astonished at the Tara Aquians. Zeander looked at her for a moment; he thought she would have realized by now but she hadn't.

"Tara Aquians do not need to speak out loud to each other..." He began to say.

"...they converse with their minds," Saphina finished his sentence for him.

"Yes, that is right," Zeander said.

"That's what the buzzing sound was in my head. I tried to read their minds before I came into the clearing, but they were talking to each other in a language I didn't understand," she said then looked curiously at Lindrella. Zeander translated and Lindrella gave Saphina the same curious look.

Aldwin had known about Saphina's gift for some time, but the other villagers standing around had not. They looked at each other in surprise. Saphina watched some of them as they mentally processed this new information. Some of them became worried and quickly tried to remember if they had thought poorly of her. She mused at the worried looks on their faces. They did not understand that it did not quite work that way. She had to be looking straight at them and it was something she could turn off and on at will. Jasper was the only one she had no control over and quite often could hear what he was thinking even if he was far away -- like now. He sat in the trolley with Lizbeth rocking back and forth fretting about her safety. Saphina sent him a mental image that she and the others were well. She smiled slightly as he received the image. She could literally feel his anxiety subside.

Aldwin sent the six villagers back to the caravan to let Zusie and the others know that it was all right to come forward, but Jasper was already telling her. Before the villagers left, Zeander warned them to stick to the path they had made coming into his village but did not offer them an explanation as to why.

Zeander put two fingers in his mouth and whistled sharply three times. The whistle echoed back to them exactly the same way several times throughout the lake side of the village and they could hear it echoing in the meadow side as well. Immediately afterward, Meadow

Imps flooded the village from every corner. They either walked out of their destroyed homes unharmed or popped right out of the ground. Saphina and Aldwin looked on in surprised confusion.

Zeander explained. "There are long tunnels several feet beneath us that connect our homes and both sides of the meadow together. All one has to do during a long tooth raid is escape through a hatch in the floor where steps lead down to the tunnels. Although the longtooths demolished much of the village, they were not very precise," he said smugly. Saphina and Aldwin looked curiously at him.

"Most of the imps were still inside eating their midday meal," he explained. "Those who were not had made it to safety through the ground-traps."

"Ah," Saphina said, nodding her head. That is why she had not seen any Meadow Imps when she reached the village. They were all safely hiding in the tunnels beneath their homes, waiting patiently for the 'all's clear' whistle.

"But what of the large claw marks on the ground? Did the longtooths make those as well?"

Zeander looked at her for a long moment but did not answer her question. She knew from experience that he only told them as much as he thought they should know. She could have read his mind but Zeander was very good at closing it shut and only let her in when he thought it prudent to do so. Saphina did not press the issue, knowing that when the time came he would tell them.

Six of the Tara Aquians continued to stand guard, with three on one side of the village and three on the other side. Everyone else worked in cooperation to right the Meadow Imps' village. Saphina had met many of them, bending on one knee as Zeander introduced her to them. She was pleased to meet Zeander's mate, Lillian, but did not question why he did not introduce her to any of the wee ones who ran about. That question would wait for another day.

Saphina and Aldwin found it most interesting that the Meadow Imps were not afraid or surprised to see strangers in their village. They welcomed them warmly and talked cheerily with them as they worked to right the village. Used to Zeander, Saphina understood them quite well and enjoyed their company. She found working beside the Tara Aquians however quite the opposite. Unlike the Meadow Imps, they never tried to communicate with her.

The Meadow Imps and Tara Aquians went about righting the village as if raids were a common occurrence. As the day wore on and the sun began to set, walking around the village became taxing at times. They had to make sure that they did not step on any of the 'wee ones,' as Zeander called them. Finally, Lillian corralled all the wee ones together near the ruined worship temple until the village cleanup was finished.

As the sunset, the Elfkins and Meadow Imps filled small stone circles with wood, lit a fire and cooked their evening meal. They lit torches as well so that when the other Elfkins and forest creatures made their way to Zeander's village, they would be able to see where they were going.

The Tara Aquians had left the village once it was righted. Before leaving, Lindrella told Zeander that they would return at first light in two days' time. Saphina, Aldwin, Bauthal and the other forest creatures ate a simple meal with the Meadow Imps and waited anxiously for the caravan of travelers from the Greenwood Forest to arrive.

CHAPTER 16
A Request

It was morning on the second day after the attack on Zeander's village. The sun was shining, the air was warm and the skies clear. It looked to be just the start of another lovely day. However, it was not. The Elfkins were running for their lives from an evil Lord only to show up in a village that was ravished just the day before by creatures that ate flesh and bone.

A disturbance at the edge of the clearing on the lake side of Zeander's village had every Elfkin da reaching for their weapons while their underlings cowered beside their ma's. Upon seeing who it was however, they slowly lowered their weapons, but kept them close. One could not really blame them. The booming noise had scared most of them and seeing the devastation of the Meadow Imps village left the rest of them jumping at every sound. The aftermath of the raid was a terrifying sight to see for such a humble, gentle race. Oh sure they had fought among themselves, but quarrels were not the same thing as mass destruction.

When they asked Old Barty if their folklore told of such events taking place in the Greenwood Forest, he sadly shook his head no. Once they heard the whole story, young and old alike, fretted so much they were afraid to sleep. Every noise sounded menacing to them, even if it was just a spiked-back cricket chirping in the grass.

They had arrived in the village a couple of hours after sunset on the day of the attack. With light from the torches, they put the trolleys in a circle, just outside the meadow side of the village. They made a quick meal and settled in for the night. Most of them however had stayed awake all night even though guards were posted everywhere. The Elfkins did not want to take the chance of one of them falling asleep, giving a longtooth grosshair or something worse the opportunity to slip by them, so they stood in pairs; the postings changing often.

The next morning, they learned that the Meadow Imps, who had declined the offer to sleep in the safety of the circle, slept in bunkers deep underground. It was unfortunate to say, but they were used to the attacks. Over the years, they made the bunkers as comfortable as their own homes. Often, during a heat wave in the summer months, many of them would sleep in the bunkers because it was cooler under the ground. By constructing underground tunnels, they could easily move from one side of the village to the other.

The Meadow Imps admitted that there had been more raids last year than any year before and it looked like this year was not going to be any better. There had already been two raids before this one. This one, however, had been the worse and the elder Meadow Imps did not know why. With the arrival of the Elfkins and forest creatures, they started to think that perhaps a force beyond their control was stirring the pot, so to speak.

The Elfkins knew the Tara Aquians would be visiting at first light and were not surprised to see a troop of them arriving in the village. But, like Saphina, they were not prepared to see such strange creatures walking amongst them. Most of the Elfkin underlings stared openly at them -- some in awe, others in fear.

The Elfkin women and men tried not to look at them, at least until they walked by that is. Then they too stared openly at them and like their underlings, some stared in awe, others in fear. However, all of them thought, upon seeing them and their weapons, that it was better to have them on their side then not.

Saphina watched as the Tara Aquians slowly and purposefully walked into the clearing. She looked around and mused at the fact that the forest creatures did not seem to react, one way or another, to their presence. Nothing seemed to faze them- not the rains, nor the long journey. They always seemed to be at ease and took everything in stride.

The Tara Aquians paid them no mind either as they walked by them. In fact, Saphina noticed they did not look at anyone. They kept their eyes straight ahead. She wondered, as they walked past her and the small group of villagers she was sharing her morning meal with, if they were taking everything in. Their eyes were so big they could probably see behind them, she smiled thoughtfully. Even though their stares looked blank, she knew they were assessing everyone and calculating everything in the village.

No doubt, they knew where everything was in the village, right down to the smallest Meadow Imp. They probably calculated how many weapons there were, who could use them effectively and who could not. The memory of Aldwin wielding a large club over his head while he screamed a battle cry came to her and she smiled. They probably knew where the best position would be for a counter attack if the longtooths or something worse should try to attack. They looked to be accomplished warriors and probably knew how to use their weapons with deadly accuracy. The last Tara Aquian, who looked like he could take on a dozen longtooths and come away without a scratch, entered the village. Saphina wondered if they dreamt battle strategies in their sleep. She would be shocked to find out that she was not far off in her assumptions.

Zeander, seeing Lindrella, stood and indicated that she was welcome to join them. Six of the warriors followed Lindrella. Saphina wondered if they were her personal guards as they were the same ones from the previous day. The rest of warriors split into two groups. One of the groups stayed and took up posts around the clearing. The other group went to the meadow side of the village.

Lindrella and Zeander exchanged their normal greeting before she sat on the ground beside the Elfkin and Meadow Imp elders. They had been sitting on the ground in a large circle waiting for her arrival. Zusie sat with Markhum, Farringdum and Gradum. Beside them was Zeander who sat with three Meadow Imp elders. Sitting on his own, on the other side of Zusie, was Bauthal. Zeander had asked Bauthal to represent the forest creatures.

Lindrella greeted Zusie and each of the Elfkin leaders in turn with her customary greeting as Zeander introduced them to her. The Meadow Imp elders she knew so no introduction was necessary and Bauthal she had met the day before. Lindrella got right to it and spoke quickly to Zeander in her singsong voice then looked blankly at Zusie. Zeander translated her words to Zusie and the others.

"She has brought you greetings from the high priest and priestess who have requested an audience with you." Lindrella spoke again but this time she looked past Zusie. "And," Zeander translated, "the Hummingmoth Messenger."

Zusie looked curiously at Zeander. She knew the Tara Aquians lived in caves beneath the water. She wondered how they were going travel to them. Zusie did not need her daughters present to know what their answer would be so she spoke for them. Jasper unfortunately would have no choice in the matter.

"Please tell Lindrella that we would be pleased to accompany her to her home," Zusie said then she bowed her head to Lindrella.

Lindrella distractedly returned the gesture as she stared across the clearing. Zusie turned to see what or who Lindrella was looking at and saw Jasper coming from the pathway that connected both sides of the village; she waved him over. When she had the time, she thought absentmindedly, she would ask Zeander why the Meadow Imps planned their village out this way.

Jasper cautiously flew over. He too had heard of the Tara Aquians and when the group of them entered the meadow side of the village, he instantly went in search of Saphina. The weapons the warriors carried looked as lethal as Saphina had said. A vision of one of the Tara Aquians knocking him to the ground popped into Jasper's mind. He hesitated halfway there as another vision of a Tara Aquian spearing him in mid-flight took over the last vision. Seeing Zusie smiling warmly at him was the only reason he continued to make his way over to them. No one noticed the smirk on Lindrella's face; she had seen Jasper's visions.

"Jasper, will you please go find my daughters and Aldwin, and tell them I need to speak with them. And Jasper…please return with them." Zusie said. Jasper looked from Zusie to Lindrella and back to Zusie again. The pit of his stomach started to churn as it always did when he got nervous. He had to wrestle mentally with the visions of great bodily harm and torture now popping into his head at random to focus on what Zusie asked him to do. He flew away hesitantly as a dreadful feeling consumed him.

The Tara Aquians and Zusie sat with the others in the circle and waited for her daughters and Aldwin. They did not have to wait for long as Aldwin and Saphina were already in the lake side of the village and Chrystalina was just entering it with a group of the Elfkin women. Zusie noticed that several of the men walked with them as guards. No one heeded Zeander's words from the night before that there were now too many of them for an attack to happen.

Zusie stood and indicated to her daughters that they were to follow her. They only walked a few paces away from the main group but it was far enough to speak in private. She told them of the request and that she had agreed to it. Their reactions were what she expected; they nodded in agreement. She then called Jasper over, who nearly dropped to the ground when he heard that he was to go with them.

"Courage little one, courage" Saphina said calmly as she placed Jasper on her shoulder. His legs hung down as he placed his hands on either side of his body and grasped nervously onto her tunic. Lindrella looked curiously at the pair of them but did not comment, only averting her eyes when Saphina looked over at her.

Zusie asked her daughters and Jasper to go and sit with the others. She then motioned for Aldwin to come over. He stood and listened closely to what she had to say. His expression changed rapidly from mild concern to a fearful apprehension. Zusie could tell he was about to disagree with the decision she had made and promptly interrupted him.

"Aldwin, I know what you are about to say, but I believe for us to make it safely across the lake to the mountains we need to trust these people." He went to interrupt her again but she stayed him with her hand on his shoulder. "Perhaps they know of a quicker route through the mountains." Aldwin sighed heavily and looked over at Saphina who was talking quietly but excitedly with her sister and Jasper. He could not understand why, but his heart sank as he looked at her.

"Why do all of you have to go?" Aldwin asked. "Our people see you and your daughters as our leaders. If you do not return, they will lose all hope."

"Aldwin, you know as well as I do that I am not the leader of this group." He began to argue with her again but she said, "But if it helps them to believe that I am, so be it. I believe we are all traveling in the same direction for the same purpose. Some of us are able to direct others, while others are able to follow. Together we are all trying to accomplish the same thing." She contemplated seriously for a moment, looking out towards the mountains to the south. She looked back at him and added, "You want to know what I think? Someone out there past the mountains in Jasper's village is the true leader. And through Jasper they are leading us to safety…calling us home."

Aldwin also looked towards the mountains and sighed heavily. A warm feeling came over him and he knew her words to be true. He nodded and they rejoined the group. Zusie raised her voice so that every Elfkin and forest creature standing in the lake side of the village could hear. If they thought she was their leader, perhaps they would listen to her as such.

"We have been asked to go to the Tara Aquians' home." Zusie started to say. She heard a gasp of concern from the Elfkins who had started to gather closer to the circle of elders, but she continued without hesitation. "While we are gone, I have left Aldwin in charge." Hurried whispers made their way around the clearing but no one challenged her words. The villagers respected Aldwin; even the elders sitting in the group nodded in agreement.

"We will return," she paused and looked down at Zeander.

He scratched his chin, thinking about how long it would take them. "Tomorrow evening before the sun sets, pending there are no problems," he said.

"Right," Zusie said and looked out over the clearing again and raised her voice so that everyone could hear. "Tomorrow evening. I suggest you gather as many provisions as you can while we are gone and think of a way to get across the lake. When we return, we will be on our way again." The crowd that had gathered dispersed quickly, most of them going in the direction of the meadow side of the village to let the others know what was happening. Jasper shivered on Saphina's shoulder.

"And how are we supposed to get there?" Saphina asked, knowing it was what all of them were thinking.

"Well," Zeander said with a giddy smile on his face. "The Tara Aquians have this...," Zeander paused for a moment, trying to think of the best word to use to describe what the Tara Aquians transported other beings in. "Vessel that you will ride in....it be like a large bubble." Zeander stopped talking when he saw their confused expressions. "Ya know a bubble? A bubble!" he said, getting agitated. "It's what happens when ya stick a hollow reed into ya drink and blow into it and bubbles come up." They still looked puzzled at each other than shrugged their shoulders. "Ya don't know what bubbles are?" he asked, unbelieving. Zeander shook his head and groaned with frustration. "How could they not know what bubbles are?" he said to the elders sitting next to him.

He started to describe the vessels to them slowly, pronouncing every word clearly. "It be clear, and has handles on either side. Two warriors will pull ya along while the other warriors swim along as guards. You will have one bubble each and enough air to last until ya get to the caves."

"Wh...why will we need guards?" Jasper stammered nervously. Saphina could feel his little body shaking on her shoulder as he gripped her tunic. The tremors shot right down her arm into her hand. Her fingers tingled from the sensation and she wiggled them. She was amazed as she turned her head to look at him that he was able to stay seated on her shoulder. She was sure if the shaking continued, he would shake himself right off.

"Calm yourself," Saphina said lightly, smiling at him. "No harm will come to you." She winked at him. "You will be with me and I will protect you."

Jasper looked questioningly at Zeander and to his relief he nodded in agreement. Jasper's nerves calmed somewhat and he straightened his back. If Saphina was not scared, then neither would he be.

Saphina read his mind and thought it best not to tell him that she was just as frightened as he was. The Tara Aquians, the water vessel and the underwater caves intrigued her more than anything else had on this journey, but they also frightened her greatly.

Jasper steadied his breathing and asked his question again without stammering. "Why do they need to swim guard?" Zeander looked curiously at Jasper and wondered if he should tell the truth. He looked at Saphina and knew she had read his mind. He grumbled under his breath before he decided to tell the truth. He was sure she would tell them if he did not. Oh, how he despised her gift and made a mental note to guard himself when she was around.

"I don't want to scare ya, but I think it wise that ya know what ya might be up against before you enter the waters of Lake Kellowash." Zeander noticed that he had everyone's attention. He cleared his throat and spoke slowly and clearly again so that they could understand him.

"There be mighty strange creatures that live in those waters. Most do not bother ya and are more afraid of ya than you will be of them. There are some creatures however, like the sharp fanged eel, the barnacle swordfish and the spiny red-legged octopus, that will attack ya, but usually only if ya provoke them first." Jasper wondered why anyone would attack them first; they sounded quite frightening.

"However," Zeander continued to say, looking straight at Saphina, "there be one species called the jawbrender that is a nasty, miserable creature and would as soon as kill ya as look at ya. It was them I thought attacked our village." Zeander looked at the confusion on their faces.

"Why do you think it was them that attacked the village? Do you mean they are like the Tara Aquians and swim in the water and walk on land?" Saphina again asked the questions she knew the others would ask.

"No," Zeander said, shaking his head. "The jawbrenders are giant, thick-scaled fish with large heads. They have large, thick whiskers jutting out from their cheeks. They have a huge spiked tail, two front legs and two thick side-fins that they use for legs. They can walk on land and breathe out of water for hours on end. They be wicked, smart, fast and deadly." The rest of them looked at him anxiously. "I knew it wasn't a pod of them that attacked the village, because if it had been there would have been no one left to tell the tale." He left out the fact that the large claw marks could have been from a jawbrender who was conspiring with the longtooths.

"There has been an uprising of them," Lindrella said in her singsong voice, recognizing what Zeander was telling them. Zeander translated. "They have even started to attack us. We are no longer safe in the water and have to travel in larger groups," she said with a deeply sad expression on her lovely face. The others realized just then that her world, Zeander's world, was changing just as theirs was.

"Why after all this time is there so much unrest among them?" Zusie asked. Lindrella looked over at the Tara Aquian named Kerchot. He was sturdily built with large, muscular arms and stood taller than the rest. His hair, tightly woven, hung down in thick braids past his shoulders. He was dressed in the same warrior clothes as the others: bare chest except for the vest, tight fitting pants, no shoes and a belt around his waist. Two sharp-looking daggers hung from the belt and he was holding a long spear with a multi-edged dagger at the end. At his wrist, he wore thick leather straps that he only had to twist once before sharp barbs came out.

Lindrella was dressed similarly to Kerchot but had a tight fitting sleeveless tunic covering the upper half of her body that flared out at her hips. She also wore tight fitting pants. Around her waist, she wore a thick belt that held two daggers hanging on either side of her hips. The spearhead, like Kerchot's, was multi-edged, but hers had a circle of red and blue crystals embedded at the top of the rod just under the spearhead. It clearly indicated her rank amongst her people. She too wore bracelets on her wrists and ankles.

"We were hoping," Kerchot said in a deep, throaty voice that resonated around the clearing, while Zeander translated his words, "that this little one might be able to tell us." Everyone in the group looked at the surprise on Jasper's face.

"M…m…m…me?" Jasper said in a squeaky voice and started to shake again.

"Yes…you," Lindrella said firmly but kindly to Jasper. Everyone looked at her in astonishment as she spoke clear Elfish.

"You can speak Elfish?" Saphina asked, as she looked accusingly at Lindrella.

"I…am…learning," Lindrella said slowly, but her words were heavily accented and difficult to understand.

"When will we leave?" Zusie asked.

"As soon as you be ready," Zeander answered.

Zusie looked at her daughters who nodded their answer. She then looked at Jasper. He hesitated for a moment but he too nodded that he was ready.

Zusie turned to Aldwin and clasped his hands in hers. "Please take care of Lizbeth for us." Still holding his hands, she stepped closer and said quietly so only he could hear. "If…," she started to say but Aldwin started to interrupt her. Zusie squeezed his hand lightly. "If we do not return, do not wait for us. Take our people to safety."

Words caught in his throat and all he could do was nod. He hugged Zusie warmly and then Chrystalina who had tears welling up in her eyes. She chuckled though when he told her to be careful and watch her step. When he came to Saphina, Jasper flew off her shoulder and landed on Zusie's. Aldwin held Saphina tightly to him and she returned the hug just as tightly. Aldwin was her best friend; they had spent many nights chatting about everything and anything until the wee hours of the morning. They argued heartily about which of them was better at tracking and fishing. Aldwin knew that Saphina was, but he liked to press the issue just to see her argue. Saphina knew that he knew she was better, but liked that he teased her about it. She never tired of hearing him talk about plants and their medicinal purposes. Saphina could not imagine life without Aldwin in it. He reluctantly let go of her and smiled as he felt the same way about her.

Jasper fluttered back onto Saphina's shoulder. Aldwin leaned in close to him and whispered, as he patted him affectionately on his back, "You are in charge now little one. Bring them home safely."

CHAPTER 17
The Magic of the Tara Aquians

Zusie, Chrystalina and Saphina with Jasper riding on her shoulder, stood on what Zeander had called a beach. They were each looking out over the crystal blue water and were deep in thought. Several Elfkins who were curious about how Zusie and her daughters were going to travel to Lindrella's home walked with them to the lake. Some of the Meadow Imps and all but one of the Tara Aquians stood with them as well.

One of the warriors, the large one that Saphina had seen marching last into the village, was to stay so they could communicate back and forth. His name was Duntar. Most of the Elfkins were pleased with this arrangement. If there was another raid, he was surely going to be able to protect them.

They had walked along a winding pathway that leads from the lake side of the village to the lake. Upon reaching it, a collective gasp resonated in the morning air. It was followed quickly by several 'oh my how lovely' and 'oh it's gorgeous.' Those used to the beauty of the lake smiled at the newcomers' first reaction to it.

It was beautiful. The clearing before the water's edge, surrounded on three sides by meadow, stretched several hundred paces along the shoreline in either direction. It was about seventy-five paces wide and filled with fine white dirt that squished between their toes as they walked on it.

"It's sand not dirt," Zeander corrected Saphina when she commented that she had never seen dirt that fine. The lake was not a big as they thought it would be. Its shape was a large, oblong circle where the banks on the other side did not quite meet, leaving a passageway through them.

"We thought the lake was going to be larger than this," Zusie voiced their collective thoughts.

"This is not Lake Kellowash. It be a small part of it called the Bay of Rowan. To get to the lake, you either have to walk around the bay and climb over the cropping of large boulders that dot the banks," Zeander pointed to the large boulders, "or swim through the passageway."

Beyond the bay, the Elfkins could see that the mountain range was indeed far off in the distance. Although they could not see the lake from where they stood because the boulders were so large, they realized that the lake was indeed much larger than the bay.

They had always known that mountain range as the Mighty Alps. However some, like Aldwin, now wondered if the inhabitants living in the mountains called them that as well. He was now convinced, after meeting the Meadow Imps and Tara Aquians, that there must be creatures living in the mountains. He fleetingly wondered whether they were friendly.

The Elfkins breathed in deeply and smiled. The bay smelled of earth, water, plant life and sun. It was glorious, they thought, as they exhaled slowly. To their delight, the bluish-green water shimmered as the sun's rays hit it. Small waves rolled in and out gently with the tide. The soft movement of the tide made the bay look as if it were breathing. They revered its beauty and speculated at how much larger the lake was. A movement to the left of them caught their eyes and they all looked as dozens of black and brown spotted flying bugs, no larger than an underling's finger, flew out from the meadow towards the lake.

"Oh look da! What are those called?" Isla inquired. She and her older siblings, Mia, Lea, Fran, Willbyn and Bran, were standing beside their ma and da. Porthos was holding Isla, and Mirabella was holding their youngest son Tom. Porthos shrugged his shoulders then looked at Zeander. Zeander looked at the other Meadow Imps who looked at the Tara Aquians. None of them knew the name of the bugs.

The swarm of bugs flew out over the water and darted here and there as they playfully skimmed the surface. The underlings giggled with joy at their antics. Suddenly however, they stopped giggling and shrieked in horror.

The Elfkins looked in shock as a large form; three feet long and almost as round flew out of the water not thirty feet from the shore. It caught as many of the flying bugs as it could in its large gaping mouth, then splashed back down into the water. The waves from the splash washed onto the shore. Those standing nearest to the shoreline stepped back a pace so that the water did not wet their feet. The Tara Aquians stood still, not caring whether their bare feet got wet or not.

"What in the name of Zenrah was that?" Chrystalina called out in fright for the arm of her mother's tunic. Jasper, just as startled as the rest, flew up in the air and fluttered nervously back and forth over everyone's heads.

"W...w...was that a jawbrender?" Marla asked shakily as she stood beside Rangous. Zeander laughed heartily as he looked up at Marla. He translated what she had asked to Lindrella and the rest of the Tara Aquians. They smirked slightly but otherwise looked bored with the question.

"All right," Zusie said sternly, looking down at Zeander who quickly stopped laughing. She looked at him curiously; something was amiss about him today, but she could not put her finger on it. "So what was it then?" she asked.

"Oh that," Zeander said, still smiling. "That was just a green back kipper, harmless to everyone…but those flying bugs, that is."

"Green back kippers," Rangous and Septer said in unison with great astonishment. Zeander looked at them.

"Well, there are green back kippers in the Bantor River," Septer said.

"But none that size!" Rangous said. His eyes were wide with delight. Quickly forgetting the reason why they were at the lake, they started talking about their fishing poles and what bait to use.

"Obviously," Septer said, "if we could catch some of those flying bugs…."

"That would be ideal," Rangous agreed as three more green back kippers of different sizes jumped out of the water. Septer and Rangous found it quite interesting that the bugs did not fly back to the safety of the meadow but continued to fly just above the water. They shrugged their shoulders and smiled at each other gleefully as they knew there was plenty of other bait that they could use. They excitedly started to list off all the things they would need until they heard a rather loud, disgruntled "ahem" from Aldwin. They looked up and saw everyone staring at them, some smirking while others looked at them crossly.

"Sorry," they both said in unison.

Zusie smiled before she turned back to Zeander. She knew they enjoyed fishing and was not upset with them. She looked at Zeander again curiously. Something was out of place with him this morning. Why was he so low to the ground, she thought. Then it dawned on her. "Where's Paraphin?" she asked worriedly. "I haven't seen him…," she paused trying to remember the last time she had seen him. "I haven't seen him since the two of you dashed into the meadow."

The others looked around as well; none of them had seen him since then either. So much had gone on since they entered Zeander's village that they did not give any thought to it. Zeander dropped his shoulders and looked sadly at Zusie and her daughters.

"When we got into the village, he went after the longtooths and…he hasn't come back," Zeander said.

Worried expressions showed on many of their faces. They had come to like and respect Paraphin. It would be a shame to lose him.

"Is that normal?" Zusie asked.

"No," Zeander said.

Lindrella looked at the saddened faces. She recognized Paraphin's name and knew they worried about him. There was nothing they could do about it. They had no idea in what direction he went. Sending out a search party for him would be fruitless. In her singsong voice, Lindrella spoke to Zeander.

"Lindrella says it time to go," Zeander said, looking at Zusie. Zusie looked at each of her daughters. Saphina was excited about the excursion beneath the water while Chrystalina showed signs that she was afraid. She, however, was not as scared as Jasper, who looked to be making his way back to the village.

"Jasper," Saphina called and he reluctantly flew back to her, sat on her right shoulder and dangled his legs down the front of her tunic. The bravery he had shown before vanished once he saw the large fish jump out of the water. He was worried. After all, he looked to be just a large bug himself. The green back kippers would think he was a meal and a fine one at that with how plump and large he was. A vision of him flying or swimming frantically away from a very large kipper popped into his mind. The vision changed to Jasper flying into the mouth of a jawbrender. He shivered in fright and Saphina looked crossly at him.

"Jasper, you really need to clear your mind of those visions," she said. Then she added reassuringly, "I won't let anything happen to you." Jasper nodded in relief as he tried to calm his nerves. Lindrella watched the exchange between them again, but said nothing.

"Where are the vessels?" Aldwin asked. The Elfkins looked around for the bubble shaped vessels that Zeander had told them about. There was nothing resemble a bubble anywhere. Perhaps, they thought, they were under the water.

Zeander looked up at Lindrella and quietly told her that they were ready to go. Lindrella motioned for Zusie and her daughters to follow her. She put her hand up to stay them five feet from the water. Everyone else standing around had followed but kept a couple of paces back, leaving a fair distance between them and the water's edge Caution and growing fear replaced their initial delight. Zeander noticed their change of attitude as they whispered anxiously among themselves. He shook his head and smirked at their innocence. They had little knowledge of things outside their village. The Greenwood Forest had protected them not just from the elements, but from time and its ever-changing ways. He shook his head again. A frown replaced the smirk. His newfound friends had much to learn if they were to survive the journey outside of the valley and the coming war that Zeander knew was inevitable.

Silence fell and the Elfkins watched with curiosity as Lindrella walked to the water's edge and bent down. The smirk on Zeander's face was back. Oh, they are going to enjoy this, he thought, as he too watched what she was doing.

Lindrella cupped her hands together and scooped up a handful of water. Carrying it carefully in her hands, she brought it back and stood in front of Zusie. She looked at Zusie expectantly. Zusie returned her look. Instinctively, she knew that Lindrella was asking for permission to do something with the water. What, she did not know, but was soon to find out as she nodded in agreement.

Everyone in the clearing stared at Lindrella as she motioned with her head for Chrystalina, Aldwin and Saphina to stand back from Zusie. Chrystalina and Saphina looked apprehensively at their mother. Zusie nodded that she was okay and smiled at them. Lindrella brought the water up over Zusie's head.

"Stand still and do not move," Lindrella said calmly; Zeander translated.

Lindrella looked engrossed as she stared intensely at her hands. Words flowed from her lips but not in her usual singsong way. They instead blended and drowned out in a soft husky whisper. Very, very slowly, the water started to trickle out of Lindrella's hands as she continued to speak.

"What is she saying?" Saphina whispered to Zeander without taking her eyes off Lindrella, as the water formed a circle three feet in diameter above Zusie's head.

Zeander answered her without taking his eyes off the scene before him. He had always found this amazing to watch. "She be chanting the ritual of aqua inversion." Zeander sensed not only Saphina's confusion, but that of all who were watching it for the first time. He tried to explain to them the magic of the Tara Aquians, which was no easy feat, as he did not fully understand it himself.

"She is able to form the water to her will. It bends to her demand like an underling to its ma," he said, trying to simplify what they were seeing. He looked around and saw that they were not grasping what he was saying. "It be hard to explain," he said. He knit his brow as he looked for the words to describe what they were going to see. They

Elfkins looked with astonishment at what Lindrella was doing as Zeander explained.

"She can command the water, but only because it chooses it to be so. They live as one. The water knows that without the Tara Aquians, there would be no order in the lake. The Tara Aquians know that without the water they would not survive. So they work in cooperation with each other." He spoke as if the lake was alive, an entity onto itself. They were even more confused so Zeander stopped talking and let them watch as Lindrella performed the ritual.

The water expanded and formed slowly over Zusie's head like a thin, clear shield. She tensed as it went past her nose; instinctively holding her breath. Kerchot, who was standing nearby, noticed this and said, "Breathe." Zeander translated. Zusie relaxed and breathed normally.

When the water reached her feet, it slipped underneath them and she was raised a fraction but was still able to stand. It felt cool under her bare feet and solid as if she was standing on a stone. The water had formed a perfect circle around her; a perfect bubble as Zeander had called it. Zusie breathed in and out and found she could do so with ease. As she turned to look at her daughters, the bubble turned with her. It wobbled with her movement. Lindrella held up her hands and without touching it, the bubble steadied.

"Can you hear me?" Zusie asked, smiling at her daughters. Her voice sounded clear to her.

"Your voice sounds muffled, but yes, we can hear you just fine," Saphina said loudly as the others looked on in amazement. Some of the underlings clapped their hands in excitement and laughed with glee. They asked their mas if they could try it next. Zusie laughed lightly at their courage. Although their voices sounded muffled, she could hear them as well.

Lindrella turned and nodded at two sturdily built Tara Aquians. They came forward, stood on either side of the bubble and held out their spears. Lindrella took one of the spears, brushed the sand off the dull end of the shaft, and placed it against the bubble. It jiggled slightly and rippled with a rainbow of colours as the sun shone off it.

Lindrella spoke again as if in a trance and a small hole appeared where the shaft touched the bubble. The water was opening against the spear and she pushed it in about five inches. To everyone's amazement, the bubble did not pop but closed tightly against the shaft. It was encased solidly in the bubble. They watched as she did the same with the shaft of the second spear. Some of the Elfkins looked fretfully at the bubble while others giggled. It looked quite strange and comical at the same time.

"The spears are used as handles for the Tara Aquians and for Zusie," Zeander said. "Otherwise she will not be able to stand upright once they start to move."

Hearing this, Zusie grabbed the spears and noticed as she did that they did not budge; they indeed were solidly encased in the bubble. She marveled at the ingenuity of it.

"The sharp end of the spear," Zeander continued, "be placed on the outside to deter anything from coming too close to the bubble." Everyone looked at him as if his words made perfect sense.

The two Tara Aquians grabbed hold of the spears, picked up the bubble, walked around in a circle with it, and then gently put it back down on the ground. Again, to everyone's surprise, the bubble did not break nor did Zusie fall through the bottom of it. Zusie realized that without the handles she would have indeed toppled over. The Tara Aquians had done this for one reason. It was to show everyone, especially Chrystalina, Jasper and Saphina, that they would be safe inside the bubbles.

Lindrella performed the ritual over Chrystalina next. She stood still as her mother had and, even though she was still nervous, she breathed normally. When it came to Saphina and Jasper's turn he was so scared he shook himself off Saphina's shoulder. He slid down the front of her tunic and she caught him in her open hands. His snout grazed the tip of her fingers but did not puncture them. Every Elfkin gasped in horror. Even Jasper gasped. Aldwin stepped forward as Saphina put Jasper back on her shoulder.

"Here," Aldwin said as he pulled out a long thin piece of cloth from his medicine bag. "Curl up your snout, Jasper." Remembering poor Lizbeth, he did as Aldwin asked without question. Lindrella asked Zeander what they were doing. Zeander explained all about Jasper's unique snout and the poisonous venom. Lindrella exchanged a look of surprise with Kerchot as Aldwin placed the cloth on Jasper's curled up snout. He quickly tied the ends of it in a knot at the back of Jasper's head. With a small blade, he cut off the excess material.

"Thank you," Jasper said, a little nasally.

Saphina suggested that he close his eyes, as he was still thoroughly frightened even though he could see that Zusie and Chrystalina were fine. Zeander told Saphina that, once the spears were in place, Jasper could fly around in the bubble without worrying that he would pop it. "The bubble," he said in a matter of fact voice. "Though made of water, is solid and can only be broken with a reversal chant."

Saphina thanked him for the information. Jasper's little fingers were digging into her shoulder and if she winced from the pain he would have flown off before the bubble was formed. She was not sure she could have convinced him to come back so she kept quiet. Once the bubble was finished she hoped he would loosen his grip or fly around as Zeander had suggested.

The group of Elfkins and Meadow Imps waved goodbye as the Tara Aquians carried them into the water. They quickly waved back; all except Jasper whose eyes were tightly shut. With his snout now bandaged, he hid his head against Saphina's neck. The bubbles submerged with ease; Zusie and her daughters vanished one at a time from sight underneath the water.

Aldwin looked out at the water long after many of the others had left. Bauthal, Septer, Rangous, Marla and Zeander stayed with him, looking at the spot where their friends had vanished from view. They said nothing, each too caught up in their own thoughts to speak. A fish jumped out of the water again, startling all of them but Aldwin into action. Rangous and Septer looked from where the fish splashed back into the water and then to each other and smiled broadly.

"We're going fishing," Septer said happily, looking at the others excitedly.

"Would you like to come with us?" Rangous asked. Marla and Bauthal shook their heads, declining the offer.

"I will walk with you back to the village to get your gear, though," Marla said. "I am sure Old Barty needs a break from watching over Lizbeth. I think I will ask some of the villagers to help me bring her trolley here. I think she would love that."

"I will help," Bauthal said.

Marla smiled. Many of the Elfkins and some of the forest creatures stopped by Lizbeth's trolley throughout the day. They said a quick hello to her or sat with her, telling her of their experiences on the journey. The only ones who did not were Paramo, her followers and their families; they thought the idea was a waste of time. On occasion however, when Paramo was nowhere to be seen, Martan would stop by and say a quick hello. Septer and Rangous offered to help Marla and Bauthal.

"No, you go fishing," Marla said as she squeezed Rangous' hand. "There are enough of us and I will ask the Tara Aquian who stayed if he can help as well. He could probably move the trolley by himself he is so big. Did anyone get his name?"

"Duntar," Zeander replied.

Before the four of them left, Zeander pointed to a cropping of rocks on the right side of the beach. He told them that just behind it was a large pool where many different kinds of smaller fish lived.

"The fish in the bay are too large for you to catch," Zeander said. Rangous and Septer looked at each other, thinking that they could take on the fish in the bay when a much larger fish, longer and fatter than the two of them put together, jumped out of the water after the bugs.

"Perhaps," Rangous said looking at Septer, "we should listen to Zeander." Septer nodded in agreement. Enthusiastically, they started to chat about what bait and fishing techniques they would use. Marla shook her head and smiled at the two of them as they walked with her and Bauthal back to the village.

Zeander and Aldwin stood on the beach looking out onto the bay. A piece of driftwood washed up onto the shore just in front of them and Zeander looked at it curiously an idea for the transportation across the lake formed quickly in his mind. He then looked up at Aldwin who sighed heavily.

"They'll be alright," Zeander said encouragingly. Aldwin did not look like he was going to move from the spot until his friends were returned safely.

"I have an idea for the vessels that will transport us across the water, if ya have a mind to listen to it that is?" Zeander added, as he watched the driftwood bob in the water.

That brought Aldwin out of his reverie, remembering that Zusie had asked him to find a way across the lake. He looked down at Zeander and nodded. They took a couple of steps before Aldwin froze in mid stride and looked curiously at Zeander who was still walking. Zeander had taken several steps, talking rapidly about his idea, before he realized that Aldwin was no longer walking beside him. He turned around quickly only to find Aldwin staring at him with a puzzled looked on his face.

"If you're here...who is going to translate for them?" Aldwin asked.

"Ah yes," Zeander said, looking at the lake then back at Aldwin. "We forgot to mention that part. Desamiha the truth sayer will translate for them." As if that would make perfect sense to Aldwin, Zeander turned around and started to walk again towards the village. Aldwin looked dumbfounded at Zeander, wondering who Desamiha was and what the heck was a truth sayer.

Again, Zeander had taken several steps along the pathway before he realized that Aldwin was not following him. This time, he had to walk back to the beach. He stood in front of Aldwin, his hands on his hips, looking up at him with an expression of scorn on his face, which quickly changed to one of mild irritation.

"Oh, that's right. I keep forgetting how little ya Elfkins know." Aldwin, not offended by Zeander's comment, looked at him curiously. "Come on," Zeander said, waving his hand at Aldwin. "Walk with me and I will tell you all about Desamiha as we work on my idea for the craft that will ride on the water; it be a great story."

Zeander and Aldwin left the lake. Zeander talked excitedly about his idea and Aldwin listened intently to each word. Neither of them saw another green back kipper jump out of the water after the bugs or the much larger fish that followed it. That fish, five times larger than any they had seen, swallowed the kipper completely then dropped back into the water, causing a huge wave to wash onto the shore.

CHAPTER 18
Lake Kellowash

``Jasper,'' Saphina exclaimed with pure delight. "You have to see this! Open your eyes. You're missing it!" Jasper tentatively opened his eyes and looked to the right. He began to shiver in fright however, as a very large white and black striped fish with three large spikes on its tail fin came barreling down on them. Its mouth was agape and large, jagged teeth stuck out from it at odd angles. Jasper thought it was big enough to eat them whole, bubble and all.

He did not see what had happened next as his eyes were tightly shut and his head was in the crook between Saphina's shoulder and neck. He shuddered pathetically. If he had kept his eyes opened, he would have seen that there was nothing to fear. Two of the Tara Aquians assigned to guard them swam forward, stopped right in front of the fish and held up their spears. Upon seeing them, the giant fish swerved and went in the other direction.

Saphina relaxed her hold on the handles inside the bubble. She had been a little afraid of the fish as well. It had been the largest one they had seen yet. However, Tara Aquians were very good at guarding and she knew she worried needlessly.

The life in the lake was much larger and definitely more dangerous looking than what they had seen in the bay. There was actually not much to see in the bay. Once they had found their balance inside the bubbles and got used to floating along, they looked all around them but saw nothing of great interest. There had been fish and plenty of them -- small ones, large ones and some even twice the length of a Tara Aquian. However, when they got near one, the fish would simply swim away. The water in the bay was also very murky; the Bantor River drained into it and constantly stirred loose sediment at the bottom. Getting a close look at a fish was nearly impossible, as it would just swim into the depths and out of view whenever they got too close.

Saphina noticed that the Tara Aquians kept the bubbles about five feet under the surface. She was going to ask her guards why they did not swim deeper, but then remembered that they did not understand

Elfish. The Tara Aquians were strong swimmers and the muscles in their arms and legs rippled. Saphina noticed that they always kept their heads facing forward, even when they swam.

The little caravan must have looked quite odd, moving along at a good pace through the water. Lindrella was in the lead with her personal guards swimming with her in perfect formation. Two on either side of her a two at behind her. Next was Saphina and Jasper. The guards that held their bubbles steady on the beach pushed them through the water and six more, three on either side, swam a couple of paces in front, beside and behind their bubble. Then Zusie and Chrystalina followed with the same amount of guards swimming in the same formation. Kerchot brought up the rear, guarding their backs.

As they neared the entrance into the lake from the bay, Saphina could see why they had not gone any deeper. About twenty feet below them, jagged rocks jutted up from the bay floor, much like the white crystals jutted down from the ceiling of the Crystal Cave. These rocks were grey in colour and looked quite sharp and somewhat sinister -- like large fingers reaching up to grab whoever was brave enough to swim over them.

Entering the lake from the bay was not as easy as going from point A to point B; joining the two bodies of water was a trench with steeply slanted walls made of solid rock. It was about fifty feet across at its widest point and in some places; it narrowed down to just fifteen feet. It was over three hundred feet long and, though it was not far from the surface of the water, it was quite dark. Like the bay floor, it had jagged rocks that stuck out from the walls. As it was, the guards swimming on the sides of the bubbles had to change positions, swimming in single file in front or behind the bubbles.

Saphina thought it was quite intimidating to be stuck in a bubble going through a dark passageway with jagged rocks that could slice you open if you were to stray off course. If not for the light shining from the crystals on Lindrella's spear, they would not have been able to see anything. The guards that held the bubbles slowed their pace through the trench. The current running through it was swift and, if not for their strength and skill, they would have crashed into the walls, possibly popping the bubbles. Even though Zeander had said that the only way to pop them was with a reversal chant, Saphina, Zusie and Chrystalina worried nevertheless.

Once they entered the lake, they all sighed heavily; glad to have made it through the trench without a scratch. The Tara Aquians had taken Meadow Imps through the trench before, but their bubbles were nowhere near the size of Zusie or her daughters'. It was a testament to their skills and strength that they safely made it through the trench.

All foreboding thoughts about safety vanished from their minds once they reached the lake. Entering Lake Kellowash was like entering a completely new world; a world that Zusie and her daughters could have never imagined existed. It was unlike anything that had ever seen in the Greenwood Forest or the Crystal Cave. It was so strikingly beautiful, in fact, that it astounded them.

The water was clear, so clear they could see several feet in front of them. Here the fish swam in large pods and did not whisk away when the caravan came close. They just moved to the side and let them pass, looking, Saphina thought, curiously at them. A hundred feet into the lake, the guards started a slow decline. They swam deeper and deeper until the sunlight filtering through the water diminished to complete blackness. They rode in darkness for about an hour. It was so dark it was difficult to see the light from Lindrella's spear, let alone any fish.

The darkness gradually gave way to a kaleidoscope of light and colour. The light, to their astonishment, was radiating from crystals in shades of pale pinks, deep purples, brilliant yellows, glowing oranges and rustic reds as well as blues and greens in every shade imaginable. It reminded them of the spring flowers on the forest floor, but their brilliance was magnified a hundred fold. The crystals lit up the water and the travelers could now see clearly in every direction.

Zusie and her daughters exclaimed gleefully as they looked around in utter delight. This part of the lake was full of life. Fish of every size and colour of the rainbow swam around freely doing whatever it was that fish do. Slithery snake-like creatures weaved in and out of the plant life that was as varied and intricate as the fish were.

Slimy, bubbled-headed creatures with long tendrils that shimmered iridescently bobbed along in the water, moving lazily with the current. Large, armor-backed, four-legged creatures with small heads and little tails swam in pods of six to nine, looking at the caravan of bubbles and Tara Aquians with interest. Chrystalina was sure that she had seen a particularly old one smile at her and nod in greeting. She wondered if her mother and sister had seen it as well as they passed, and made a mental note to ask them.

Unfortunately, they were too far behind her to yell to them. She quickly forgot about the strange creatures as a rather large pod of fish came barreling down on them. The fish did not have a chance to get close however, as the guards quickly blocked them. Saphina shivered. It was a beautiful, but also very dangerous place: a place where the rule of the day was survival of the fittest or the fastest. She wondered how there could be so many little fish swimming around with such ferocious, larger ones lurking in the water.

Saphina realized, as she looked at the crystals, that they formed a natural habitat. The crystals cascaded in every direction -- large ones on smaller ones, smaller ones on larger ones -- creating a stack of caverns that the smaller fish could live in. She saw that her assumption was right as several small yellow and white striped fish quickly dashed into the holes as a much larger, thin, black-scaled fish with a long snout and two buck teeth sticking out from its upper jaw swam towards them.

Zusie had seen a similar situation and wondered at the beauty and brutality of the place. Life in the lake was so different from life in the forest. She turned her head away in horror but not before she witnessed a pod of fish with razor, sharp teeth swarm around a beautiful blue fish five times their size. They tore into its flesh and hungrily ripped it apart.

She said a quick prayer to Zenrah that their new life on the other side of the mountain would be like the life they had in the Greenwood Forest. However, she knew that Zenrah would not be able to answer her prayer. Her thoughts then turned to the Light of Goodness that Jasper spoke of and wondered about it for quite some time as they continued to travel through the water.

Time passed as time does, but under the water, it was harder to gage how much as there was no sun or shadow to work with. The scenery changed often, from crystal beds with all manner of fish living among them, to barren rock where little lived, to lush beds of green plant life that looked like the grasses in the meadow. Here, snake-like creatures watched the procession from behind the plant life but never ventured out to take a closer look. The girls' legs started to tire and their hands itched to let go of the handles but they dare not for fear of toppling over.

Their stomachs rumbled and their mouths felt dry. The noonday break must have passed and each of them wished they had brought a pouch of food. They wondered why no one had suggested it; perhaps they thought the smell from the food would have attracted unwanted attention. Thankfully, they had relieved themselves before leaving; this journey would have been a little harder to stand through if they had not.

More time passed by and the scenery changed yet again. Grayish green coloured boulders surrounded by long thick blades of grass-like plants stood out in regular intervals on the lake floor. Finally, they came to what looked like the end of their journey through the lake.

Before them stood a wall of solid green vines that rose up about hundred feet or more and spread out as far as they could see on either side of them. The vines looked more like a waterfall of snakes as they coiled and uncoiled with the movement of the water.

Kerchot came forward. Lindrella nodded at him and then spoke -- not in a chant this time, but in her singsong voice. It sounded as if she were talking with someone. The girls watched in wonder as the vines stopped moving and loosely hung down. Three more Tara Aquians came forward. They swam up to the vines and, with Kerchot's help; they pulled open the vines. The vines, though heavy, went willingly. The girls looked from the wall to each other, as they were now close enough to see each other's expressions. They were all amazed at what they saw. Each of them wondered what would happen if someone or something other than a Tara Aquian tried to make their way through the curtain of vines. Would the vines go willingly or encase them in a death grip?

Behind the vines was a rather large hole that looked to be the entrance to a channel. Lindrella and her guards led the way in. The procession entered the hole in the same formation as they had traveled through the lake.

The channel was a long tunnel that was so dark they could not tell if rock or vines surrounded them. Again, the only light they could see was from Lindrella's spear. Occasionally, the light would disappear as if she had swum around a corner before quickly coming back into view. They had journeyed through the tunnel for quite some time before they saw a glimmer of light ahead. Suddenly, they burst out of the channel and into a cave that was completely submersed in water. The greyish green rocks they saw on the other side of the curtain of vines formed a stairway. It looked just like the stairway that went up the side of Mount Aspentonia.

Zusie and her daughters looked curiously around as the Tara Aquians closed the gap between the bubbles, swimming closer together and in single file just as they had through the trench between the bay and the lake. On either side of the stairway, rocks, much like the ones at the entrance from the bay to the lake, stuck out. They found it quite odd that they followed the steps up instead of just swimming up the side of the cave until they heard a low rumbling sound that is. They watched in amazement as several jets of water shot out from between the jagged rocks. This happened often and not in the same place twice. The only place it did not happen was on the stairway.

They continued to follow the steps up but slowed the pace to a crawl the closer they got to a large, thick, black ledge that stuck out from the cave wall. Saphina, being ahead of the others, noticed that the top half of the ledge was above the water and that something on top of the ledge was glowing. Saphina wondered if the golden glow was an archway like the one to the entrance of the Crystal Cave.

The two Tara Aquians carrying her bubble stepped out of the water and onto the thick stone ledge. They walked a few paces away from the stone staircase and gently set the bubble down but continued to hold it steady. Saphina shrugged her shoulders to wake Jasper. "Jasper, we are here. Open your eyes. You have to see this," Saphina said in a mystified voice as she started in amazement at something straight ahead of her.

During the journey through the lake, Jasper had opened his eyes a couple of times but preferred to travel with them shut; he eventually fell asleep. Slowly, he opened his eyes and started to stretch his arms and legs before abruptly stopping in mid-stretch. He too stared at what Saphina was looking at.

Zusie and Chrystalina arrived and were just as astounded as Saphina and Jasper were; so much so, they were speechless. No words could describe what they saw before them. They blinked their eyes several times to make sure they were actually seeing what they were seeing: a cave bathed in gold.

CHAPTER 19

The Golden City of Awnmorielle

Nothing they had seen thus far on their journey could surpass what now lay before them: the Golden City of Awnmorielle. Zeander had told them about it; however, they could not envision how large it would be. The ledge they were standing on was about a hundred feet wide and thirty feet deep. At the back of the ledge was a large archway leading into a massive cave. On either side of the archway, intricately carved stone pillars, four feet round, stood flush against the walls and spanned from floor to ceiling. The pillars were made of gold crystals. Intricate scenes like on the stone table in the Crystal Cave were carved into them. However, where those scenes depicted life on the land and the changing of the seasons, these carvings depicted underwater scenes. Zusie and her daughters wanted to take a closer look but, being encased in the bubbles as they were, all they could do was look around.

The pillars were an impressive entranceway to the city itself. Awnmorielle was a massive cave twenty times wider than the Crystal Cave and five times taller. To say that it was a cave was to diminish what it was. However, how else do you explain a city inside a mountain -- whose only access was through a long tunnel hidden behind a curtain of vines and a flight of stairs submerged in a couple hundred feet of water -- other than to say it was a cave? That, however, was where the similarity ended.

Along the walls of the cave, stone staircases led way to large balconies that stuck out about three feet from the face of the wall with handrails made of petrified wood. There were three rows of balconies stacked on top of each other ten feet apart. Along each balcony, several golden archways ten feet in height and three feet wide led into smaller caves. The newcomers to the city would soon learn that the Tara Aquians used these smaller caves as their sleeping quarters. The main cave curved back into the side of the mountain, much as the entrance hallway to the Crystal Cave did; the balconies and stairways stretched the length of the walls, curving out of sight with the hallways.

The city was alive with noise and movement as Tara Aquians young and old went about their business. They paid no mind to the caravan of travelers standing at the entranceway. Zusie found that odd and wondered how often a troop of Tara Aquians brought three bubbles carrying strange beings to the city. She did not have time to ponder her thoughts as a commotion caught her attention.

In the center of the city, a large stone statue of a female Tara Aquian dressed in what looked like a traditional gown stood erect facing the entranceway; her arms outstretched in greeting. The statue stood about twenty feet high and had a five-foot circumference at the base that tapered up to the head, which held a crown of jewels and white glossy shells. The statue was carved from crystals. They looked just like the ones in the golden archway on the side of Mount Aspentonia. A rainbow of colours radiating a shimmering light surrounded the golden statue. It lit up the center of the city in a soft, colourful glow. At closer look, the rainbows of colours were small carvings of all manner of fish and underwater plant life. Someone had painstakingly carved each character from a different colour of crystal like the ones they passed on their journey through Lake Kellowash.

The statue was the middle of a large stone fountain, twenty feet in circumference, four feet high and less than a foot thick, depending on the size of the stone. The stones were the same greyish green ones that dotted the lakebed before the wall of vines, only smaller, and were stacked neatly on top of each other. Along its ledge, a smooth stone bench two feet off the floor curved completely around it. Carvings of fish made from the greyish green rocks held the bench up. Water jetted out at different heights from little holes on the floor of the fountain. They bathed the statue in a constant stream of water.

Three rows of smaller half-moon shaped benches that were solid rock with a smooth top for sitting on, surrounded the fountain on all sides. This was where the commotion was. A small group of young Tara Aquians were playing a game of chase and tag, a game the underlings played back home. An older Tara Aquian, holding a staff in his hand, interrupted their game. He reminded the newcomers of Old Barty and they smiled at the comparison as the young ones ran off.

Lindrella came forward to stand in front of Saphina and Jasper; both of them leaned their heads to the left, trying to peer past her. They quickly brought their eyes back to her when she reached out her hands. Touching but not touching the bubble, she spoke the words of the reversal chant.

The bubble jiggled a little and she took her hands away and stepped back a couple of feet. Jasper asked Saphina what was going to happen; she shrugged her shoulders. She looked at each of the Tara Aquians who had brought them through the water but they stared straight ahead.

They continued to hold the bubble steady with their spears. Saphina, not knowing what else to do, held on as well.

The bubble jiggled some more and Saphina looked up. She squinted her eyes, thinking that she and Jasper were about to be drenched with water. To her amazement, a tiny hole appeared at the top of the bubble. Gradually the hole got bigger and bigger; going down the side just like it had formed. Only now the water was disappearing as the hole got larger. Jasper nudged her cheek with his elbow and, when she looked at him, he pointed a little finger at her feet. Saphina looked down and noticed that the water was slowly pooling around her. Within a few minutes, the bubble was gone; Saphina and Jasper looked curiously at each other and smiled. Lindrella bowed her head before the water at Saphina's feet and quickly spoke to it again. It jiggled in response then trickled over the edge of the ledge they were standing on.

Saphina shook her head in astonishment and looked up at the two Tara Aquians who had brought her through the water. They were looking at her expectantly and, for a moment, she was confused at their look until she realized she was still holding the ends of their spears. She smiled at them, embarrassed, and let go of the spears. They stayed beside her, looking expectantly at her again. Now what do they want? She wondered then whispered her thoughts to Jasper.

"Perhaps they want to make sure you don't stumble with your first step," he said wisely. Saphina took a tentative step forward and wobbled a bit but was able to move without collapsing to the ground. They bowed to her and Jasper and walked a couple of paces away, turned sharply with their backs to the city, and watched as Lindrella walked over to Zusie. Saphina flexed her fingers and rubbed each hand in turn. She had not realized how cramped they had become. Jasper stood up on her shoulder and was about to fly off.

"Stay close," Saphina whispered to him. Instead of flying off her shoulder, he stretched his arms and legs then sat back down on her shoulder. Saphina turned to watch Lindrella perform the reversal chant on her mother's bubble. Zusie had no problems with being able to stand and took a step without falling after she let go of the spears. She rubbed her hands and stretched her fingers as Saphina had.

Lindrella finished the reversal chant on Chrystalina's bubble but as she took a step forward, her legs gave out. The guards caught her before she fell to the ground. Holding her arms at the elbow, they walked with her back and forth until she was able to take a couple of steps on her own without falling. The three of them looked at each other and smiled broadly, relieved that they had made it through the journey safely.

"That was quite the experience," Zusie said, looking at each of her daughters.

"Yes it was," Jasper said. Saphina looked strangely at him.

"How would you know, Jasper? You slept most of the way here," she teased lightly. Jasper chuckled in response and raised his hands and shoulders, as if to say, "Oh well." Saphina, Zusie and Chrystalina chuckled at his response.

All the guards walked to Kerchot and, after listening to what he said, they came back in single file and bowed their heads to Zusie, her daughters and Jasper. Not knowing what was going on and hoping that it was the right response they bowed their heads as well. Once the guards received their bow they left, each of them went in a different direction. Lindrella motioned for Zusie, her daughters and Jasper to follow her. She did not wait to see if they complied; they fell in line behind her. Kerchot once again brought up the rear.

They walked side by side; Saphina and Jasper were in the middle, with Zusie on their right and Chrystalina at their left. The Tara Aquians still went about their business, not giving the newcomers a second look.

"Have either of you wondered how we are supposed to communicate with them when Zeander is not here to translate for us?" Saphina asked. Zusie and Chrystalina shrugged their shoulders and shook their heads. "Hmm," Saphina said, looking back at Kerchot who was walking a couple of paces behind them, staring straight ahead. "Hopefully there is someone here who can translate or we are in for a long night," Saphina said. Zusie and Chrystalina nodded as they continued to follow Lindrella through the city.

The grasses in the meadow moved slightly back and forth about a hundred feet from the sandy clearing before the lake. However, they only moved in one spot, and the wind was not blowing. Rangous raised his weapon, a bow and arrow, at the spot where he saw movement. Seeing this, Duntar raised his weapon as well and waited for the movement to come again.

They had been standing watch. Rangous looked out over the meadow to the right while Duntar looked out over the meadow to the left. The elders of both villages, after much discussion, thought it wise to post guards there, as well as on both sides of the village. Earlier on in their shift, Duntar and Rangous tried to communicate. After a frustrating half hour, they only learned each other's names, so they gave up the attempt to communicate verbally. Instead, they made noises with their mouths if they saw a movement or heard a noise to get each other's attention. In between these times, they stood in silence, watching, waiting, and periodically switched sides.

The sun had almost set and the sky was turning darker, making it more difficult to see. They peered at the spot, trying to see if something was moving around and coming closer. Duntar quickly looked back to the left, making sure that no one was trying to sneak up on them while their backs were turned.

The movement came again, only this time it was closer. Something or someone was slowly making its way towards the clearing. Duntar looked at Rangous and motioned that he was going to walk into the meadow where it met the water, circle around and sneak up from behind whatever was out there. Rangous understood and nodded. He wondered however at how someone as big as Duntar could walk through the meadow unseen and unheard. Duntar disappeared from Rangous' view five feet into the meadow.

The movement came again, now just twenty feet away from the clearing. Rangous nervously raised his bow and arrow, ready to shoot at whatever it was. Duntar called out his name, not in pain or aggravation but calmly. He slowly raised his head up at the last spot where Rangous had seen movement. Holding his hand in the air, he calmly called Rangous' name again. Rangous understood and lowered his weapon as he watched Duntar stand with some difficulty. He was holding something very large and dark in his massive arms, cradled it as if it was a small underling.

Duntar walked slowly through the meadow towards the beach, not caring about how much noise he was making. He tenderly carried the thing in his arms and talked to it soothingly. Rangous looked strangely at Duntar and wondered what he could be carrying so tenderly. As Duntar stepped into the clearing, Rangous' jaw dropped open in shock when he realized that the large dark shape was Paraphin.

The mighty snake looked near death's door but had enough strength in him to scold Duntar weakly. "Put me down...you big oaf. I can... ssslither along on my own...without your... asssissstance." Paraphin's words came slowly with labored breaths and he winced with each step that Duntar took.

Duntar did not put him down, either because he did not understand what Paraphin was saying or because he was simply ignoring him. Rangous motioned that he was going for help but Duntar stayed him with a shake of his head. Kneeling down, he gently placed Paraphin on the ground. Duntar stood as Rangous knelt beside Paraphin and looked him over. Rangous winced as if in pain himself as he looked at all the open sores and long scratches.

He looked curiously at a large, odd mark just below Paraphin's head. He wanted to ask Paraphin what could have made such a mark, but Paraphin's eyes were closed. He seemed to be resting. Duntar put two fingers into the belt at his waist and pulled out a reed about three inches long and an inch wide. Rangous looked up at him curiously, as Duntar put the reed between his lips and blew.

The sound, like a very loud honking noise, vibrated in the night air. It was so loud it startled a flock of tiny yellow birds with black tipped wings who were sitting quietly on the very tips of the grasses on the left hand side of the clearing. Rangous had watched them earlier with interest. They sat very still, not making a sound until bugs flew by them, then they moved with quick agility, catching the bugs in their beaks; chomping down on the bugs a couple of times before they swallowing. Not liking the sound the whistle made, they nosily squawked in annoyance at Duntar before they flew away.

Rangous put his hands over his ears as Duntar blew into the reed again. It was the same sound he and the others heard the last time they were with Paraphin, before he took off with Zeander on his back towards the Meadow Imps' village. Rangous understood now why Duntar stopped him from leaving to get help. The whistle would call help to them. It was wiser than have one of them leave, making the other vulnerable to attack.

Rangous knew at that moment that he had to find a way to communicate with the Tara Aquians, for they knew and understood battle strategies far better than he did. He knew in the coming weeks and months that he would need to know how to protect his people and he hoped the Tara Aquians would teach him. Duntar blew into the reed again then slipped it back into his belt. Rangous stood and walked to the edge of the clearing where Duntar had entered from the meadow, cocked his bow and arrow and peered out. He wanted to make sure nothing had followed Paraphin back to the village. He quickly looked back at Duntar who nodded to him. Rangous felt pleased that he had done the right thing. Duntar stood with his legs apart behind Paraphin, holding his weapon steady at his side, waiting for someone from the village to arrive.

Paraphin moaned in pain. Duntar looked down at him. His concern quickly turned to hatred of those who had done this to his friend. Instantly, his mind started to calculate the necessary steps for retaliation as they continued to wait for someone from the village to come to their aid.

They only had to wait a moment before several Meadow Imps, led by Zeander and Lillian came running into the clearing followed by Septer, Aldwin and Bauthal who were all holding torches. Zeander, seeing Paraphin on the ground by Duntar's feet, ran straight to him and fell to the ground. He gently stroked Paraphin's head.

"Paraphin what have ya gone and done to yourself? Why did ya leave? Why did ya not wait for me?" Zeander asked. The others standing around looked sadly at Zeander as Lillian put her hand on his shoulder to comfort him. Zeander had beaten himself up over the fact that he had not gone with Paraphin and fretted about it. They had been inseparable ever since Paraphin saved Robby, Lillian and Zeander's only wee 1 from an attack. That had been three summers ago while Zeander and Robby were hunting in the meadow. Robby unfortunately died from his wounds. Paraphin was the only one who could convince Zeander to heal first before they went out to get revenge.

"Too…many," Paraphin replied weakly. His eyes were still shut as Zeander stroked his head.

"Too many…what," Zeander asked? He looked up at Duntar then over to Rangous as if they knew what Paraphin was talking about. They shrugged their shoulders and shook their heads. He leaned his ear closer to Paraphin's mouth as he could barely make out what he was saying. "I can't understand ya. What's too many?" Zeander questioned as his voice rose with aggravation.

Paraphin opened his eyes, smiled then said clearly, "Quessstionsss."

Zeander looked in disbelief at Paraphin then gently clipped him across the top of his head; Paraphin winced in pain and moaned. He was sore from the tip of his head to the tip of his tail.

"Ah, you deserve that ya big dolt. I thought ya were dying. And ya laying there, being all cheeky with me and smiling." Zeander got up off his knees and stood with his hands on his hips, looking crossly at Paraphin.

"Not today…my dear friend…not today," Paraphin said weakly. Zeander smiled in relief and put his arm around Lillian's shoulders.

"Here, let me look at him," Aldwin said, taking his medicine bag off his shoulder. He knelt down and quickly prodded and poked Paraphin before he declared that it was safe to move him and that, with rest and medicine, he would be all right. Gently, Duntar picked Paraphin up, cradling him again as if he were a wee one, and carefully carried him into the village. The rest of them followed except for Rangous and Septer. They peered out over the meadow to the left and right of the beach. Nothing stirred, not even the little yellow birds with the black tippcd wings that had flown back to sit on the tips of the grasses.

A roaring fire burned in a stone pit in the lake side of the village. Beside the fire, Paraphin lay on a stack of blankets while the others sat around waiting for him to speak. He had complained about the blankets, but Aldwin insisted on them, telling him that he needed to keep his freshly cleaned and medicated cuts and scrapes away from the dirt. Aldwin assured him that he would only have to lie there until the sores scabbed over, which would be by the following midday; then and only then could he move about.

It was quite uncomfortable for Paraphin to rest on blankets. He was used to lying on the ground or on a nice warm rock. However, he was too sore and weak to argue so he conceded. He did say an audible no to medications that would put him to sleep. He needed to tell the others what had happened to him from the time he left the village to when Duntar found him in the meadow. They would need to hear what he had to say first, and then he would take the medication that would help him sleep without argument.

"Asss you know it wasss the longtoothsss who had raided the village," Paraphin said quietly so that only the small group sitting beside him, eating their evening meal, could hear. Zeander and Aldwin thought it best for only a few to hear what Paraphin had to say. They did not want there to be mass hysteria and have the Elfkins and forest creatures leave the safety of the village before Zusie and her daughters returned. Zeander, Aldwin, Rangous, Marla, Septer, Bauthal and Duntar nodded; they knew it was the longtooths.

"But what you don't know," Paraphin said, lowering his voice even more as he looked straight at Zeander. The others, except for Duntar who could not understand what was being said, leaned forward to hear what Paraphin said next, "isss that they were not alone." The others looked questioningly at him as he said, "They were being led by a jawbrender." Marla gasped in fright; Rangous quieted her with a harsh shush.

Zeander sighed heavily as the others looked with great concern at each other.

"I thought as much," Zeander said, shaking his head. "When I saw the great claw marks…I was just hoping…I was wrong."

Zeander translated to Duntar what Paraphin had said. He fisted his right hand and pounded it into his left hand; it made a loud smacking sound. The others, sitting in small groups on the other side of the fire eating their evening meal, looked curiously at Duntar. He managed a weak smile; they turned back to their meals.

"What do you think that means?" Bauthal asked, looking at Zeander and Paraphin.

"I will answer that in a minute," Zeander said, holding up his hand. "Let's see what else Paraphin has to tell us."

Zeander looked expectantly at Paraphin, knowing that the worse was still to come.

Paraphin leaned over and lapped up some water that sat in a large round stone bowl beside his stack of blankets. His red forked tongue darted out several times while the others waited, their evening meals going cold on their plates. He was too weak and sore to eat but Aldwin insisted that he have something to drink to keep him hydrated. Paraphin finished drinking what he could then looked up at them.

"After Zeander and I reached the village and he jumped out of the sssaddle, I took off after a longtooth that I sssaw dasssshing into the wessst ssside of the meadow." He looked apologetically at Zeander, "Sssorry but I lossst the sssaddle."

"Yes, yes. I can see that," Zeander said hurriedly and more harshly than he meant to. "Finish telling us your story." Not fazed by Zeander's harshness, Paraphin continued as Zeander translated for Duntar.

"Well they had ssscattered in every direction excccept for north ssso I followed a group of them going wessst. They had ssstopped after about an hour to ressst, I suppossse. There were jussst four of them. I ssssnuck up on them and took out three of them, letting the fourth one get away. He wasss easssy enough to follow asss he thrassshed around in the meadow, not caring that he wasss leaving a trail almossst asss noticcceable asss your caravan of travellersss doesss," he said, nodding his head feebly at Aldwin.

Aldwin returned his look without expression or comment, as there was nothing they could have done differently.

"Ssso I followed the lassst one who went due wessst for quite sssome time, perhapsss five hoursss, then he turned and went sssouth towardsss the lake. He followed the ssshoreline continuing to travel wessst for three or more hoursss until he came to that clearing that'sss sssurrounded by thossse ssstrange coloured bouldersss." Zeander and Duntar nodded their heads; they knew the clearing. It was quite a distance away and everyone who knew of its location stayed clear of it as the rocks gave off an eerie humming noise.

"I waited in the meadow on the north ssside of the clearing, hoping no one in the raiding party would come up behind me. Gradually, over the nexxxt hour, they trickled in one or two at a time. I ssssnuck clossser asss it was getting quite dark and I needed to sssee where my bessst attack point would be."

Marla breathed in sharply. "You attacked them on your own?" she asked skeptically, not quite believing that he would attack so many.

"That wasss the idea but I never go the chanccce. Asss I wasss ssspying on them, a jawbrender had come up from the lake and sssomehow sssensssed I wasss there. While I was busssy trying to figure out my bessst vantage point, he came up behind me and before I could ssstrike out at him he caught me by the throat." Paraphin tilted back his head so the others could see where the jawbrender had grabbed him. A twelve-inch gash just below his head down his black body glistened with the cleansing and healing salve that Aldwin had tenderly spread on it -- It was the same mark that Rangous had wondered about earlier. Everyone had seen the long jagged gash but did not know until now what had caused it. They looked at him in horrified silence.

"It carried me into the clearing and ssspat me out onto the ground. I was dazed from the pain and, before I could gather my witsss, ssseveral of the longtoothsss yelled 'throw him in the lake.' The jawbrender didn't even wait. It picked me up again, climbed up on the rocksss and ssspat me into the water."

Everyone in the small group could hear Zeander and Duntar's sharp intake of breath. The others looked confused at Zeander, thinking that that was probably what saved him.

"Paraphin can't swim," he said to them, "plus that be where the red legged octopi live," said Zeander. The others looked fearfully at Paraphin they were not sure they wanted to hear the rest of the story but could hardly wait for him to tell them. Zeander and Duntar were very interested in knowing how he escaped and waited patiently for Paraphin to drink a little more of the water.

"Well," he said, "thisss particular jawbrender wasss not very sssmart. He threw me over the sssside but didn't wait to sssee if I had landed in the water, nor did any of the othersss. There were rockss below the oness he threw me off. I waited, trying not to moan from the pain. Sssseveral other jawbrendersss came into the circle asss well, one of them being Bosssto, their leader. They talked at length about what they were doing there but I could hardly hear them. I am not sssure exactly what they were sssaying. I waited until they left then I crawled back over the rocksss and ssstarted to make my way back to the village." Zeander looked questioningly at his friend knowing that his tale was not quite finished.

"Your story tells us how you got the jagged cut down your throat and the bruises, but it doesn't explain how you got all those other cuts."

"Well I wasss pretty sssore and exhausssted from my ordeal and…well…I sssort of…fell asssleep," Paraphin said, embarrassingly. Zeander looked at him strangely.

"Please don't tell me…ya didn't…did ya?" Zeander asked. Then he added, disgustedly, "by a muddle puddle?"

Zeander slumped back on his blanket while he translated for Duntar. Duntar groaned loudly and looked at Paraphin in disbelief.

"What is a… muddle puddle?" Marla asked, curious. "It doesn't sound very scary or threatening." Zeander looked at her crossly.

"Muddle puddles are home to the pigmy muddle fish." The others looked at him with confused expressions.

"Sorry I keep forgetting ya not from here." In a softer voice, he said, "so much to teach in so little time. Okay," he said, looking at the Elfkins and Bauthal. "Pigmy muddle fish are nasty little creatures. They live in mud puddles and are kin to the mammoth muddle fish whose home be in the bay, but they are nothing like them. The mammoth muddle fish are kind and gentle. They be very large, about twice the size of Duntar, but they only eat plankton and nibble on underwater vegetation." Marla smiled; they sounded nice.

"Now the pigmy muddle fish are quite the opposite," Zeander continued. "They're tiny…not much larger than my hand," he said, holding up his hand for all to see. "But they're aggressive and have razor sharp teeth." Seeing that he had everyone's undivided attention, he went on. "They attack in droves of twenty or more. They eat only things born of flesh and bone, mostly birds and small mammals. But," he paused for effect, looking at Paraphin who should have known better, "they be known to take on larger prey." Paraphin groaned.

"You don't go anywhere near their puddles, let alone fall asleep near one. That's the reason we zigged and zagged through the meadow so we could stay clear of them." The others nodded, some of them saying "Ah," like the winding journey through meadow made sense to them. None of them however, at the time, had questioned the reason for the zigging and zagging. Nor, did they ask why Zeander or Paraphin had to go with them to the river each night. It now however made perfect sense.

If Paraphin could blush, his cheeks would have been red from embarrassment as the others looked at him. He could not return their looks and instead, looked down at a loose thread on the blanket. Aldwin, seeing the great snake's vulnerability, took pity on him.

"Come on all," Aldwin said standing, "why don't we let Paraphin gct some sleep?" Paraphin yawned as if on cue.

Everyone rose, wished Paraphin a speedy recovery, and left in search of another fire to sit by. Zeander and Duntar, Aldwin noticed, went in the direction of the clearing near the lake. He wondered, as he took a little red berry out of his medicine bag, if they went to send a message to Lindrella. Aldwin placed the berry under Paraphin's tongue who took it without complaint, unlike Old Barty. Paraphin instantly fell asleep on the pile of blankets.

Aldwin rose and walked not towards another fire but towards Lizbeth's trolley to check in on her and give Mirabella a break. She had offered to help take care of Lizbeth while Zusie and her daughters were gone. It was Mirabella's idea to move just Lizbeth rather than the whole trolley to the beach. Aldwin agreed and they were able to convey their wishes to Duntar. For most of the afternoon, she lay under a makeshift shelter on a thick stack of blankets while Marla and Mirabella sat with her.

Mirabella's children and some of the wee ones played a game of chase and tag. The wee ones were smaller than the underlings were but could really run. Aldwin thought the children's laughter and being out of the trolley did Lizbeth a wealth of good and knew that Zusie would agree with him. He walked through the path to the meadow side of the village; Lizbeth was back in her trolley. Aldwin's thoughts as he walked slowly down the path were of Saphina. He sighed heavily and wondered about the things that Desamiha the truth sayer would say to her; now understanding, thanks to Zeander, who and what Desamiha was.

CHAPTER 20
Desamiha the Truth Sayer

After Zusie and her daughters ate, Lindrella escorted them to Desamiha's cave. It was in stark contrast to the others they had seen after arriving in the city. Those caves had been welcoming, bright and airy.

First, Lindrella had shown them to the caves they would sleep in. They were small, about ten feet by ten feet, with smooth walls and rounded ceilings. A sleeping cot covered with bluish grey blankets and an off-white pillow sat against one wall. Against the other wall, a small table stood with a washbasin on it. Beside the basin were three medium sized decanters with a different coloured liquid in each of them.

Along that wall was also a shelf unit that was built right into the wall. The shelving unit had five deep shelves that were packed with provisions. On the bottom shelf, folded neatly, were two bluish grey blankets. The second shelf held two stacks of fluffy off-white towels. The third shelf held off-white tunics made from a soft material that had Chrystalina anxious to feel them. The fourth shelf held two woven baskets. One basket was full of candles; the other basket was full of soap bars. The fifth shelf had an arrangement of small figurines; Saphina looked at them curiously before they left the room, making a mental note to look at them again before she fell asleep.

Each cave had been the same except for the paintings on the walls. Someone had gone to great trouble to paint scenes of water and land life. Saphina and Chrystalina could hardly wait to look at them again. After seeing their sleeping quarters, they walked further along the main pathway that led deeper into the mountain. They came to another large cave that had several hallways leading from it. It looked very much like the Crystal Cave, only there were no etchings above the doorways or statues on the walls. The ceiling however did have pale yellow crystals hanging down; they bathed the cave with light.

At the far end of the cave and dead center to where they had entered were a set of wide stone steps that led up to another brightly lit cave. Although they could not see any one moving around up there, they heard a buzz of commotion. Lindrella, instead of going up the steps, turned and went down the first hallway to right. It was not as long as the one that led to the Crystal Cave, but it did curve several times before it entered another large cave.

This cave, Zusie and her daughters quickly realized, was an eating chamber. All around were round stone tables with four curved benches surrounding each; they looked like the benches that sat center of the city around the statue. These benches however had soft cushions on each of them. Along one wall was a bank of large stone tables that sat out a couple of feet from the wall. Several dishes, bowls, cups and eating utensils sat neatly stacked on the ends of the tables.

The four guests watched as several Tara Aquians came out of an antechamber on the other side of the tables. Each of them was carrying a large platter that was heaped with food. They placed the platters on the tables. The platters were full of fish, baked goods and, to their delight, fresh vegetables and fruits. The four of them looked curiously at each other and wondered where the vegetables and fruit came from. As the delicious aroma from the platters wafted over to them, their stomachs rumbled loudly from hunger.

Lindrella smiled. She did not have to communicate with words to understand that they were hungry. Her stomach rumbled as well. She walked them away from the food and into an antechamber just to the right of the main door. They followed her reluctantly until they realized that she had led them to a bathing chamber. She motioned for them to join her when they had finished using the facilities and washing up.

They reentered the eating chamber and were surprised to see that it was almost full of Tara Aquians. They looked around for Lindrella. Seeing her, they quickly walked to the table she was sitting at. They had to pass several tables on the way and were not surprised that the Tara Aquians did not falter in their conversation or eating. This was how it had been since they first arrived in the city. No one looked at them nor tried to talk with them.

Zusie and her daughters wondered at this. It was the first question they would ask the interpreter, whoever that might be. During their meal, they tried to communicate with Lindrella, asking her questions that she could not understand. Seeing their frustration, she said in broken Elfish. "La...tr, af...tr...yo met...wit Desamiha," Zusie and her daughters nodded that they understood; all would become clearer once they spoke with Desamiha.

Saphina sat with her mother and sister on large, thick, squared cushions on the floor of the cave of the truth sayer Desamiha. The cushions were cream white in colour and had golden thread woven throughout them in a floral pattern. In each corner were white and gold tassels that dangled onto the floor. The cushions looked almost too lovely to sit on, but Zusie and her daughters sat on them comfortably as they looked around the cave.

Six candles glowing from little arched cubbyholes in the walls dimly lit the room. The cubbyholes were like the ones in the Crystal Cave. These ones however were not as large. They were evenly placed around the room at the same height, about four feet off the floor. In each of them, an ornate candleholder made from bones that were scrubbed white held the candles. The light flickered through the holes of the candleholders casting eerie shadows on the walls and ceiling. Chrystalina shivered in spite of herself.

Other than the candles and cushions, the only other object in the dark cave was a large throne. The visitors to the cave were sitting five feet from it. They looked curiously at it and wondered about the mysterious person who held court from it. The throne sat on top of a green stone dais three feet high and twenty-five feet squared. The throne itself sat in the middle of the dais. It was quite large, and made from white scrubbed bones as well.

The four of them sat nervously as they waited to have an audience with Desamiha. All of them were thinking that they should have asked Zeander more questions about what was going to happen before they left on the journey to the city. Jasper was so nervous at seeing the monstrosity of a throne that he flew, as usual when he was upset or nervous, back and forth over the tops of their heads.

"Jasper, will you please stop doing that? You are making the rest of us nervous," Saphina said. Seeing that he was not about to stop, she added tolerantly, "Zeander would not have let us come if he did not trust the Tara Aquians. No harm will come to us. Please, come and sit on my shoulder."

Jasper thought for a moment, he liked Zeander and Paraphin, a lot for that matter, but how well did they really know them? He was about to say so but stopped when he heard a sound like sticks rapidly rubbing up against each other coming from somewhere behind the throne. He quickly dropped to Saphina's shoulder and buried his head in the crook between her neck and shoulder. Saphina was thankful that she had kept his snout bandaged. The cloth scraped against her skin as Jasper shivered in fright.

"Calm yourself, little one. There is nothing to fear," Saphina said. Her words quickly reminded Jasper of the times that Aldwin had said those exact words in that exact manner and something awful always happened right afterward. Saphina continued to gently pat his back and coo softly to him. It did not calm his nerves.

The noise became louder. Chrystalina, sitting to the left of Zusie, leaned over and tried to peer around the throne. Saphina, sitting to the right of Zusie, did the same in the other direction. They spied an entrance to a hallway that they had not noticed earlier. They could not see anything beyond the entrance; the hallway was pitch black. The noise came again; it was definitely coming from the hallway.

"It must lead to another antechamber," Chrystalina said. However, they could not see anything or anyone walking down it. They sat upright again, looked at each other, and shrugged their shoulders before looking at Zusie -- she told them not to worry.

The noise became louder and sounded as if it was coming towards them at a faster pace. Chrystalina and Saphina leaned over and peered around either side of the throne again. This time, to their surprise, they did see something. Along with the noise, a light appeared. It weaved back and forth as if someone was carrying a lantern and running.

They sat back upright as the light and sound came nearer. They all looked oddly at each other as they heard, along with the sound, someone muttering breathlessly. Saphina chuckled as she heard a curse and understood the words spoken. Whoever was carrying the light had tripped over something in the hallway. She looked over at Chrystalina who also chuckled. Zusie, however, looked puzzled; surely, the person speaking such words could not be Desamiha.

A flash of light suddenly erupted into the cave and a red blur wildly sped by them. They quickly turned around to see that the red blur was a woman. She abruptly came to a stop at the entrance to the cave and quickly turned back around to stare at them in disbelief. She looked at them as if she was not quite sure that what she saw was what she saw.

"Oh, oh my...here you are!" the person said as she tried to catch her breath. She walked back towards them and stopped when she reached the throne. Her face was very animated as she spoke and her manner of speech, though tinted with a slight accent, was clearly Elfish. However, she was not Elfish; nor was she Tara Aquian. Zusie and her daughters looked curiously at her. Even Jasper looked up from Saphina's shoulder to look at her.

Her skin was a creamy light brown and her dark brown hair was twisted into tiny braids that hung down past her shoulders in varying lengths. Her eyes twinkled from the light of the lantern she held in her left hand. She had a similar build and facial appearance to Zusie but she was not as tall. The only noticeable difference between the two of them was the colour of their skin and their eyes. Zusie's were blue and this woman's were dark brown. As they looked at her, her eyes changed to a bright green.

Her manner of dress was the most unusual thing about her. A flowing red skirt that hugged her hips covered the bottom half of her body. A sleeveless white tunic covered the top, or almost the top. It did not quite meet the waist of the skirt. Her belly button peeked out at them. On each arm, she wore several white rings that made a pinging sound whenever she moved her arms. The sound was much different than the sound they had heard earlier.

A thick belt was tied around her waist- its ends hung to her knees. It was woven with a brown material that Zusie and her daughters did not recognize. The belt also had feathers and small beads tied onto it. Over her left shoulder, she wore a brown bag similar to the medicine bag that Aldwin carried. In her right hand, she held a lantern with a glowing white crystal in it. In her left hand, she held a long staff that was taller than she was. At the tip of it was a skull and from it several hollow, dried reeds hung down in varying lengths.

"Well now, isn't it lovely to meet you" she said, composing herself rather quickly. She put the lantern on the stone dais and leaned the staff against the throne. She then turned back and greeted them just like Lindrella. She then introduced herself.

"I am Janilli." She said. As Zusie and her daughters returned the greeting, they wondered if she was Desamiha's apprentice. Jasper looked curiously at her from Saphina's shoulder.

"Oh," Janilli started to say once they finished their greeting. "It's rather dark in here, isn't it? Well, we cannot have that, can we? This room is ominous enough without it being in shadows as well. " The light in her eyes danced mischievously as she smiled.

Without waiting for them to respond, she clasped her hands together again but this time she rubbed them vigorously back and forth. As she did, the candles on the walls flickered and shone brighter and the eerie shadows disappeared.

"It's a rather dismal room, isn't it? Janilli said as she looked about her. They did not know what to say so they continued to look at her with befuddled expressions. Seeing their expressions, she said lightly, "Why don't we go into my sitting room? It's cozier in there." Without waiting for them to agree, she picked up the lantern and staff, and started to walk towards the hallway behind the throne.

Quickly, Zusie and her daughters stood. Jasper was still hanging onto Saphina's tunic. "Do you think we should go?" he asked nervously.

"I don't think we have a choice in the matter," Saphina said. They followed Janilli to the hallway. The reeds hanging down from the top of the staff bumped softly against its sides, creating a hollow sound as Janilli walked. The noise coming from them was the same noise that they had heard earlier.

As they reached the entrance to the hallway, Zusie looked knowingly at Saphina. Saphina, knowing what she wanted, shook her head. She could not read Janilli's mind. She had a strange feeling that Janilli was blocking her attempts.

Janilli stopped at the entrance to the hallway and waited for her guests to catch up. She smiled warmly at them. Once they reached her, she leaned the staff against the wall and snapped her fingers. The candles on the wall slowly dimmed, placing the throne room in eerie shadows again. They followed her as she walked down the hall; this time, she did not trip on anything.

Upon reaching the sitting room, they noticed that it was indeed cozier. It was a round chamber with a high, arched ceiling. Curved shelving units lined the walls. They held all manner of things like scrolls, small decanters with coloured liquids in them, small statues, writing utensils and inkwells. One shelf held large clear jars packed with floating frogs, bugs and other strange creatures they could not put names to. There were also several woven wall hangings with beautiful detailed pictures on them -- In front of them, sat a comfortable chair with a thick cushion.

In the middle of the room was a small pit built into the floor of the chamber. A small, smokeless fire burned in it. From the ceiling, crystals hung down just as they did in the Crystal Cave. However, the ceiling was not as high and the crystals were not as long. On the far side of the fire pit, across from the entranceway, sat a rocking chair with a thick cushion on it. Janilli walked to the chair and rested her hand lightly on a dark green robe that lay over the back of the chair.

"Please, bring a chair forward," Janilli said as she smiled warmly at them.

She watched with interest as her guests picked a chair. They didn't realize that the chair they picked spoke of their character and interests. Zusie fetched a chair that stood in front of a wall hanging that had all manner of creatures looking up at a large shimmering tree. Saphina picked one that sat in front of a wall hanging depicting a couple embracing while a battle raged around them. Chrystalina picked one that sat in front of a wall hanging depicting the stars and moons and a lone stranger who was standing on a rock by a raging river.

Once her guests seated themselves comfortably around the fire, she looked at Saphina and Jasper. He was holding tightly onto Saphina's shoulder.

"You have a question you wished to ask?" Janilli said. Without looking at Zusie for permission, Saphina asked the question they all wondered about.

"Why do the Tara Aquians ignore us?" Saphina said as her mother and sister nodded.

"The Tara Aquians do not speak with anyone until that person has spoken to Desamiha first," Janilli said.

"Why?" Chrystalina asked.

"Because that is the way that it is," Janilli said.

"But Lindrella spoke to us," Saphina said.

'Yes," Janilli said. The four of them wondered if she was being vague on purpose. They decided to change their line of questions.

"Will Desamiha be joining us? Are you her apprentice?" Saphina asked. "Ah, right to the point,'' Janilli said. "Just like Lindrella, you are," she added then smiled. "No… no," she said. Then she looked up at the crystal ceiling and knitted her brows together. She scratched her head lightly with one finger as she thought deeply. "Well, yes, yes," she said changing her mind as she nodded her head and lowered her hand. "I suppose, you could say I am Desamiha's apprentice. In a roundabout way," she added. They looked at her oddly, as she lowered her hand. "It's all rather difficult to explain. You will see once we get started."

Without further ado, she picked up the dark green robe from the back of the chair and put her arms through the billowing sleeves. The robe hung loosely over her shoulders and cascaded in shimmering rivets down to her toes. It had two large pockets on either side of the front panels. Out of the right pocket, she pulled a belt made from the same material as the robe and tied it around her waist. In the left pocket, she took out, with great care, a blood red stone attached to a long piece of braided rope that looped around and reattached to the stone. The stone shimmered gold and silver as the light from the fire sparkled off it. She put the braided rope over her head and the stone hung down and lay against her chest. Janilli sighed heavily and welcomed the weight of the stone against her flesh as if it were an old friend. An odd thought crossed her mind; she never felt at ease in her own skin until the stone touched her. Shaking her head of the strange thoughts, she continued.

She rubbed her hands together as she walked from the back of the chair to the front of it and all the lights, save the light from the fire in the pit, dimmed to blackness. Even the crystals in the ceiling dimmed to nothingness. She picked up a small decanter that was sitting on the seat of the chair and opened it with great exaggeration. Zusie and her daughters looked at Janilli with baffled expressions. Standing in front of the fire, Janilli held the decanter over the fire and, speaking words that the others could not understand, she emptied the contents of the decanter into the fire.

A luminescent liquid slowly poured out from the decanter as if time itself had slowed to a crawl. The fire crackled fiercely as the liquid caressed the flames then dripped onto the wood logs that were fueling it. Zusie and her daughters leaned back in their chairs, resisting the urge to move the chairs away from the pit. A minute or two passed before the fire started to spurt and sputter. Suddenly, to their astonishment, four little white balls of light exploded out of the fire and zoomed around the room.

Zusie looked at her daughters; both of them, along with Jasper, were caught up in the strangeness of the moment. They were surprised that the balls of light did not come into contact with anything in the room, nor did they crash into each other. It was as if they had a particular path to follow. Zusie looked at Janilli who was smiling broadly and looked to be on the brink of giddiness.

One of the small balls of light touched down on the bridge of Zusie's nose between her eyes. She jumped, thinking that it would burn her, but it was not hot. Before she could raise her hand to brush it off her nose, a warm calmness enveloped her. She sighed heavily and slumped down in her chair as if a great weight dropped on her lap. Her arms lay limply at her sides and her legs dangled loosely over the edge of the chair. She was alert and could see and hear everything around her, but it was as if time crawled by.

Slowly, Zusie turned her head from right to left and realized that a little ball of light had touched both of her daughters as well. They too were slumped in their chairs. The warm calmness prohibited her from having any feeling of concern or fear for her daughters' safety. Instead, she smiled at them, and they smiled back at her. The last ball of light did not touch Jasper. He sat stiffly on Saphina's shoulder. Concern and fright started to bubble to the surface. Before he could do much more than think about how he was going to help his friends out of this predicament, a voice spoke to him.

"Steady little one, do not be afraid." He looked at Janilli. She had not spoken. He looked about and no one else was in the room. It took him a minute to realize that the voice speaking was inside his head.

"Are you a Hummingmoth messenger from the Whipple Wash Valley?" the voice asked calmly. He nodded.

"You will need to recite to your friends the message I give to them today." Jasper nodded again, understanding now why they insisted he come along. Although Zusie and her daughters were alert, they were also in a trance much like the one he had been in, and he would have to retell them what he was about to hear.

With great expectation, Janilli looked at each of her guests in turn and nodded to Jasper. He nodded back at her, understanding without her asking if he was ready. She smiled warmly and winked at him and, without moving her lips, he could hear her say, "This is the best part of what I do. You are going to love this."

Janilli looked at Zusie then Chrystalina and finally to Saphina, who all looked back at her. She smiled broadly and they smiled broadly as well. She nodded her head and they nodded their heads as well.

"Okay," she said and giggled with glee.

"Okay," they said in unison and giggled with glee.

With great excitement, she asked, "Okay who wants to go first?"

All three of them eagerly shot their left arms in the air and waved their hands excitedly. It was good, she thought, to have such eager participants as she wondered whom to choose first. Janilli however would have been greatly upset to find out that no one had told them about her or the journey of truth they were about to partake in. If she had known, she would have taken the time to explain it to them and let them decide for themselves if it was right for them.

She looked at their eager faces, blissfully ignorant, and decided that she would first read for Chrystalina then Saphina, leaving Zusie for last. She watched as the last ball of light circled her head then sat, not between her eyes like the others, but on the stone hanging around her neck; the light disappeared into the stone.

Janilli breathed in deeply as the warmth from the now brightly glowing stone spread throughout her body. Desamiha the truth sayer was now with them. Janilli could feel her take over her body and her mind, and she welcomed her with great joy. She was now whole and her aura shone brightly from the connection. Janilli was as much a part of Desamiha as she was of her; together, when united with the ancient bloodstone of Awnmorielle, they were one.

She never questioned it; it had been this way for as long as she could remember. Truth seekers would come to her; she would put on the green robe and the bloodstone and pour the liquid with no name from the vial into the fire. Once Desamiha joined them, she would give the truth seekers readings, predictions and answer any questions they might have. She never questioned the process or the order in which they came to her or who she answered first. Her belief in Desamiha was so strong that she had no need to question why she chose to speak through her. If she had realized that greater powers than hers had destined the order she chose that day, she might have rethought having an audience with Desamiha. However, she did not, and for that slight oversight Janilli was soon to discover that not only were Chrystalina, Saphina, and Zusie's lives going to change forever, but so too was hers.

CHAPTER 21
The Dawn of Realization

A sound blared loudly from the lake side of the village, announcing the Tara Aquians' arrival. Zusie, no longer startled by the noise, jumped down from Lizbeth's trolley. Wiping her palms down the front of her tunic to straighten it, she looked worriedly in the direction of the sound. Her stomach began to churn. Zusie was not sure she was ready for the visitor the Tara Aquians brought with them. It was inevitable, she knew, but it still made her nervous.

"The Tara Aquians are here," Zusie said, looking over her shoulder at Lizbeth. She tried to calm her nerves. Lizbeth, still in a deep sleep, did not respond but Zusie spoke to her anyway. She had been having a one-sided conversation with Lizbeth. She was telling her that they would soon be leaving the valley, their home, and traveling south over the lake to the mountains, hopefully to safety and a new home. Zusie also told her how nervous she was and wished that Lizbeth would respond and tell her all would be well.

Zusie sighed heavily; time sometimes passed by too quickly. A full moon rotation had turned since their fateful visit to the city of Awnmorielle and their audience with the truth sayer Desamiha. In those few short moments that they sat with her, their lives changed forever. None of them would be able to go back to the life they had. Knowledge, rather good or bad, has a way of doing that. Knowledge changes ideals and perspectives, and there is no recourse for the recipient other than to accept it as truth and move forward.

For Zusie, the knowledge of who her people were and where she came from was bittersweet. She had always hoped that once she learned the truth she would be elated with joy. However, she was not. No one could really blame her. After all, how could she be overjoyed to know that the only reason she lived was because her mother hid her from her father. A man who would have killed her without a second thought if he had known she survived birth, just for being female.

Her father, as it turned out, was none other than Lord Canvil; A ruthless, conniving, heartless man who took over lands by force killing everyone who did not bend to his will. Those who chose to live became slaves to his army of warriors. Only the strongest and most skilled of the male slaves survived the training process and became warriors, losing all they knew and thought to be true to the tyranny of the king.

From the females, he took a woman and made her his personal slave. If she gave him a son, the child and the mother lived. If the woman gave him a daughter, the king had them both killed. His sons grew to be as ruthless, conniving and heartless as he was. They fought beside him, greedily taking the spoils of war. She sighed heavily as she wondered if they too, like their father, would kill their daughters.

Her thoughts turned to her sister. Yes, she had a sister; a younger sister. The same despicable man had fathered them, but they did not share the same mother. Janilli's was from another homeland, far from Zusie's, to the northwest. Even though time had passed, it was still hard for her to believe and to know that they had lived in the same valley for most of their lives but neither knew of the other. Zusie said a silent thank you to Zenrah for shining on both of them and keeping them safe.

The king had been away plundering another land when each of them was born. Their mothers, at great risk to themselves, stole their daughters away to safety but did not survive themselves. Each of the girls at the same age found their way to the valley. Zusie came first and made her home with the Elfkins. Her sister came three summers later and, with a stroke of luck, made her home with the Tara Aquians.

A stirring at the edge of the clearing had Zusie looking there. Janilli stood just inside the clearing, looking cautiously at Zusie. She was not sure that Zusie would welcome her. They had not spoken since the session with Desamiha. Janilli had not taken the news well, and had stayed away as she tried to rationalize why Desamiha had not told her of Zusie before now. If she had known she had a sister living in the Greenwood Forest, she would have gone looking for her. The omission confused Janilli and she refused to speak with Desamiha or conduct an audience with her.

Chrystalina and Saphina, who had been standing by one of the trolleys, walked over to Janilli and greeted her warmly. They were excited about having another family member. Janilli was excited to have family as well and returned their greeting. Jasper, at ease with Janilli, flew off Saphina's shoulder and sat on hers. Janilli looked at him and said something that Zusie could not hear. The three of them chuckled; Jasper smirked then curled up his snout. Janilli looked back at Zusie and waited for her welcome.

Zusie sighed heavily again. It was not Janilli's fault; she had no more control over her parentage than Zusie did. She looked kindly at

Janilli and smiled warmly. Janilli understood how she felt; the knowledge gained from the session was a surprise to her as well.

Janilli was not worried about being sisters because she instinctively knew that Zusie would welcome her. What disturbed both of them was that blood bonded them to the same evil lord who was coming to destroy the lovely valley that they found sanctuary in and called home. Their allegiance was to the people and creatures of the valley and they would fight to keep them from harm, even if that meant warring with their brothers and father.

How angry the king will be when he finds out that this valley is not the Whipple Wash Valley, Zusie thought as her family walked slowly towards her. Her heart pounded with concern for the Elfkins who stayed behind in the Greenwood Forest and the Tara Aquians who would stay to fight to give the rest of them more time to get to safety. When they reached Zusie, Jasper flew off Janilli's shoulder and hovered above their heads.

Janilli and Zusie looked intensely at each other then hugged warmly for the first time. Keeping her tears at bay with great difficulty, Janilli gave her sister another squeeze before she stepped back. They were valued leaders among their adopted people and they would need to stay strong if they were to survive the rest of their journey. Zusie looked at her daughters as she brushed tears from her eyes and smiled brightly as they did the same. Even Jasper, who resumed his spot on Janilli's left shoulder, wiped the tears from his eyes and sniffled loudly. The other four laughed lightly; he smiled awkwardly and shrugged his shoulders.

"Can anyone join in on this crying fest or is it just for the four of you?" Aldwin said as he walked up to the group. Hearing Jasper sniffling loudly from Janilli's shoulder, Aldwin corrected himself. "Oops sorry, I mean the five of you,"

"Definitely an Elfkin like you can join us," Saphina said, wrapping her arms around Aldwin's waist as he wrapped his arms around her shoulders; smiling lovingly at her. This too had changed.

Zusie looked at her daughter and Aldwin, standing before them in a warm, loving embrace. She had a feeling it would have changed in due time but the words of Desamiha had sped it along. During the session, Saphina learned that she would be in a great battle to save the Whipple Wash Valley; beside her would be a man, her mate. Saphina had asked whom. Desamiha, speaking through Janilli, looked at her and asked her own question. 'Is there no one you can think of who would stand by you while war rages around you?'

Saphina did not have to think about it; Aldwin's name instantly came to her. When the four of them made it safely back to the Meadow Imps' village and right after the reversal chant finished, Saphina ran to Aldwin. He had been waiting impatiently on the beach for their return. She threw her arms around him and kissed him passionately. Aldwin stood for a moment in shock then wrapped his arms around her and kissed her thoroughly back. Everyone standing around clapped and shouted with glee. Once they finished kissing, Aldwin quickly bowed before the elders who were standing near and declared his intentions for Saphina. Saphina, not wanting to be outdone, also bowed before the elders and declared her intentions for Aldwin. The elders happily nodded their approval and everyone standing around clapped their hands and congratulated the couple. They postponed the celebration until they reached the Whipple Wash Valley. There they would celebrate their union at the same time as Rangous and Marla.

Desamiha told Chrystalina that she and another would teach the Whipple Wash fairies how to read the stars so that they might find their way home. When Chrystalina asked whom the other one was Desamiha answered that she was not sure. Desamiha also warned Chrystalina about a stranger and told her to err on the side of caution while dealing with him. When Chrystalina asked what she meant, all Desamiha would say was that all would not be, as it seemed. There had been more to each of their readings about what they needed to work on or accomplish on their journey to the Whipple Wash Valley.

After their session with Desamiha, they each stared at Janilli in shock. She retuned their stares. They had all kinds of questions to ask her, but before they could ask them, she told them that it was time to meet Lindrella's ma and da. Janilli was quite solemn as she escorted them to a large chamber called the throne room. Towards the back of the room, Aldus, the high priestess, and Gando, the high priest, a direct decedent of Awnmorielle, sat in large blue crystal thrones. They had been waiting for Zusie, her daughters and Jasper to arrive.

Lindrella sat in a smaller throne beside Aldus. Kerchot sat in a chair several feet away from Gando. Janilli silently escorted them to cushioned chairs that were set before the thrones in a semi-circle. Three rows of empty chairs sat behind them. Janilli sat in a chair beside Lindrella and forlornly looked straight ahead. The others in the room looked questioningly at her. Normally, after a session with Desamiha, she was giddy and talkative. However, this session with Desamiha perturbed her greatly. They would find out why afterward.

Aldus and Gando greeted Zusie and her daughters cordially; their real interest, however, was with Jasper. They had heard about him through Desamiha and were very eager to hear his message. For an hour, Janilli translated back and forth. Aldus and Gando believed every word of the message and immediately put the Tara Aquians on high alert.

Afterward, a young Tara Aquian maiden named Emi escorted Zusie, her daughters and Jasper to their rooms. Lindrella and Janilli stayed behind to discuss battle plans with Kerchot. Even though Zusie and her daughters were tired, they stayed up while Jasper recited to them the words of Desamiha. Chrystalina carefully wrote down everything he said. Afterward, she gave each of them their own copy, which they rolled up and placed in a wooden tube that Janilli gave to them. They tied the tubes securely to their belts.

In the morning, Emi escorted Zusie, her daughters and Jasper to the eating chamber. While they sat with her, they noticed that the Tara Aquians no longer ignored them. However, none approached them either. Instead, they nodded if Zusie or one of her daughters smiled at them. After they ate and freshened up, Emi escorted them to the entrance of the city where Lindrella and Kerchot waited with the Tara Aquian guards to take them back to Zeander's village.

"You are deep in thought, sister," Janilli said, looking curiously at Zusie. Zusie looked at her. She had not realized that her thoughts had drifted.

"Yes, yes," Zusie said, nodding. "I was just thinking about how much has changed since we came to visit you."

"I am sorry, sister, if the message you received from Desamiha has upset you or given you distress."

"No," Zusie said, putting her hand on Janilli's arm. "Most things have changed for the better." They smiled at each other.

A mournful noise split the morning air and everyone flinched. It was coming from the lake side of the village.

"What in the name of Zenrah was that?" Aldwin asked to no one in particular.

"It sounded…like someone…trying to blow on a summoning whistle," Janilli said, looking at the others. "But they are playing it very badly."

Just then, the mournful noise came again, but this time is was a little louder and smoother. Everyone in the meadow side of the village looked curiously towards the lake side; some grabbed their weapons while others put their hands over their ears. A commotion stirred at the entrance to the meadow side of the village, making everyone reach for their weapons. They quickly lowered them when several Meadow Imps strolled into the clearing, shaking their heads in dismay. Zeander walked beside Paraphin, who was completely healed. They were the last to arrive.

"Zeander, what is that awful noise?" Aldwin yelled over to him.

"Duntar gave Rangous a summoning whistle as a gift and he be trying it out." As if on cue, the horn blared again, only this time it was much louder but still not in tune.

Everyone screwed up their faces and most of them put their hands over their ears. Zeander took his hands from his ears.

"He be teaching Rangous how to use it and what the different notes mean." Zeander shook his head, looking back from where they came. "I hope it doesn't take him all day to get the hang of it." The sound blared again, only this time it sounded more like a wounded animal. Everyone moaned and screwed up their faces as if the sound caused them physical injury.

"I will go have a talk with him," Aldwin said, looking at Zusie and Janilli.

"Thank you Aldwin," Zusie said.

Aldwin held out his hand and Saphina took it in hers. She motioned for Chrystalina and Jasper to come with them. When neither of them moved, Saphina looked at them again with an 'I think they would like to be alone to talk' look on her face. Chrystalina, understanding, held her hand out for Jasper to stand on. Jasper looked over at Saphina who raised her eyebrows and pointed towards the entrance. Jasper then understood and they left to speak with Rangous.

The horn blared again, only this time it was a piercing whistle. Everyone moaned again. Chrystalina, Aldwin and Saphina, with Jasper now on her shoulder covering his ears, quickened their steps.

An awkward moment followed as Zusie and Janilli watched the four of them enter the pathway leading from the meadow side just as another group of Elfkins, Meadow Imps and forest creatures entered from the lake side. Most of them were shaking their heads. They had come to that side hoping that there would be some relief from Rangous' attempts at the whistle. The whistle blared again; the mournful sound was back, only this time it was much louder and they all moaned in unison.

"I think he is getting better," Janilli said. Zusie looked at her and shook her head; they both chuckled lightly and turned around.

"Oh my," Janilli said in astonishment. Zusie also looked but gasped loudly. Lizbeth was sitting upright. Her eyes were closed and she was muttering something.

"No more…no more," she said breathlessly. The horn blared again. Lizbeth screwed up her face as the others had then fell back down onto her sleeping cot. Janilli reached out and touched Lizbeth.

"I knew she could hear," Zusie said with glee as she grabbed Janilli's other arm. Janilli however did not move; she stood stiff as a tree trunk as her hand lightly touched Lizbeth's arm. Zusie looked at her fearfully, gingerly shook her arm and called her name. Janilli's expression was blank as she looked down on Lizbeth's resting form. Zusie panicked and shook Janilli's arm but she did not move nor did her expression change. Zusie went to call for help but stopped when Janilli's body started to glow brighter and brighter. As if scorched by hot water, Zusie let go of her arm and took a step back.

A voice low and lovely came from Janilli's mouth. Zusie looked at her curiously. She remembered the voice from the first time she met her in Awnmorielle. She tried to calm her nerves but her heart beat quickly. There was no reason to fear what was to come next but it was eerie all the same. Zusie had no idea that her sister could pop in and out of a trance at will. She also did not know that Janilli had stopped giving readings. Janilli had no control over what was happening to her. Desamiha was with them, whether Janilli agreed to it or not, and there was nothing they could do about it but listen.

"Your prayers have been answered, Zusie," the voice said hauntingly. Janilli turned her head to look at her and smiled warmly. "Lizbeth will survive the journey to the other side." As quickly, as the words were out and before Zusie had a chance to react to the message, Janilli came out of the trance. She looked confused at Zusie for a moment then weaved back and forth. She took her hand off Lizbeth's arm and held onto the trolley, steadying herself. She felt like she was going to faint.

"Desamiha," Janilli asked as she breathed in deeply. Zusie did not miss the scared look in her eyes.

"Yes," Zusie said, nodding. "Would you like to sit down? You look like you are about to faint."

"Yes," Janilli said and abruptly sat on the ground. She leaned her back against the side of Lizbeth's trolley and put her hands over her face as she tried to calm her nerves.

"I gather by the look on your face you weren't expecting that?" Zusie asked.

"No," Janilli said, shaking her head. "That was the first time she came forward without the blood stone and the vial with no name. I had no idea it was even possible. It was so strange. As soon as I touched Lizbeth's arm, my senses flooded with your concern and love for her and then Desamiha took over."

Zusie handed her a pouch of water. Janilli thanked her before taking a long drink. She looked worriedly at Zusie. Desamiha turned out to be someone you did not want to mess with and Janilli shivered as the last effects of the trance wore off.

"Was the message for you then?" she asked as she passed the water pouch back to Zusie. She tried not to worry about Desamiha's ability to use her as a vessel for communication so far from Awnmorielle.

"Yes," Zusie said. Then she reached out and held Janilli's hand. "Are you sure you're alright, sister?"

"Yes," Janilli said and smiled weakly at Zusie. "What did she say?"

Zusie sat down beside her sister and drank deeply from the water pouch. Putting it down beside her, she dabbed her mouth lightly with the sleeve of her tunic and smiled cautiously at her. There was much for them to talk about, starting with the latest message from Desamiha and Janilli's reaction to it.

The two of them sat and talked until the sun was just about to set. They talked in earnest about their father and the coming war, comforted each other over their mothers, wondered about their homelands, planned a strategy to get their adopted people to safety and laughed as if they had known each other forever. It was good. Janilli smiled a thank you to Desamiha, forgiving her for keeping Zusie from her.

A quiet moment passed and then Janilli looked strangely at Zusie. An odd thought was blossoming in her mind. She told Zusie what she speculated and she agreed. Janilli would no longer need the bloodstone of Awnmorielle or the vial without a name because she, Janilli, was Desamiha. With the realization, Janilli wept. After the tears subsided, Janilli looked at Zusie as another thought quickly formed.

"Do you think my gift is why Lord Canvil," neither of them could bring themselves to call him father, "executes his female heirs?" Janilli asked.

"Perhaps," Zusie said. "But why do you have it and not me?"

On the other side of the clearing Saphina laughed heartily at something Chrystalina said and wrapped her arms around her, telling her that she was the best older sister she ever had. Janilli looked at Zusie.

"Was Chrystalina born first?" Janilli asked slowly, already knowing the answer.

"Yes," Zusie nodded and looked at her sister questioningly.

"Yes," Janilli echoed.

"Without an older sister there can never be a younger sister." Zusie said now understanding her sister's train of thought.

"Yes," Janilli nodded and looked over at Saphina and Chrystalina. The gift was passed down to the second daughter.

"Do you think that is the reason why Saphina can read minds?" Zusie asked as she too looked over at her daughters.

"Without an older sister there can never be a younger sister." Janilli echoed.

Zusie nodded then smiled awkwardly, "But that doesn't explain the connection with Jasper, why Saphina's gift is not as strong as yours or why the king wants us dead," Zusie replied.

"No it doesn't," Janilli chuckled nervously. "That my dear sister will need more thought."

"Well should you tell them or should I?" Zusie asked.

"I would like to if you don't mind," Janilli said. Zusie smiled and nodded.

As they made their way towards Saphina and Chrystalina neither of them heard the soft beat of wings or saw the small creature who had heard everything they said. Nor did they see the smirk on its face or the red glow in its eyes as it flew with purpose towards the Greenwood Forest.

CHAPTER 22
Paramo and the Watercrafts

The day Aldwin told Old Barty that he no longer needed him to watch over Lizbeth, Barty's first thought was that Lizbeth had passed over while he ate his morning meal. However, seeing the broad smiles on Aldwin and Zeander's faces, he knew it was not true. When they told him they needed him to oversee a special project, Old Barty whooped loudly with joy. Then he swung his cane at their heads and told them off for scaring him. He then whooped again for joy.

"Not that watching Lizbeth isn't useful," Old Barty said while they sat around the fire that night discussing their plans at length. "But this," he said beaming, "Is what I was meant to do."

Everyone sitting around the fire that night chuckled at Old Barty's delight and had to admit that he looked years younger as he talked on and on about the watercrafts with Aldwin and Zeander. The Elfkins, listening from the other campfires, looked skeptically at the three of them. They were not convinced that their plan would work -- especially so after Paramo said that the watercrafts would probably sink and whoever was on them would be food for the fish.

Old Barty heard her words and the urgent murmuring that followed quickly afterward but did not care. He was doing something meaningful again and that was all he cared about. He had started to feel like a bump on a log. There was nothing more for him to do than sit in a trolley while everyone else worked around him. He fretted about it every day. At least in the village, he had woodworking to keep him busy. However, on the trail there was no need for chairs and flutes.

Zeander and Aldwin smiled contently, as if making Old Barty feel useful again had been their intention. In reality, Old Barty was the right Elfkin for the job. After all, his chairs lasted hundreds of years before they broke down. Old Barty had been so excited about the project that he barely slept that first night. He was anxious for the morning to come so that they could start to demolish the trolleys, which had been his design, and start building the watercrafts.

Zeander's idea for the watercrafts had indeed turned out to be very clever. From the six trolleys, they were able to make three large watercrafts. They bound the planks of wood together with several yards of braided bimble yarn. The sides of the trolleys they used for the sides of the watercraft. They set the sides in place with thin pieces of hard metal sticks that the Tara Aquians called nails. Then they coated everything with tar from the river so the water could not seep through the cracks.

Several of the women sewed thin blankets together. The Meadow Imps and Elfkins looked with skepticism as the blankets were fastened to the cross beam of a T-shaped pole structure. With the help of four burly Tara Aquians, they fastened the pole to the middle of the watercraft. Then they fastened the bottom edges of the blankets to the deck of the watercraft with thickly braided bimble yarn.

The watercrafts were now ready to carry them across the lake. The wind blew up, caught the blankets, and pushed the watercrafts forward, but because the poles stopped them from going anywhere, they bumped noisily into each other. The Elkins who were standing on the beach looked on with worried frowns.

"How are the blankets to keep us dry if it should rain when they fly in midair like that?" Paramo asked quite rudely as she looked at Zeander with contempt. The watercrafts had taken a full moon rotation to build and every chance Paramo got she undermined the work that was being done on them. Her manners and attitude had not improved while in Zeander's village. The Meadow Imps had ignored her after Paramo had insulted Lillian by saying the meal she brought for her was not fit to feed a pig. Everyone noticed that even though she complained about the food, she ate everything on her plate.

Zeander and Old Barty did a double take as if they were not quite sure they heard her right. Seeing the expectant look on her face, they realized she was serious.

"It's not for keeping the rain off of ya," Zeander and Old Barty said in unison.

"It's for catching the wind," Zeander said, shaking his head as Old Barty nodded, and smiled broadly at the genius of it.

The villagers standing around looked strangely at the pair of them as if they had lost their minds. Old Barty looked down at Zeander and told him to explain.

"The blankets will catch the wind and move the craft along faster," Zeander said. "Just like when the wind catches a bird's wings, lifting it higher or faster." The Meadow Imps understood but the Elfkins still looked confused. "Surely," Zeander said, "you've wondered how birds fly before."

Many of them shrugged their shoulders and shook their heads at each other. Only a few nodded that they understood the concept.

"First bubbles, now this. How have ya managed to survive this long?" Zeander added, shaking his head back and forth.

"What will happen when the wind isn't blowing then?" Paramo said smartly.

"See those long pieces of wood?" Zeander said patiently as if he was speaking with an underling. He pointed to the six long flat-sided spears that stuck out on either side of each of the watercrafts. Without waiting for Zeander to explain further, Paramo raised her voice so that all could hear.

"Surely you don't expect us to get in the water and push them along?"

"Don't be ridiculous," Zeander said with contempt. He had not forgotten how much trouble Paramo caused while crossing the meadow or how she had insulted Lillian's kindness.

"You," he said pointedly, "Wouldn't know a hard day of work if it sat on your lap and slapped you in the face while you were stuffing it full of food." Paramo gasped in horror at the way Zeander spoke to her and looked around for Martan.

Some of the villagers chuckled behind their hands; Paramo always seemed to be chewing on something. Spying Martan, she called him over. He walked to her with purpose and an angry scowl on his face.

"Did you hear," Paramo said pointing her finger down at Zeander, "what this little imp said to me?" Paramo said imp as if Zeander was a bothersome pesty gnat that she wanted Martan to squish on her behalf.

Zeander, standing his full height, stood his ground even though he only came up to Martan's knee. He liked Martan -- he was a hard worker, a willing learner and was fair minded and good with his underlings -- but Zeander was not about to back down no matter how tall or well-built Martan was. Paramo had it coming to her; someone needed to put her in her place.

Martan looked down at Zeander thoughtfully. He liked Zeander as well. He looked slowly from Zeander to Paramo. With her arms crossed at her chest and her right foot tapping quickly on the ground, she waited impatiently for Martan to say or, better yet, do something to Zeander. Martan could tell by the satisfied smirk on her face that Paramo truly expected Martan to have a fight with Zeander.

Paramo squeaked loudly with shock however, when Martan grabbed her arm and pulled her in the direction of the village. He loved Paramo in spite of her bullish, ungrateful faults, but by Zenrah, she was going to get an earful today.

Paramo shrieked again as Martan unceremoniously marched with her past the other villagers. They frowned as she cried obscenities at Martan and turned their heads, indicating to her that they would not interfere. She tugged and tugged, trying to break his hold on her arm. She screamed that he was breaking her arm.

Everyone standing in the clearing turned quickly in shock as Martan bellowed, "Enough," and let go of her arm. His face had turned red with embarrassment; he clenched his hands into fists. His whole body shook with anger as he paced angrily back and forth in front of Paramo. Paramo shivered with genuine fright. Martan had never yelled at her before.

Everyone wondered whether he had finally had his fill of her whiny, demanding ways. He had never once contradicted her to their knowledge. Several of the men took a step forward; worried that he might strike her. Although many of them felt that she deserved it, it was not in the nature of an Elfkin to strike another, let alone one's mate.

Everyone relaxed as Martan's hands slowly opened. "There are two ways we can handle this, Paramo. Either you come with me now or when it is time to go you and the underlings can leave without me." Martan gulped down a lump of emotion that had formed in his throat.

Several of the villagers standing nearby groaned or gasped in astonishment. They would leave no one behind. However, they collectively thought, that if someone had to stay it should be Paramo. Paramo, seeing the deadly serious look on her Martan's face, sighed heavily and conceded. He turned and walked into the pathway leading to the lake side of the village with his head held high. Martan was now in charge. Paramo walked slowly behind him with her head bowed. Seeing that she was several paces behind him, he stopped and waited for her to catch up, which she did quickly.

The villagers turned back around and an urgent whisper erupted from a group of Elfkin females as they giggled. They were the same women who had backed Paramo when she had confronted Zusie. Zusie, who was standing with her daughters and Janilli, scowled at the group of women. She had purposely not interfered when Paramo had started to speak with such disdain. Even though Zeander was small, he was mighty and could hold his own.

Besides, Zusie had her hands full keeping Saphina from lashing out at Paramo when she started trashing the design of the watercrafts and speaking to Zeander with such disdain. Zusie knew that things had to play out as they did. Paramo was due a lesson and Zusie was glad that Martan stepped up to teach it to her.

Seeing the disgusted look on Zusie's face, the Elkin women quickly stopped and blushed embarrassingly. Zusie nodded at Zeander and Old Barty. The two of them finished explaining how the watercrafts would carry them to the other side.

Two hours later, Aldwin tied the first watercraft back to its post. The maiden voyage of the first ever watercraft went ahead without a hitch. Rangous, Septer, Aldwin, Kerchot and Duntar maneuvered the craft over the water effortlessly. They practiced raising and lowering the blankets several times. Each time they raised the blankets, the wind caught them and the craft lurched forward and moved faster across the water. When they lowered the blankets, the craft slowed. Rangous used a boot shaped stick attached to the back of the craft to steer it.

Zeander and Old Barty watched from the shoreline and took great pride in their invention. It pleased them to hear the Elfkins exclaim in excitement as the watercrafts skimmed effortlessly over the water. Everyone came up to Zeander and Old Barty afterward and congratulated them on their most ingenious design.

CHAPTER 23
And so it begins

The last of the caravan of travelers, fleeing for their lives from the valley that time forgot, sat forlornly around a fire on the lake side of the Meadow Imps' village. A storm was brewing overhead and they huddled together in silence as they ate a meager meal of bread and fried fish. Seventy-five of them remained -- Fifty Meadow Imps and twenty-five Elfkins. They had enough provisions to last them until they caught up with the others who had already started the next leg of the journey without them. There had been tearful goodbyes and several reassurances that they would leave no one behind. To make sure of it, Zusie, along with Saphina, Aldwin and Janilli, stayed with the last group. Chrystalina, Jasper, Septer, Zeander and Paraphin led the first group. Rangous, Marla, Lindrella and Old Barty led the second group. That group also had Lizbeth with them.

The provisions for the last group were already neatly stacked in the centers of the watercrafts along with the packs that held their personal belongings. The watercrafts had done Zeander and Old Barty proud. With the help of the Tara Aquians, the first and second groups made it safely across Lake Kellowash with all their provisions, and the crafts were still sturdy enough to carry the last group.

The first two groups had a combination of Meadow Imps and Elfkins but they also had all the larger forest creatures from the Greenwood Forest that chose to go with them. All the smaller creatures, like the red dapple spider ants, had already left, choosing to find their own way out of the valley. Just after they met Zeander and Paraphin, Zusie and Bauthal spoke with the winged creatures. Bauthal gave them a very special task to perform. They were to spread the word of Canvil and his army to every creature they came across. They flew out in two large groups; one group flew east, and the other west. The plan was for them to fly around the mountain range, spreading the word of the pending battle, and eventually meet up with the rest of them in the Whipple Wash Valley. The best-laid plans however, can sometimes go astray. No one could have predicted that after leaving the sanctuary of the Greenwood Forest, life for all of them would change drastically, even for the winged creatures and the small red dapple spider ants. Life was not the same outside of the Greenwood Forest.

The last group of travelers would sleep one more night in the village then be on their way at first light. As they sat around the fire, they spoke hesitantly of how different their lives were since leaving the forest. It was as if the Greenwood Forest had protected them from more than just the passage of time. The strangest aspect, they all agreed, was the fact that Elfkins could not converse with any of the creatures in the meadow except for Paraphin. They all looked expectantly toward Janilli who shrugged her shoulders; she did not know the reason why. Eventually, their conversations drifted off and all sat quietly as they listened to the rumbling of the approaching storm.

A sound blared, disturbing the silence, and several of them jumped. They all grabbed their weapons; always just a finger touch away. They calmed their nerves when they realized that the sound came from a summoning whistle. The whistle announced that the rest of the Tara Aquians who would travel with them across Lake Kellowash were there. With the help of the Tara Aquians, they would climb the great stone steps that led up the side of the mountain to a landing. At the end of the landing, a huge trench, much like the one between the Bay of Rowan and Lake Kellowash minus the finger-like rocks, wound through the mountains. The trench, named The Hollow of Rock, was a hundred feet wide and thousands of feet high, with a clearly defined path going through it.

The Tara Aquians, having no need to travel down it, had no idea how far it went through the mountains, nor did they know if it reached the other side. They had no choice; staying would mean certain death as none of them would succumb to Canvil's demands. They were mistaken though, because there was one who had already betrayed them, they just did not know it yet.

Once they reached the other side, the plan was to burn the watercrafts. They could not take the chance that they would float back to the bay and straight into Canvil's hands. If the trench did not go all the way through, they would have to retrace their steps and take the long route around the mountain. It was Zeander's idea from the start to destroy the watercrafts. He asked Chrystalina to keep records and detailed drawings of them. She had the plans and the hand-drawn pictures of them tucked safely away with the rest of the scrolls.

The tar they used to waterproof the watercrafts they found out, quite by accident, was flammable, so the crafts would burn easily. Chrystalina had tripped with a candle in her hand. The candle landed on a stack of blankets- the ones the Elfkins had covered with tar to protect them from the rain. The stack of blankets instantly burst into flames and, even after the Elfkins doused them with buckets of water, they still smoldered well into the night. Many of the Elfkins shuddered at the thought that if the wind had caught a spark and carried it to their makeshift shelters, most of them would have perished in the meadow. They all said a silent prayer of thanks to Zenrah that that had not happened.

One thousand Tara Aquians would stay behind to fight if necessary. They had made detailed plans of how to foil the king's way across the lake. Some of the plans included the flammable tar. They prayed to Awnmorielle that none of them would lose their lives. Unfortunately, that would not be the case.

Just as fifty Tara Aquians, led by Kerchot and Duntar, entered the lake side of the village, a heart-wrenching scream came from the meadow side of the village. They looked around frantically and counted quickly; it was not one of them. The scream came again. Kerchot and Duntar raced along the pathway leading to the meadow side of the village. Aldwin, before leaving, ordered the rest of the villagers not to panic and to stay put. While Zusie and Janilli calmed the Elfkins, the Tara Aquians stood guard.

It was very dark in the meadow side of the village and difficult to see. Duntar and Kerchot moved stealthily forward while Aldwin guarded the entrance to the pathway. Hearing noise coming from behind him he quickly turned and stepped out of the way just in time as Zusie and Janilli ran into the village carrying two torches each. Saphina had followed them.

"Be careful with those. It hasn't rained in weeks," Aldwin said harshly. "And put that out," he said, looking at the flaming arrow in Saphina's bow. She drove the tip into the dirt and reloaded her bow with another arrow. Kerchot and Duntar each took a torch. They walked to the far side of the village, looking behind every hut as they passed. They each had a spear in one hand and a torch in the other their daggers hung at their waists. The Tara Aquians were always ready for battle. While Zusie and Janilli looked around the village Aldwin and Saphina stood guard at the entrance to the pathway. Aldwin had an arrow loaded in a bow. Saphina looked at him; his stance was strong and primal. He looked as if he had always been a warrior and not a kindhearted healer who just recently learned, with quick agility, how to use a weapon. Although he had gotten quite good with a bow and arrow, it was odd for her to see him carrying one. She smirked at the memory of him running into the village wielding a club over his head while he screamed a battle cry. She doubted that she would ever forget that day. The day her kindhearted hero came to rescue her. Saphina smiled broadly. Her smiled quickly vanished as another heart-wrenching scream pealed through the night air.

"It's coming from the meadow," Duntar said, now able to speak fluent Elfish thanks to Rangous, who could now speak fluent Tarawyn. Duntar and Kerchot drove their torches into the ground, burying them, and ran into the meadow. All Zusie, Aldwin, Saphina and Janilli could hear was Duntar yelling "muddle puddle" before he and Kerchot raced off. Knowing where the nearest one was, they speedily ran towards it. The small group standing in the village could no longer see them as the meadow and the darkness, swallowed them up.

They anxiously waited, looking frighteningly at the spot where Duntar and Kerchot had left the village. Several minutes later, they heard them running back through the meadow and spotted them entering the village at the same spot where they had left. Duntar was carrying something very small in his massive arms while Kerchot whacked pigmy muddle fish off Duntar's legs. He stabbed the fish with his spear as they tried to clamp back on.

Zusie's heart lurched as Duntar came closer, and then she cried out. With the light from her torch, she recognized the prone figure in Duntar's arms. It was Benly, Camcor's oldest son. Aldwin dropped his bow and arrow and ran to Duntar. He quickly looked Benly over.

"He looks bad, really bad. Run ahead and ready a bed for him," Aldwin ordered. Zusie and Saphina ran through the pathway. As they entered, the Elfkins swarmed around them. Saphina ignored them as she pushed her way through. Zusie walked to the side of village away from the entrance. The Elfkins and Meadow Imps followed her. As they stood around, Zusie told them whom they found and what had happened. Saphina readied a bed on the other side of the village.

"Are there others?" one of the villagers asked anxiously.

"We don't know," Zusie said.

Duntar and Aldwin entered the clearing. The Elfkins and some of the Meadow Imps cried out. Benly did indeed look quite bad. Wounds covered his little body and his eyes were closed. They feared the worst. They started to move forward to take a closer look just as Kerchot, carrying Aldwin's bow and arrow entered the clearing. Janilli was right behind him. Kerchot quickly stepped in front of them and looked menacingly down at them. Janilli stepped between Kerchot and the Elfkins.

"Give Aldwin room to do his work. We will let you know as soon as we can how Benly is doing." Zusie stood beside her sister and the Elfkins nodded that they would stay there. The Meadow Imps comforted the Elfkins and invited them to sit with them at the edge of the village.

Duntar gently laid Benly on the blankets then got up quickly and stood beside Zusie, Janilli and Kerchot. Aldwin motioned for Saphina to take Benly's soiled and blood-soaked clothes off as he poured fresh water into a bowl. She did so as quickly and as carefully as she could.

Aldwin quickly and gently washed away the dirt and blood. Benly's eyes flickered open as the cloth scraped at his open wounds. He moaned in agony. Everyone standing around let out the breath they didn't realize they were holding. Reaching into his medicine bag, Aldwin pulled out long strips of cloth to wrap the wounds with, salve to spread over them and a purple lizben berry. Saphina soothed Benly with kind words.

"Calm yourself, little one. You are with friends. It's Saphina and Aldwin from the village." Benly looked at them strangely for a minute. Recognizing them he started to cry. He had made it to safety. Aldwin spread salve onto Benly's open wounds. Benly cried out in pain. Aldwin reached for the berry to slip under Benly's tongue.

"No," Kerchot said loudly, recognizing the berry. Aldwin looked at him indignantly. Duntar quickly stepped forward to finish what Kerchot was trying to say.

"We need him awake so that he can tell us what happened. Hopefully, Awnmorielle will look kindly on him and he will survive long enough to tell us his tale."

Aldwin turned back to Benly. He understood the reason to keep him awake in case the rest of them were in danger, but he was just an underling and his wounds were severe. Aldwin feared that Benly would not make it through the night.

Aldwin finished his administration of the ointment, bandaged Benly's wounds then laid the blanket over him again. Saphina, seeing that Aldwin was finished, brought a water pouch to Benly's lips and held his head up so that he could drink from it. Benly tried to gulp down mouthfuls.

"Easy, little one," Saphina said. "A little at a time." Benly understood and lay back down on the blankets. Looking about him, he sighed as he recognized Zusie who smiled warmly down at him. He stared strangely at Janilli. When he looked at Kerchot, his eyes went wide with fear. Saphina looked up and scowled at Kerchot.

"Kerchot, you're scaring him; smile," Saphina said. She smiled at him so he could see what she meant. Kerchot understood and smiled down at Benly. His fright however did not ease.

"Benly," Zusie said as she knelt down beside him. "Can you tell us what happened? Where are your ma and da and siblings? Where are the others?" Benly looked at her as if he did not understand the questions.

Several moments passed. Zusie looked up at Saphina, hoping she was able to read his mind. However, he was so deep in thought she could not penetrate it.

"Dead," he whispered. "All of them…dead." Tears welled up in his eyes as he looked mournfully at them.

They did not have to prompt him to say more, as he knew he had to tell them his tale; his ma had told him to. No matter how painful it was to remember, he had to tell them.

"My ma and I had been working at the pottery hut. I am ten now and she was teaching me how to make a bowl. We heard the gong of the summoning stone then screams coming from the village. We ran quickly back but my ma shoved me behind a hut when she saw what was happening in the village square." He gulped down the pain of sorrow that was rising and continued.

"Strangers had arrived in the village," he said, looking strangely at Zusie, "like you. One of them was fair-haired and asked my da all sorts of questions. Da did not answer him so the stranger punched my da in the face so hard he fell to the ground. He drew out a large knife and stabbed my dad in the chest with it. The other villagers ran for their lives but the strangers were faster and killed them all." Benly's lips trembled at the memory.

"My ma picked me up in her arms and quickly carried me back to the river. She gave me her pouch of water and the little food we had packed for our lunch. 'You are a smart and strong underling,' she said. 'Follow the river until you get to the meadow then follow the path through the meadow until you find Zusie and the others.' He looked at Zusie and smiled weakly, "I found you." Everyone standing around looked at him with pride.

"So you did, little one. So you did," Zusie said. She brushed his hair from his eyes. He thought for a moment then sniffed loudly as tears welled up in his eyes.

"Jasper was right," he said, nodding, then looked apologetically at Aldwin. "They are coming."

Duntar quickly hushed everyone as he strained to hear something. No one else standing in the village could hear anything other than the usual night sounds. Kerchot listened as well. They had mentally sent a message to a dozen Tara Aquians to search the meadow for signs of someone following Benly; they were now mentally reporting in. Duntar and Kerchot looked gravely at each other before Duntar spoke. "They are coming," he said.

"Who is coming?" Zusie asked anxiously.

"Kerchot sent scouts out, right after we found Benly." Zusie looked around; she could see there were indeed about a dozen Tara Aquians missing. Duntar continued, "Our scouts came across half dozen of them making their way back towards the forest."

"Did they catch them?" Zusie asked anxiously again while the others now looked fearfully around.

Duntar nodded. The expression on his face spoke volumes; the scouts would be coming back alone and the members of the king's Venom Horde would not be making it back to report to their leader.

"We cannot be sure that there are not more of them watching us," he said as the Tara Aquian scouts entered the village. Elfkin women cried out. The Tara Aquian scouts looked more terrifying than usual. The others could see that they had indeed been in a fight. Blood dripped from their spears and knives, their eyes still shone with the light of battle, their breathing was slightly labored, and the muscles in their arms bulged from the effort of being used. None of the Tara Aquians seemed to be hurt as one stepped forward and reported to Kerchot and Duntar.

"They are coming! We need to leave now," Duntar said.

"They're coming," Benly repeated hauntingly in a hushed whisper.

"We leave now," Duntar said again.

"Now! What do you mean, now," Aldwin said, as he got to his feet. "We can't move him," he said angrily, pointing at Benly. "At least for a day or more."

Duntar took Aldwin's arm and pulled him roughly to a large rock that the Meadow Imps used as a lookout point. With Duntar's help, Aldwin climbed to the top of it. He looked out over the meadow. Off in the distance a bright orange light glowed. It was too dark to see the smoke but he knew that in the light of day it would be billowing upwards, hiding the sky and the sun from view. In retaliation for killing their comrades, the Venom Horde had set the meadow on fire and it was quickly racing towards the Meadow Imps' village.

Aldwin jumped down from the rock and ran over to Zusie and the others.

"We have to leave now.' Aldwin said. "They have set the meadow on fire."

"But Benly," Zusie said with worry, looking down at him resting on the blankets. "Moving him might very well kill him."

"Zusie," Aldwin said grabbing her arms. "Think logically. We have no choice. The fire will soon reach the village. Besides, we can't be sure it wasn't one of them who threw Benly into the muddle puddle to distract us." Zusie's breath caught in her throat.

The wind changed direction and smoke from the fire quickly reached the village. The Elfkins, smelling it, started to panic. They jumped up screaming and ran frantically around. It was all the Meadow Imps could do to keep out of their way.

"Enough," Kerchot roared with anger. Everyone froze and looked in fright at Kerchot who held his spear above his head and shook it in anger. Duntar stepped forward and ordered everyone to make their way to the watercrafts as orderly and quickly as they could.

"We have already sent a message for them to be readied." Zusie looked around. A large group of Tara Aquians stood guard, the rest of them must have left to ready and guard the watercrafts. She said a silent thank you to Zenrah for sending them the Tara Aquians. The Meadow Imps, use to raids, knew that hysteria did nothing but get you killed during traumatic events. Calm and intelligence got you out alive. They stood aside and let the Elfkins go down the pathway first. As they hurriedly ran by, bumping and tripping over each other, the Meadow Imps shook their heads. The Elfkins still had a lot to learn.

The Meadow Imps followed the Elfkins in an orderly fashion through the pathway followed by Zusie, Janilli, Saphina and Aldwin. The Tara Aquian guards followed them. Duntar scooped up Benly, pile of blankets and all, and walked quickly down the pathway, trying not to jostle him. Kerchot followed, guarding Duntar's back.

By the time they reached the bay, the first two watercrafts were already on their way with Tara Aquians swimming guard and pushing them through the water. Duntar waded into the water and handed Benly to Aldwin who handed him to Saphina. Kerchot cut the line holding the watercraft to the shore. The craft leapt forward as the wind caught the blanket. The Tara Aquian guards strained to hold the watercraft in place while they waited for Kerchot and Duntar.

Kerchot turned back. Duntar, seeing the rage of battle shining in his eyes, stayed him with a hand on his massive chest with great difficulty.

"Our fight with them will be on the water...there," Duntar said, pointing to the shore. "We will both die." Duntar would stay to fight beside Kerchot if need be, but he hoped Kerchot would listen to him.

Kerchot, understanding his words, agreed. As they turned to join the others, they heard battle cries coming from the meadow side of the village. The Venom Horde had indeed been lying in wait for them. Quickly, they swam to the watercraft and pushed it with the help of the rest of the Tara Aquians. The wind was with them and it blew the watercraft and its passengers quickly towards the mouth of the bay. Zusie and the others watched thankfully as the first and then the second craft slipped through the opening between the bay and the lake.

Their watercraft was halfway across the bay when they heard screams of rage coming from the pathway between the lake side of the village and the sandy beach. A troop of the Venom Horde ran into the clearing. The Elfkin women cried out. It was dark but they could see enough of the Venom Horde to be frightened of them. They were large, savage-looking men dressed in dark clothing with thick metal plates on their chests, arms and legs. They brandished lethal-looking, long, curved, polished swords in one hand and torches in the other. They ran to the water's edge but did not follow.

Instead, they shouted again with rage and angrily swung their mighty swords in the air. The fair-haired man that Benly had talked about walked assuredly up to the front of the line and barked out orders. The Venom Horde quickly ran along the shoreline towards the rocky outcropping that separated the Bay of Rowan from Lake Kellowash.

Duntar and Kerchot smiled as the wind picked up and shot the watercraft forward. The Venom Horde would not make it to the rocks in time before the watercrafts slipped through the opening. The fair-haired man, seeing this, roared with anger and took a step into the water then retreated as several very large fish poked their heads out. Duntar and Kerchot smiled again. There may have been a huge army of them, but they were afraid of the water and had not brought their demon fireflies with them.

The skies opened up and rain pelted down in droves, quickly dousing out the torches and the fire in the meadow. Effectively it shrouded the Venom Horde in darkness and made the fair-haired man scream with rage. The sound chilled the Elfkins and Meadow Imps to the core. Benly whimpered in Saphina's arms and she held him closer as Janilli threw a blanket over Saphina's head; sheltering them from the rain.

The winds picked up again and the passengers held securely onto straps on the sides of the watercraft. The last caravan of travelers slipped though the opening to the lake and they cheered with joy as they left the Venom Horde far behind them. As Aldwin expertly steered the watercraft towards the stone steps Zusie looked at her sister. She thought optimistically as Janilli smiled back at her that perhaps Lord Canvil's reign of tyranny had finally come to an end on the shores of Lake Kellowash, in the valley that time forgot.

The End

EPILOGUE

All night and the following day, the wind was on their side and they reached the other side of the lake a day early. With the help of the Tara Aquians, the caravan of Elfkins and Meadow Imps made their way up the great stone stairs to the Hollow of Rock and the second leg of their journey to safety and freedom.

The others, as planned, had gone on ahead without them. They, being the smaller group with less to carry, would catch up to them. Most of the last group had already started down the path through the crevice; Zusie, Saphina, Aldwin and Janilli remained.

Zusie stood beside Saphina, her arms wrapped around her in a comforting, soothing embrace that only a ma could give to her child. They both were deep in thought as they looked over the lake towards the Bay of Rowan. Zusie was thinking of Chrystalina, Jasper and the others, wondering if they were alright, how far ahead they were and how long it would take to catch up to them. She had given orders that at all cost Jasper must be kept safe and under no circumstance was he to fly ahead of the others. His safety, she knew, was paramount to their survival.

Saphina's thoughts were of Lizbeth's trolley. She wondered how the Tara Aquians had carried the trolley up the stairs. They must have been successful as there were no signs of debris. Lizbeth and Old Barty would still need the use of it and it carried the scrolls, statues and Aldwin's supply of medicines. A burly Tara Aquian named Barton, was put in charge of carrying Lizbeth up the stairs. He was Duntar's brother and was just as big and gentle. Another Tara Aquian named Sander carried Old Barty up. He grumbled about it at first, but was secretly thankful for the gesture.

Tears filled Saphina's eyes as her thoughts turned to the animals in the Outer Bound Meadow -- the midnight blue butterflies, the ground snorkels, and the bugs with no name -- how many of them lost their lives in the fire before the rains doused it out. The Venom Horde was indeed a band of heartless, ruthless men who gave no thought to life or consequences. Did they not realize that the fire they set could have killed them as well? Aldwin stood a few paces away from Zusie and Saphina, giving them privacy. His thoughts were of the Tara Aquians and their ingenuity. They had fashioned several small hammock-like carriers from the tent poles and tar covered blankets to hold the provisions. Hundreds of loaves of bread were baked every night a week before the first crew made the journey across the lake. The Tara Aquians wrapped the bread in leaves to keep it fresh then put it into large cloth bags.

The bread would last for several weeks in the bags. Water barrels that the Tara Aquians used were fitted with poles so that four carriers could divide their weight. Everyone had a new backpack to carry thanks to the Tara Aquians who supplied the blankets that went into making them. The backpacks, like the ones the Elfkins carried, held personal items like clothing. The Tara Aquians, Aldwin thought, were an ingenious race of people and he was thankful they chose to fight alongside the Elfkins and Meadow Imps.

Janilli, standing beside Aldwin, sighed heavily. Her thoughts were also of the Tara Aquians, but of those who chose to stay behind- a thousand brave souls. They had been the only family she had ever known and she worried immensely about them. She looked over at Zusie and Saphina; they were her family now too and it pleased her greatly. Her heart ached as fat tears dripped from Saphina's eyes onto Zusie's tunic.

The four of them stayed to watch the burning of the watercrafts -- Zeander's most ingenious idea realized by the Elfkin and Tara Aquian carpenters and supervised by Old Barty. It was a shame they had to destroy them. Each of them sighed heavily as they looked down at the crystal blue water of Lake Kellowash, shimmering in the noon sun.

Far below, smoke from the burned watercrafts lazily wafted up to them. The winds that brought them across the lake had died down just as quickly as they had risen. Zusie wondered if Zenrah had heard her prayers. Janilli wondered if Awnmorielle, the goddess of the Tara Aquians, had provided the winds that whisked them away before the Venom Horde could block the only exit out of the bay. They would be surprised to learn that a power far greater had brought the winds that carried them to safety.

Kerchot, Duntar and the other Tara Aquians had long gone, leaving the watercrafts to burn on their own; they had been anxious to put their battle plans in order. The Venom Horde that had arrived just as they were leaving, they knew, was not all of them. They had no idea how long it would take Canvil and the rest of his army to get to the

Greenwood Forest. In the time that they had, they would strategize, recruit the help of the creatures in the lake and spy on their enemy.

Saphina sniffed loudly again as she stepped away from Zusie. She wiped the tears from her eyes with the sleeve of her tunic. Trying to mask how sad she was, she walked over to Aldwin and playfully punched him in the arm.

"Ouch!" Aldwin cried out in mock pain and rubbed his arm where she had hit it, "What was that for?" "I swear," she said with a scowl on her brow, "loving you has made me a puddle of mush. All I seem to do these days is cry." Zusie looked over at her daughter and Aldwin in shock as they picked up their backpacks and started to walk towards the Hollow of Rock. Saphina's innocent words resonated with Zusie. They took her back many years when she first realized she was with child.

Zusie looked questioningly at Janilli who, before picking up her sack, smiled and nodded that her assumption of her daughter's condition was right. She did not wait for Zusie to join her; instead, she picked up her backpack and skipped over to Aldwin and Saphina. Beaming brightly she started to tell them the good news.

Zusie stood alone looking out over the lake to the Outer Bound Meadow that she could barely see. She looked further still towards Mount Aspentonia and tears welled up in her eyes as she wondered sadly at the lives lost there. None of them, not even Camcor or Bertrum, deserved to die that way.

Zusie sighed heavily again as a tear dripped down her face. What lay ahead for them, she wondered. Not just for her, her daughters and now her grand-underling, but all of them. What was to become of them? Was it safety they fled to or was there something worse waiting for them, just around the next bend? Would they make it to the Whipple Wash Valley? Would they meet the Whipple Wash fairies and help them in the war against Canvil, her father, as Desamiha predicted? How many more of them would die before they reached the safety of the Whipple Wash Valley?

Zusie felt a hand on her shoulder. Startled, she quickly turned; her hand instinctively went for the handle of her knife. Saphina, Aldwin and Janilli -dear Janilli, their fates ever entwined by their dreadful father and their courageous mothers, stood looking at her with expectant happiness. Seeing their happy faces, she pushed all foreboding thoughts to the back of her mind. She bent down and picked up her backpack.

"Come, a grand adventure awaits us," Zusie said smiling as she slung the pack over her shoulder. The others chuckled at her words as they walked happily away from the stone steps. Little did any of them know how grand the adventure was going to be.

Far below them, at the base of the steps, a lone stranger dressed in dark hooded clothing stood in the shadow of the trees waiting for them to leave. Then he too turned, but jumped on the back of a large black roan that was darker than the night sky and had feathered wings of the same colour. Instead of following them, he urged his winged roan into the air. They flew low over Lake Kellowash towards the Outer Bound Meadow and the fair-haired man who waited impatiently for the dark stranger's return.

ABOUT THE AUTHOR

The Valley Time Forgot is the first book in The Whipple Wash Chronicles, and S.D. Ferrell's debut novel. A designer and artist for over 30 years, Ms. Ferrell has discovered her passion for writing and knack for storytelling. Having grown up on a small hobby farm with six sisters and one brother, she was able to seek inspiration from her childhood experiences, and found subtle ways to reflect upon them throughout the novel. With colourful characters, vivid imagery and a few plot twists, Ms. Ferrell has created a fantastical world that is sure to delight, engage and leave readers of all ages wanting more. She currently resides in Southwestern Ontario with her youngest daughter, and is working on the second book in the series, *The Wrath of a King*.